Grisly Tales
from
Northumbria

First published in the United Kingdom in 2020 by Northern Heritage Services Limited

This publication is a compilation of previously published books and other material.
Grisly Trails and Ghostly Tales 1992 (Virgin) 9780863695889
Nightmare on Your Street 1993 (Virgin) 9780863697166

Northern Heritage Services Limited
Units 7&8 New Kennels, Blagdon Estate, Seaton Burn,
Newcastle upon Tyne NE13 6DB

Telephone: 01670 789 940
www.northern-heritage.co.uk
Follow us on Twitter & Facebook

Copyright © Alan Robson MBE

ISBN: 9781916237636

Typeset in Garamond Premier Pro

Design and layout by Ian Scott Design

Cover design: Chloe Roddham/Ian Scott

Skull illustration: Neil Jackson
E-mail: neil@media-arts.co.uk

Printed and bound in the UK by Martins the Printer, Berwick-upon-Tweed

British Library Cataloguing in Publishing Data
A catalogue record for this book is available from the British Library
All rights reserved. No part of this publication may be reproduced, distributed, or transmitted in any form or by any means, including photocopying, recording, or other electronic or mechanical methods, without the prior written permission of the publisher, except in the case of brief quotations embodied in critical reviews and certain other noncommercial uses permitted by copyright law.

The FSC certification
is considered the "gold standard" designation for
wood harvested from forests that are responsibly managed,
socially beneficial, environmentally conscious, and economically viable.

Grisly Tales from Northumbria

Alan Robson
MBE

CONTENTS

Introduction

The Border Country

The Berwick Vampire	01
Berwick River of Blood	03
Berwick Castle and the Blood of the Borderers	05
The Cannibals of Berwick	07
The Auchencrow Witches	11
Knock Knock: Death's at Your Door	13
Carnwath: Planning Permission Denied by the Devil	13
The Castle Craig Flying Saucer	14
Dalkeith: Thomas the Rhymer	14
The Scottish Fisherfolk and the Fingers of Christ	16
Fatlips of Dryburgh	17
The Scarborough Skate Scuttler	17
The Hobkirk Poltergeist	18
Jedburgh's Bony Finger of Death	19
The Lammermuir Outcasts	20
The Mansucker of Melrose	21
The Weird Wizard of Oakwood	23
The Golden Thread of Rutherford	24
The Horse Witch of Yarrow	25

Northumberland

The Phantom Horseman of Allendale	27
The Divelstons of Dilston	29
The Hexham Extraterestrials	30
The Featherstone Phantom	31
The Ghost Battle of Langley	31
Murder at Knarsdale Hall	32
Nafferton Castle and Welton Hall, Cursed Forever	35
The Black Bitch of Black Heddon	36
The Bellingham Peddler	37
The Brigand of Bardon Mill	38
The Norman of Prudhoe Castle	39
The Alnwick Zombie	39
The Dirty Bottles of Alnwick	43
Murder at Alnwick Fair	43
Gorgeist of Alnwick	45
Hanged at the Hotspur Tower	47
Alnwick Castle: The Sightings	48
Alnwick Castle: Home of the Wispery	51
The Barber of Belford	55
Buckton's Grizel	55
The Dissected Saint of Bamburgh	56
Bamburgh's Laidley Worm	58

Bamburgh: Oh my Darling	61
Beadnell: Where There's Life There's Hope, When There's Death…?	62
The Flower of Bedlington	63
Warning in Bedlington	65
The Bonny Lass of Belsay	65
The Murdered Minstrel of Bellister Castle	66
The Lord Crewe Arms, Blanchland	66
The Spry Family and the Blanchland Horrors	68
The White Lady of Blenkinsopp Castle	70
Refugees from the King at Burroden	71
Chillingham Castle	72
Chillingham Castle – Home of The Torturer	74
The Cursed Cattle of Chillingham	79
The Roman Legion of Corbridge	79
The Rudchester Roman	80
The Cragside Queen	81
The Druid Curse of Craster	82
Cresswell: There Is Nothing Like a Dane	84
The Dead Walk at Dunstanburgh	86
Death at Dilston	87
Ellingham: The Fried Friar of Preston Tower	88
The Curse of the Elsdon Gibbet	89
The Embleton Piper	90
The Farne Island and Cuthbert's Ghost	91
Haughton Castle: Man Who Ate Himself	92
The Haltonchesters Lightning Curse	93
Haltwhistle: Here Comes the Bride	94
Hazlerigg: We All Fall Down	96
The Hexham Walk of Death	96
Tricky Dicky of Starward	97
The Kraken of Holy Island	97
The Holy Island Sea Sirens	98
The Big-nosed Ghost of Holy Island Castle	98
Holy Island Ghost of St Cuthbert	100
The Treasure of Broomlee Laugh	101
Meg of Meldon	102
The Haunted Loveseat of Morpeth	102
The Battle of Otterburn	103
The Ghastly Cavalier of Rock Hall	104
The Saltskin of Seghill	105
Thropton: Going Boo for the Booze	106
Queen Mab of Whittingham	107
Who Walks at Warkworth	108

Tyneside

The Black Magic Woman and the Geordie	111
The Disco-Dancing Monk of Newcastle	112
The Ghost of the Blaydon Races	114
The Hoppings' Head Boy	114
The Black Plague of Elswick	115

The Flaming Ghosts of Gateshead	116
It's Raining Dosh!	118
Gosforth's Singalongaghost	118
Newcastle's Phantom of the Theatre	120
Newcastle's Willie Watcher	121
The Phantom of Windows Arcade, Newcastle	122
The Jarrow Reaper	122
Jarrow's Black Death	124
The Spirit of the Swan	125
The Newburn Screamer	126
The Ghost of the Bigg Market	126
The Gateshead Grunt	127
Auld Clothie of the Cooperage	130
The Laughing Cavalier	131
The Massacre of the Moor	132
The Floating Faces of the Newcastle Flood	133
The Body Snatching Business (Tyneside Ltd)	134
The Cathedral Phantoms of Newcastle	135
The Black Friars of Blackfriars	136
The Ghostly Eloper	137
The Ghastly Head of Earl Grey	140
Ghosts Galore at Newcastle's Castle	140
The Witch House of Claremont Road	142
The Power of the Northern Mind	143
Rowlands Gill: The Ghost That Would Not Be Recorded	145
The Viking of Rowlands Gill	146
The Jackhammer Man of South Shields	148
The Phantom Fortune of South Shields	149
South Shields Old Hall and the Signs of Murder	150
Tynemouth's Viking Phantom	150
Walker's Weeping Madonna	152
The Fire Woman of Whitley Bay	153
The Witches of Winlaton Mill	155
Wherever You Go, You're Sure to Find a Geordie	156

Wearside

The Pesky Poltergeist of Chester-le-Street	159
East Rainton: The Ghost of Mary Ann Cotton	160
Fatfield: The Horror of the Havelock Arms	162
The Fairy Minstrel of Houghton-le-Spring	162
The Spooks of Houghton-le-Spring	163
The Sexy Spirit of Houghton-le-Spring	164
The Terryfying Trio of Houghton-le-Spring	165
The Maneater of Seaham	165
The Lambton Worm	167
The Ghostly Avenger of Lumley Village	169
The Phantoms of Lumley Castle	172
The Curse of the Marsden Grotto	175
Pelton's Metamorphic Sprite	177
The Miracle of the Sunderland Sand Eels	177

The Cauld Lad of Hylton Castle	178
The Sunderland Body Snatcher	183
Ghost Ship on the Wear	184
The Freemasonry Plot	186
Washington's Lady in Red	186
Washington: The Ghostly Pilot of Nissan	188
The Silkie of Washington Hall	189
The Whitburn Poltergeist	189

Durham and Teesside

The Shepherd and Shepherdess at Beamish	191
The Bishop Auckland Boar	191
The Cursed Land of Beamish	192
The Faery Folk of Bishopton	197
Branspeth: Bobby Shafto and the Love He Left Behind	197
Darlington's Curse of St. Barnabas	198
Touch of the Dead: Beamish Hall	199
The Durham Forcefield	199
Durham: The Story of Mary O'Brian	200
Sanctuary Denied in Durham	203
The Ebchester Incineration	206
The Fairies of Ferryhill	206
The Footless Man of Waskerly Moor	207
God's Assassin in Guisborough	208
The Serpent of Handale	209
Toad in the Hole, Hartlepool	210
The Saintly Poltergeist of Hartlepool	211
The Hawk of High Force	211
Langley Hall: Any Body For Me?	213
The Pickled Parson of Sedgefield	214
The Spinning Saucer of Shotton Colliery	215
Sir John Conyers, Dragonslayer of Sockburn	215
Stainmoor and the Bloody Hand of Glory	216
The Teesside Airport Spook	218
Witton Castle Ghosts: The Surgeons Room	218
Witton Castle Ghosts: The Stage Room	219

A Final Word

The First Live Broadcast from a Black Magic Ritual	220

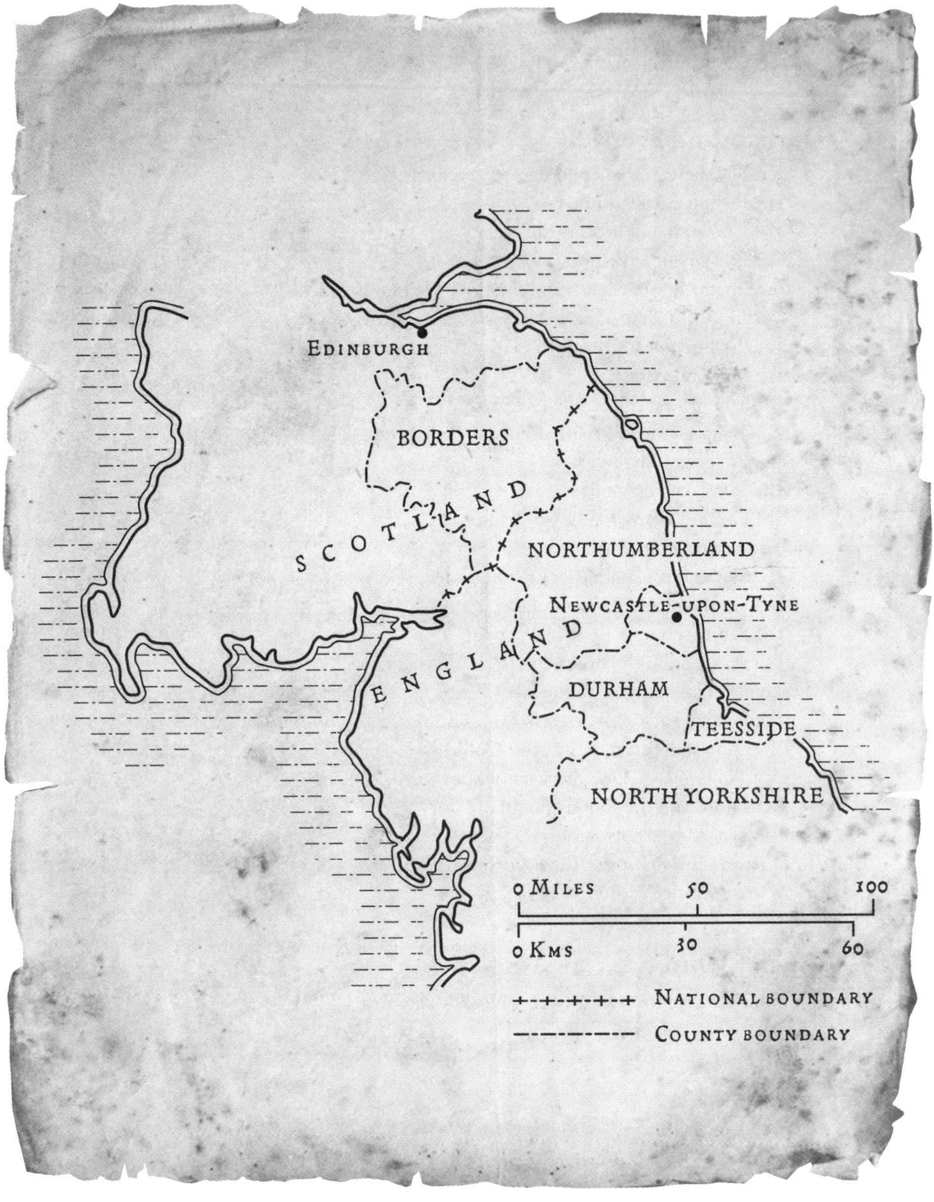
Edinburgh
Borders
Scotland
Northumberland
Newcastle-upon-Tyne
England
Durham
Teesside
North Yorkshire
0 Miles 50 100
0 Kms 30 60
National boundary
County boundary

INTRODUCTION

Over the last forty years on radio and television, I have been lucky enough to travel across Britain and the World seeking out the strange and bizarre. I am proud to finally create a compilation of the best of the North East, all in one package. The North East has an incredible history and with that a gory and blood-curdling array of grisly tales. Many older stories brought right up to date, others guiding you through a teeth-chattering tour of terror, all on our own doorstep.

Old Northumbria spread way down the country and up to the Scottish borders, so I ask you to follow these amazing trails, seeking out where these stories took place. The North has the most castles and the greatest history, yet so many of us don't know what has happened on our own doorsteps.

Available for the first time in over twenty years a mixture of incredible stories about local people and their experiences with phenomenon of every kind. Zombies, ghosts, demon's, witches, vampires, curses, murders and even alien cattle ripping, all right here in the place that we love.

Dig out a picnic basket, set a day aside and head off to visit the haunted castle used in Harry Potter, or the home of the torturers at Chillingham, or select half a dozen tales and seek them all out.

This is a must for believer and sceptic alike, the perfect guide to finding ghosts, and more importantly the incredible history of how they became ghosts in the first place!

Read what ordinary people encountered when they went on their own 'Grisly Tale'

If you experience anything on your visit, make sure you let me know!

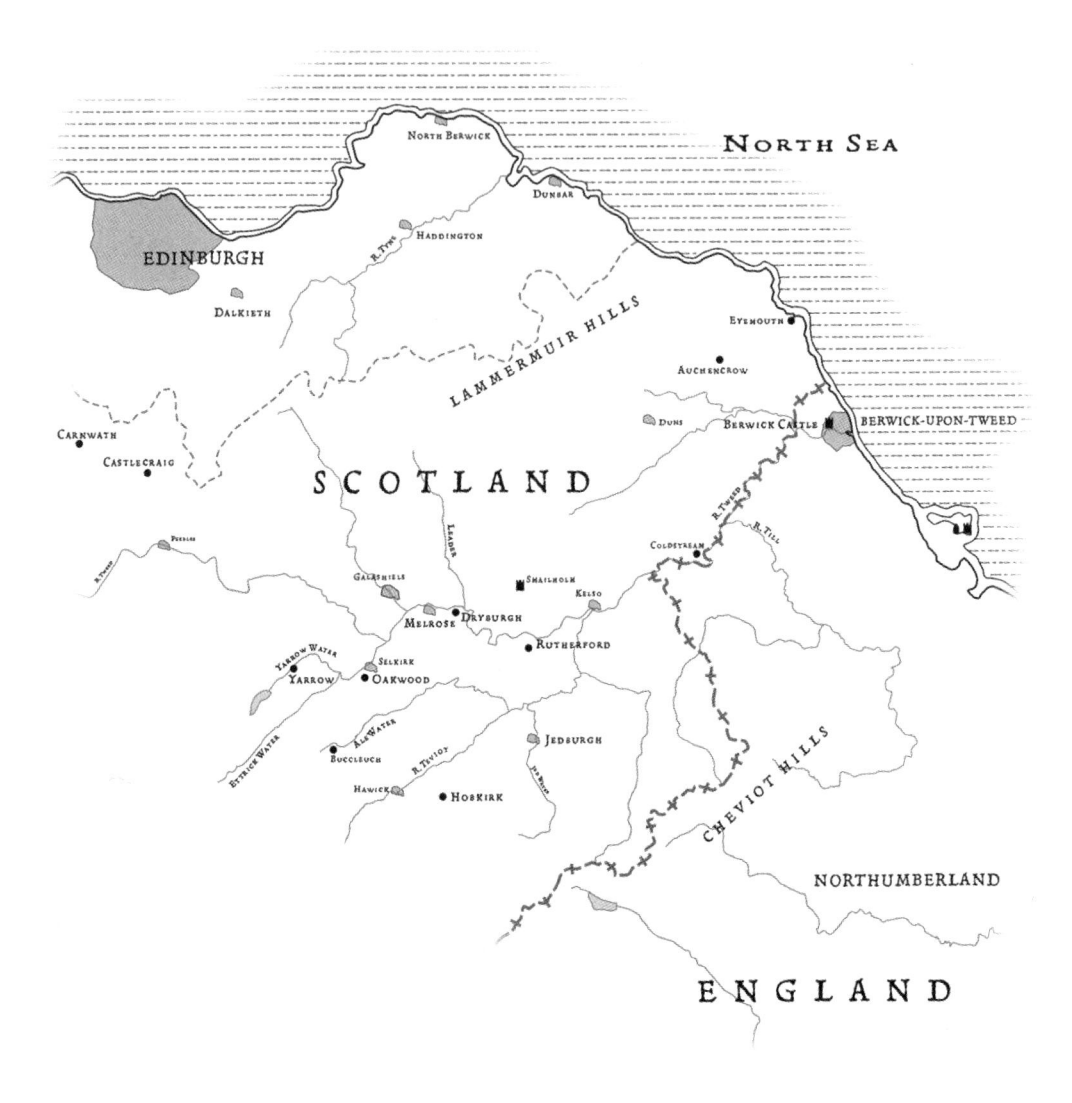

THE BORDER COUNTRY

THE BERWICK VAMPIRE

Many people think that vampires are merely the work of fiction, Bela Lugosi saying 'I don't drink wine!' then plunging his clay fangs into a poor unfortunate actress's neck. It is surprising that just about every culture, race and religion has its vampire tales. To some the vampire is known as wukodalak, to others, wampior, vampyr, pen-nangglan, nosferatu, muronys – the list goes on and on! It, therefore, should be no surprise that such creatures have seemingly invaded Britain too. This story is set around a small village that is now part of Berwick, being swallowed up in the early 1900s. A man by the name of Colin McFaddon used to survive on growing his vegetables and breeding sheep, scraping a modest living from the land. His fiancée was Betty Hough: some legends say she was a prostitute, others that she was 'unemployed'. We'll give her the benefit of the doubt! Colin had sworn that as soon as he could earn enough to look after her they would be married, and this was their great aim in life. He devoted every spare moment into trying to transform a 'cottage' (more a hovel) into a building suitable for a new bride. On a Friday night, they would meet in a local tavern overlooking the coast, share some drinks, have a sing-song, then head off into the countryside to find a quiet nook or cranny to make love. Halfway through the evening, both having downed a few jars of the loopy juice, Betty excused herself and headed out to visit the old farmyard toilet, a hole in the ground with a plank over it. She never returned. Several other women tried to make use of the plank, but the door was bolted. After half an hour Colin asked the landlady, a portly, fun-filled woman known to all Berwick residents as Bella, to investigate. Off she went and found the door locked, so asked her husband to force it open. There still seated on the plank was Betty, whose throat had been ripped out, and the blood was still trickling down across her grey and purple dress. Her face was ashen pale as if life had been sucked out of her – maybe it had. The local gossips made the most of the only bit of excitement Berwick had experienced for years. Throughout the countryside, lambs had been found drained of blood and their throats were torn open. At first, farmers blamed foxes and domestic dogs that roamed in packs down country lanes, but now they had another possibility: a vampire might be on the loose.

The murder of Betty Hough was put down to a crime of passion: claiming that she was a prostitute and had been selling her body in the toilet, an argument had erupted, and her punter had slit her throat. This failed to take into account that her boyfriend awaited her return, that her body was drained of blood and that the wound to her throat was made by teeth, and not a blade.

Three months later a young girl was picking blackberries by a farm cart track when night began to close in. The eighteen-year-old had been told not to be out later than six in the evening, but it had been a glorious summer's day. She had swum in the Tweed, slept in the fields, picked flowers and hadn't collected the number of blackberries demanded by her mother, so she was trying to catch up. The sky was beginning to blacken when a figure approached, shoulders hunched, a dirty tramp-like man with eyes of fiery red. She turned to walk down the lane, only to be jumped on and pushed into the hedgerow. As he lay on top of her, she screamed as he opened his mouth showing two huge fangs. She tried to push him away, keeping his snapping mouth away from her skin. At that moment, a group of labourers returning from the fields saw what was happening and captured him. They took him to see the local magistrate who declared he was a madman and not a vampire, despite the fact he did have enlarged teeth resembling fangs. He gave orders to lock up the tramp, and they placed him in a barn until he could be moved to a proper prison. On his way to that barn, the man leapt on one of his guards biting out his Adam's apple, leaving him writhing on the ground as the other guards glared in horror. He was off over the fields and before the others could reach him he had disappeared into the darkness.

The following morning dogs were brought in to complete the search. They followed his scent to a small copse of trees deep in the woodland interior. There was a make-do shelter, twelve planks of wood leaning against a tree, no cooking utensils, only a bowl of blood. No sign of anyone, but there was a hole dug into a bankside. It seemed too big for rabbits, foxes or badgers so they reached inside and felt a man's foot. Recoiling in horror they were unsure of what to do until Colin McFaddon stepped out of the throng to say 'Dig the bastard up!' He grabbed a spade and began hacking away at the earth until you could see the outline of a body. As the soil fell away, the man's eyes opened and he screamed as the light of the sun hit his face. He struggled free of the ground, and dived into the shadows, trying desperately to avoid the rays of the sun. Colin shouted 'See, he is a vampire! Kill him or it'll be your woman who dies next!' McFaddon struck the first blow and using the edge of his spade he swung at the tramp's neck almost severing the head. The others began belting away at the helpless torso, and scythes, clubs, old swords and shovels battered the body until there was nothing left but pulp. They scraped up the remains and hurled them onto a bonfire, and the 'vampire' was consumed by the flames.

BERWICK'S RIVER OF BLOOD

When King Edward II was put to death on 21st September 1327, no one had the right to cheer louder than the people of Berwick. Not a household stood that had not paid for his throne in blood. Edward I had died in 1307 on his way to invade Scotland and his son felt duty-bound to continue his quest. It took him years to make any headway at all, as the tough and rugged Border Scots were pot keen on a king who ruled from so very far away.

It was in 1314 that English forces suffered their greatest and most humiliating defeat at Bannockburn. They were completely hammered by Robert the Bruce, who confirmed himself King of Scotland. Edward decided that one of the few weapons left to him was fear, and this he used to the full. He would single out a village, then raze it to the ground, slaughtering anyone who stood in his way. Never before had a king adopted this sort of tactic against innocent civilians, and the people despised him for it. Edward would justify his actions by saying he was 'rooting out the Scottish rebels', but it seemed to the people it was nothing but sheer blood lust.

The worst example of this tactic was meted out against Berwick on the chilly North-East coast, straddling the border with Scotland. Edward's reputation was in tatters after his abortive assaults against the Scots, now highly organised. He decided that he must teach someone a lesson, and decided that Berwick would be his target.

What made this such a cowardly and loathsome thing to do was the fact that Berwick was merely a market town, not particularly involved with the conflict at all. Certainly, everyone you spoke to voiced an opinion, but 'a nest of rebels' it certainly was not. It was a freezing morning when English troops were spotted by men working on the land. They thought nothing of it - English soldiers passed through regularly, they would buy food, make some money for local prostitutes and innkeepers, then they would move on. A similar arrangement was had by the Scots on their forays South. This day was different, the troops were not the same laughing and jolly Englishmen that has passed through Berwick some weeks before, they were not in any mood to smile.

As they approached the farm labourers they drew their swords and cut them to the ground. As they marched into Berwick, it was barely dawn. Most people were still in their beds, and it was there they died. Innocent men, women, children and even babies in their cots were put to the sword. Holy men, teachers, farmers and peasants alike were stabbed or hacked to death. A group of fifty or sixty locals decided to fight back, rallying on the outskirts of town near the low bridge. They killed up to thirty English until they were overwhelmed by the sheer mass of soldiers facing them. The tide was coming in and the blood from such a mountain of bodies didn't just trickle into the Tweed, it flowed like a mountain stream. The Tweed was red with the blood of Berwick's innocent townsfolk. Other villages further upriver were warned of the massacre by the scarlet message sent on the tide. When the English soldiers left this 'stronghold of the rebels', not a soul survived. The only Berwick citizens to live through that day were those working in fields a mile or so away, some farm workers and those that had scurried into the countryside, hiding in the undergrowth. King Edward announced his 'great victory'; against all odds, he had conquered Berwick. The town was full of insurrectionists, a nest of insects biting the hand that fed them. The truth was it was bloody murder.

Since that day many people in Berwick have witnessed various strange phenomena, including screams after midnight, when the town is silent. The clunking and clanking of swords and shields, the marching of men clattering along.

* In 1966 Mrs L. Holmes from Sandyford, Newcastle, was visiting Berwick and was walking along the river, beside the low bridge, when she saw the water change colour. It seemed to last for minutes, yet it probably lasted only seconds. Instead of the clear consistency, it seemed to be turning from pink to a glimmering red. She thought the sun was playing tricks on her eyes, but after focusing again, it was indeed bright red. She happened to mention this to a local clergyman who told her the story, and she was quite petrified.

* In 1977 young Philip Gill from Edinburgh was out fishing for tiddlers with his little net, when he dipped his jam jar into the river. On pulling it out the water was murky red, his father even commented on the fact saying 'No fish could survive in that!' On scooping out more water it all seemed tainted, and it was only after drawing water some hundred yards downstream that it seemed to clear.

* Frances Marshall was driving into Berwick for a day trip in August 1981 and she claims to have seen what she described as a sword fight. On approaching the town she saw, once again close to the riverside, a group of up to a dozen men dressed in sackcloth and armour fighting with swords and claymores. She presumed there was a war society restaging of a battle, acted out by interested townspeople. On visiting the Tourist Information Office she was informed that no such event was currently happening. Frances now firmly believes that she has not witnessed ghosts, saying this: 'I think that maybe places can act rather like a video recorder, capturing things, and occasionally playing them back. What I was seeing may well have been something from days gone by that actually happened!'

It's an interesting theory, imagine if we could rewind life, just think of all the things we'd change. I don't believe in fate, as it makes people stop trying, thinking whatever will be will be, and it takes advantage of those who choose to believe in it.

BERWICK CASTLE AND THE BLOOD OF THE BORDERERS

The fortified town of Berwick has always been the centre of controversy. Is it Scottish or is it English? Where does its allegiance lie? To this day amongst the good folk of Berwick opinions still differ, yet back in 1377, it was rather more clear cut. Berwick was controlled by Sir Robert Boynton who was firmly in the pocket of the English monarch Edward III. The history books differ as to the nature of Sir Robert: English folk believe he was a kindly old gentleman who looked after the interests of everyone, a selfless fellow who would give his last crust to the needy, willing to assist in any case of hardship. The people of Berwick at the time described him in very different terms. To them, he was known as 'Boynton the Butcher' or 'Rab the Rapist' and each local hostelry had its own list of atrocities purported to have been carried out by the governor.

One tale told of how a young girl on her wedding day was taken away from her husband to be, her virginity taken by Sir Robert. An old custom of feudal times misused and abused by a man with more power than he knew what to do with. Berwick was a long way from London, so what Sir Robert Boynton decided was what carried the most weight. The Border folk also claim that he lined his own pockets riding on the backs of the poor. It is claimed that the last straw was when he ordered the death of a farmworker because he had 'spoken ill' of the governor. Three soldiers walked into his home while the family were eating, and in front of his wife and their five children, he was hacked into pieces.

As Sir Robert Boynton dined on venison and wine seven Borderers decided that they had to act to stamp out this cruelty. They waited for a night with a crescent moon, when it was at its very darkest, and began to climb into Berwick Castle. On reaching the battlements they came upon a sleeping guard. The guard would never wake again, his throat was slit, and with a gruesome gurgling gush he slumped to the ground, the blood welling into a pool, around his head. One by one they picked off that night's guard patrol. Stealthily they entered the castle, and on finding the barrack-room, they set about surprising and killing a further dozen soldiers.

Sir Robert was in the Great Hall warming himself against the chill of the night when three Borderers kicked open the door.

'How dare you!' yelled Sir Robert. 'Guards! Take these men away. You'll hang for this!'

Without saying a word the three roughly dressed men walked towards him. 'Get back!' he ordered. 'Look, I'll give you anything you want, just don't kill me! I'll make you all rich men!'

His pleading was to no avail, they stood a yard away from him and laughed loudly, as the mighty Sir Robert Boynton shrunk before them. From the man with the iron fist to the trembling coward in minutes. 'This is for Tam!' said one of them. 'Aye and for the thoosands of ither poor buggars!' added another as the blows rained down upon him. At first, they hammered him to the floor with the hilts of their claymores. Once he lay on the ground, his hands waving in a desperate attempt to protect himself, they lifted their swords and cleaved his skull in two. His reign of terror was over.

That morning the entire castle was in the hands of only seven Borderers, and the people of Berwick rallied to their side. Soon almost fifty of the townsfolk were in control of their town.

All the soldiers in Berwick Castle were butchered, but those who had shared their night with the women of the town made good their escape. As soon as word reached London a huge military force was sent to recapture one of England's furthest bastions. These untrained border folks battled to keep control of the castle against entire battalions of soldiers numbering somewhere between nine and twelve thousand men. They fought like tigers and the English army believed that there were thousands of people in the castle. Every time they came close to assailing the walls they were forced back by a rain of missiles, arrows and boiling pitch. Eight days later the English had hacked a hole in the main gate, and they were finally inside. They swarmed at the hapless Borderers who were all on the walls, and within minutes every one of them lay dead. Once again Berwick belonged to England. Although much of Berwick Castle has been destroyed by both time and civic planning, the walls and towers remaining have been the setting for several strange experiences.

* In March 1958 it was reported in an American newspaper that Mrs Winona Harrison, the wife of a US soldier, had visited Berwick Castle and had this to say: 'I visited Edinburgh Castle and it was just as I imagined it to be, but my tour of castles had to end on reaching Berwick. I was standing on these steps when I was thrown to the ground. I heard groans and cries and I could not move for fear! I heard clanking as if I were in the middle of a sword fight. I was looking around but could see nothing! The awful thing was that I felt as if I was splashed with something warm. I felt this fluid running down my face, yet when I used my hand to wipe it off there was nothing there! It felt just like blood. It wasn't thin like water, rather thicker than that. I must have sat there for up to an hour while all this was going on, then I ran back to the town for a gin!'

* Dorothy Thorpe of Glasgow visited Berwick on a coach trip over the August Bank Holiday in 1968 and felt someone breathing down her neck whilst looking at the White Wall of Berwick Castle. On turning around there was no one there!

* In August 1991 young Tony Davidson from Berwick claims he was pushed over by 'something invisible'. He felt a weight on his back as he lay there and it would not

let him up. He reached around to feel what was pinning him to the floor, and said 'I felt a leg on my back, yet I could see my own shadow on the wall, and there was no one else in view!' It vanished as swiftly as it had happened, and Tony has sworn never to visit Berwick Castle ever again.

* In 2018 radio producer Tony McShane visited the ruins of Berwick Castle along the dark path next to the River Tweed. On reaching where one of the towers once stood, he felt something touch him and swung around whilst holding a video camera. He caught a man-shaped dark shadow, moving as if running, around the corner of the castle. He said "It bumped me out of the way. When I checked the footage I was stunned to find that I'd caught it on camera'.

THE CANNIBALS OF BERWICK

In those dark days before the motor car choked chickens with its fumes, no one could travel more than thirty or forty miles in a single day. Travelling from London to Scotland on horseback was far from enjoyable, no matter how good a rider you were. So people endeavoured to break up their journey by staying at the many inns dotted along the way. The most favoured route through the North East took them across a tiny bridge in Newcastle, long since replaced by the Swing Bridge.

It was this route that the newlyweds Elizabeth and Rodney Thorpe had taken, on their journey to their new. matrimonial home in Edinburgh. They were married in York at Elizabeth's request, as all her family, the Campbells, lived thereabouts. Ever the gentleman, Rodney had suggested that they travel by coach, but his wife, a keen horsewoman, decided it would be more exciting and romantic to ride.

Exciting it was, but any hopes of romance were soon ground into dust. They spent their first night in Durham in a coach house; ailing to get much sleep due to the revelling of drunks in the inn below their room. The honeymoon began in Newcastle where the couple spent three days and nights at lodgings near the Quayside.

It was in Newcastle that they were told by a blacksmith of the perils of travelling through Northumberland. For three years over a hundred people had disappeared. The government of the day had presumed that it was the work of innkeepers, robbing and murdering their customers.

The Thorpes' journey North along the magnificent Northumbrian coast continued, and it seemed as if they were following in the footsteps of a troop of soldiers. On reaching Tynemouth they saw a gallows, and there swinging in the biting wind was a portly fellow bobbing like a dead bird in a water tank. A decree had been made that thirty innkeepers would be hanged for the murders of their guests. Innocent or guilty no one knows; there was no trial, just a basic execution.

As they proceeded along the coastal road, every five or six miles they came across another gallows, bodies were eaten away by the salt air, eyes pecked out by crows, weevils and flies swarming over the rotting corpses. They were welcomed at every inn by those hollow sockets staring at them, teeth clenched in agony, another twisted body with a snapped spine. They were only three days away from Edinburgh when they set off for the last leg of their journey. The road ahead took them to Berwick, then across the border into Scotland. On this warm sunny day, they could have no inkling of the horrors ahead.

They had both stopped to gaze at the waves beating into the craggy cliffside, as tiny rainbows appeared in the water cascading back into the sea. They had been hypnotised by the beauty of it all, and they smiled at one another, leaned into a lingering kiss, then headed back to the road. Suddenly they were surrounded by dozens of filthy ruffians in rags, all shouting and waving clubs, axes and crudely made spears. Elizabeth was dragged from her horse and brutally hurled to the ground, in less than a second her dress was torn from her. Rodney believed she was to be raped so rode at her attackers striking them with his riding crop. As he hit out at them he saw a glint of steel being raised above her and a long curved blade struck down, blood spurted into the air as a gurgling scream sent shivers down his spine. He gazed down in horror to see her stomach wide open as they ripped out her innards, and then proceeded to eat her alive. A white-bearded man, Sawney Bean, seemed to be in command of this ragtag gang. He stared at Thorpe, blood trickling through his bleached whiskers, and he yelled 'Get him!'

As the life mercifully drained from Elizabeth the brigands stood up, some clenching bloody intestines, others crazy with excitement. As they charged towards him his horse took it upon itself to veer away from the throng. It galloped North with Thorpe swaying in the saddle. He was dizzy with fear, his brain failed to comprehend what he had seen. He begged that God would let him wake up and end the nightmare, but sadly fate had taken him too far. The horse's mouth frothed as it began to tire, and the last few miles of his journey he managed on foot.

On arriving at Edinburgh Castle a detachment of soldiers was immediately dispatched to accompany him back into Northumberland. They had been told to find Elizabeth's body, and apprehend the murderers. It took almost two days for them to get there, thirty troops at a forced march, two officers on horseback and Thorpe. It was a late May evening when they arrived, there was no one about. The only evidence of the crime was a huge patch of clotting gore being feasted on by maggots and beetles, as fat blood-gorged flies buzzed into the faces of anyone who got too close.

They searched for tracks and found those of a group of around fifteen men dragging something down to the beach, the footprints disappeared into the sea. Had they escaped by boat? Pirates were commonplace along the North East coast, but they drank rum, not blood!

The officer, having checked the area, decided that there was nothing more that could be done, so the following morning they would begin their trek back to Edinburgh. They camped in a copse of trees near the sea, supped on a deer they had trapped, then settled down for the night.

Rodney Thorpe was sickened by his experience. Why couldn't they have taken him, Elizabeth was so beautiful, only twenty-three years of age, it was all such a waste. Just as the snores of the hardened fighting men were at their height Thorpe awoke with a scream, he was sweating and gibbering like an idiot. It would be many a month before he could face the pictures in his dreams, pictures painted by a troubled mind. They calmed him down, gave him a tot of whisky from a small silver hip flask, then tried to snatch what rest they could.

Morning crept up on them unnoticed, and as they collected their muskets and packs, one young soldier noticed that the tide had gone out. Once this had been brought to the attention of the officer he ordered that a search be made of the area. Within minutes they had located a lace shawl caught up in rocks and seaweed. The shawl her mother had given her, the shawl she had been wrapped in as a baby, as her mother and grandmother had been before her.

At the end of the beach, the cliffs began to rise and looked as if they were going to crash down on to the sand. One soldier had begun searching the dark clammy nooks and crannies when suddenly he took off his tricorn hat and began to wave furiously. As everyone raced across the wet sand they were ordered to be quiet, so as not to give advanced warning of their presence.

What the young soldier had discovered was a cave that wound up from sea level into the cliff. When the tide was in, the entrance was completely underwater, yet the inside of the cave was dry and safe.

As they made their way deeper inside, they could smell something, the faint aroma of crackling pork, and way off in the distance the shimmer of a burning torch. Creeping silently towards the light the soldiers eventually peered into a huge hollow cavern where lived the incestuous family of Sawney Bean. Ragged remnants of humanity huddled around a huge campfire, men, women and children all twisted and bent.

As their eyes adapted to the darkness, they felt their stomachs tighten when they discovered that what they thought was roast pork was a child turning on a spit. Vomit fought its way into the throats of the soldiers, one man turned to run, only to bump into something hanging from the cavern wall As they looked up they spotted bodies, dozens of them sliced into pieces, salted and dangling against the cool rock passage. The eyes of the soldiers were wild with fear and revulsion, the officer knew that he would have to act now or lose control of his men who were on the verge of panic.

He ordered his men to cock their muskets and fix bayonets, then they began walking into the main cave area. Many of the men grabbed clubs, yet after three shots exploded into the cave, killing two and wounding a third, all fighting stopped. Thorpe told the officer that their leader was a small pock-faced man with a white beard and mad staring eyes, and he had yet to be found. As the soldiers began to bind the crowd of cannibals, Thorpe made his way back down the tunnel, mercifully not noticing that one of the joints of human flesh he strode past was that of his beloved Elizabeth. He was twenty yards from the cavern entrance when out of nowhere a man stood eye to eye with him. Mad eyes, a white beard – it was Sawney Bean! Thorpe grabbed him and they wrestled to the floor, Bean had managed to draw a long curved knife and was about to use it when a soldier loomed out of the darkness to knock the knife spinning from his hand. Seeing he was outnumbered Bean began to run back towards the beach. Thorpe and the soldiers, slipping on the seaweed and the green slime-covered stones, pursued him along the beach. He was heading towards the horses tied up by the campfire. On reaching Thorpe's horse he clenched its mane and was about to pull himself aboard when a rifle butt appeared over the horse's back and sank into the old man's face. He fell like a sack of potatoes, his blood soaking into the grass as had that of so many of his victims. Over forty people were taken back to the garrison camp, where they were charged with murder, and all were found guilty. One baby boy was born while his mother was in prison, and that child was given to a family called Ross, who raised him as their own. The men were hanged and the women were taken to the outskirts of Edinburgh where they were burned at the stake. It's said that on Hallows Eve if you look out from the battlements of Edinburgh Castle towards the hill known as Arthur's Seat you can still see the glint of flame as these devilish women sink into the pit. If a strong wind whistles along the castle's rocky escarpment, it echoes the cries of torment as the fire consumed them.

Sawney Bean's name became a legend because he ate people, and hanging was not enough for him. He was taken from his rat-infested cell, stretched on a rack until many of his bones were broken, throttled with a knotted rope and then, once revived, he was gutted. His stomach was opened and his innards removed one at a time. It is claimed that he was still alive as they tied his arms and legs to four horses. After a count of five, a musket was fired and the horses all ran off in different directions, wrenching Sawney Bean into quarters.

Although this was a long time ago in the Border Country they still talk of the baby, raised not on the breast, but on the blood of the innocent.

THE AUCHENCROW WITCHES

In the 1600s and 1700s, the area around Berwick was infamous for its covens of witches, they abounded in almost every village and certainly in every town. The witch that was most feared was known as Eliza, a dark-eyed woman with teeth worn down to blackened stumps. Her skin was pale and white, prone to peeling if ever she dared walk out in the sun. Her place was in the darkness, this was her power. When darkness reigned so did she, terrorising the locals and exacting from them whatever she wanted, as a price for leaving them alone.

It is said that Eliza could make sheep miscarry, cause cattle to perish and even make infants die in their cots. Those that were cursed by her almost certainly met with disaster. It is thought in some quarters that far from being a mystic, she was, in fact, a clever murderess, who employed members of her coven to do her dirty deeds. When she cursed a family, saying their youngest child would die, one of her 'witches' would creep into the home and smother the babe with a pillow. The following morning nothing could be proved, other than that another of Eliza's curses had worked. After over thirty years of living in fear, the people of Auchencrow decided to seek help from a 'white witch' who lived in Blackadder. This goodly witch told them that the only way to break the spell of a black witch was to draw blood from her face anywhere 'above the breath' (above mouth level).

This was the time when things were to get extremely nasty. Each time a local was cursed by one of Eliza's henchwomen, they would pull out a knife and slash their faces. There are several cases of people being indicted with this crime. In each case, their excuse was that they were merely trying to break free from a spell.

Eliza realised that her power was waning, despite over the years killing thousands of animals and hundreds of young children in Marygold, Lintlaw, Houndwood, Ayton, Cairncross, Berwick, Eyemouth, Preston and Clappers. This made the head witch seek out the woman who had led to her destruction, and both she and her coven of over forty witches set off to Blackadder to confront, the white witch. They would kill her and carry her body through the villages as a warning to the locals not to dare mess with her again. She got rather more than she bargained for. Eliza was not a witch, merely called herself so, and ruled by fear. Her fellow witches were nothing but murderesses. They presumed that the white witch was also a charlatan, this was not the case.

The white witch of Blackadder was known as Cissie, a lady in her forties who could mix up potions to cure bellyache, gout or infertility. She could cure animals and birds and was not known to harm a living soul. Yet she was about to start.

On finding her small thatched cottage on the southern outskirts of Blackadder the witches surrounded the house, hurling burning tapers onto it, setting it ablaze. Within seconds the house was an inferno, yet still, Cissie refused to leave. It took almost four hours for that cottage to burn to the ground, as the witches danced around, drinking, laughing and even cooking the white witch's chickens in the heat.

They were revelling in their victory when from the ashes stepped Cissie completely unharmed, she crossed her arms and suddenly from the remnants of her home burning tapers filled the sky, each one landing on the witch who had thrown it. They began to burn, and yet no matter how hard the witches tried to cast them away, they remained firmly fixed, in the same way, that iron filings are solidly affixed to a magnet. All but six of the 'witches' were dead. Eliza ordered the others to kill the white witch. They were less than enthusiastic having seen so many of their coven incinerated, even so, they grasped their knives and dubs and rushed at Cissie who stood her ground. As the blows rained down she merely smiled. Each blade point was unable to get any nearer than an inch from her body. She pursed her lips and blew, and each dub began to batter the person carrying it, and each blade was pushed into the body of its murderous host.

So there stood the power of good and the very essence of evil. Eliza declared that she knew what the witch's power was: 'Ye cannot harm me, but ye can make me hurt myself if I were to attack ye! So I won't and then there's nought ye can do!'

Eliza was right, the white witch could only return any assault backwards on her assailant. So Eliza began walking away. At this, the white witch picked up a pitchfork and walked slowly behind her. She heard Eliza laughing saying 'Your magic can't harm me now!' She heard the white witch walking behind her, and on spinning around she barely had time to register the picture before her when Cissie rammed the fork into her stomach and began to twist it.

'This is not magic, this is justice. I kill ye as ye would kill a snake!'

Eliza couldn't speak, the sparkle in her eyes merely began to fade as her life melted away. It is believed that her body was thrown into an abandoned well near Whitsome.

KNOCK, KNOCK, DEATH'S AT YOUR DOOR

The Scottish Borders are renowned for having a variety of ways of finding out that death is due. Here are some of the commonest:

Herries is one of the oldest family names in the Borders, the name originally evolved from a family who settled in Scotland from Gaul around AD200. The word herisson means hedgehog in French, and whenever a member of the Herries family dies a hedgehog is seen nearby.

The Imlachs, the Martins and the Donaldsons are all supposedly tipped off that death is coming their way by seeing a white dove flying around the eaves of the house.

The Robsons, Gallaghers and Forrests are given a warning by tapping on a window or door that wakes you from your slumbers. Within twenty-four hours someone will die.

The Fosters, Forsters, Grahams, Williams and Thomases are all supposed to be told of impending death by items moving in the house. Plates falling from walls or ornaments turning to face the wall.

*In Yorkshire the Middleton Family all see a brown-clad monk before they die.

CARNWATH: PLANNING PERMISSION DENIED BY THE DEVIL

At Carnwath in Lanarkshire lie the remains of Couthally Castle, once home to the mighty Somerville family who ruled the roost for generations. The castle was taken by armed Somerville men in the early 1100s, and from that day they kept tight control by the lash and the gallows. Whilst capturing the castle they had breached three of the walls, and Laird Somerville decided he would demolish the entire structure and start again from scratch. So whilst living in 'huge marquees he ordered his men and hundreds of locals to begin erecting a new castle two hundred yards away. They worked very hard, yet each evening the walls erected that day would be pushed to the ground. That night Somerville armed with the family claymore stood guard himself over the work. If any rogue dared damage his property he would slay them. It was three minutes past midnight when the Devil appeared, and the Earth opened and a million demons poured out of the pit and began to wreck the work that had been done. Somerville, rigid with fear, ordered his men to begin work there and then, at restoring Couthally Castle to its original condition. It is said that the tormented ghost of the old Laird remains on the site of the castle, hoping that the gates of Hell never open up and swallow him.

In 1965 a group of picnickers from Denmark visited the area on a trip to Scotland. Whilst they were eating, they claimed to hear 'voices underground'. They could hear hundreds of people, but all speaking in a language they could not understand. Lars Pederson of Copenhagen said 'it was not Danish nor English, it sounded Asian to me!'

*Whilst researching for a radio programme on strange phenomena, I visited Couthally Castle, or rather what's left of it, and there are areas where things quite simply do not grow. I spoke to one local farmer who said 'Dina ye mess wi that, Hell's Gates lie yonder!' I couldn't find them, even though my name is probably already on the guest list!

THE CASTLE CRAIG FLYING SAUCER

Ever since some charlie declared that he had seen a light in the sky that had resembled a flying saucer, the term has been used a thousand times a day in various parts of the world. Yet long before it was coined, the residents of Castle Craig in the Border Country had witnessed what is believed to be the very first sighting of a 'saucer'-shaped UFO. In 1592 they heard huge loud booms from the sky, this is long before we discovered sonic booms or were able to break through the sound barrier. Having investigated they saw that the sheep and cattle were in a total panic, as overhead there came a huge shadow blotting out the sun. As farmers and village folk alike gazed up into the sky they saw a long saucer shape glowing brightly as it moved as slow as a cloud overhead. It then disappeared at incredible speed leaving behind a huge explosion of sound that 'scattered animals and people alike!'

DALKEITH: THOMAS THE RHYMER

Throughout the Borders, there are thousands of strange tales of a prophet and seer known as Thomas 'the Rhymer' so-called because each prophecy or curse he made would be done in rhyming couplets. Throughout the 1200s he journeyed far and wide, leaving countless tales wherever he appeared. He covered an area from Glasgow across to Edinburgh travelling down the country as far as Alnwick. One such legend surrounds Dalkeith, when 'the Rhymer' saw a man mistreating his three daughters. On investigation one of the daughters broke down in tears saying that her own father had been raping her since she was eleven years old. The same could be presumed of her two older sisters. The man's wife had died, and he had transferred his carnal needs to his own children. Thomas shouted at the man, demanding he releases the tight grip he held on the arms of the two older girls.

'For each of your sins great pain, great pain,

For thirty years may it never wane.
May a plague of boils cover your head,
And your only release comes when you're dead!'

Within seconds the man began writhing on the floor in agony. The good people of Dalkeith were appalled as they watched huge septic lumps begin to grow onto his head. The young girls screamed and ran from him. Thomas gave the girls a handful of gold, saying, 'There my children, make a life for yoursells!'

Despite his amazing powers, he was despised by many who feared him. He could create spells to make people fall in love, to make folk rich or to make them suffer. He denied he was a wizard or a warlock, maintaining he was merely a simple 'Rhymer', a poet and balladeer who travelled around giving people entertainment. But everyone knew he was far more than that.

His death is shrouded by many different tales, yet the most common is that of how he became bewitched by a beautiful woman, who was, in fact, a witch herself. She poisoned his wine, and he died in agony. However, seven years after they recorded his death Thomas the Rhymer returned with a new bride, a woman he claimed was an Elfland Queen. She appeared to be a child barely sixteen, small and attractive.

Admittedly there are hundreds of different tales about Thomas, who was a thirteenth-century Indiana Jones, but my favourite involves a man known throughout the Selkirk area of Scotland as 'Campbell the Bloodseeker'.

The Campbell clan had their fair share of rogues, and this man was by far the worst of them all. He had no castle, no camp and no clansmen who would follow him. He liked killing people, it was all he could do.

He had worked as a mercenary for Simon De Montfort who had tried to curb the powers of King Henry II. After De Montfort was beheaded the vicious Scot returned to his Border country. The following year he had fought against the Norwegians, winning the Hebrides for Scotland. His problems began when he could find no one to kill legally. This is when he became maybe the worst brigand ever to roam the North country.

He didn't stop people to steal their money, he stopped them so he could kill all the men, then rape and murder the women. How many would die in so savage a fashion no one will ever know. But one day he was raiding a farmhouse, cutting down the farmworkers with his double-headed axe. On kicking open the door, he found three women and an old man sitting down to supper. He raised his axe above his head, ready to decapitate the elderly chap. At that very moment Thomas the Rhymer stepped out of a back room.

'Hurt no more, you Devil's spore,
You no longer go to war.
Tie his legs and to him saw

Never will ye kill no more!'

The farmers watched as Campbell's axe flew from his hand and stuck into a tree. He began floating in the air, his legs wide apart, as he began to hang upside down. At that very moment, an old gnarly-toothed saw was raised above him, came down between his legs and began sawing. It moved to and fro as the blood spurted and the flesh was sliced until it started to cut its way through his head. As the saw reached air on the other side it fell with a clunk to the ground, being joined by the perfect halves of Campbell the Bloodseeker. He had reaped what he had sown.

Many believe that Thomas was merely a prophet and a kindly philosopher of a man. That may well have been so, yet his more colourful legends are certainly more entertaining.

* **Steeleye Span recorded a song about 'Thomas the Rhymer' produced by Jethro Tull star Ian Anderson.**

THE SCOTTISH FISHERFOLK AND THE FINGERS OF CHRIST

Whenever you have a close-knit community you often discover that you're wading chest-deep in superstition and myth. Such may be the case on the Scottish coast particularly around Dunbar, St Abbs and Eyemouth, yet you would never doubt them to their face. They're a hardy lot, red noses weathered by many a storm, tiny veins like a facial road map, having surfaced in the chill winds from the North Sea, and a sense of humour that can turn you into an instant friend.

The Scots for over two hundred years have looked upon the haddock as their 'lucky omen' and if they catch any early in the season they know that it will be a good year ahead.

A legend told me by an old fellow called Big Jackie from Eyemouth in 1968 was about a giant haddock over seven feet long, that lived in the 1780s and had rescued two fishermen after their boat had hit rocks near Reed Point. They were drowning in very rough seas when they felt something beneath them holding them above the water. On getting into the shallows near Thorntonloch they gazed through the driving rain to see a giant haddock swimming back out to sea! Whenever they caught haddock in their nets in future they would always release them, and since then the fish has been special to all fisherfolk.

There are other legends too, for many Scottish fishermen believe that when Christ fed the multitudes he fed them haddock. They say that the black spots on the side of each haddock's head were made by Jesus Christ when he divided the fish out amongst the five thousand.

FATLIPS OF DRYBURGH, BERWICKSHIRE

On 14th June 1645 King Charles I suffered his most crushing defeat at the hands of Cromwell's men at Naseby in Northamptonshire. So fierce and determined were the Ironsides that many hundreds of the cavaliers just scattered and ran, knowing the day to be lost. Weeks later Charles's soldiers were being tracked down and arrested. One woman was so distraught about the way the Civil War was going she decided to become a hermit, living in the cellars of ruined Dryburgh Abbey near Berwick. She vowed that she would never look at the sun until her lover returned. Four months later she was told that his body had been buried near Naseby, shot down by a Roundhead musket. This condemned her to remain in the cellar forever, only ever venturing out late at night, to sob and cry beneath the stars. She was befriended by a tiny dwarf of a man called Fatlips who would tidy away the rubbish from her cellar, bring her food and remove all of her toilet matter in a wooden bucket. Fatlips wore a pair of heavy iron shoes and clanked as he walked. Some say he did this to frighten away rats and mice, others that it miraculously stopped the musty old cellar from suffering from damp and condensation.

Visitors to Dryburgh often claim to have heard clanking footsteps. Some believe they are the footsteps of some gallant knight of old, that once protected the abbey from evil-doers, but the locals know it's just little Fatlips cleaning out the netty (toilet).

THE SCARBOROUGH SKATE SCUTTLER

The most horrible story that I have been informed of in recent years involves the skate, yet another flatfish, but this time of much greater size. I was told by Fred from North Shields that throughout the centuries sailors had used skate for sexual purposes. I discounted this completely, but was stunned to have it confirmed by the fishing fraternity from Dunbar down to Hull. When I asked why, the answers that I got were bizarre, to say the least, particularly one legend that stretches back as far as 1743.

It involves a young boy called Philip from Scarborough who was a cabin boy on a tall-masted schooner, The Hawk. He was seventeen years old and was travelling up the North-Eastern coast to Edinburgh with a cargo of fruit. Also travelling on board was a young lady, Elizabeth Munro, the pretty daughter of Iain Munro, an Edinburgh businessman. Young Philip was very taken by this attractive young girl, and during the voyage, they became friends and, while docked in Edinburgh, lovers. It was no surprise that Elizabeth chose to travel back to Scarborough aboard The Hawk when two weeks later it made its return journey. Yet merely three hours out to sea there was a horrendous storm and water was sucked into the sky by a waterspout creating a terrible whirlpool in the sea off North Berwick, east of Aberlady. As the tall ship spun into the whirlpool young Elizabeth had been swept off the deck and sucked into the sky by the violent winds and disappeared in seconds into the funnel.

Philip saw this and was about to leap after her when his crew-mates held him back. The Hawk did manage to survive the storm, with ripped and tattered sails and a broken foremast, and limped back to Edinburgh. That night Philip had a vision that his love, Elizabeth, had been transformed into a huge white skate, and was now swimming the seas waiting for him to join her. Most people would've blamed a dream like that on eating pickled onions late at night, but not Philip. He had never been at a lower ebb, and with the tide, he had borrowed a single sailed yawl and was off towards North Berwick to seek out his beloved.

The story goes that close to the shore he spotted a huge white skate, and he dived into the water and swam towards it. In Philip's eyes, this huge fish became Elizabeth, so he kissed it, then made love to it. Having done so, the water began to steam and transform into the beach, and there lying beside him was Elizabeth Munro. He returned to Edinburgh in glory, they married and her father gave him a job onshore. I suppose this was to stop him being tempted; remember there's a lot of other fish in the sea!

This seems very peculiar, yet the male skate has a sex organ very similar in size and shape to a human male, and the female skate has genitalia almost identical to a human female! This is why in supermarkets you never see a whole skate, only skate wings. Also, according to fishermen when they prepare these fish for sale they have to curtain off the filleting area because it so shocks tourists and passers by. They also say that to satisfy lust at sea in the 1700s, 1800s and early 1900s they used to strap a skate to a mast and let the sailors 'relieve their sexual desires' as it is claimed to feel similar to a woman. It brings a whole new meaning to the phrase 'get your skates on'!

THE HOBKIRK POLTERGEIST

Many a canny Scot knows the story of the Hobkirk poltergeist, that caused endless concern in a church in Roxburgh in the 1700s. This troublesome phantom would crack stained glass windows, pour holy water onto the floor, set fire to curtains with candles and breathe onto the necks of the choir. It was decided that something had to be done.

The Reverend Edgar was sent for and he carried out a complex exorcism, and the ghost was chased away.

Suddenly this amiable Reverend, known to most in the vicinity as Nichol, his Christian name, became quite a celebrity. He had defeated Satan and had proved he was indeed sent by God to serve them. Some decades later Reverend Edgar died, and because of his ghostbusting reputation, it was believed by the more superstitious that he might choose to wander from his grave in Hobkirk churchyard. Preempting any phantom strolls they decided that they would rebury him, on the outskirts of the village.

This seems to be a fairly stupid course of action, but it proceeded with the full permission of the new Reverend. He believed that Nichol Edgar was a tough act to follow, so out of sight, out of the congregation's mind.

So the coffin was dug out of the clay soil and carried on the shoulders of six local men across the barren lavender-shaded moor. It was almost halfway to its new resting place when one of the pallbearers stuck his foot in a pothole and the coffin lurched to one side. The deceased Reverend's hand popped out of the coffin slapping one of the bearers in the face with its deathly cold palm. The coffin was dropped there and then and the bearers and their entourage all ran home in sheer panic.

The poor dead Reverend lay in amongst the heather until the following morning when sufficient courage was mustered to return his body to where it belonged, Hobkirk graveyard.

There have been sightings of glowing light at the cemetery, yet whether it's the Reverend no one knows.

JEDBURGH'S BONY FINGER OF DEATH

Jedburgh Abbey was proudly chosen as the site for the royal marriage of Alexander III to his beloved Yolande in October 1285. They were the Charles and Diana of their day and thousands flocked to witness this union of souls. A huge wedding feast was held following the elaborate ceremony, and the castle resounded to merrymaking of the rich and poor alike. There were jugglers, wizards, jesters and a masked pageant culminating in a musical play performed to the music of the flute, fiddle and pipes. The masked ball ensued when everyone in their fancy dress costumes enjoyed the dancing.

Amidst the joyous throng, a skeleton suddenly appeared. At first, Alexander thought it was merely a costume of outstanding construction, but on getting close he could see the floor through its rib cage. It stopped directly in front of him and pointed a grey bony finger into his face. Hypnotised, yet fascinated, he gazed at this horrific vision. The entire ensemble froze with fright until the apparition disappeared as swiftly as it had appeared.

No one could concentrate on merrymaking after viewing such a horrendous thing, so the party ended, and the newlyweds made their way to their bed-chamber. A local wise woman warned Alexander that the vision was a warning from God to obey his rules, lest death would befall his household. Alexander was neither religious or superstitious so totally ignored her.

The following March, King Alexander decided to enjoy a feast, even though he should be abstaining because of Lent. So following the downing of a brace of thickens and some quails' eggs he rode off to meet Queen Yolande for an afternoon's riding. He approached her group near Kinghorn in Fife when his horse began to gallop, he pulled back on the reins, and unable to stop, both horse and rider plummeted over cliffs to their deaths. Alexander's ghost is said to walk in both Jedburgh Abbey and the castle, witnessed by hundreds over the years.

THE LAMMERMUIR OUTCASTS

In 1744 and again in 1825 there were strange sightings over the Lammermuir Hills in the Scottish Border country. Over a hundred people in all watched in amazement when they saw injured kilted Scots marching with donkey carts and horses across the sky directly over the hills. In 1744 people gathered over nine hours to watch this pictorial that remained in the sky until night fell. Sworn statements were produced and even doctors swore that they had seen the strange happenings in the sky.

In February 1825 a group of eight people travelling between Berwick and Haddington saw 'pictures in the sky' directly above Cranshaws Hill, in the same range of hills. This time it was a fight between thousands of men, and they had seen the execution of around forty men in kilts. Unarmed they were hacked to death by red-coated soldiers. Three figures were also seen not in the sky but running over the hill itself.

* This story remained buried for many years until in 1848 one of the witnesses was invited to a party where one of the other guests mentioned that back in 1692 three men had escaped from the massacre of Glencoe, and had hidden on Cranshaws Hill. Had they really watched a heavenly re-enactment of 13th February 1692? The day that soldiers under the orders of King William III put forty unarmed Scots to the sword for refusing to give their allegiance to him. Had those three shapes on the hill been those phantom refugees, escaping forever from the bloodstained hands of the English king?

THE MANSUCKER OF MELROSE

Death in the Middle Ages was one of the very few things that seemed to flourish, fed by disease, war and neglect. So when the people of Melrose, Galashiels, St Boswells, Selkirk and Kelso began finding bodies, they would put it down to the various warring factions that tried to incite friend against friend, family against family. Clan conflicts were still commonplace, and whenever someone died, the opposing group was always blamed. The one man who benefited was the local priest, who would tend to the needs of bereaved families, and take money for burials. Little did they know that it was that very priest, based in Melrose Abbey, who was responsible for killing up to thirty people over twelve years. The murders were so violent that people chose to stay indoors between sunset and sunrise. If anyone did venture to the cluster of inns, they would always go out in groups, rather than risk being on the streets alone.

The priest was never happier than when he was hunting, the locals even nicknamed him 'the hundeprest', and would see him riding across the fields chasing a stag, running down a fox or even out for rabbits. It was the hunting he did when the sun went down that would ultimately cause his own destruction. Bodies had been found with puncture marks in them, not just around the neck, but sometimes through the skull or chest too.

They believed they were merely caused by a sword point, yet the truth was rather more disgusting. The priest would greet passersby as they walked around the streets, dim and dark in those days before streetlights. On seeing a churchman they would relax and chat, only to have their skulls cracked with a club. While they lay unconscious the priest inserted a hollow sharpened metal funnel into them and would begin to drink their blood. It was thought that he would also drink in the juices around the brain too, to give him some kind of extra-sensory powers. Miraculously the priest had been seen doing this early on, after having murdered his first victim. Two passers-by saw the priest crouched across the body of a young girl, but put it down to him giving her the last rites. No one had thought that this vampiric activity was going on. The priest was able to eat garlic, walk in the daylight and obviously carry crucifixes around with him. All of the vampire legends dictated that of all the people in the village, a man of God could never be such a thing.

His undoing was to change his pattern of killing. He had successfully preyed on people who wandered about late at night and had he continued doing so he quite probably would never have been found out. However, as people would not venture out after dark, his perverted lust for blood got the better of him. He found a house where an elderly woman lived and decided to visit her and take her blood and brain. He entered the house, pushed the woman down onto a straw bed, and smashed her over the head with a heavy candlestick. He had just pushed the metallic blade into her neck, when from a back room came three relatives who had been staying with her, having visited Melrose from their homes in Lauder. They grabbed the priest, leaving the funnel still sticking into her neck, as it brimmed and frothed with dark red blood. They punched and kicked him until the priest lost consciousness. The people of Melrose found it impossible to believe that their worldly-wise and dedicated priest could possibly be a depraved killer. They even tried to blame the widow's own family, for blaming the priest to cover up their own murderous deeds. So they released the priest but accompanied him home, and during a search of his quarters in Melrose Abbey, they found old green bottles filled with blood. They also found cudgels stained with blood and many personal items that had been taken from the victims. The one article that damned him was a cameo painted by a local miller of his wife, taken from his blood-drained body.

The priest claimed that he was doing the work of God, purging the area of all the sinners. The blood found was the blood of Christ, and anyone who tried to stop him would be destroyed by the power of God's almighty hand. Many locals believed the old priest, but sufficient numbers of the others damned him as a demon, a devil-worshipper or a madman, who must be burned at the stake. He was taken by ox-cart out from Melrose Abbey to a local beauty spot known as Scotts View, where they planted a wooden stake, surrounded it with twigs and tied the priest to it. They ignited the fire and it began to burn. At this very moment, the priest began to tear the stake from the ground. His cassock was aflame, his hair was burning, yet he managed to struggle towards the assembly of villagers and locals, screaming out his curses, and yelling of his agony. He got within feet of them when he collapsed in a heap. At this many ran home, others continued piling wood on the smouldering corpse, to guarantee that the evil would never return.

*Visitors to Scotts View have claimed to have seen something bright on the hillside. A floating something that glows then disappears.

*In 2020 Derek Lang, an architect from Leeds visited Melrose Abbey and decided to walk around the countryside, finding himself on the hillside at Scott's View. He fell asleep on a glorious sunny afternoon during the Covid-19 lockdown, he had chosen the town to exercise just as the rules were relaxing. He woke up three hours later with an almighty pain on his neck. On getting home he discovered what appeared to be human teeth marks on his neck as if someone had sought to bite out his throat. He rang his doctor, but due to the virus precautions, he refused to see him. The doctor said it was probably an allergic reaction, but what reaction of that kind has teeth?

THE WEIRD WIZARD OF OAKWOOD

Once more a Scottish wizard with amazing powers came forth to surround his entire community with countless stories of mysticism. Michael Scott lived at Oakwood Tower, about five miles from Selkirk, and became known as Scotland's most loved warlock. He could not be killed by the hand of man; many attempted to stab him, poison him, set fire to him but all to no avail. He was protected by a magic cloak that could withstand anything that mortal man could throw at it. When he was attacked by rogues sent to drive him out by a local landowner, he sent out a demon who drove them all mad. The same demon demonstrated its powers by splitting Eildon Hill into three, those peaks can still be seen to this day. The following night to prove to everyone how powerful he was he commanded his 'pet' demon to dam the River Tweed, this resulted in a huge ridge of rock appearing at Kelso that is also still standing. Finally, he ordered his mighty magical worker to twist ropes of sand at the mouth of the River Tweed. If you go down to the tide line at low tide you will see amazing twined sand patterns curling along the shore. There are four different tales as to how Michael Scott died, so I've picked the juiciest:

Scott was visiting Berwick when he was stopped by a traveller who begged him to help, as his daughter was seriously ill. Being a kindly wizard Scott ran inside to see that the girl had been bitten by a rat and was dying of infection that it had given her. So he asked a villager where the rat had bitten her and demanded that everyone returned to that spot. They were by a riverside, and the feverish child was placed where she had been playing. Scott clapped his hands and suddenly the girl stood up and began walking backwards. To his astonishment the villager watched as the stream flowed backwards, birds flew backwards and his own daughter sang to herself in reverse. Then as she sat down, a rat appeared backwards, unbit the child, then vanished into a bush. At that second Scott clapped again, freezing time. He told the worried father to get out his knife and stand next to his daughter. Then he clapped his hands again and everything returned to normal, the stream flowed downstream again and the rat appeared running to bite the young girl. The father swished the knife down and missed the beast, it was far too fast. Realising that it would bite the girl, and she would surely die, Scott dived in front of it, and it buried its teeth in the bridge of his nose. He clenched it in his hands and smashed it onto a nearby rock. The girl was returned to the bloom of health and Scott made his way back home, realising that his intervention would cost him his life. He could not be killed by anything mortal man could throw at him, but this was an infected rat. Death came swiftly, and he was buried in 1234 with his book of spells in Melrose Abbey.

THE GOLDEN THREAD OF RUTHERFORD

In the Scottish Borders there stands the pretty little village of Rutherford, and in the 1300s and 1400s, a Scottish woodcutter called Rooney used to homestead there. He was known for his fables, creating different stories for every situation, and often made more money for entertaining in the local inns than he did chopping wood. He always swore that his stories were true, and no matter how fanciful, he would never admit that he had made them up. He was greatly loved by the people of the vicinity and was in his seventies when he lay on his deathbed, quite an age to reach at that time when the average age expectancy was around fifty-four.

He was close to death when he gathered all of the villagers from Rutherford, Roxburgh, Manor Hill and Maxton, and ordered that his cot be carried out into the yard. It was there that Rooney told his final story, all about a fairy princess who had flown here from a land far away. Once arriving she began to fascinate a local giant called Stich, who begged the fairy to marry him, this she declined, as fairy princesses could only wed men of good heart and this the rough giant certainly didn't have. So one night as she slept the giant lifted open the roof of her thatched cottage, and lifted her out. She struggled and screamed and all her neighbours tugged at the giant's leg, prodding it with pitchforks, but the monster just shook off their puny assaults. The huge Scot carried the fairy to his hilly hideaway, a place now known as Sweethope Hill (near a place now called Stichill), where he held her captive for a year and a night. Then on returning from his adventures, he discovered that the princess was working on a spinning wheel, weaving her hair into golden thread. No matter how much hair she used, she always seemed to have plenty. She spun and spun hair by the sackful. The giant thought himself a lucky ogre, not only did he have the most wonderful fairy princess in all the world, but now he had riches beyond his wildest dreams. Sweethope Hill was completely surrounded by this golden thread when the princess declared that unless he released her she would cast a spell to make the golden thread vanish down a worm hill and disappear into the centre of the Earth where it would melt in the fiery furnace. The giant refused to let her go, so with a wave of her hand, the end of the golden thread began to disappear underground. Slowly the thread began to disappear, ream after ream, mile after mile, until the giant shouted 'Nay ye'll not take my riches, fairy princess or not!' and taking hold of the thread he wrapped himself in it, and dug his huge heels in. This was of no use at all, for as the thread became entangled around him it forced his head into the earth, and kept pushing him further into the damp ground. It took only minutes before the huge frame of the giant disappeared beneath the ground, as the thread kept going further and further towards the centre of the Earth. The fairy princess was released and was able to fly back to her people far, far away.

The villagers applauded old Rooney for another great story, and his very last words were: 'You think me an auld liar, but time will prove me right!'

In 1844 near the River Tweed, not far from Rutherford, local quarrymen uncovered a long piece of gold thread embedded into a layer of rock between eight and twelve feet below the ground. The Kelso Times and The Times both carried stories about its authenticity. It had been there since around 1380.

Maybe the mighty bones of the giant lay only a few more feet below that thread, had they dug further!

THE HORSE WITCH OF YARROW

Winning an apprenticeship has always been very important to the working class. Like my father before me, I tried hard to get 'the tools' behind me as an apprentice electrician, yet it was not meant to be. I had so many electric shocks I used to glow in the dark. My fingers were so brown everyone thought I was a heavy smoker, yet it was merely electricity burns. By the time I quit, I was carrying almost as much electricity on my body as they do in the National Grid. Yet long ago you couldn't walk away from your trade, you had to see it through. Usually, you went into your father's profession, and he would be your teacher. Such was the case in Yarrow in Scotland where two brothers were learning to be blacksmiths at the local forge. Yet they had been cursed by a local witch, who had taken a fancy to the handsome lads. Every night of the week this ugly crone would sneak up to one lad's bedside and place a horse's harness over his head, casting a spell to transform him into a black stallion. She would climb upon his back and ride him to her coven. No one understood why the one lad was so weak and floppy the next morning, when his brother was strong, with much greater stamina. Yet one evening the other brother saw what the witch was doing, so planned his revenge for the following evening.

He moved his brother into his bed and waited for the wart-ridden hag to appear, and as she kneeled across him to place the bridle on his face he threw her down and placed the harness over her craggy face, transforming her into a huge black mare. He galloped her to the very smithy where he worked, and shod her, hammering horseshoes onto the horse's feet.

He then set the witch free, and he returned home, well pleased with that night's work. When morning broke they found the old witch lying in a ditch bleeding profusely, with horseshoes nailed to both her hands and feet.

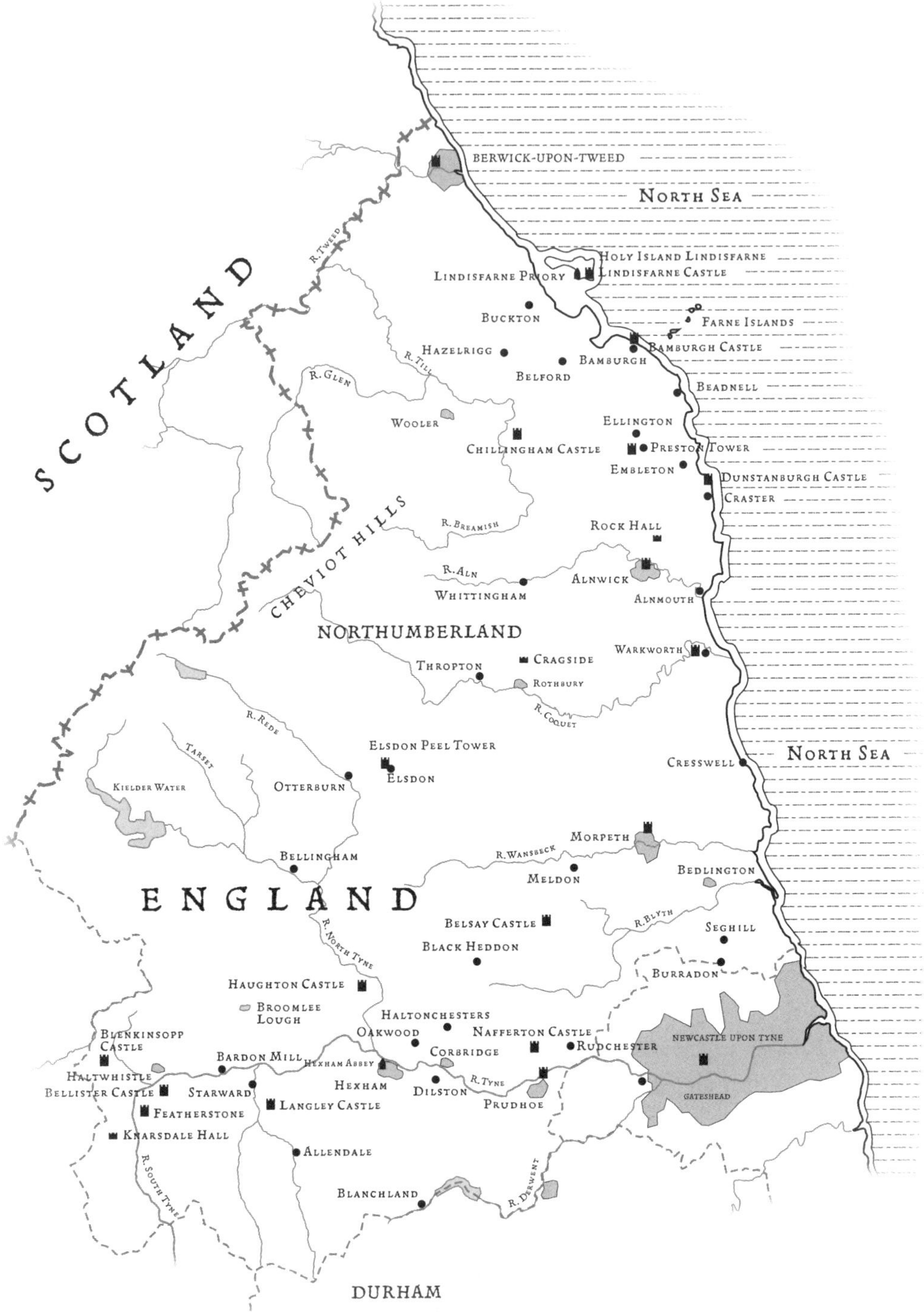
BERWICK-UPON-TWEED
NORTH SEA
R. TWEED
SCOTLAND
HOLY ISLAND LINDISFARNE
LINDISFARNE PRIORY
LINDISFARNE CASTLE
BUCKTON
FARNE ISLANDS
HAZELRIGG
BAMBURGH CASTLE
BAMBURGH
R. TILL
BELFORD
R. GLEN
BEADNELL
WOOLER
ELLINGTON
CHILLINGHAM CASTLE
PRESTON TOWER
EMBLETON
DUNSTANBURGH CASTLE
CRASTER
CHEVIOT HILLS
R. BREAMISH
ROCK HALL
R. ALN
ALNWICK
WHITTINGHAM
ALNMOUTH
NORTHUMBERLAND
WARKWORTH
CRAGSIDE
THROPTON
ROTHBURY
R. COQUET
R. REDE
TARSET
ELSDON PEEL TOWER
ELSDON
KIELDER WATER
OTTERBURN
CRESSWELL
NORTH SEA
MORPETH
BELLINGHAM
R. WANSBECK
MELDON
BEDLINGTON
ENGLAND
R. NORTH TYNE
BELSAY CASTLE
R. BLYTH
SEGHILL
BLACK HEDDON
BURRADON
HAUGHTON CASTLE
BROOMLEE LOUGH
HALTONCHESTERS
BLENKINSOPP CASTLE
OAKWOOD
NAFFERTON CASTLE
NEWCASTLE UPON TYNE
BARDON MILL
CORBRIDGE
RUDCHESTER
HEXHAM ABBEY
HALTWHISTLE
R. TYNE
BELLISTER CASTLE
STARWARD
HEXHAM
DILSTON
GATESHEAD
FEATHERSTONE
LANGLEY CASTLE
PRUDHOE
KNARSDALE HALL
ALLENDALE
R. SOUTH TYNE
R. DERWENT
BLANCHLAND
DURHAM

NORTHUMBERLAND

THE PHANTOM HORSEMAN OF ALLENDALE

There is something special about mining communities: a spirit exists among them that you cannot easily put into words. A closeness of kind, where every neighbour would share his last slice of bread or lay down his life to protect your life, and a sense of real community. Such was the case with the leadminers of Allendale in the 1700s, for all the hardships of their lives. Each week they struggled (and some died) in the damp, sodden lead mines, earning a pittance and scraping barely enough to keep their families alive.

Once a year, though, at the beginning of December, the mine owners would send out their paymasters to visit each community and reward their employees with the amount of bonus which was their due. Heavily laden with gold as they were, the paymasters were attractive prey to robbers and highwaymen, and many had already been shot and killed.

But in April 1739 tales were spreading that the notorious highwayman Dick Turpin had been hanged for his robberies and murders. Turpin was arrested after he accidentally shot his partner Tom King during a scuffle with some people they were trying to rob. As King lay dying, he confessed his crimes and told of Turpin's hideaway.

Many of the paymasters felt that Turpin's execution would calm the blood of those rogues who might think about robbing them. The public hanging of a notorious highwayman was bound to discourage others from sharing the same fate. Reassuring themselves, off the paymasters went, loaded to the gunwales with the bonus money.

One of the paymasters had travelled from his home in Penrith, in Cumbria, to make deliveries in Leadgate, Alston, Nenthead, Coalcleugh, Allenheads, Sinderhope and Allendale. Little by little, he was paying out the eagerly-awaited money to the mining families that were scattered around the countryside. Just as he was leaving Carton towards Haydon Bridge, he hit a tiny forest path. The trees formed a darkened vault overhead as the branches clenched together like hands in prayer. It was an eerie place; even the birds seemed uncomfortable there, never daring a song.

Rather than riding down this dark and dangerous road so late in the evening, the paymaster decided to cut across country. Passing through a gate into an open field, he cantered across the rough pasture.

Unbeknownst to him, a group of thieves had been trailing him, often robbing the homes of the miners after he had delivered their money. This time they decided to stop him in his tracks. As he rode over the field illuminated by a moon barely full, he saw four men on horses riding towards him. In such circumstances, you can understand why he jerked back at the horse's reins and began to gallop away. On reaching the gate he had opened to enter the field he discovered it had been roped closed. As he stared down at the fencepost two men leapt from the trees and hurled him to the ground.

The local farmer later remembered hearing horses and voices, but as that was the main road 'across the tops' he was used to hearing travellers making their way past his property.

Although the family of the paymaster visited the area searching for him, no sign was ever found. If some of the quiet country-folk of those parts had suddenly become wealthy, it seems that none of their fellows enquired too closely into how they had been able to leave the mines and buy land of their own.

This story was told for many years, often changing slightly, until many doubted whether it had any truth to it at all. In 1911, however, during the construction of a decent standard road from Cowshill to Lowgate near Hexham, workmen were channelling through the field where the dirty deed had been done. Barely two feet down, the labourers came across a spherical lump. They cleared away the boggy soil to push their fingers into gaping eye sockets of a skull. As they kept digging down and down, they discovered that beneath the skull was the neck, the rib cage, torso and entire body of someone who had died over a hundred years before. Despite the searches and investigations, the body of the paymaster had never left the field where his life was taken.

Between 1911 and 1987 there were eight reports of a phantom horseman riding across the Northumbrian moor. The first report was, the most grisly.

* An elderly man from Whitley Chapel was walking his two sheepdogs at dusk in September 1911. 'I heard this sucking noise. It was very loud, and I remembered thinking it was the noise you hear if a cow becomes trapped in mud, struggling to free itself. Then I looked across the field and spotted an animal trapped in a huge quagmire at the lower edge of the field. I didn't go too close as this creature was up to its neck. The mud looked black in the twilight, and as I neared it wasn't a cow's head I saw, it was a horse with steam snorting from its nostrils as it struggled free of the mud. Then as its front legs pushed onto the firmer ground I noticed that from below the level of the mud pool came the shape of a man on the animal's back. the dogs were barking and yapping and I shouted out, "Here, fellow, do you need any help?" And it was at that moment that this mud-covered shape turned to look at me, and I couldn't see his eyes, just two bright red holes. All around his shoulders there was a collar of red that seemed to drip from him. I don't think it was blood but it could've been. I stood there hypnotised by these bright red glowing eyes as the horse cantered around. I couldn't take my eyes away from his. Then the horse stood back

on its hind legs and then galloped straight past me, actually splashing both me and the dogs with the grey mud. I watched as he covered the field leaping over the hedge at the bottom. Although I couldn't see him after that, I could still hear horse's hooves off away into the distance!'

* In 1987 Ian Robson of Hexham wrote: 'I know that this horseman exists: my grandfather and uncle both saw him in the 1960s. They were fishing on the River Derwent, west of Blanchland, and they saw a man on a horse riding by around six in the evening. It wasn't dark, so they thought nothing of it. The rider glanced at them and they saw bright red eyes that looked like rubies. They thought it was a trick of the light, in the same way as when you take a flash photo of someone, it looks as if they have red eyes. Yet my grandad, Harry Henderson, said that when the rider rode off after glaring at him, his shoulders were covered in blood, and the eyes were vivid red. He doesn't believe it was a ghost, but he did say it was weird.'

Almost monthly, even now, someone hears the beating of hooves on grass or sees the prints of hooves in mud in the middle of a field that had locked gates. The Phantom Horseman of Allendale lives on . . .

THE DIVELSTONS OF DILSTON

Dilston Castle was one of the many castles seized by the Crown when its owner the Earl of Derwentwater chose the wrong side during the Jacobite Rebellion in 1715.

However, there is another legend that goes back many more hundreds of years. The Divelstons owned the castle, and it became accursed not long after John Divelston's marriage to a woman called Elizabeth, who was born in York. He did not know, when he fell under her spell, that she was a witch. Their marriage soon soured when he discovered his wife bathing in the blood of a slaughtered cow. He was appalled by this, and from that day they lived separate lives.

Elizabeth contented herself by 'romancing' practically every other man in the castle and many from local villages. It was obvious to Divelston that he was becoming a laughing stock; he had to get rid of this woman.

One evening he crept into her bed-chamber and found her in bed with a servant. He killed the boy with a sword blow to the head. To his utter horror, the woman began bathing in his fresh blood. 'Try and kill me and this castle will be cursed!' said Elizabeth, reaching into the boy's open skull and eating his brains.

As Divelston vomited at this vile sight, Elizabeth stood up, her naked body covered in gore, and walked to him saying 'You and I must become husband and wife again. I shall take no more lovers, but you must return me to your bed.' He looked at her, a beautiful creature with long black hair, the blood dripping off her every curve. She smiled, and a trickle of blood dribbled from the side of her mouth, as she reached out to caress his cheek, smearing it with the servant's blood.

Divelston forced an answering smile and turned away, and then in a flash, he swished his sword around and severed the witch's head. The body remained standing; the head fell upright on the bed, and to his horror, it spoke. 'Now you've done it, John Divelston. Within a hundred years your family will be gone, and all of the occupants of this castle will live in misery!' At that, the eyes closed, and the tongue hissed between the lips like a snake, until eventually, the vibrations ceased.

John Divelston had the body carried over the border into Scotland and cast into a ravine.

THE HEXHAM EXTRATERRESTRIALS

During the winter of 1904/5 some very strange things happened all over Britain. What I am about to describe happened not only at Hexham, but also, at precisely the same time, in Gravesend, Norwich, Badminton, Aberdeen, Abingdon and Hull.

Twenty days running, from Christmas Day well into the new year, local farmers discovered that their animals were being butchered as they stood. Bodies torn open, literally wrenched into pieces, were found on both sides of the River Tyne. Many had their internal organs missing; in others, the hide and innards were there and undamaged, but not a bone was to be seen. To remove an entire skeleton and leave the internal organs untouched is an impossibility, yet that is what had been done, and without even disturbing the fleece. Despite keeping them closely guarded, animals continued to be butchered – cattle, pigs, chickens, goats and eight horses from a nearby riding school. It was almost as if someone or something were shopping for parts, taking certain items from different creatures.

It is alleged that three locals disappeared during that period. Some said that they had merely moved further south; others believed that they had been taken by whoever was conducting this strange, almost scientific dismembering of animals.

Local newspapers, of course, ran stories about these killings; they also ran a story about 'swarms of strange aerial lights in the sky, reminiscent of airships'. Was there a connection? As always, the authorities played down these stories as 'fanciful in the extreme', but they could not explain the animal rippings.

Was Hexham visited by people from outer space? Were they responsible for the dissections? We will never know, but it is an interesting coincidence.

THE FEATHERSTONE PHANTOM

Strange bumping and banging can often be heard at Featherstone Castle, near Haltwhistle, by visitors and staff alike, and they know exactly what it is.

Sir Reginald FitzUrse used to rule the area with an iron fist, swift to clamp down on anyone who stood in his way. There are stories of how in the castle grounds he would take pleasure in whipping stable boys with a cat-o'-nine-tails just because they hadn't polished the saddle of his horse sufficiently. He and his cronies had once ripped the clothes off the back of a young girl and were on the verge of committing rape when her father intervened to stop them. Later the father's body was found with a knife in his back.

FitzUrse was eventually stopped, and he was locked up in the tower of Featherstone Castle. No one knew what to do with him, so they did nothing; they didn't feed him, they didn't give him water. They just ignored the fact that he was there. It took him almost three months to die of starvation.

He ate his leather boots and anything else he could find and drank what little rainwater he could catch and his urine. All the while he would scream out in torment, begging anyone to open the door. He would hammer on the thick oak doors until his hands were bruised, he would claw at the wood with his fingernails until they bled.

Now the ghost of the knight can still be heard most nights at Featherstone Castle, walking across the floor, emitting deathly groans, and hammering on doors and walls.

THE GHOST BATTLE OF LANGLEY

Langley Castle is one of the most magnificent of buildings set in idyllic countryside in Tynedale, Northumberland. Yet in the course of the past 250 years, several passers-by have claimed to see it burning.

*In 1799 one of the Duke of Northumberland's servants went to deliver a message to the castle, but returned home to report 'seeing it being sacked by rebels'.

On returning to the castle he discovered it was in perfect condition.

*In 1885 John Douglas Hope of London was visiting Langley Castle with a variety of haberdashery items and draperies. As he was looking at the castle he witnessed hundreds of soldiers burning and looting it.

*In 1979 Robert Fulton researched 'ghost battles' and was told by Mrs Rose Robertson from Leeds that she had witnessed a ghost battle at Langley Castle.

An incumbent at the castle when telephoned said, however, that 'It's the first I've heard of it. The castle does have several ghosts, but I've not heard of a battle.'

*Research into the castle's history shows that it was destroyed in 1405 when Henry IV brought his forces north to destroy the joint forces of Archbishop Scrope and the Earl of Northumberland. Could it be another case of the videotape of history being replayed?

MURDER AT KNARSDALE HALL

Four miles from Haltwhistle stand the proud portals of Knarsdale Hall, rugged stones which hide a most terrible secret.

Legend tells of a selfish and arrogant lord of Knarsdale Hall, who by the time he was in his middle forties had still not found a wife. This was no great surprise for he had a face like a ripe tomato, jowls like a bulldog, and the form of a sack of horse manure tied with string.

They say that money talks, and it spoke most clearly to the parents of the most beautiful girl in the Tyne Valley.

On meeting him she thought him a loathsome creature and told her father how disagreeable she found him. However, he was the richest man in the area and the parents thought it a great honour that their lovely daughter would become the Lady of Knarsdale Hall. So the bands were read, the marriage arranged and the sweet beautiful blonde became the wife of the jelly-bellied Lord.

Honeymoon nights are remembered as a time of passion and joy, of the fulfilment of mutual desire: their honeymoon was equally memorable. Not for passion, however, but rather for temper. The servants heard voices raised in anger, china being thrown and windows were broken as the battle ensued. The arguments continued throughout their unsatisfactory marriage. The people watched, describing her 'as the most perfect beauty trapped in a cage of gold'. She seemed to become accustomed to her lifestyle, and just got on with life, but never showed the least glimpse of affection towards her portly and dribbling husband.

After some months, however, everyone began to comment on how happy the Lady of the Hall had become. You would hear her laughing, she was wearing new dresses, and she always made sure she was wearing the latest scents from abroad. Many believed that she was beginning to love her husband and that things would be happier for everyone now.

The truth was that she had taken a lover, a young man – some say he was her husband's nephew, others his cousin – who also resided at Knarsdale Hall with his sister.

As often as they could they would meet under the light of a single candle, kissing, exchanging chit-chat and being young and in love. They always made sure that her husband was out hunting, visiting town or away on business. Some servants were sworn to secrecy and bribed to ensure their discretion.

It was a chilly November evening, the wind was howling up the valley, and the young wife shivered with anticipation; her lover would be coming to her on that stormy night. He padded along the cold wooden corridor, sneaked into her bed-chamber. There she was in the candlelight, her long blonde hair hanging in ringlets, a long, white satin nightgown hanging off her shoulder. Surely there had never been a more beautiful woman. They kissed, a long lingering kiss, and then they made love.

It was at the very height of their union, as two voices moaned in unison that the bedroom door opened, and there in the shadow stood a figure. It was the young man's sister; shocked at what she had seen, she scurried back to her room. The lovers held each other tightly, sick to their stomachs at the thought that they had been found out. They reassured themselves that surely she would not tell the husband, if only to protect her brother and their tenancy of the Hall.

Worry nagged the lovers like a sore tooth. Whenever in her presence they felt on a knife-edge. What if they were to quarrel with her? What if she were to talk in her sleep? What if she made a deal with the nobleman? It was all irrational, for she had sworn to her brother that she would not breathe a word to a living soul. But the young wife had already decided that the only sure way of the girl keeping their secret was if she took it to her grave with her.

It was another wet and windy night, thunder crashed in the darkness, lightning flashed and the errant wife lay in bed with her foul husband. The darkened room exploded with light as the electricity charged atmosphere turned night into day. The wife complained that a banging door was keeping her awake and that she would only be able to sleep if it were closed. Her husband sat up and reached for a dressing gown, but she stopped him, suggesting that he should send his young niece to close it. So he called to the girl, and off she went to the other side of the house in her flimsy white nightgown to undertake the task.

She reached the door that was swinging wildly back and forth with the wind, and as the rain gusted in upon her soaking through her nightgown, she shivered with the chill. Then a strong hand grasped her across the mouth, another round the waist and she was carried out into the storm.

She struggled and bit the hand, then screamed, but with the storm at its height, her cries were lost. Eventually, she wrenched free from her attacker and turned to see it was her brother.

He told her to follow him, grabbing her arm roughly and dragging her. She lost her footing but he refused to stop, towing her through the mud, scraping the flesh from her feet on the gravel paths and dumping her unceremoniously next to the Hall's small lake.

Although the lake was only small and not terribly deep it had overflowed with the torrents of water falling from the sky. He held her in his arms tenderly, looked into her eyes, and she began to feel a little more reassured. Yet as his hand cradled the back of her neck, his grasp began to tighten and he forced her face towards the water. She clawed at him, she wriggled and writhed but all to no avail. He held her face under the murky water until all life had drained out of her.

He then picked up a huge stone, knotted it into her nightdress, and waded out with her into the lake until the weight took her body down.

The Lord and his Lady snuggled into their blankets, content that the banging had stopped, and sleep soon took them over.

Nearing four in the morning the Lord was awoken by a particularly loud crack of thunder, and the noise of his hounds baying in his stable. He walked out of his bedroom to a window overlooking the stable and all seemed well – but why were they making that racket?

As he turned back towards his bedroom he saw his young niece standing in the firelight; she was soaked to the skin, and her face was ashen pale. Her hair hung like rats' tails, and her nightgown was ripped and muddy. 'What's wrong, child? Why aren't you in your bed?' he asked, and then in a blink of an eye, she was gone. When morning came they searched the grounds but she was never found. The nobleman always blamed himself for not having secured the door himself and often chastised himself for his selfishness. He may have been an ugly old cuss, but he had more humanity in him than his callous wife. The relationship between the lovers was never as fiery again, the passion had died on that stormy night. Soon the lover disappeared too. There were many stories. Some claimed that she had murdered him whilst in a rage because he was said to have made pregnant a girl in Haltwhistle. Others that he rode into Scotland to escape from her clutches. The most commonly related story tells of how his lordship discovered his wife's infidelity and strangled the young man. Whatever the truth, he was never found, dead or alive.

Ten years later the Lady of Knarsdale Hall was a psychotic paranoid and believed that everyone was against her. She would cry for no reason, often for hours, and would rant at anyone who would take it. She was burdened with guilt, knowing she was responsible for one, maybe two deaths.

One night she was shouting at her husband and said, 'Don't you ever treat me like that again, or you'll end up on the bottom of the lake, just like that little witch did!' He wondered what she had meant by this, and had the servants drag the lake, and there to his horror he found the body of his niece!

He thundered back into the house and accused his wife of her murder, and drove her even further over the edge of sanity. Her remaining days were spent locked in one of the bedrooms, stark raving mad. She was completely incapable of doing anything for herself and had to be looked after like a baby. But she often lashed out and injured her helpers and had to be tied down even to be fed. She was possessed with huge unhappiness of spirit, and it was a mercy for everyone when she died.

*Every year visitors see the ghost of the young girl travelling from the Hall to what is left of the lake, her silken gown gliding over the grass. It is said that she is only seen on the anniversary of her death, yet many people have seen her in different parts of the Hall.

One guest also complained of hearing mad laughter echoing around the upstairs rooms; others hear a slamming door whenever there is a thunderstorm. Maybe houses remember what has gone on within them, and require no excuse to share the experience.

NAFFERTON CASTLE AND WELTON HALL, CURSED FOREVER

It is written that a 'twisty-faced man' known as Lang or Lanky Lonkin built Nafferton Castle with his construction gang for Lord Wearie. Wearie was a cunning swine and managed to use some fine print on their agreement as an excuse not to pay them. They had laboured for years to create the magnificent hall and had only received their basic living expenses, Lonkin decided to wreak his revenge on those he felt had done him down.

There are about nine different versions of this story; I have chosen the most entertaining one.

Lonkin heard that Lord Wearie's family were staying at Welton Hall, barely a stone's throw away. He bought the co-operation of Lord Wearie's grandchild's nurse and she left a downstairs window open, through which he crept in. First, he and his accomplice stabbed Wearie's baby grandson dead. When she heard her baby's cries subside so swiftly the child's mother ran into the room to find her baby dead in his crib. She saw the murderers but was so distraught that all she could do was collapse on to the cot, hugging her murdered child to her breast. Her other child, Betsy, aged about fifteen, rushed in while Lonkin and the wet nurse were poised to stab her mother, and she begged them to spare her mother, offering her own life in exchange. Lonkin said, 'Nay, lass, Lord Wearie must get his deserts, for Nafferton Castle and Welton Hail are cursed for evermore!'

He ordered the girl to watch as they stabbed her mother, forcing young Betsy to catch the blood in a golden washbasin as it oozed out of her.

When the rest of the household came running, attracted by all the screaming, Lonkin and the wet nurse managed to escape. Three days later, however, they were cornered. Rather than be captured, Lonkin hanged himself from an oak tree near Whittle Dene. First, though, so that no one else should have the money and jewels he had stolen, he wrapped them in a leather pouch and threw it into the swirling water. It is said to remain there to this day.

The nurse wasn't courageous enough to follow his lead, not after witnessing his agonies of dancing in midair until his neck snapped. She was to meet an even more painful death, burnt at the stake by Lord Wearie's men on his return from London.

*The lady's ghost is said to walk Welton Hall, looking in anguish at the death of her child. She is often heard crying, or seen in the downstairs rooms, seated in one of the chairs, wringing her hands. *The oak tree near Whittle Dene is said to carry the outline of the hanged man, and whenever anyone sees it a deep pool known as `the whirl dub' begins to swirl and bubble.

THE BLACK BITCH OF BLACK HEDDON

In the 1700s a woman visited Black Heddon, claiming that she was collecting for the poor. People gathered up their old clothing, shoes, food and whatever pennies they could afford, and sent her happily on her way. She always dressed in black and tried to squeeze as much kindness as she could out of people. It was believed that this woman may well have been the first charity collector in the North of England. The sadness is that she never gave any of the goods or money to the poor. She kept it all for herself and lived quite a fine life. Much of the stuff was sold, once again to 'raise funds for the poor', who would of course never receive a penny.

She was finally run out of Black Heddon by a landowner who had spotted her drinking in a tavern in Newcastle and boasting of how she was 'conning those country bumpkins out of their shekels'. So when next she appeared he tipped all her collected sundries on to the ground and chased her out of the village with his horsewhip, threatening to 'hang the bitch if she ever returned'.

The story goes on to tell how this woman was killed in the vicinity, trampled to death by two horsemen who had heard how she had fooled them. They had meant to frighten her but had gone further than planned when one of the horse's hooves crushed her throat.

Since then, many people riding horses have been surprised by a woman in black wearing a long rustling gown. The horses shy and try to throw their riders. Then suddenly she just disappears. Many riders find their way barred by the ghost, and have to turn back or find another, longer route to avoid the spirit.

Some say the only way to force the 'bitch' to get out of the way is to wave a hangman's noose or a riding-whip, others recommend some witch wood from a rowan tree. Yet, while she may be deterred, she cannot be got rid of, as, it is said, she still walks the country lanes of Black Heddon in search of a horseman or woman.

THE BELLINGHAM PEDLAR

When the aristocracy are away the great halls and mansions are run by the servants, who do their best to keep the place neat and tidy with the minimum of effort. Such was the case in the early 1720s when the home of Colonel Ridley, Lee Hall, was visited by a pedlar carrying a huge rucksack on his back. He politely enquired if they would put him up for the night.

As the Colonel was away on business, the servants felt that they could not invite him into the house, but allowed the traveller to spend the night in one of the stables with the horses. He asked if he could leave the rucksack inside, as it contained all of his wares, and he did not want them stolen while he slept. The maid said that that would be all right, so the pedlar placed the pack up against the fireplace in the kitchen. While the maid was locking up before making her way to bed, she saw the pedlar's pack move and heard a noise like a sigh. She tore around the corridors crying out for help, as the pack began to wriggle all the more. Members of staff hastened to her aid, one carrying a musket. As the pedlar's pack began to roll around the kitchen floor, the man fired into it, and blood splashed the wall and began to trickle into a red puddle on the floor.

When they opened the pack, out fell the lifeless body of a tiny man. It seems that the pedlar had planned to rob the house, with his accomplice hidden in the pack, ready to sneak out once the house was quiet to let in his partner. (Some say it was a gang of cut-throats ready to murder the entire household; a two-man operation seems likelier though.)

The legends vary at this point, some say that the servants found a horn in the pack, and when they blew it the pedlar arrived. This fails to explain how, if it was a prearranged signal, the entire household wouldn't be woken by it. More likely is that one of the servants opened the door, and in the early hours the pedlar crept into the house to be surrounded by the staff and to be brought face to face with his dead companion. He was badly beaten up, his nose broken, and his right hand stamped on until it was utterly useless.

*If you visit the churchyard in Bellingham you can see the gravestone of the tiny robber, carved in the shape of the rucksack he was killed inside.

THE BRIGAND OF BARDON MILL

Hardriding Farm, Bardon Mill, near Haltwhistle, was once the home of the legend of a brigand who caused a great deal of suffering in the 1300s. The legend seems to change each time I am told it, so I will present the mainstream version of quite a gruesome tale.

From 1345 to 1371 a brigand used to prey on travellers and farmers alike covering an area between Wark in the north and Alston in the south, Brampton in the west to Hexham in the east. It was a sizeable patch and he became quite a thorn in everyone's side, with crimes attributed to him ranging from murder, arson, and wounding to rape.

Described as a round-shouldered man, with a pock-marked face and bloated jowls, he must certainly have been strongly built, for it is said he once physically picked up a horse with rider aboard and threw them to the ground.

The final straw from this wicked man came in August 1371 when he stopped two young lovers as they walked along the banks of the river at Hexham. It was midday and the riverside was choked with people, yet still, the rogue drew his sword and demanded money. The man refused and was stabbed through the heart. As he lay there dying the brigand emptied his pockets and pushed the girl into the river. She was almost nine months' pregnant and could not swim. Despite all attempts to save her, she was swept to her death. As he made his escape he trampled two three-year-old children, leaving them both in critical condition.

Two locals out riding witnessed this and decided to follow at a discreet distance, so they could guarantee his eventual capture. The brigand not realising he was being followed, returned directly to Hardriding Farm, secreting his horse, and counting his gold. The men decided to finish him on their own, bursting into the house with swords drawn and hacking him to death. They said that even once it was severed his right hand had crawled across the table to grasp at the gold coins, so insane was his desire for money.

They swept the remnants of his butchered carcass into the front yard, where they placed scrub wood around it and set it on fire.

The robber's ghost was regularly seen up to a dozen times a year until 1900; since then it has appeared only twice.

*In April 1927 a young woman felt a man's hand reaching for her purse as she sat in front of the range at Hardriding. She turned to see the hand disappear over the back of her chair. On looking around there was no one there.

*In 1933 the owners of the farm heard yelling and screaming from the living room, as from a violent fight. On rushing into the living room they found all was at peace.

THE NORMAN OF PRUDHOE CASTLE

After the Norman Conquest, William the Conqueror rewarded his knights by giving them huge areas of land, and much of Northumbria came to belong to the French. One lucky knight was Robert de Umfraville, known locally as 'The Bearded One' or 'Robert of the Beard', who inherited the entire area of Redesdale, including Prudhoe Castle. Many who have told of seeing a strange bearded figure there, knew nothing whatsoever at the time about the knight or the history of Redesdale and Prudhoe.

*Louise Cuthbert from Battle Hill in Wallsend stopped off at Prudhoe one day on her way home from Hexham. Not knowing that Prudhoe had a castle, she spotted it, she decided to take a look. On getting close she caught sight of a Norman soldier wearing a bright green tunic over chainmail. His helmet, which had a nose-guard, did not completely cover a big black bushy beard.

*Colin Ryder, a canny lad I worked with many moons ago, told me that he knew of several people having witnessed 'things'. He, himself, lived a street away and had no run-ins with phantoms.

*One of the most dramatic sightings was by two American tourists, Roy and Irma Mankowietz from Boston. They were visiting the castle, and after they had finished taking photographs Irma asked where they would go next; they took out a map, spread it on the ground and pored over it. While they were crouched down they caught sight of a pair of chainmail-clad feet behind them. They glanced around to see a Norman soldier with a sword in hand, mad staring eyes and a long black beard. They left the map and ran into the village where no one took them seriously.

They wrote their story in an American magazine called Phenomena.

*The Umfraville seat passed to the Percy family when Gilbert de Unifraville's widow married Henry de Percy in the 1380s. There had been no ghostly occurrences until Prudhoe Castle lost the Umfraville name.

THE ALNWICK ZOMBIE

Some theologians say that men may die, but the evil that men do lives on. Such was the case in Alnwick, a place steeped in tradition, over which looms the castle, lending a touch of grandeur to this market town.

Tourists today hear many tales of the valour and gallantry of the men who defended those mighty ramparts. There are tales of their cunning too, for when the castle once seemed about to be overrun, and when most of the defenders were dead, those who remained carved statues, standing them on the battlements. The enemy arrived expecting to walk into the undefended castle but found it apparently bristling with troops, and thought better of it. These silent. sentinels remain there to this day, their eyes staring out over both town and country, defending the townsfolk, and confusing their enemies.

But what of the enemy within?

There was once an aged hermit who lived in a dilapidated and rotting cottage close to Alnwick Castle, and who was known to be a nasty piece of work. Soldiers from the castle would see him beating his dog and spitting on passers-by, and once had to restrain him as he attacked a young girl, ripping the clothes off her back.

The townspeople feared the hermit and gave him a wide berth. He, in turn, bristled with resentment for their lifestyle. They seemed to have so much, he had so little – so he began his intimidating escapades. He would kill pigs, sheep and even dogs, often leaving them soaked in blood outside front doors. Several children disappeared, their bodies never to be found, and although the hermit was questioned nothing could be proved against him. A young girl was knocked unconscious and raped, and when she recovered, she could not say who her attacker was, as her tongue had been torn out.

The hermit made everyone's life a misery. He even openly defied the Church during a Sunday service. While the mass was underway, he burst into the chapel swearing and pushing the congregation, his profanities echoing around the sacred building. When the men of the congregation restrained him, he punched one to the ground and stamped on him. He yelled that Satan protected him and that these Christians were fools to follow such a weak God.

While the townsfolk were preparing to have the hermit jailed, he died. It surely was not very Christian of the people to be so happy over his death, but happy they were. Celebrations were held in local hostelries, and the soldiers from the castle shared in the rejoicing.

After the hermit's death, some local farmworkers were sent to his hut to collect the body. They had been told the hermit had been laid out, and pennies placed over his eyes. Entering the darkened building, they made their way through dust and filth and swathes of cobwebs to reach his straw bed. To their horror, there sat the hermit sitting upright, his eyes staring but lifeless. Terrified, they bolted and ran.

Eventually, the soldiers took charge and removed the body under a sheet, the joints stiff with rigor mortise. To place him in his cheap wooden coffin they had to break dozens of his bones. That done, they set fire to the hut where so much evil was thought to have taken place.

When it was announced that the hermit was to be buried in holy ground, the people began protesting, for he had proclaimed Satan as his saviour and had denounced God. Despite the protests, however, and although he had never confessed his sins, the hermit was given a Christian burial. Words were said at his funeral to indicate that although he had lived a wicked and evil life, he was now in the hands of God, and it was up to God alone to judge him.

Within two days of his burial, a farmer whose duty it was to tend the churchyard noticed that the hermit's grave had been disturbed. Someone, or something had scraped the shallow covering of light soil away and the casket was open and empty. Turning around, the farmer saw the body propped against a tree. … There were packs of dogs in old Alnwick, but surely, they would not dig up an entire corpse? Had the townspeople decided to remove it? Or had the accursed body escaped from purgatory to wreak his revenge on those so overjoyed at his passing? This time the townspeople buried him deep, laying heavy stones on the grave so he would not escape again. Or so they hoped…

But Alnwick soon became a very changed place. People would see a shadowy figure lurking in bushes, in gardens and outside houses; they would often feel the sensation of someone breathing down their neck, and on turning, their lungs were filled with the rancid stench of a carcass long dead! Dogs howled throughout the night hours, keeping people awake and shattering their nerves. No one dared step outside after dark, and the local inns were forced to close their doors for a lack of custom.

The local farrier said it was stupid to fear the dead, for surely the living can do you more harm, and he continued his hobby of snaring rabbits in the rolling Northumbrian hills. One morning a shepherd found his body lying in the valley beneath Alnwick Castle, his throat torn out.

This death caused yet more terror amongst the townsfolk, and some began to leave Alnwick to set up homes elsewhere. Still, people saw the shadowy figure, now beginning to foul the air as his body began to rot on his bones. Rats were attracted by pieces of the hermit's decaying flesh as he continued his deathly patrol through the streets in search of his prey. Having feasted on the tainted and rotten skin and sinew, the rats infested the homes of the people of Alnwick, and soon a second horror spread through the town streets – the plague!

A plague bell accompanied the dreadful cry of 'Bring out your dead!', and the scab-covered bodies were dragged out and piled on dozens of others. There was not a house in the town which did not lose someone during the pestilence that followed. The cottages of the dead were burned, their clothes and possessions were thrown onto the bonfires that lit up the skies like hell on earth.

Superstition began to overtake what remained of the community. The people began to blame the Church for allowing the defiled presence of one of the Devil's children into holy ground, and it was then that the sons of a local man decided to take matters into their own hands. The young men gathered the people together in the market square and marched towards the graveyard, determined to put matters right. The pawn of Lucifer lay buried deep in the Lord's earth: only when he was out of there and burned would there be peace…

It took all of the crowd's strength to move the rocks placed on the grave, and then there were six feet of water-sodden earth to get through. Yet within moments of their starting to dig, there, poking through the soil, was a hand reaching upwards, and the crowd gasped as someone shrieked, 'It's moving!'

The Alnwick Zombie was only inches beneath the ground, yet with their own eyes, the horrified townsfolk had seen the hermit's vile corpse planted two yards deep.

Scraping away at the soil, they finally uncovered his remains, not thin and bony, but gorged with blood, a human leech, reddened and puffed, fattened on the blood of the honest citizens of Alnwick! The body as once more out of his coffin, his shroud was ripped and tattered, and there was soil under his long claw-like nails.

The women averted their eyes and crossed themselves, for surely this creature had been feeding on the agony and torment of all of Alnwick. The men could only stare; a silence had come over them as if they were hypnotised by this bloated and disgusting creature. Although dead for over seven months, he had not decomposed but had increased in size. This was surely the Devil's work!

As the panic began to surge within him, one of the brothers picked up his crude shovel and swung it down with all his force on the body. The swollen corpse exploded with blood at the impact. A torrent of gore rained down for yards around as the others joined in, hacking and chopping in a frenzy of blood lust as they attempted to exorcise the power of this fiendish soul from hell.

At long last, they were exhausted. Summoning their remaining energy, they carried the scattered remains away from the sacred ground, piled them up at the crossroads on the outskirts of Alnwick and set them on fire. They say that the body didn't burn red, but gave off a blue flame.

As the flames grew in ferocity many onlookers swore that the pieces were knitting themselves back together again. Once consumed by fire, the ashes were collected and thrown into the River Aln.

The following morning birds sang again for the first time in months, the mist lifted and the sun shone. From that day forth no one was lost to the plague, but people still believe that a shadowy figure can be seen wandering the long streets of Alnwick.

* **In January 1970, a student (Malcolm Hardy from Wales)** was working on a local farm. Seeing the bent figure of a man with staring eyes, dressed only in rags, he approached him to offer him a drink from his flask and a piece of KitKat, but as he got within three feet of him, the ragged figure disappeared.

* **Cheryl Potts of Pallion in Sunderland** was asleep in her car, parked on the main street in Alnwick when she felt someone fondling her right breast. She had locked the car door, so thought she was dreaming until she awoke with a start. She described what she saw for Metro FM's 'Night Owls' programme: 'There was this dirty, smelly tramp sitting across me and he was trying to rape me. I pushed him and screamed and suddenly he wasn't there anymore. I'll never forget his eyes, he really had crazy eyes. People were walking past the car and they must have thought I'd lost my mind. I have never told anyone this because no one would believe me!'

* In 1986 Mrs R. Young, visiting Alnwick from Edinburgh, said that while sitting on the grass with her family just below the castle, 'I began to smell something so vile I was almost sick. The smell kept returning every couple of seconds and I felt as if someone was breathing right in my face!'

THE DIRTY BOTTLES OF ALNWICK

Old Cross Inn on Narrowgate in Alnwick used to be a wine shop and bakery. Now it's a quality 'olde-worlde' pub.

They have an old ledger dated around 1810 telling of an incident involving a man who was creating a window display with the latest collection of sherry. As he was installing the bottles he felt a sharp pain in his chest and collapsed backwards on to the floor and died. The lady owner of the shop declared that his display must never be touched again, and had the entire window boarded up.

The window is said to be cursed, and anyone who dares to move the bottles now shrouded in dust and cobwebs would suffer the same fate as the man.

The staff of the Old Cross are very worried indeed at present as the heavy wooden casks that the bottles stand on are rotting away, tie cask has already crumbled, smashing some bottles, sherry quaking into the floorboards, and the others are going the same way. The staff don't know whether to clear up the mess, leave it it is, or try to restore what is a legend that has lasted close to one hundred years.

MURDER AT ALNWICK FAIR

When Northerners think of Alnwick Fair they think of happy locals wearing costumes of days gone by, milling around stalls and having fun. Yet there was a time when the fair would attract a different sort of crowd, a crowd with a lust for death.

Many people believe that it was at Alnwick Fair that the very first ducking stool was ever used in the North. I have heard many different stories of the Alnwick Fair ducking stool, but the only one to crop up twice is about an old woman called Annie who lived in a tiny village now known as Shilbottle.

Her husband was a seafarer, never at home, believed to be a member of the crew of the Discovery. Whilst he was involved in a mutiny against the explorer Henry Hudson, she was at the centre of a murderous plot at home.

The year was 1611, and Annie found her daughter Esther in a state of distress. An Alnwick man had tried to rape the girl, but she had managed to escape. Her clothes were ripped and one entire side of her pretty face was swollen and bruised.

Annie gathered together her family and friends and they 'visited' the young man as he worked in the fields near High Buston. When they charged him with the crime, he merely laughed. Rape in the 1600s was commonplace, and women had almost no rights at all, but goaded by the young man's arrogance, Annie and her companions decided to carry out their own sentence. Annie ordered that he be held down on the ground, and as he lay there wriggling and cursing each of them he glimpsed a small campfire being built. He taunted each of his captors, saying that his uncle was the local magistrate and they would pay a great price for hurting him. So confident was he that no harm would befall him that he burst out laughing, saying 'This is ridiculous! She's only a girl, what harm is a little bit of fun? Anyway, it's not as if I done her!'

He was in mid-laugh when he saw Annie approach him carrying a large iron bar. Her hand was wrapped in cloth lest she burn herself. The end of the bar glowed white-hot. Two men pulled down his trousers as his confidence turned to horror and he squealed 'For pity's sake, no!'

Annie thrust the sizzling iron into his groin. He screamed until he passed out, as the smell of burning flesh filled the lungs of his captors. They had gelded him!

Things returned to the rural norm once again, but by the end of 1611 word reached Alnwick of how witches were to be persecuted throughout the country. It was then that a plot was hatched to pay Annie back. Her victim began collecting stories about how Annie was a witch. He persuaded his friends to spread the word, and when she appeared at Alnwick Fair she was pointed out. Although this was in the days before the witchfinders would gain notoriety, a ducking stool had been erected. The local magistrate saw how the crowd had been incited against the old woman and was powerless to help. Superstition and the fear of witches had eaten away at the folk of old Alnwick; if this woman was a witch she had to be destroyed.

Despite the protests of the few sane-minded citizens, Annie was tied to the primitive stool. Surprisingly, she did not put up a fight. She knew who the ringleader was, and seemed content knowing that he would never molest any other woman. As the stool took her down for the first time she merely held her breath, returning to the surface gasping for air. The second time was not so easy for her, and the third time her tormentors waited for a huge stream of bubbles to rise to the surface. She screamed underwater as the water poured into her body and took her life.

The man she had gelded had taken his revenge, but it was not something he would savour for long. That night he was walking past an inn on the market square when a slab of stone fell from a window's edge and killed him. Many said that before she died Annie had cursed him. This may well be true, but she was certainly not a witch – though she was only one of many to be wrongly drawn into the savage rooting out of witchcraft.

GOREGEIST OF ALNWICK

Sometimes we find ourselves trapped in the same space as something we just cannot understand. Such was the story of Scots Mary and Jack Lynch who found themselves in a nightmare of the worst kind. It would destroy their careers, their marriage and their lives. They moved to Northumberland from London where they ran a successful bed and breakfast establishment. They sold well and with their hard-earned nest egg, they escaped the fumes of the city and set up a new business in the countryside idyll of Northumberland. They found a small dilapidated hotel and set about restoring it. After weeks living in a caravan, the building was finally taking shape and ready for guests. They were ahead of schedule, things had gone well, too well!

The first guests arrived, spent two satisfactory nights and were gone. This was all so easy. Until they moved into their accommodation in the B&B. Mary began having severe migraine headaches, it felt like there was extreme pressure on the sides of her head. Jack began having strange flashes across his mind of blood, people dying and people screaming in pain. At first, he did not mention anything until Mary described a dream that had woken her the night before. She described how she saw dark shadowy figures hacking men, women and children to pieces. "It was so real" she explained "and finally this brute picked up a baby by its ankles and just slammed it into a wall shattering its skull and leaving a bloody trail across the stone! I woke up screaming, my daughter in Bayswater was pregnant and I thought of her!"

Realising that she was seeing similar pictures to him, he unburdened himself of the daily horrors he saw.

Then one morning Mary was making up a bed in a room for guests due that evening. She looked down at the empty bed and saw the body of a young woman, her head hacked into two and her body torn open with entrails dripping down over the end of the bed. As she screamed for Jack the eyes opened and the bloody face contorted into a smile. The poor woman was so shocked a doctor was called and she needed sedating. The pressure was also affecting Jack, his daily visions of vile brutalities were beginning to transform this confident Scotsman into a gibbering wreck. After three months of having no sleep, they were both at the end of their tether when they put their dream enterprise up for sale. They had planned to stay on until a buyer could be found, until the cold night of November 11th 1993. Mary was putting face cream on whilst sitting at her dressing table. In the mirror behind her, she saw a group of figures, one man had a knife and was drawing it across his arm over and over again. Blood dripping down onto her side of their bed. She spun around and squealed, waking Jack, but the figures had gone. Her husband's nightmare interrupted, he struggled to get back to his uncomfortable unrest with Mary unable to sleep. Suddenly the bed moved, not a little, as when someone turns over, it moved four feet and hit off a bedside chair. They both jumped up and got out of the bed when something pushed them both to the ground. Jack explains "I was trampled on by what felt like a dozen men. Then I was kicked and what felt like a knee hitting me in the face split my lip. All of the ghost stories I had ever heard said that these things go through you, believe me, they can be as solid as you or I. I grabbed Mary and we ran down into the dining room. We had about a dozen guests all sleeping in their rooms, what could we do? We could not leave!"

Jack went to the toilet and as he sat there the light bulb exploded. He felt a hand reach into his stomach and grip him, it squeezed his stomach and he vomited across the door. When he opened the door allowing light from the hall he could see that the spatter of his vomit had the shape of a man clear for all to see in the middle. By this time, Mary was weeping, quivering in fear. "Every time I closed my eyes I saw horrid images of people being murdered, women and children attacked and blood... so much blood. My doctor told me I was suffering from stress, but something was doing this to us. I kept seeing this one woman, her head hacked open, she was forever staring at me, laughing and trying to provoke me. While Jack was at the toilet she appeared in front of me. I could see her shattered bones in her skull, veins and arteries pumping blood and this horrible gurgling noise. As I looked down she looked like an octopus, her intestines were just hanging down wrapping around her legs"

This 'goregeist' phenomenon is rare when people see bloody images from a time before. The following morning Jack gave refunds to some of his guests and told them all to leave. He hired a wagon to collect all their belongings and they moved back to London. The bed & breakfast remained unsold for eight years before being sold and redeveloped into a shop.

Historian Paul Baker researched the area of north Alnwick and found that it is an area where a betrayal took place. In the 1500s, a common way to stop Border Reivers from attacking villages was to offer 'Days of Truce', the equivalent of a Bank Holiday and where spectators would travel to settle their scores. Without fighting, all disputes would be discussed and resolved. However, in 1574 a group of Scottish outlaws stumbled into one of these festivals. A woman Meggie Carmichael told them they were welcome and all their sins would be forgiven on that day. She even allowed the eight of them to sleep in her house and barn. It was then that she hatched a plot to get them to murder a man who had wronged her. They did this as most of Alnwick slept in a drunken slumber. However, whilst the Scots were dispatching the unfortunate ex-boyfriend, Meggie was sending a boy to inform the soldiers what the Scots were doing. She was overheard and the boy was killed. In a drunken rage, the Scots murdered her three children and brutally killed her. Just as she was dying she was heard laughing.

The Scots were confused until the soldiers burst in and arrested them all. Meggie's laugh could be heard as they were shackled and taken to Alnwick Castle for sentencing. "They've done for me and mine," said Meggie, "but this day shall ne'er be forgotten. Not as long as Meggie is here to remind them!"

HANGED AT THE HOTSPUR TOWER

One of Alnwicks greatest landmarks is the Hotspur Tower that stands on the entrance to Bondgate. Today only the gate survives and shows the entrance to the old walled town. Its name comes from 'bondagers' as it was built by men and women who were in effect slaves to their landlord. During the mid to late 1400s, all of Northumberland fell victim to the plague that had killed its way across Europe. The land around Alnwick was particularly badly hit. Some villages were completely wiped out and they built a plague pit in the rolling ground that currently lies across the river from where Alnwick Castle now stands. Such was the terror created by the 'Black Death' that bodies of plague victims were placed in a pit up to ten deep, the dead and the living coiled together whilst lamp oil was poured in, then covered with kindling then put to the flame. Town folk watched from a distance as their friends and family were burned. Hundreds of bodies remain as ash beneath the ground, and there have been reports of screams and floating apparitions in that area ever since. In 1986, a fair was held on the land and whilst packing up their stall the Jobson's of Berwick saw a ghost. "It was the strangest thing," said Edward Jobson "We had been selling farm produce and had done quite well when I heard my wife scream from the back of our tent. I ran in and saw her cowering in the corner and standing over her was a figure. I shouted and it turned to face me. It was a man in his fifties with a beard and pockmarked skin. He took three steps towards me and I thought he was going to attack me. His eyes were jet black and he looked terrified, but not half as terrified as I was. He looked solid but went straight through me. At that second I felt this enormous fear and I could not help myself from crying. My flesh became itchy too and I had to scratch myself over and over again. The following morning I woke up with three boils on my chest. I had never had a boil before or since. My wife and I know what we saw and swear to it. It was the oddest experience of my life. If that is what a ghost is, I never want to see another bugger!"

Following the plague there was a great shortage of workers, so the Lord decreed that all men and women living in their cottages had to work free if they wanted to keep their homes. Months of unpaid labour in the fields followed, usually carried out by the women and children, as the man had to tend their farms and smallholdings. One worker, James Merrick disappeared around this time and gave birth to a legend. His wife said that he had left her, moving up to Scotland to start a new life without her. However, there is a story that a man was found hanging from the Hotspur Tower gate whilst construction was underway. Rather than taint the construction of such a fine structure they threw his body into a foundation trench and just carried on. Between 1870 and the 1950s many people saw a dark shadow late at night in this area. An American couple in the late 1960s claimed to have driven through the gate and saw a man hanging from a rope. They presumed it was a dummy as it was the week of Alnwick Fayre. It was not.

ALNWICK CASTLE: THE SIGHTINGS

This truly beautiful castle, reconstructed in the 1700s, seems to have soaked up the amazing history it has been such a great part of. The world-renowned architect Robert Adam was hired to recreate a castle with a pristine Gothic outlook. Used as the school Hogwarts in the Harry Potter movies, it gathers tourists from across the world. In the mid-1800s, Anthony Salvin stripped away many of Adam's internal designs, replacing them to bring back the castle's medieval features.

If you seek to search for spirit in a place where so many lives were taken, let me give you a plan. Essentially Alnwick Castle remains as it was first built as a circular keep, two baileys and a wall with numerous towers. The road from Alnwick town centre will lead you directly to the castle gates. The gates should be your first photograph, as during one of the many insurrections the bodies of tortured prisoners were hanged on the gates. Numerous photographs have strange swoops of light, transparent figures and particularly in the first light of morning, there have been sightings in this area. During one of the early battles against the Scots, a war chief gave an ultimatum to the castle to surrender. Instead, the Captain charged with negotiation drew his sword and told the chief to run. He did not and had his head sliced clean off. It was placed on a spike so 'He can see the destruction of his men'.

Next to the entrance, there is the barbican that was built to help protect the main gate from attack, as it regularly was. It is said to deter any adversary for trying to force their way in. The proud emblem of the Percy Shield with its rampant lion and motto can still clearly be seen on the archway. The barbican and gatehouse were separated from the castle by a ditch, once flooded into a moat. This moat was once so full with dead Scotsmen that their comrades could run over their backs. The Alnwick soldiers got in and out over one of the countries biggest drawbridges and at the end of its huge heavy bolstered doors was a razor-sharp portcullis. This huge barbican was often the only part of the castle attacked and it always held it's own during a siege. Often people have claimed to see faces peering down on them from this structure.

In 1962 Elizabeth Murray from Berwick-upon-Tweed reported that she had seen someone fall from the barbican. She told the staff who investigated but found no one. Others confirmed what she had seen, but was it some ghostly replay of some time in the past being repeated?

Nowadays, the public enters through the stable courtyard to the right of the gate complex, but the original way in was past the barbican. The stable area has had its moments too. On one occasion when thousands of arrows were fired over the walls, the Scottish prisoners in manacles were sent out into the yard to be killed by their own people. The torrent of arrows only stopped when a prisoner was released to tell what was happening. A long and irregular curtain wall, broken by tall medieval towers rims the outer bailey. Each tower has had its share of ghostly sightings, including several where people feel the touch or breath of some invisible entity. Margaret Sturrock took a group of friends to the castle and suffered a severe panic attack whilst in one of the towers. She explains "I was enjoying my day out until I walked into the tower and I felt as if I had walked in on something. I felt as if I should not be there. Something black moved along the edge of the room and another behind me. I had never seen a ghost before, I was not even sure I believed in them, then these two black shapes wedged me into a corner. I could smell breath on my face, a rotten cabbage smell so strong I started choking. I tried to scream but couldn't and eventually just passed out!"

To the right, you see the Clock Tower and the Auditors Tower with the original stonework from the 1300s. In this area, there have been regular sightings of a soldier who appears to follow visitors who sense his presence. He has also been captured on numerous photographs. The auditor's tower used to keep animals on its ground floor. Between the two towers, there are chambers and administrative offices, yet they used to be the billets of the defenders of the castle. This in these area's have moved, electrical gadgets switch on and off and many cameras, particularly camcorders fail to work. Across the bailey, to the left of the keep and gatehouse, you can see the Abbot's tower. This was built in the 1300s where the Abbott of Alnwick Abbey could reside in safety while his monks were being regularly slaughtered and attacked. This is now the home of the regimental museum of the Royal Northumberland Fusiliers. If you walk along that side of the curtain you reach the Falconers Tower, the best area to capture images of the rest of the castle. The strangest phenomenon here is the sound of crying. Visitors often feel an overwhelming sorrow, some weeping for no reason, and many seeking to get out of that area of the castle.

Behind the keep, you find Alnwick Castle's middle bailey surrounded by its long curtain wall. At night, visitors and staff have both seen numerous shadowy shapes gliding along this lush grassy area. On nights when the sea fret and fog rolls in you can see it moving unnaturally as if figures are moving around in it. Many of these segments go back 800 years with people losing their lives in every direction. The rather more modern Warders Tower, the 14th Century Eastern Garrett and the Record Tower are all popular with visitors, yet all with ghosts attributed to them. Hotspurs Seat is a 14th Century guard Tower and it's said that any Scot to visit this place will be unsettled by it. You must stand in the centre of the tower, close your eyes and allow the 'wisper' to speak to you and give you visions of the blood that was spilt there. Hundreds of reports of voices here, shouting, screams and even one case of a fatal heart attack back in the 1950s.

The Constables Tower and the Postern Tower both built by the first Lord Henry Percy remain as they looked in the 1300s and many of those who lived there through the years appear to remain therein. This is where the majority of clear sightings have been made, noises, footsteps, darting black figures, rustles of dresses, the clanking of armour, voices and the patter of children's feet.

The Constable lived in the Constables Tower and some believe a few of them remain. It was also used as an armoury and defended by archers firing through the tiny slit windows, and has huge battlements on top of its majestic form. The Postern Tower has the castle's last escape hatch, the sally port, designed to help defend the rather isolated keep.

If you go through the Middle Gateway, you find two baileys and you get to the keep across a short wooden bridge. It was on this bridge that two traitorous Northumbrian tribal leaders were bent over and decapitated as a warning to any others who dared betray the Duke. You pass through a dual towered archway built in 1350 and designed in an octagonal shape to warn visitors of malicious intent. It is four stories tall, once with a portcullis and with heavy wooden doors. Just inside the door, there is the Bottle Dungeon, barely lit with arrow slits. When not housing prisoners, it became just another area that required defending. Many prisoners died in this room, either being starved to death or being allowed to die of their wounds. Some say you can smell death in this place. On the battlements that feature stone from every period in its history right the way back to the Norman Conquest of 1066. You can also see the life-size stone soldiers guarding the castle and acting as a deterrent against any approaching enemy. Add them to the real soldiers and it looks to anyone that the castle had a formidable garrison.

Inside the castle, another ghost watching area has to be the Grand Staircase where many have watched the white figure of a woman swishing down, yet floating a foot from the ground. Ghosts seem to have appeared everywhere over the centuries. In the fine library, the Red Drawing Room, especially the Drawing Room that had previously been the medieval banqueting hall. Here the knights would speak of their conquests and their plotting for and against various sides. If you place your hand on the fireplace you are said to connect to the spirits of Alnwick. That night you will dream of those who died to keep it safe.

An amazing place with an above-average opportunity to experience it's great history and things not of this physical world.

ALNWICK CASTLE: HOME OF THE WISPERY

Alnwick Castle, forever home of the Dukes of Northumberland who still resides in one of Northumberland's true gems. Although it has been changed and restored over the years, it remains essentially what it always was designed to be a symbol of power and wealth. The first castle on this site was built in the 11th century when William the Conqueror's standard-bearer Gilbert de Tesson acquired the castle. Some say that it was ceded to him as the Norman King rewarded the men who had fought by his side. The locals were less enamoured being ruled over by the French, but any hint of rebellion was swiftly crushed. Rather than risk a long, drawn-out conflict with the rebellious, they bought information to locate dissenters who were put to the sword. Eventually, people were too frightened to even think about talking openly about their new rulers, lest their entire family would be killed. The spies used this as a way of getting rid of people they had a grudge against. Rivals in business or love were named as rebels, then once they were out of the way the spies got what they wanted. Such was the case of a family that history merely describes as 'The Weavers' whether this was their name or profession we'll probably never know. This innocent family were fingered by a spy as plotting against De Tesson. The reality was that 'The Weavers' husband, wife and seven children lived on land next to the River Aln, land needed by a neighbour to water his animals. The Weavers' refused him permission for his animals because he had stolen from them in the past. For being law-abiding they were named as rebels. The Norman's sent out twenty men at midnight who surrounded the cottage and set it on fire as the family slept. As the fire began to intensify, the families awoke and tried to escape but were forced back inside at sword point. One of the son's made it out and attempted to get to the woods in the darkness. On tripping over an exposed tree root, the Norman's were on him and cut him to pieces. By this time several neighbours from across the river were watching the fracas one of them bore witness 'The woman was on fire, her hair burning as she howled like a wolf; They pushed her back in and above the screams all we could hear was the laughter of the Norman'.

All the while, the Scot's aided by many of the Northumbrian Celts kept attacking the invaders looking for any chance to give the land back to the people. Then in 1087 William the Conqueror was back in Normandy fighting the French who had attacked his homeland. As he rode over cinders after raiding Rouen his horse stumbled and they both fell, his horse rolling over the top of him. His angular armour that he had designed himself cut into his abdomen rupturing several internal organs. This Norman Duke had become King of England and had built eighty castles across England and had his men placed at each one to keep hold of the power. The Scot's and Celt's kept battling away and not far from Alnwick the Scottish King Malcolm Canmore was killed in battle by Robert Mowbray the Earl of Northumberland.

A rhyme of the day from a Northumbrian who cared not for the Norman's.

With slash of sword and flash of spear

Fought well against the Norman

A King struck down in shame

By the blade of an Alnwick man

Two years later Gilbert de Tesson, known locally as Tyson, rebelled against the new English King William Rufus. As soon as this uprising failed he was turfed out of Alnwick Castle and all of his possessions', including his army, were taken from him. The castle and lands were given to Yvo de Vescy who immediately started building an even greater fortress. His daughter Beatrix was also his only heir and she married Eustace Fitzjohn who would be given the title of Baron of Alnwick. He would eventually team up with anarchist Empress Matilda who was the daughter of the late King Henry. Her men had just slaughtered a third of the population of Lincoln and King Stephen watched his cavalry flee in panic. Matilda, who was best known for her bad temper, became Domina Anglorum 'Lady of The English' and prepared herself for her coronation. It never happened after she exchanged the King for her half brother the Earl of Gloucester. Stephen took back his thrown and all of Matilda's allies were undone. Fitzjohn had to give back the castle but began working on King Stephen until eventually, having successfully switched sides, the traitor got his castle and land back. The first ghost sighting followed the death of Fitzjohn in Wales in 1157. Workers at the castle said that three days after his death, Fitzjohn was seen walking across the battlements as he always did in life. Several approached him believing that he was still alive only to see the apparition fade away before their eyes.

The descendants of the De Vescy dynasty continued to keep control of one of England's most northerly outposts. In 1172 and again in 1174 the Scot's besieged Alnwick Castle defended by William De Vescy. The Scottish King William the Lion was captured in a battle whilst trying to escape in the fog. In an amazing contradiction of likelihood, De Vescy's son eventually married The Lion's daughter. Then all hell let loose when King John came to the throne because William the Lion claimed that he owned all Northumberland. Whilst that was still debatable, King John came to Alnwick Castle at least twice and an uneasy truce fell into place.

Over the years, the owners of Alnwick had regular rebellions against the King and in 1212 he ordered that Alnwick Castle be torn down 'twas a carbuncle on the arse of my reign'. Fortunately, it was never carried out as Alnwick joined forces with the Scots again and allied them to King Alexander of Scotland when he invaded Northumberland. The people living there had no great love for the English but knew they were stronger than the Scottish and Celts combined. Many tried not to get involved, just tilling the land and hiding at the sight of warring factions. Yet Alnwick was burned to the ground in 1215. Those who had not fled were captured and placed in Market Square. They were surrounded by armed men and began pleading for mercy, only for the four lines of soldiers to march into them, hacking them to pieces. 350 men women and children were executed to quell 'Northumberland's nest of vipers'.

To his credit, Eustace de Vescy kept rebelling until he was killed by an arrow in his neck whilst besieging Barnard Castle.

Forty years of relative calm followed until John de Vescy joined Simon de Montfort in an attempt to overthrow King Henry III. He was eventually wounded in the bloody battle of Evesham in 1265 and forced out of Alnwick, eventually having to buy it back. Following his death, his brother William took it over and was immediately in conflict with the Scots. William Wallace, 'Braveheart' besieged it in 1297 but this superbly defended castle stayed strong and Wallace had no choice but to fight around it. Following the death of de Vescy, the Bishop of Durham was awarded control until he could find a purchaser. In 1309 it was bought by Henry Percy.

Even then, the Percy family were one of the most powerful in all England. Henry, the first Lord Percy would continue the Alnwick legacy and go against the English King but also fight the Scots simultaneously. In 1314, he led a revolt against King Edward II and declined to fight with the King against the Scots at Bannockburn. He was taken prisoner and was ransomed back to the English. The following seven Percy lords were all called Henry too, fighting with bravery across Europe.

Yet it was the fourth Percy Lord who is perhaps the best known. He was a born warrior, not just fighting for a cause but loving it. He was skilled with every weapon of the day and battled for over thirty years against all comers. William Shakespeare in Henry IV made his son famous as Harry Hotspur. At the age of twelve, this chunky boy took to the field in the Battle of Otterburn and took dozens of lives. Even at such a tender age, he inspired his troops leading a nighttime attack against the Scottish. Even though he failed and was captured he earned a name as a warrior that would stay with him. His ghost is regularly seen leaping from battlements at the nearby ruined Warkworth Castle.

In 1399 the Earl of Northumberland and his son were accused of treason by King Richard II, so they immediately began a revolt against him. They succeeded in unseating him and replacing him with their favourite King Henry IV. True to their fickle alliances they would later rise against him for he was not remotely grateful to them for putting him on the throne. Hotspur was killed and his father surrendered and the castle held out until it was confronted by one of the King's huge wooden siege engines. It had been pushed all the way from Leeds to show they were serious about taking Alnwick Castle. Following the release of Henry Percy he started another rebellion and was forced to flee up to Scotland and live in exile. His final effort to bring down the King ended in his death in 1409 at Bramham Moor. He was unseated from his horse and dragged through the English who all stabbed and hacked at him.

The next Henry Percy was a close friend of the future King Henry V and never was a friendship more necessary. The Scot's managed to besiege and eventually burn Alnwick Castle. The marauding Scot's had lost thousands of souls to the castle so were determined to destroy it, and the men who defended it. All those who did not perish during the assault were taken down into the cellars and cells. They placed barrels of oil and wood among them then locked the door after rolling oil down the stairs and setting it afire. No one knows how many were there, but they died the vilest death. The cellars are filled with a unique feeling, to describe it as a presence would not be accurate. There is a weight on the chest. Those people who are open to such things have felt smokiness on their lungs and the grip of panic. Visitors have had to leave swiftly following nausea and twisting in the stomach.

Four years following the fall of Alnwick Castle the Second Earl of Northumberland got involved in the War of the Roses between the Houses of Lancaster and York. He was killed at the Battle of St. Albans in 1455.

The third Earl of Northumberland was another Northerner who enjoyed to fight. He sided with the Lancastrians and fought against the Yorkists whilst also having to fend off the Scot's. He played a huge part in the battle from whence the rhyme 'The Grand Old Duke of York' comes. One of the bloodiest events to take place on English soil was the Battle of Towton. The Earl was killed along with 38,560 others as the Duke of York defeated the Kings forces and seized power. It was written 'I waded up to my chest in the limbs and entrails of the dead. There was so much blood it ran in rivers down the hill and those trying to reach the fight slipped on it. The cold land steamed as bodies were opened up and skulls split by sword and axe. So tired was I from battle, I lost will to go on and hid beneath the bodies of the dead as those from both sides walked over me. After the battle, we (the Yorkists) were victorious but looked around and saw death on all sides. The weeping of the women and children in search of their men was a grip to the soul'.

The Yorkists besieged Alnwick Castle twice, on one occasion firing captured Alnwick town's folk over the walls by catapult. The castle eventually fell but would later be returned to the Earl of Northumberland when Edward IV came to the throne.

In 1489 the sitting Earl of Northumberland declared that he had to double the taxes, and to his surprise, the people rose against him. As he sat in the great hall, a mob of townspeople stormed in and helped by some of the soldiers upset they had to pay tax, and rather than negotiating, they beat him to a pulp. They carried his body to a window and threw it to the cheering crowd below.

This incredible castle has always been the home of controversy and that wondrous Northern trait of stubbornness. The Seventh Earl Thomas Percy was beheaded by Queen Elizabeth in 1572 because he supported her adversaries Mary Queen of Scots and the Catholic Church. The Eighth Earl supported Mary too and was put into the Tower of London and died in mysterious circumstances. Some say he killed himself, others believe he was just executed and even that the other prisoners had turned on him. There was a suggestion some years later to say that they had refused to feed the prisoners and the plump Earl was eaten by his cellmates. The truth is we know for sure.

The Ninth Earl's cousin was one of the members of the Gunpowder plot where Fawkes attempted to blow up parliament. The castle fell into disrepair until Sir Hugh Smithson became Duke of Northumberland in 1755, from that day the Northumberlands were an integral part of Royal society. His wife was a Percy and to gain control of the lands he changed his surname to that.

THE BARBER OF BELFORD

In the 1880s there was a barber in Belford known as Watty, serving both the living and the dead. For even after someone had died, Watty was called in to shave him so that he would look decent when laid out in the parlour, as was the custom of the day. He did not have sufficient work in Belford to keep him going, so he was also well known as a travelling barber throughout the area, from Beadnell and Bamburgh, Bellshill, Chatton and Wooler. Although Watty was getting on in years when he suddenly quit, questions were asked – he had, after all, been a local institution for over forty years. Watty explained that the last three months of his working life involved nothing other than shaving or cutting the hair of the dead or dying. Then, during the last shave of a dying merchant, Watty claimed, the Devil appeared in a cloud of fire and brimstone and declared, 'That'll do, Watty, I'll take him as he is.'

BUCKTON'S GRIZEL

At Buckton in Northumberland walks an interesting ghost known as Grizel, short for Grizelda, the daughter of Sir John Cochrane who lay rotting in a dungeon in Edinburgh Castle for the part he played in Argyll's rebellion against James II.

When he succeeded his brother, the rather randy Charles II, the King declared that the role of the monarchy would never be tainted by debauchery again. His new order was far from popular, particularly when he ordered his soldiers to arrange that the Whigs were defeated, assuring that the more manageable Tories were elected. At 'the Bloody Assizes' Judge Jeffreys sentenced 320 of the Duke of Monmouth's supporters to hang, 840 to be sold into slavery and many others to be lashed with the whip or the cat-o'-nine-tails. The Duke of Argyll's supporters met with a similar fate, and the Judge sent out execution warrants throughout Britain to mete out what was loosely termed justice.

Knowing her father's death warrant was to be delivered to Edinburgh by coach, Cochrane's shapely daughter Grizel dressed as a highwayman and held up the coach. She took all of the mail including the death warrant.

It was her timely intervention that gave Cochrane's followers sufficient time to half-plead with and half-bribe officials into getting Sir John a pardon. Near Buckton, there is a copse of trees known as Grizzy's Clump, the cluster of bushes where she lay in wait for the coach.

The ghost of that girl on horseback, dressed as a highwayman is said to appear at the end of every month.

*Mrs Marjorie Burke said: 'I was one of the sceptics who had heard of Grizel but refused to believe it. Yet one night in 1987 I was driving home in my Ford Fiesta when I heard a horse. I turned to see someone riding a black hone, wearing a black cape and tricorn hat. It was almost eleven o'clock at night and I can't imagine anyone riding about in fancy dress at that time. You don't think I'm stupid, do you? And I hadn't been drinking!'

THE DISSECTED SAINT OF BAMBURGH

One of the greatest castles left standing anywhere in Great Britain has to be Bamburgh. Used as Macbeth's castle in Roman Polanski's film, it is the archetypal Northern fortress. Earlier structures on this site were probably used by the Romans and the Celts, who called it Dinguaroy. Yet only when the walls were changed from wood to stone did it begin to be known as 'impregnable'.

The fate of the Northumbrian king, Saint Oswald, leads to one of the creepier stories about Bamburgh Castle. Oswald was determined to kill off a wave of pagan worship and ritual by restoring Christianity to the confused Northumbrian tribes. He was helped in this by dozens of monks who landed in Cumbria, travelling across Britain with Oswald's help, and setting up a monastery on Lindisfarne (Holy Island). Northumbria lived in peace under Oswald until Penda, the pagan king of Mercia, murdered him at Maserfelth.

Perhaps it was the fact that a deeply religious king had been put to the sword by a Devil-worshipping warlord that sparked the fierce legends. The terrifying tales began when Penda returned Oswald's body to Bamburgh in pieces. His head and hand were embalmed; the rest was buried in sacred ground. Then strange things began to happen when, in the mid-700s, Oswald's head disappeared. Some say it was stolen, others suggest it had been taken by the angels because he was such a holy man.

As if cursed, the fortunes of Bamburgh went into rapid decline. Viking raiders raped, pillaged and murdered the people of the town, and many were forced to live further inland. Even religious figures began to steal the silver and gold crosses and crucifixes.

In the time of William the Conqueror, Bamburgh Castle became a Norman stronghold. Yet another British fortress to protect our new rulers from their new slaves. It was during this unsavoury time that one so-called monk crept into the chapel where St Oswald's hand remained as a sacred relic, hid it on his person and fled. It is said that the monk was found strangled some days later, and the less educated swore that it was Oswald's hand that choked the life out of him!

The fortunes of Bamburgh continued to seem cursed with bad luck. Robert of Mowbray was trapped by William Rufus at Bamburgh late in the tenth century. In the sixteenth century, the rich Forster family owned Bamburgh, only to become bankrupt. In later years, the castle and associated lands were bought by the Bishop of Durham, Nathaniel Crewe, who subsequently became Lord Crewe. The hotel The Lord Crewe Arms in Blanchland still bears his name and has suffered countless hauntings. Lord Crewe would die without ever having the child that he so deeply desired, and after his death, the castle fell into disrepair.

The fortunes of Bamburgh seemed to change as soon as Oswald was made a saint. Almost at once, the curse of Oswald's hand was brushed away. The very first Lord Armstrong bought Bamburgh Castle, restoring it to its present glory.

*The curse may be gone, but many visitors have suffered an unpleasant shock. Harry Reed, a local fisherman, was reeling in his nets just off Bamburgh when he saw a human hand in them. In shock he dropped the net back into the water, losing his catch and the hand. He had not known anything about St Oswald, so it seemed best to leave him happy in his ignorance. He said he had not reported it to the police in case they thought he was crazy!

*When a school party visited the castle in 1963, one of the girls had to be rushed to hospital in a screaming fit. On reaching the hospital in a teacher's car she had calmed down. The teachers had had all the children holding each other's hands, so none would get lost. The girl told doctors, 'I was holding Susan's hand, but when I looked back Susan wasn't there, just a hand with no one on it!' The doctors and the teachers put it down to imagination.

*During the making of Polanski's Macbeth, starring Jon Finch and Francesca Annis, two extras dressed as soldiers had a shock. Roger and Brian, two likely lads from Bedlington, both swore they saw a hand crawling across the sand while they took a break. They thought at first it was some electronic gadget being used by the special effects department. Both had watched a few horror films when hands had done this before and presumed it was a practical joke. Both commented how clever it was until they realised there was no one else about!

BAMBURGH'S LAIDLEY WORM

The causeway between Holy Island and the Northumbrian Coast has always been surrounded by myths and legends, none more famous than the mighty Laidley Worm.

In Saxon times Northumberland was ruled by King Ida, a fair man, greatly respected by his people. The king had two children, the prince and princess, both thoughtful and kindly folk. The prince took to the high seas for adventure, travelling abroad and embroiling himself in many adventures. Life at home on the windswept Northumberland coast was far more sedate, however, and at times very lonely.

The king was a widower, but no one was more surprised than the princess when he decided to seek out a new wife, to share the burden of his kingdom. So, a huge procession began, as King Ida visited all the noblemen throughout England in search of a bride.

Eventually, a dark and dusky beauty was found, and King Ida was hypnotised by her. Swiftly he agreed on terms with her father and set off on the journey back to the North with his new bride. What King Ida did not know was that this woman was feared for miles around, many said she was a witch, others that she was the daughter of the Devil. Her father was more than pleased to accept any dowry that would remove his daughter from beneath his roof.

Many stories were told about her: how she once turned a blacksmith into a fish, then ate him for her supper; how she had turned into a huge sea serpent and overturned fishing boats; how one lover rejected her and she turned into a huge wild cat and ripped him to pieces.

This was not the pouting innocent that King Ida believed, this was a viper he would clench to his bosom.

King Ida's people all loved him dearly, and there was a lavish feast at Bamburgh Castle to welcome the new queen. The princess made sure that there would be no animosity between herself and the queen, presenting her with a huge bouquet. All the princess wanted was her lonely father to be happy again. But the queen soon became very jealous of the young princess, as she heard how everyone for miles around spoke of her stepdaughter's beauty, and how she was the most beautiful woman in Northumbria.

The twisted mind of this Southern witch soon began to boil and bubble, plotting on how she could draw all the attention away from the princess and towards herself. There seemed to be nothing else for it, the princess had to go.

To kill her own stepdaughter was going too far, so she created a spell to transform the flaxen-haired beauty into a long and loathsome Laidley Worm some forty feet long.

The disappearance of the princess greatly distressed the king, who sent out many search parties, all to no avail. Stories did return from Spindlestone Heugh, far to the West, of a horrid monster which was described as an enormous worm, with bright shining red eyes and a gaping mouth. It would coil itself around the Spindle Stone, hissing at anyone who dared go anywhere near.

Inside this strange creature was the trapped spirit of the beautiful princess, her silent screams emanated only as a serpent's hiss!

You may believe that you have breath so bad in the mornings that it could wilt a pot plant, but it's as nothing compared to this vile creature's stench. It is said that no grass or trees would grow for miles after the Laidley Worm had passed, so acrid was its venomous breath.

Stories of this strange and weird creature spread around the world, and eventually the Childe of Wynde, King Ida's princely son, heard of his kingdom's plight and began preparations for his return home. He ordered a ship to be built with two huge masts made of rowan trees, and within the year he was under sail and heading back towards Bamburgh.

In the meantime, the queen had consolidated her power, and the king was completely under her spell. The good people of Northumbria were beginning to despise their rulers – things had changed, and not for the better. But news of the prince's return cheered them, and word spread around the Bamburgh community like wildfire; he would be home any day now!

The queen gathered a brood of fearsome witches, all toothless hags who were sorceresses in the black arts. Together they would summon up a whirlwind to sink the prince's ship as soon as it came into sight. And indeed, within the week a sail was sighted, far off on the curve of the horizon. The witches got to work, and from the battlements of Bamburgh Castle, the queen began the incantations that would doom the brave young prince.

But to the evil queen's astonishment, her spell did not work. Her powers, like those of every witch, were useless in proximity to rowan wood – and the prince's masts made a sturdy defence against her black magic.

So the prince landed in a small boat on Budle Bay and set off in search of the long-tailed demon that had cursed his land. He was determined to kill this creature, so that good fortune would return to Bamburgh and the rest of Northumbria.

On arriving at Spindlestone Heugh he saw the creature coiled twenty times around a wedge of stone. He drew his sword and stepped forward to face the beast. The princess looked out from behind the monster's eyes and screamed at her brother, but all that came out of its mouth was an unearthly hiss. Not wanting to harm her own flesh and blood, the Laidley Worm backed away, retreating towards the dark recesses of the cave where the creature slept.

The prince advanced, his eyes glinting with hatred for this ugly creation that had lived like a parasite off the backs of the poor. Then to his astonishment the forty-foot monster simply laid down its head, awaiting the final death blow. Deep inside the

Laidley Worm, the spirit of the young princess wouldn't allow the creature to harm the brother she loved more than life itself.

The prince heard a voice from nowhere, maybe the sort of telepathy that brothers and sisters are said sometimes to have, telling him to kiss the monster three times. Travelling adventurers had been known to romance women who were rather less than beautiful, but to kiss a forty-foot long, foul-smelling green monster seemed nonetheless to be going a bit far. But, dosing his eyes and gritting his teeth, the prince bent down and kissed the slimy and scaly skin of the worm.

A blinding flash of light hurled the prince backwards into the rocks. What had he done?

At first, he thought he had given the monster even more power, so he picked himself up, grasped his sword and headed into the smoky haze to finish the beast. He searched through the haze, but though there was no sign of the worm at all, at the base of the Spindle Stone sat a tiny, weeping figure, dressed in white. It was his sister, the princess.

He gathered her into his arms, hugging her so strong it was almost as if he would snap her spine. She explained how her wicked stepmother had ruined Bamburgh, totally captivating King Ida and gaining full control of the kingdom.

The evil queen knew that she was in deep trouble. The prince was returning with the princess that she had wronged so cruelly. So, summoning up the last remnants of her black magic she began casting spells towards the couple as they approached Bamburgh Castle. However, the prince held up his sword and the spells rebounded back on the wicked queen, draining her of all her powers. Once inside the castle, the prince stood over the cowering witch as she spat out her hatred towards him, and he gathered all his white magic powers to turn this vile woman into a venomous toad, casting her out of Bamburgh Castle and cursing her to walk the dunes forevermore.

So next time you're walking up to visit the amazing castle at Bamburgh, mind how you tread, for somewhere in the undergrowth lurks a poisonous and evil toad with shining eyes just waiting to steal your form, and return to take back the lands that once were hers.

* In March 1969, Frank Good from Sunderland was visiting the area around Spindlestone Heugh, collecting rocks for his fish tanks. It was around 5.30 in the afternoon when he spotted a strange white figure crouching in a corner next to a pile of stones. He thought it odd that anyone else should be out there on a wet and rainy evening, so went across to say hello, and also to make sure that the coast was clear while he filled his haversack with rocks for his fish.

Frank described what he saw: 'It was like a piece of luminous chiffon, sort of a pinky white. It just floated up into the air and moved across the fields. I was as close to it as you are to me, and could almost touch it.'

*Locals say that in that area you can often hear weeping, and the worms in the vicinity are the biggest and the juiciest to be found – presumably trying to live up to the example of the Laidley Worm.

BAMBURGH: OH, MY DARLING

Grace Darling was born on 24th November 1815, and for most of her young life she was with her father, who was the keeper of the Longstone Lighthouse on the Farne Islands, near Bamburgh.

It was a stormy night in September 1838 when Grace spotted a ship, the Forfarshire, in distress. Its rigging had collapsed, and the sails were flapping in the gale-force winds. The storm was so fierce that they couldn't launch the lifeboat at Seahouses, so the entire crew seemed doomed to die. Both Grace and her father were so close to the vessel that they could see men leaping into the sea and drowning and could hear screams of terror as the huge ship was tossed around as if it were a cork.

Grace couldn't bear to hear their tormented cries so decided to take out their longboat themselves, regardless of the likely consequences. If a lifeboat with full crew couldn't withstand the battering of the twenty-foot-high waves, how could a 23-year-old girl and her father manage? Yet out they rowed, hands slipping off the wet oars, the boat filling with water and the rolling Forfarshire heading across to meet them. Had they collided, the longboat would be crushed into matchwood, yet miraculously one of the seamen managed to get a line to them, and eight seamen and a woman were rescued. Struggling against the waves they managed to get them back to the Longstone lighthouse. A tremendous story of incredible bravery, yet tragedy lay around the corner, for Grace would die aged only twenty-six on 24 October 1842. In Bamburgh, there is a museum dedicated to her memory. The ghost of Grace is said to walk on the Farne Islands and witnesses have spotted a figure in a long brown skirt standing on the very top of the lighthouse, looking out to sea.

A spokeswoman from the Grace Darling museum says 'It's all a load of old rubbish!'

*Mrs Frances Coleman from Berwick said: 'I saw a young woman on the lighthouse while we were on a boat from Seahouses going out to see the seals. She was small and brown-haired, in her early twenties. She was wearing a dark dress and had a shawl around her shoulders. I was so shocked to see someone dressed like that on a freezing day, I took a photograph of her. On getting to the museum at Bamburgh later that afternoon I realised the woman I had seen was Grace Darling! And even though she was right in the middle of my viewfinder, when the photo was developed, she wasn't there.'

BEADNELL:
WHERE THERE'S LIFE THERE'S HOPE, WHEN THERE'S DEATH ...?

Beadnell Tower was built by the Forster family who also owned Adderstone Tower, both in Northumberland. When the family sold it off it became part of a public house called the Bull Inn, latterly The Craster Arms. The Craster family had owned Beadnell Tower and its coat of arms is still proudly placed in the centre of the building. The motto reads 'Dum Vivo Spero' Where there's life there's hope'.

But what of when there's death? I spoke to an elderly Craster man who had come back from Australia to visit his family in Alnwick. He told me the story of Frank Charlton who used to work in the Bull Inn in the early 1820s. He was a bar/cellarman who also did odd jobs around the local villages. Frank was greatly loved, a man of immense good spirits, always with a smile or a joke.

He was also greatly loved by several of the ladies who lived thereabouts, especially when their husbands were out in their fishing cobles or tending their land. It came as no surprise when Charlton told the landlord that he was going to have to move on. He didn't give any reason but the landlord surmised that one of the husbands was on his trail. That night, in a barn not 300 yards from the pub, Frank's headless body was found. He had been lashed with whips and was only recognised by a heavy silver ring he always wore.

As in all small villages, rumours spread like milk over cornflakes, no one would speak of the incident. Although at least eight women had been his secret lovers, none spoke out. The authorities sent in people to investigate, and eventually, it was catalogued as an accidental death. They didn't know how his head had been detached, nor where it was, but at least the case was tied up very neatly that way.

This was only the beginning of endless strange happenings, sightings of a headless man walking the streets crying out in pain (I wonder how he did that?). Drinks would move across the bar, women would feel hot beery breath on their neck, dogs would refuse to enter the pub.

Things seemed to be getting worse and worse until a very odd thing happened.

One day the landlord of the inn opened his doors to find the carved stone head of Frank Charlton on his step.

There was a note with it, apparently written by one of the tonged husbands. 'He took my wife, so I took his head. It seems he can't rest without it. As I cannot return the real one, here is one he can wear.'

The landlord had the carved head built into the wall of the inn, where it remains to this day.

THE FLOWER OF BEDLINGTON

During the late 1700s, Bedlington was a sleepy Northumberland farming village, surrounded by lush green fields and woodland glades teeming with wildlife of every description. Jimmy Robson said it was his 'Garden of Eden' and in his paradise, he met his 'Eve', a local farmer's daughter, so beautiful were her eyes they made the most devastating blue sky appear muddy and grey. Her parents were strict puritanical types, who were bitter and crusty and disliked by most of the Bedlingtonians. Jimmy would watch her whenever he could, and often she would walk in the woods with her long auburn hair waving in the wind, like tiny tentacles plucking at the air.

Despite being a goodly soul, well-liked by everyone, it was considered by her parents that young Robson was 'not good enough for our daughter'. The name of Robson had been widely feared across the 1500s and 1600s because they were Border Reivers and rogues, but Jimmy Robson was far from that! They were miserly folk positive that their beautiful daughter would marry a rich man, and they would have some degree of security too. In an attempt to separate the lovers they even decided to send her to their relations' farm in Stokesley in the North Riding of Yorkshire.

As she was taken south by pony and trap, Jimmy Robson riding a huge Shire horse clumped along as fast as he could, swearing that he would love her forever and that no matter how far they were apart he would love her 'till eternity'.

Jimmy Robson believed that she would never return. Nowadays the distance between Northumberland and Yorkshire is barely an hour by train, an hour and a half in a car, but it was three days' journey way back then. Young Robson was destroyed at being parted from the woman he was sure was his only true love. He fell ill, losing his will to live, he took to his bed in a terminal depression and literally willed himself to die. This he did within seven days. His corpse was barely cold when the puritan family began to make arrangements for their daughter's return and her imminent wedding to a rich landowner's son.

Before the news of his death had reached Stokesley, Jimmy Robson arrived telling her uncle that he had her father's blessing to take her with him. The uncle, unsure at first, noticed that he was riding his brother's finest grey mare. Knowing that his brother treasured this horse more than his wife, he agreed that she should leave with Jimmy.

As she rode behind him on the horse she noticed that he was very cold, and commented to him about this. He gave no answer, just hugged her closer to him, and rode on. As they crossed the river Tyne using the tiny wooden bridge where the Swing Bridge now stands, she noticed that he cast no shadow on the water. On reaching Dudley Jimmy told her that he had a headache so severe he could barely see. So she took off her scarf, wet it in a nearby burn and wrapped it lovingly around Jimmy's head.

The girl was elated that her disciplinarian of a father had relented, allowing her to marry for love rather than money. On arriving home she kissed Jimmy on his frozen cheek and leapt down from the sweating mare. Grasping her petticoats she ran up to the door, and on opening it she shouted that she was back with James. She cuddled her father so tightly she nigh squeezed the life out of him. 'Thank you father, you have made my life complete. Thank you for sending Jimmy for me!' The father was surprised and shocked, yet on hearing that a man who had been placed freshly into his grave two days before was waiting to meet him outside, his surprise turned to horror. Half pushed by his daughter he found himself outside staring not at Jimmy Robson, but his favourite horse soaked with perspiration and frothing at the mouth.

'Jimmy!' cried out the daughter: 'Don't be afraid, everything is all right now!' Jimmy never returned, and her father told her the full story. She swore that he had come for her, bringing her back north. On hearing the sad tale she fainted into a coma from which she would never recover. Only seconds before she had been elated, thrilled with joy and excitement for the future. Now she was in despair. Her father carried her to the couch where he watched the colour drain from her face, the twinkle in her eyes became dull and glassy and she began to twitch uncontrollably. The doctor was dragged from his bed, and despite trying everything from bleeding her with leeches, pumping her chest and even slapping her face, nothing broke this deathly spell. Within a day she was dead. Her last words were whispered into her mother's ear seconds before she passed away: 'Swear that you'll bury me with Jimmy, I want to be in the same coffin, in the selfsame grave. You parted us on Earth, you must not part us in Heaven!'

At first, her father said it could not be done, but he did give his final consent as the last gasp of air escaped from her chest with a sighing grunt.

She was placed in the farmer's parlour for two days while friends and family including Mr and Mrs Robson respectfully filed past. Yet that following Thursday when they opened Jimmy's coffin he lay there, arms outstretched ready to enfold his beloved into his arms. To their horror, they saw he still wore the scarf around his sore head, placed there by their daughter on the journey home.

*The figures of two ghostly lovers have often been seen between Bedlington and Cramlington, also in Plessey Woods. A tall man hugging to his side a beautiful girl with auburn hair. They have been spotted walking for miles, then finally disappearing into nothing.

*In 1987 Mr L. J. Josephs from London was visiting relatives in Gosforth, Newcastle, and they took him to visit Morpeth, Bedlington and Alnwick. Whilst sitting on a bench in Bedlington centre he felt as if he were being watched. On turning around he saw a couple caressing about ten feet behind him, sitting on a church wall. He thought it was romantic that two people should be so willing to kiss openly in front of so many people. As he watched the couple began to fade. He could see the metal fencing of the church through them until they were no more than a haze.

WARNING IN BEDLINGTON

Over the centuries there have been thousands of stories about people being warned by 'a knocking on the window', 'a tapping on the wall' or being confronted by a ghost who says nothing, just stares at you.

Death usually ensues.

Such was the case at a house in Millbank, Bedlington, in the mid-1960s. A woman was lying in bed when she felt as if someone was watching her. In a cold sweat, she sat up to be confronted by a World War 1 soldier. 'Who's that?' she asked, and the figure faded out in front of her.

Eventually, she managed to get back to sleep. The following morning she learned that her elderly next-door neighbour had passed away at the exact time that she had come face to face with the apparition.

On describing him to her neighbour's family they all became convinced that it was the old woman's husband, who had travelled back from 'the other side of the curtain' to guide his wife's spirit.

THE BONNY LASS OF BELSAY

At Belsay, near Morpeth, there is the tale of 'the bonny lass' who would tempt the red-blooded Northumbrian lads with pouty glances and beckoning eyes. She would just appear from nowhere, her eyes so beautiful that they would transfix any man who stared into them. It was as if men could see their every dream for the future realised in a single glance. It was said that men would follow her for miles and then just as she arrived in a flash she would vanish in a small puff of smoke, often leaving the puzzled man several miles from home, often totally lost.

One of her favourite haunts was the lake near Belsay Craig. She would wander there, placing a wisp of hair between her lips, laughing endearingly and walking slowly in her long rustling skirts. The locals call her 'Silkie', as they often do mysterious ladies in long dresses, yet. it is believed that her real name could well have been Carolyn and that she was a rich Newcastle businessman's daughter.

There was a terrible horse-riding accident near Belsay in the mid-1700s when a young girl called Carolyn was thrown on to a pile of stones, splitting her skull. Since then the apparition has been catalogued thousands of times. Once this strange girl led a man into the lake, as he was so hypnotised by the vision he glimpsed in her eyes he wasn't aware of where he was. The irony was that he couldn't swim and had another local not pulled him back on to dry land he surely would have drowned.

The 'bonny lass' used to be seen for hours sitting in a tree near a waterfall, and to this day it is known as 'Silkie's Chair'. Legend tells us that anyone who dares to sit in that chair will be wed within twelve months. Between 1800 and 1850 spinsters visiting the locality would ask to try it, and many were indeed wed within the year!

MURDERED MINSTREL OF BELLISTER CASTLE

The Lord of Bellister Castle, near Haltwhistle, once hired the services of a talented minstrel whose songs and parodies entertained many a guest. The old nobleman believed, however, that the young man was also wooing his young wife. So one day he decided to spend the whole day at home, to see if his suspicions had any foundation. As he turned the corner into the rose garden he heard some laughing and giggling. There in a mountain of petticoats lay his young wife, with the minstrel astride her, both totally lost in their lovemaking. The Lord bellowed out his anger, calling for his servants to come and apprehend the man who had seduced his wife. The minstrel ran for it, racing away from Bellister Castle toward the river. He was just beginning to relax when he heard the baying of hounds, and, looking back towards the castle, he saw half a dozen of the Bellister hounds. And he was their prey!

He fled along the banks of the River Tyne but was pulled to the ground by one of the dogs, as the others tore him to pieces. The only part of his face that remained remotely recognisable was his beard.

*Things at Bellister Castle were never quite the same again. It is said that the heartbroken ghost of the old nobleman still walks the halls, and is known as 'The Grey Man'.

The spirit of the minstrel is said to inhabit the woods near the River Tyne, where he can be seen running, or standing pointing towards the castle with blood running from his beard.

THE LORD CREWE ARMS, BLANCHLAND

Out of all of the haunted pubs and hotels in the North, the Lord Crewe Arms is by far the most famous, and yet why it should be is a complete puzzle. No one there has ever suffered a tragic death, as far as is known, no one has even hurt themselves particularly, yet the string of strange happenings over the year is hard to match.

The Lord Crewe sits in a wonderful woody hollow, surrounded by the kind of countryside that could have saved Hammer Films a fortune in sets. The weather often obliges too, enveloping the area with a thin, eerie mist, that has your knees knocking long before you enter the house. And that is the kind of chilly building that is custom-built for a haunting. It has a good restaurant, is charmingly run ... but you sense that there is something not quite right somewhere.

The ghost is supposed to be that of Dorothy Forster whose brother chose the wrong side in the Jacobite Rebellion and ended up in Newgate Prison, later being sent into exile as a traitor. Although Dorothy missed her brother, she could do nothing to bring him back to England, and, it would seem, accepted this. She got married and settled elsewhere, and happily lived out the rest of her natural life, never returning to the Hall that is now the Lord Crewe Arms; in fact, she was never ever seen in Blanchland again. So why she would choose to cross that great divide to haunt this pub forever is a complete mystery. Yet it is claimed that she still does, and many people claim to have witnessed a woman in long skirts waiting at a window. Visitors have been woken up by someone in their room, knocking on their doors, doors opening even when they are locked, lights flashing on and off, pictures moving and articles being moved about.

I have put this to the test twice. The first time, I placed Mrs Kay Williams from Redcar in the Lord Crewe overnight, linked to me by telephone. Kay had this to say: 'It was a lovely modern room, nothing like what I expected, but I could not rest. When I did begin to nap I felt someone close to me as if they were tucking in. I don't think it was my imagination, but it was as if my husband was cuddling into me. I sat up with a start when it happened. Later that night I was reading a magazine when I felt the end of the bed go down as if someone was sitting on it. It took me almost five minutes to gather the courage to peep over the top. There was nothing there, but I could have sworn that the bedding did have the signs that someone had sat on it! I didn't believe in ghosts, but this has made me think.'

If it isn't real, what is it? Imagination running rampant? Well, I had to test that theory too, using a simple technique. I had an assistant working for me on the late-night phone-in on Metro FM, Alice Keens-Soper, a right charlie of a lass, whom I thought the world of. She was always game for a laugh, with a sharp sense of humour and a dirty laugh. When I was seeking a volunteer for a ghost hunt, she was swift to put her name forward, and in due course was taken by taxi from her trendy Jesmond home to Blanchland. Unbeknown to me she had smuggled her current boyfriend along too. On discovering this, I asked her to assure me that he would not be in her bedroom with her. I needed her to be alone for the experiment that was to lie ahead. To tell Alice to keep a boyfriend at bay was rather like pouring sugar on the ground and telling an ant to leave it alone. Even so, she was as good as her word, and was placed in 'Dorothy Forster's room'.

I decided to play with her imagination, to see if I could plant ideas in her mind, and create a reaction. Once again linked only by a telephone, we kept in touch, live on air to over a million people dotted around the North. At first, she had nothing to report, except that the window had rattled a little bit. At that I told her that it had been from that very window that Dorothy Forster had kept vigil, and every fifteen minutes it would creak, as she looked out, waiting for her brother to return to her. This had the desired effect, and the next time we spoke she was definitely getting nervous. Then she mentioned hearing footsteps, certainly nothing unknown in any hotel, but I suggested it was Dorothy Forster pacing the room as she did every night. Later Alice told of how the chair next to the bed had suddenly started squeaking a little. This gave me another excuse to fib, saying that that was Dorothy's seat, and how she must be sitting next to Alice at that very moment. These mind games culminated in Alice being very, very frightened and quite convinced that the Lord Crewe Arms was haunted.

It proved something very different to me – that the imagination is rather like plasticine; it can be sculpted and moulded to fit what people want to believe. Alice swore that ghosts existed for some months afterwards until she finally began questioning what had happened to her.

*Many phantoms have been witnessed over the years at the cemetery in Blanchland. Figures of women in long skirts, monks, Roman soldiers and weeping children. The most enduring ghost is a ginger-haired monk with a ragged habit, who many believe lived in a monastery that existed in Blanchland from about 1150 to 1588.

THE SPRY FAMILY AND THE BLANCHLAND HORRORS

In 1987, I was sent a tale by P. Stokoe based on the experiences of the Spry family. It was the true story of what happened to her Auntie Angela and her family, who eventually moved house to Waskerly.

The house in question was on top of a hill at West Roughside, Blanchland, and its nickname was 'Wuthering Heights' as it resembled the house from the classic movie. Angela moved in with her husband and two young children Karen (aged 3) and Christine (6 months). From the very first day, they felt as if there was something very wrong, a sense of dread, something indefinable but most-definitely evil.

The family had a history of having what they called a 'sixth sense' and even young Karen had shown evidence of this. Despite having been involved in three other house moves in her three years the child would not sleep in the house at Blanchland. When bedtime came around she refused to go upstairs, and should her parents try to carry her upstairs she would lash out. These tantrums became nightly events with the youngster punching, kicking, snarling and spitting at her parents. On one occasion she bit

Angela so badly she thought she might need stitches. Karen was such a calm, loving child, what could possibly make her into such a demon? So Angela would allow Karen to fall asleep on the sofa each night, and then when they went to bed, they would gently carry Karen up to her bedroom.

Their dog Shep also refused ever to go upstairs, despite having bounded up the stairs of previous homes. Often it would sit at the base of the stairs just looking up and cowering, it's tail tight between its legs. On several occasions Shep would go berserk at the foot of the stairs, barking and clawing at the living room door, trying to attract the family's attention. It was as if he were able to see something, or someone, that human eyes could not.

But Angela began to feel quite comfortable about the house and had it not been for Karen and Shep acting so strangely she would have thought nothing of it. Then one by one other strange things began to happen. Despite the master bedroom being warm and snug, greasy dampness began to appear in the bed. A stickiness that you could feel on your skin, and it was thicker and more unpleasant than any substance the body could exude. They discovered a false wall had been erected at the end of a corridor. There was nothing behind it, and no apparent reason for building it. They discovered the house had previously been owned by drug dealers who may have used the hidden panels for stashing their product.

More research uncovered that when the police raided the house they found everyone sleeping downstairs, as no one, even then, could bear to sleep upstairs. Karen's room was the one that no one could face, least of all the tiny child herself. Why was it that all of the rooms had a door that locked from the inside, yet Karen's room only locked from the outside?

On the wall ran three perfectly straight lines, drawn in red, blue and green. You can imagine a child scribbling on the wall, but not three perfect parallel lines. Karen used to say that she could see people in her room and had to keep the light on and the door open so they could get in and out. At first, this was written off as 'imaginary friends' but when the child was becoming literally white with fear, a psychic was invited to investigate.

The medium made a thorough investigation and claimed that there was indeed a presence in Karen's room, of a man wearing a doublet. He was not going to harm her, rather to the contrary, he intended watching over her. The medium was paid and sent away. Although at first, it reassured Angela, she knew that what the child had seen was far different from what the psychic had described.

Babysitters would stop going to the house, for even when the children cried the sitters were too terrified to go upstairs.

Angela had been free from actual contact with 'whatever was there' until one night when she lifted Karen and proceeded to carry her up to bed. As she neared Karen's bedroom the child's eyes opened 'as wide as plates' and all the colour drained from her face as she proceeded to shake and shiver. She took her down the stairs and as she did so the colour returned to her cheeks, and her eyes closed in peaceful slumber.

Although there is no history of any violent crime taking place in that house a local clergyman, who does not wish to be named, said, 'A man lived there in the thirties and he went stark raving mad after his mother died. He became so violent that his brothers used to lock him into his bedroom. He once escaped after climbing out of the window but fell on to the ground, breaking both of his legs. He was never able to walk again and remained in that house until he died. He never moved from the first floor and refused to allow anyone to sleep up there but him. I honestly don't believe all this mumbo jumbo, but, oddly, this family couldn't rest comfortably on the first floor.'

The family, not surprisingly, moved out after less than four months. Angela was relieved to escape until she remembered that she had left a parcel of baby clothes under the kitchen table. She knew then and there, to her horror, she would have to go back. On entering the house, to her surprise Shep ran straight upstairs, something he had never done before. She quickly grabbed the bundle of clothes and headed for the door. It was at that moment that Shep began to go crazy, barking in the same excited fashion that dogs do on disturbing a rabbit, or spotting a cat. Angela froze with fear: stood there paralysed, my heart was beating so loudly I could hear it getting faster and faster.' She ran from the house with the dog and as she dived into the car it stalled. Swiftly she turned the ignition again, it started, and she calmed herself as she drove away.

The irony is that this house was essentially evil although no murderous deeds were ever carried out there. Yet the Sprys now live in a house at Carterway Heads, Waskerly where a brutal murder was once carried out! So far the Sprys have experienced nothing untoward at their present home, and I hope they can now live in peace.

THE WHITE LADY OF BLENKINSOPP CASTLE

In the 1500s Blenkinsopp Castle was at the height of its powers, commanding a splendid situation near Haltwhistle on the River Tippalt. It was owned by Bryan de Blenkinsopp, an imposing warrior who ruled the savage countryside nearby with a kindly hand, though he was known to deal harshly with anyone who caused him problems. It was said that one day he came upon a robber assaulting a young woman near Gilsland, took his lance (he had been hunting boar) and chased the man away, cornering him in the woods and running him through. He chose to leave the body in the forest, to feed the land as his lands fed him.

His people loved him, for he kept them safe, yet they knew he was a most materialistic man, so tight he could peel an orange in his pocket. He made it commonly known that he would never marry because then he would have to share his riches. The most common version of this tale tells of how he 'promised to marry only a woman capable of filling a chest of gold that it would take ten men to carry'. It is said that this is how rich he was and that he would only take a bride whose wealth could equal his.

Sir Bryan went off to fight in the Holy Land and ten long years later he returned to flourishing Blenkinsopp Castle with the daughter of a sultan as his bride. Her skin was black, and you can imagine the stir that made among the locals who had never in their lives seen a living soul that colour. And to marry a 'heathen' – that was worse than if he had married a peasant. But then the Sultan had given her a dowry of treasure so huge it took twelve of Sir Bryan's entourage to carry it.

At first, the marriage seemed a happy one, his bride filled the castle with laughter, only occasionally feeling homesick for Arabia. As time went by, however, she began to suspect that his love was more for her treasure than her company. To test her husband's affection, she sent her two personal hand servants, believed to be eunuchs, to bury the treasure where her husband would never be able to find it. In a fury Sir Bryan stormed out of Blenkinsopp Castle with four of his soldiers, never to return. Many stories circulate, some that he went back to the Holy Land, others that he travelled to Scotland where he was killed by Border Reivers.

His wife tried many times to return to her home but never managed. After five years of waiting for her husband to return she died of a broken heart, in the dungeon where she had dug up her treasure.

It is said that Sir Bryan's wife walks the castle walls late at night, and can be seen sobbing in the dungeons. Wearing a wispy white robe, she glides across the floor, her dark features often invisible in the darkness so that what is seen is the white gown floating by apparently of its own volition.

REFUGEES FROM THE KING AT BURRODEN

There has been a fort or tower at Burroden since Roman times, and the village gets its name from Burgdon-Fort Hill and has quite an interesting history. Although a great many don't believe the legend surrounding it, the tales told are many and diverse. The most interesting revolves around King Henry VIII and goes back to August 1546. I have found no proof that it ever happened, but this is how it goes anyway:

A group of Northerners visited London to appeal to King Henry for help to support their families. Taxes were very high, and unlike in the South where the crops were forthcoming, the North had suffered quite a barren year. So Thomas Robson and

Wilfred Armstrong, the patriarchs of large Northern families, took it upon themselves to petition the King. They never met Henry, though they did plead to Catherine Howard, his sixth wife, who listened most sympathetically, and promised that she would do all that she could. Armstrong and Robson were offered a bed for the night by Catherine but politely refused, having already sought lodgings at the Nag's Head on the outskirts of London. The following morning Catherine spoke to King Henry about it and drove him into a terrible rage. He ordered that Robson and Armstrong be arrested and executed, for daring to 'affect matters of state using the Queen's petticoats to hide behind'.

Nothing was more assured than their certain execution, so while Henry's soldiers were out searching for them, Catherine sent one of her handmaidens to the Nag's Head, warning them that they were to be arrested, and beseeching them to return home. This they did, and Henry dispatched orders to arrest them, wherever they could be located. It took almost two months to get back to the North, and Robson and Armstrong thought it unwise to return to their homes, so they sought refuge at Burroden Tower. The three troopers responsible for manning it were Jack Armstrong, Henry and John Robson. Two sons and a cousin of the escaped men. So the soldiers acted as if nothing had changed, and no one, not even their own families, knew where they were. The only clue was that all of the soldiers were asking their wives to put up more food each day for their 'bait'. The extra food was of course for their guests.

They remained there for almost three months, not even daring a visit home at Christmas. Instead, they sent letters back, delivered anonymously. On 28th January 1547 King Henry VIII died, and kindly Catherine was widowed (for the third time). Edward VI's uncle, the Earl of Hertford, became Lord Protector of England and declared an amnesty for all prisoners, allowing the refugees of Burroden Tower the chance to return home.

* The ruins of Burroden Tower still stand, and some strange sights have been beheld, including men peeping out from over the top wall. Just glancing out and sneaking away again . . .

CHILLINGHAM CASTLE

Probably the most haunted of all of the northern castles.

In 1995 a group of 13 sceptics were taken there, placed into individual rooms alone, and four hours later they all totally believed in spirit. The most sceptical was a taxi driver, who made plausible excuses for every glimpse of a shadow, every bump, noise or whisper. Then finally in the torture chamber alone, he asked: "I don't believe there are ghosts and if there are, prove it to me now!". At that, the wheel on the rack noisily turned twice right in front of his eyes.

In 1998 a school teacher visited the oubliette, where the open grave of a small girl still exists. As a tribute, she dropped a single unopened rosebud through the grill, onto her bones. Within a second something incredible occurred "Just as it landed the entire room filled with the scent of roses. It was overpowering. Yet that bud had not even opened and had no smell to it at all. I believe it was the spirit of that child letting me know she was grateful!"

In 2000 I was involved in a BBC TV series called 'Trouble in Store' and took their crew to Chillingham Castle. The cameraman was particularly cruel in his total disbelief in all things spectral. Yet during filming, he was pushed, heard voices and caught several moving shadows. Finally in one room, the King Edward Room, he caught hundreds of thousands of bluebottles all flying around the top window. He filmed them, then came out, shutting the door and shouted for us. We raced up, he opened the door and there was not one single fly on view. One lady, Susan from South Shields, was so shocked and terrified that she had to sit in the office with staff, after being touched harshly during her time in the Great Hall.

One of the greatest tragedies took place in the noughties. Cyril was one of the castle's guides, he loved the building so very much, and often told people that if and when he died he would love to come back to the castle. One day a listener to my late-night show 'Night Owls' had decided to visit Chillingham and was questioning Cyril about the place when this wonderful chap fell dead at her feet. Bless his memory and love to his family.

Over the years I filmed several TV shows for Fox Family's 'Scariest Places On Earth' and during one episode a family member quit the challenge, saying that he was in the Great Hall when something or someone, looked him in the eyes. On film, we could not see anything other than his terrified reaction. Yet when we turned the image to negative you can clearly see a smoky man-shaped figure walk up to him and stare him out. As soon as he ran away, the figure disintegrated. I also performed an ancient chant said to open a portal into the next world. When I did it, the power in the castle went off, a woman said she had been pushed, by unseen hands downstairs, requiring an ambulance and crew members heard a horrifying scream. The Vice President of Fox, Eytan Keller was also pushed down the tower stairs, he was in Ashington's Wansbeck Hospital for almost a week.

An entire TV special in Los Angeles was made about the incident, because when they came to edit that precise footage, all of the power went out but just for their building, something impossible because they shared a grid with forty other premises.

In February 2020 Neil Walker visited Chillingham for the very first time. He experienced the fluttering heart of walking through the ley line in the witchy woods opposite the castle. In the great hall, he clearly saw the chandeliers moving and in the torture chamber felt someone stroke his hair.

HOME OF THE TORTURER

If you should walk up the long drive at the side entrance to this incredible castle, through the spookiest woods imaginable, especially at night, you are met with the most intimidating sight. A castle designed to frighten you away. This one, very special castle, means so very much to me, and its history is unique. Originally a simple Mott and Bailey castle that was extended outwards, pushing its original torture chamber deep into the heart of the building.

The first original fortified house was built in the late 1290s, and the castle built and opened by 1344.

At the castle, they have simple drawings on tiny coffins thought to be from the original fortification, showing images of extreme torture. It seems long before this giant of a castle's construction the people on its land already enjoyed the spilling of blood, and knew how to terrify the locals. Yet the main story begins around 1271 when a young man was born to a farmer living on a croft on the outskirts of Chillingham. Young John Sage had watched many a nearby farm robbed by marauding Scots, and it took little persuasion for him to join the English Army in Alnwick. He flew through the ranks because of his great Northumbrian tenacity, and his hatred of the Scots. His first regiment was based along the Borders, often billeting at Chillingham Castle. At the time that one castle was probably the safest in all of the area, it had fought off Viking marauders, Irish pirates and vagabonds, the Scots and the Picts, and even the English on occasion.

During one stay at the castle, the Scottish poured down to remove the castle once and for all. About a thousand well-armed and battle-hardened warriors decided to enter the land from the South where a tiny stream currently stands, it was a gushing river back then. Unaware an English regiment was housed there, they attacked uphill, only to find a nest full of their worst enemy, the English Army. They were all but massacred, yet almost won, for, within seconds of the battle beginning, a Scottish archer killed the English Captain. Yet, as he fell Sage mounted his horse, rallied the men, and from a certain defeat, he led them to a key victory. The local villages knew about the battle because the rivers were red with blood for almost two weeks.

Sage suggested that Scottish prisoners were shackled along the weir at the side of the castle, then as it rained the water would eventually get deep enough to drown them. He told his men to leave their bodies there to deter any other Scots from attacking.

His reputation across England was beginning to grow. In Northumbria, he was a hero, similar in popularity the great heroes of common man, like Jackie Milburn or Alan Shearer today.

Within two more years he was a lieutenant, and King Edward the First, chose to do battle with the Scot's only when he led his troops. King Edward the First was a tall, rather gangly man, so gained the nickname 'longshanks'. His other nickname was 'the Hammer of the Scots', he dealt brutally with them at every opportunity. Using murder and rape as weapons often against entirely innocent towns and villages.

On one occasion they butchered almost everyone in Berwick because three of William Wallace's men had been seen at a market there.

Everyone, including the King, believed Sage would eventually rise to be a General in his army. He was just about to be given the rank of Captain when his regiment was called upon to wipe out a few Scottish survivors who had been caught by English troops trying to steal cattle from the Chillingham farmers. Sage volunteered to lead this minor altercation, as his Father farmed the cattle there, and he took the attack personally. Along with twenty other cavalrymen, he rode at speed towards the six fleeing Scots, sword in hand to cut them down. On this occasion he was rather arrogant, thinking the job was simple, and to their surprise, the marauders turned to fight them. Two fired longbows, knocking two of Sage's men off their horses. As the Lieutenant reached them, he failed to see one had a pike, he had sunk the base into the ground and faced the point at the oncoming horse. It sliced into Sage's horse, and then up his entire leg until it skidded off his hip bone. He fell from his horse bleeding profusely, and had a farmer not applied a tourniquet swiftly, he would surely have died.

The Scots were ended, and Sage was carried back to Chillingham, the nearest castle where his wound was tended. King Edward visited the castle, many believe to see how long it would be before Sage could be back by his side. However the pike had done great damage, and the wounded man knew his riding days were over.

Sage implored the King to let him still fight the Scots, but being unable to ride meant he could not lead a regiment any more. He could barely walk. For the rest of his life, he had to drag his left leg behind him, gaining the nickname 'Dragfoot'.

The King thanked him for all he had done and offered him any job he felt capable of doing, outside the military. Sage, who had spent three months at Chillingham, had watched the parade of Scottish prisoners arriving after battles. His loathing for them was now greater than ever. He asked if he could become the castle's torturer, getting information from these rebels, so he could continue serving his King. Richard readily agreed and from that day, a brand new extended torture chamber was built. He built into it every kind of horrific treatment he had ever seen and created numerous ones of his own. The chamber had a rack to stretch his prisoners, a wheel to bend and snap their backs, and almost 350 years before Vlad Dracule he began impaling people. His technique was to have a blunt pole, place a prisoner on it, the pole at his rectum. At first, he was strong enough to hold himself in place, then as gravity began to work little by little it would force its way through him, eventually bursting out of his neck or into his skull. A disgusting way to die.

Sage created a chair with spikes on it, so whoever sat in it could not move as he sliced the flesh off him.

He even asked his King for help in bringing an iron maiden up to Chillingham that had been captured from a French chateau. Inside that human-shaped beast, spikes pierced your chest, tore into your viscera and also ripped into your genitals. Sage used vices to crush knees and elbows, grinding stones to pedal into their skulls and created a double-edged saw to literally cut the enemy in half. He would hang them upside down from a door, legs wide open. Then two men would draw the blade back and forth, long slow strokes so the victim could scream or give the answers required. Once started they always ended up in two pieces. He had cages built to put people in to hang from the castle walls to starve to death. If there were too many to give individual tortures to they also had an executioners axe to decapitate them. Sage was very keen to show one of his inventions. It was a huge cooking pot, big enough for two human beings or four children. Once placed into it, a lid was placed on to stop them from climbing out. With gaps in it big enough to hear what they said and to watch their flesh cook and eventually fall off. Over the years the reputation of Chillingham was similar to Hell for the Scots. On one occasion too many prisoners were captured, Sage had all of the women gathered in the courtyard, each one tied to the other. He then brought in bales of hay, surrounding them with it then set them ablaze. Over forty died that day. At the back of the current castle, there is a fairly recently built lake, yet back then it was a nasty stinking bog. Rather than dig graves, Sage ordered the bodies of the Scots would be taken to the bog and sunk beneath the surface. Then suddenly the war with Scotland was over. The King wanted things to return to calm, as he was about to begin a conflict with France. He ordered that every Scot still in captivity was to be set free, no exceptions. Sage refused to say that he had eight sons of Clan Chiefs, all aged under ten years of age. They would return home and sooner or later would return to seek revenge. This generated a strong letter from one of the Kings advisors saying "Any child leaving their prison must be allowed to go free if he walks through the door!". The cunning Sage then walked up to the Tower Room (now used as a museum) opened the window and threw them out one at a time. The last one a four-year-old little girl who had been captured only that day.

Every time he dragged his leg, the hatred for his prisoners increased, and yet he knew he would have to release them. So one Thursday he mounted a coach and drove around the local villagers, telling each one what was about to happen that Saturday at 3 pm. All of those Scots that had attacked their land killed their family, robbed them, raped them and had been their worst enemies were due to be released. He invited them all to come to the main gate of Chillingham. It is exactly one mile from the castle gate. By the time Saturday arrived almost five hundred locals armed with bows and arrows, scythes, clubs, swords, spears, hammers, picks, shovels and rocks waited for their appearance. Sage was obeying his King, he was setting them free. Out of around 215 men, women and children released not one made it to the gate. They were massacred, some beaten to a pulp, and Sage vowed to leave them where they lay to deter any thought of revenge. Wild dogs fed well for months to come. Even to this day you occasionally find a human bone or an ancient toenail along what is now known as 'the Devils Mile'.

So what was Sage to do now he would have no prisoners? Well, he opened his torture chamber up to visitors and gave them tours. Many were keen to be regaled with how he cut pieces from the Duke of Argyll and many other leading enemies.

'Dragfoot' even found love, with a young lady called Elizabeth Armstrong, the daughter of the leader of a local gang of Border Reivers. One evening he invited her to his torture chamber where he was showing off. He began to make love to her on the rack, he began to choke her, in an attempt to heighten their sexual intensity. To his horror, she simply stopped breathing. He tried to suggest it was, what it really was, a horrible accident, but her father would have none of it. The local Army at Alnwick refused to arrest Sage, so Armstrong wrote to the King. He said that unless Sage was executed for the murder of his daughter, the Reivers would incite another war with the Scots. There were over fifty groups of thousands of men who could certainly create another war. The King knew that could not be allowed to happen. Advised by the Duke of Northumberland, a warrant for Sage was released. He was dragged out and on the tallest tree near the main gate, he was hanged. Once a hero, now a villain the locals all wanted a souvenir. Some cut off fingers or toes (whilst he still lived) others genitals, ears and nose.

My first dealing with Chillingham was when kitchen staff sent me a recording of the empty building captured on cassette. Pans hurled about, doors slamming and grunting voices.

This castle loves to show off and if you are of sincere heart it will show you its wonders. On every visit I have been there I have seen or heard them.

There is a chair in the Great Hall where any photo taken of it has a smoky image of a man sitting on it.

The Blue Boy is another ghost, often photographed there. He overheard the castle owner offering to help the Spanish Armada. He ran off to tell the authorities only to be captured and walled up into a chimney.

It is said that if you put your hand into the Lake at midnight the dead rise up and pull you in.

There is a tree in the valley at the side of Chillingham where they tried to burn a priest alive. The tree refused to burn because God refused to allow it. It is said to be lucky if you take off a single leaf.

In the outbuildings often used as lodgings ghosts are regularly seen, most usually ragged, tortured Scots.

One caretaker called Chris once told me that he thought it wasn't real, till he returned to his tied house and there was an old woman in his kitchen cooking. As he approached her she disappeared.

I have seen swarms of bluebottles that disappeared, full figure entities and felt someone touch my head in the chapel.

One of Sage's imported torture was ran oubliette, a French word meaning oblivion. It is a dark tiny cell that you can see to this day. They would break your arms and legs, then hurl you ten feet into the lower chamber where you would starve to death. Often the poor souls tried to stay alive by cannibalising the other bodies and drinking their blood. Up to fifty bodies were in there at any time. The lowest surface liquefied corpses, on top of the new fresh meat. If you look through the grid in that oubliette you see the open grave of a girl believed to be the last killed there, a youngster called Sarah aged 11 or 12.

Outside the castle directly opposite was the remains of a Christian monastery that only lasted a few years before they were driven out. Yet on the hillside nearby there are standing stones still erect after 6,000 years.

Through the monastery opening is the witchy wood with ley lines you can feel. The witches and pagans were pinned to the trees, others buried in heaps there. They were pinned to trees alive, to kill a witch brings pain back to you ten times. So they allowed the beasts of the field to kill them. Many of the trees still have the marks of pinning on them.

Sir Humphrey Wakefield once said to me "Thank you, for you and our ghosts have saved this beautiful castle!" I have made three TV shows and twenty one radio shows there, this place truly is unique, and loaded with spirit.

THE CURSED CATTLE OF CHILLINGHAM

Around Chillingham Castle, you find the herds of Chillingham cattle established since the mid-1200s. They are fine white beasts, with the tell-tale red ears, the last survivors of the wild herds of cattle that used to roam all over Western Europe and Britain.

The cattle are said to be protected by the fairy folk, who used to have small white cattle of their own. When they all died off, the elfin folk adopted the Chillingham herds, and agreed to protect them forever.

The cattle are still flourishing, and it is written that if anyone tries to harm any of these animals the fairies will kill them.

*During a school trip in 1967, Roger Gill of Durham wandered across the field and started chasing the cattle. As he ran he felt something or someone grab his foot, and he broke his ankle. He phoned 'Night Owls' on Metro FM with this story in July 1988 without knowing the legend.

THE ROMAN LEGION OF CORBRIDGE

Corbridge in Roman times was known as Corstopitum, and the centre was almost two miles away from the current town square. It housed a huge Roman fort built on Stangate. The Romans had constructed a mighty bridge, a model of which exists in Corbridge museum, and a few remnants of this can still be found in the river. This was the Romans' main supply base for legions on their way to Caledonia (Scotland) and countless thousands of soldiers passed through the town each week.

In AD126 the Fifth Legion visited Corbridge, to build up their food reserves and dally with the camp followers who made a good living from their Roman rulers. They assisted local craftsmen to rebuild their aqua duct and needed many men to repair it swiftly. Once that work was complete they set off through Portgate along the Devil's Causeway towards Hartburn. There were many rogues and Reivers in Northumbria at that time, but not many would tackle a fully armed Roman patrol. Yet they would never reach Hartburn and were never seen again. It is believed that they either ran away, hard to believe of such a disciplined army, or that they were attacked and killed, all signs of the battle removed so that the Romans had no reason to take vengeance on any particular village.

*In February 1777, Frances Murray from Leith was visiting a friend in Stamfordham and claimed to see a Roman legion marching across the hillside and vanishing into a copse of trees.

*Lesley Dundas from Newcastle was out with friends on a bike ride when she neared Matfen, and saw what she swears was a Roman soldier carrying a square shield and sword.

THE RUDCHESTER ROMAN

A bizarre event took place in 1971 when the Dobson family from Filey decided to spend a week camping along Hadrian's Wall.

They had no particular knowledge of the history of the area, although they knew that several forts along the wall, which stretches from the east coast across to the west coast, had been inhabited by Roman soldiers. They were far more interested in the breathtaking scenery of Northumberland and the Border Country than in the various piles of stones.

They spent their first night parked on the seafront outside South Shields and started moving inland along the northern bank of the Tyne. As Newcastle's West End peters out into suburbia they had a meal at a local pub, then set up camp near what used to be called Vindobala or the Rudchester Fort. They had first parked down a dark road near a quarry but had decided to move.

The two children were bedded down early in the cramped caravan, and Frances and Bill Dobson brewed a pot of tea on their Calor gas stove. It was a warm, balmy evening and reinforced against the wind by a drink or two, Bill decided to take a walk out into the darkness. The moon was full, and the sky was illuminated by the reflections of the streetlights of Fenham, Benwell and Slatyford, a few miles down the road.

Frances had a cup of tea and a fig roll and impatiently waited for her husband to return. She couldn't stray far from the caravan because of the sleeping children. So instead she walked towards a rough, dry-stone wall and lit a cigarette. As she did so she put her hand behind her to rest on the wall and felt something cold and steely. Startled, she jumped up and turned around to see a man covered with dirt. She asked him what the hell he thought he was doing, and received an unintelligible answer, obviously in a foreign language.

She tried to look him up and down, but with the moon constantly dimming as the clouds relentlessly rolled by, she was unable to see much. She did, however, catch sight of a glimmer of metal, and of a dark ruddy-coloured robe that had the most obnoxious smell.

She walked slowly back towards the caravan, and the man walked behind her; her sandshoes made no sound, but he flip-flopped along in what seemed to be sandals. When Frances got to the caravan she reached inside the door for a torch, but when she turned around the man was gone. All that remained was a horrendous stench that filled her chest. The smell was similar to that of a boneyard.

Slowly but surely Bill ambled back and refused point-blank to believe his wife's story. She, however, had been so alarmed that the following day she stopped at a tourist information centre and asked about the fort. She was neither the first nor the last visitor over the years to claim to have seen a Roman soldier, or soldiers, along Hadrian's Wall.

*The most famous sighting was when a coach party of over forty men, women and children saw four fully-armed Roman soldiers running along the top of the wall. The truth was less than dynamic: it was a group of four clerks from the DHSS Longbenton raising money for charity by running the length of the Wall in fancy dress.

Frances Dobson even phoned a lecturer at Newcastle University, who confirmed that the Romans at Rudchester Fort would indeed wear a ruddy-coloured tunic, as they were the First Cohort of Frisiavones.

On discussing what this stranger said, the lecturer spoke in a strange tongue and asked if that resembled the man's words. It may well have been Roman but it wasn't close to the original. Then the lecturer tried again, and at once Frances said, 'Yes that's it, that's definitely it!' The lecturer was speaking Dutch.

That particular Roman cohort was made up of 'honorary Romans', containing an entire tribe from Holland.

There was no way Frances Dobson could have known about the Dutch connection, and to this day she swears that she saw a Roman soldier, still guarding Hadrian's Wall.

It explains the smell too, if you're over 1,900 years old I think you can allow yourself a hygiene problem.

THE CRAGSIDE QUEEN

Cragside Hall near Rothbury is, in my opinion, the most beautiful house and grounds in the North. Lord Armstrong had it built, taking about thirty years from 1864. He was the first to have electricity in his home, creating it from a water wheel at Debdon Burn. He took a heavily forested area, and transformed it into a paradise of rare and exotic plants. He installed lakes, bridges, trails and rock gardens. Any bare rockface that he had was transformed into the most wonderful of landscapes. Yet I have been told of a shy ghost that is said to wander the grounds, witnessed by very few. On researching the book two people wrote in with the following stories:

*Gordon Craggs from Amble wrote: 'In 1956 I first visited Cragside, and I was looking down the valley from the house when I saw a tiny girl wearing a long white gown. Her arms were bare and her hair in a kind of bun on her head. She was very delicate looking, and as she looked up towards me her face looked so calm and peaceful. I couldn't take my eyes off her, and despite her outfit being quite unsuitable for where she was walking it didn't seem to be getting dirty, although it trailed along the ground. I started down towards where she was, and I was within twenty feet of her when she disappeared. I couldn't believe it, I almost chatted up a ghost!'

*Mr and Mrs Steiner were visiting their daughter Ursula who had married an oil rig worker from Wallsend and were taken to Cragside on a day out in 1988. The Steiners were from Dusseldorf and were used to visiting castles, it is a favourite pastime of theirs back home in Germany. Neither believed in ghosts in the slightest, yet what happened at Cragside changed their mind.

They parked their car in an area just down from the house and decided to take a walk through the woods while the weather was still bright. Ursula's husband Frank was offshore, so the threesome enjoyed a sandwich as they casually took in the spectacular scenery when they saw a young girl peering at them from around a tree. They shouted 'hello' but the girl just ran backwards behind another tree. It was as if she were playing a game! This went on until finally Maria Steiner, Ursula's mother, said 'Enough' and they turned to make their way up to Cragside Hall. At this, the young girl appeared. She was wearing a long cream silken gown, buttoned high to the neck, where her shoulders were covered by strings of pearls and a light orange feather boa. She was wasp-waisted and kept a silken handkerchief protruding from the puff sleeves of her dress. Her hair was light brown and she had a serene expression. Aristocratic yet full of fun. The Steiners turned back to introduce themselves and stood not a yard from the figure as it completely faded away. Mrs Steiner passed out and they carried her to the car and gave her a drink to revive her.

On getting to the house they told one of the men guiding cars to the parking areas, and he said that it sounded just like Winnie'. They didn't know who Winnie' was, but I'm led to believe that he was referring to Miss Winifreda Watson-Armstrong who died in France when she was only eighteen. She was always very playful, and loved the gardens at Cragside, once saying to Lord Armstrong, 'This is the happiest place I know!' It seems as if she has chosen it to be her home even now.

THE DRUID CURSE OF CRASTER

Craster is known as the kipper capital of the world, worth a visit purely on the grounds of dunking one in butter and letting it melt on your tongue. But many years ago, long before the Norman conquest, it is believed that Craster was one of the North's early Druid settlements. The only legend appertaining to the place concerns a family who lived in a small house on the ground where Craster Tower now stands.

A local family of fisher folk had built a primitive home, close enough to the sea to ply their trade, but far enough away to escape the bitterly cold North wind. Life was hard, but they were managing. There were five in the family, Jacob, a fisherman, his wife Ruth and their three children, including a ten-month-old baby. It was on Hallows Eve when around thirty men were seen coming towards their home, they were dressed in long dark robes with hoods over their heads. At first, they thought they were monks proceeding towards Lindisfarne, but on closer inspection, they saw that each one carried a long curved dagger. Jacob offered them water and some food, fish with bread hot from the oven. All seemed to be going well until the leader of this group asked if Jacob had any children. Jacob nodded, and in that very second felt someone grip him from behind. He also felt hot, very hot and weak, growing weaker all the time. Whether he had realised that one of those strange knives had been plunged into his back we will never know, but he didn't make a sound. His eyes tried to puzzle what was happening as his life drained away.

Ruth was in the house feeding the baby when the robed figures pushed open the door. She thought no wrong of it until one reached down and snatched the child from her. With the fury that only a mother could create, she pulled one of the men towards and past her and he fell into the open fire, staggering out screaming in agony as he struggled to remove his clothes. It was to no avail as he fell on a bundle of cloth and within seconds the entire cottage was burning. The thatched roof began to take hold and burning straw landed on top of all the house's occupants. Ruth had managed to wrestle free her child and was under the window as the fire consumed her home.

Miraculously both she and her baby escaped and she stood underneath a tree and watched her entire life change within a period of half an hour. At that moment the remaining robed figures walked towards her, daggers were drawn, ready to avenge the deaths of around twelve of their number. Just then, Ruth's other two children were returning home with two or three wagon-loads of fishermen, back from a day's fishing. They had promised Jacob they would look after his two teenage sons, and that they had. On seeing the smoke they had galloped towards the house and were now racing towards them to offer assistance. They reached Ruth and the baby a matter of moments before the black-robed group and immediately began to fight with them. Grabbing axes and pitchforks the brave fishermen of Craster managed to scramble a victory, killing all but one of the strange men in black. The remaining attacker stood at the doorway to the burning house and began chanting what is now believed to be an obscure Druid prayer, and then he turned and walked inside.

The flames were subsiding, but the heat was intense and no human being could survive it. As smoke continued to pour from the windows and doors the assembly heard 'A curse on thee, a curse on thee and gradually the voice faded away.

It is said that on entering the cinder-filled room they found the Druid, dead but completely smoked and cooked. Many believe this is how the fishermen came up with the idea for creating 'smokehouses' to cook their kippers and other fish. No house could be built on that spot ever, again, and even now there is said to be a square of land near Craster Tower where no plants will grow, so it is now covered with paving slabs. What happened to Ruth is unknown, and she was never heard of again.

*The only sighting reported near to this spot was made by a motorist called Judith Wilson who did an emergency stop on the Craster to Dunstan road when she saw a tiny baby in the middle of the road. Having screeched to a halt, she dived out to check on the child to find that there was none in sight.

CRESSWELL:
THERE IS NOTHING LIKE A DANE

At Cresswell near Druridge Bay, one of the most picturesque landscapes on the North-East coast, stands the Peel Tower, for many years the only lifeline the local villagers had. Not only had it been used to summon worshippers to prayer, it also warned them when the Vikings were set to raid. This area of the beach was the perfect place to land, they could bring their longships close enough to the shore for them to walk in. Some say as many as 5,000 raids began at Druridge.

It came as no surprise that over the years some Norsemen decided to stay, building homes for themselves and their families. One such man was actually a Danish Prince, who so fell in love with the place he ordered the Vikings to stop their raids, pushing them either further north around Berwick, or south to the mouth of the Tyne. This pleased the locals who befriended the Prince, and soon all animosity had disappeared, except the family who lived at Cresswell Tower. They had lost three sons in vicious and bloody battles with the Danes and refused to accept one into their community. The Danish Prince was a peace-loving man, and never having taken up arms against the Britons, he did not believe he had anything to fear.

His only mistake was to fall in love with a pretty Northumbrian girl, the youngest daughter of the family who lived in Cresswell Tower. She felt the same towards him, even though she knew that hatred for the Prince festered throughout her brothers and cousins. After a decent time of courtship, the Prince approached the family to ask for her hand in marriage, and to everyone's surprise, they agreed. They negotiated a suitable dowry and the Prince left the Tower cheering and singing, such was his joy. He invited every single man, woman and child to the wedding to be held at Cresswell Tower. He prepared his entourage and forwarded cartloads of food, freshly killed deer, boar and cattle. There had never been a happier man, he had left the warlike Vikings to settle in a peaceful land and was about to marry the most beautiful woman he had ever known. His fiancée was Scandinavian in appearance, with long plaited blonde hair. So the great day arrived and the Prince with an escort of four men began to ride down the coast towards Cresswell. At the tower, hundreds of people were gathered awaiting the groom's arrival. The bride-to-be was stunned at how little resistance to her marriage she had received from her brothers who detested the Prince. She took her place high up at the very top of the Peel Tower, scanning the horizon for any sign of the man who was set to share the rest of her life.

However, her brothers were a cunning pair and had employed three Scots to murder the Prince on the way to the ceremony. They were barely half a mile from Cresswell when arrows flew into the chests of two of the escort. The others were so surprised they were easily pulled from their horses by the Scottish attackers. The Prince could easily have escaped had he left his men, instead, he drew his sword and proceeded to attack. He never saw the man who killed him, for as he raised his sword to do battle with one Scot, his clansman had pushed the head of a spear into his back, forcing the point upwards piercing his heart. The Prince swayed in his saddle as the horse began to gallop off towards Cresswell.

The crowds all cheered as they saw the Prince galloping towards them, his bride gave a smile as bright as a Mediterranean sunrise and all would surely be well. Yet as the Prince approached his bloodsoaked body slipped from the horse, his foot remaining entangled in the stirrup. The wedding party gasped as he began bouncing off rocks and greenery alike as the horse dragged him right past the Tower. Eventually, some of the guests managed to stop the horse and found that the Prince was dead.

As the news was shouted up to that fated woman on the Peel Tower she looked as white as her pearl-laden gown. Whether she fainted or whether it was by choice we will never know, but she fell from the tower to her own death, landing between her two brothers. Not only had they murdered a good man, who would have made a decent and honourable husband; they had killed their own sister too.

The bride that never would be is said to haunt Cresswell Tower, and on a few occasions has re-enacted the moment she fell, much to the surprise of visitors. Sounds of agony can often be heard from the nearby dunes, and this is always followed by the pounding of a horse's hooves, dragging something large and bulky through the brush.

*Miss D. D. Knight from Penrith in Cumbria wrote to me in August 1985: 'You should visit Cresswell because I am positive that I saw a ghost there last summer. We were having a beach barbecue at about 11.00 pm when my boyfriend and I went for a walk. We were standing beneath the tower when we looked up and saw a lady dressed all in white. She was so clear we could make out all of her facial features, even in the moonlight. I shouted up to apologise if we'd woken her up. We were playing music on the beach and having a bit of a dance. She didn't answer, just looked really sad, and then turned and walked away. She was wearing a long white dress.'

THE DEAD WALK AT DUNSTANBURGH

Dunstanburgh Castle was known as the largest castle in Northumberland. Its occupants had been Roman, Norman, Saxon and originally maybe even Druid! Some believe it has the ghost of John of Gaunt, others that of a lonely girl who weeps at the top of Lilburn Tower, but by far the most famous is that of Sir Guy. Whether this is legend or fact no one knows, but it has outlasted any other.

The story tells of a brave knight who had travelled throughout England seeking adventure, and this brought him to the 'uncivilised' North. He came across Dunstanburgh Castle and it was in such a poor state of repair he believed that any decent knight would return it to its rightful condition. The rescuing of damsels, the jousting and the search for the Holy Grail would have to wait for a while. As he approached the castle a thunderbolt struck the earth and this burst open the door of a tiny cottage outside the castle walls. A strange half-man half-beast appeared, proclaiming himself a warlock and told Sir Guy that a most beautiful girl (some legends say a Princess) was waiting to be rescued, as she had been trapped by an evil spell.

So Sir Guy kicked open the castle gates, climbing the portcullis and over the secondary wall. There he met a huge monstrous serpent with fiery green eyes and huge poisonous fangs that dripped with a venom so filled with acid it melted even the stone that it touched. The valiant knight lashed at it with his sword but the beast was too quick for him. It coiled around his armour and was just about to sink its teeth into his neck when the wizard stepped forward-thrusting a torch into its mouth and it crumbled into ash around him.

Although the castle had appeared unoccupied the truth was far more frightening, for as Sir Guy entered the main courtyard he saw row after row of knights, each one armed to the teeth with visors closed ready to attack. This was the army of the dead, raised by a magic spell from all the local graveyards to act as demon guardians for this kidnapped lady. Through the slits in the visors Sir Guy could see no skin, merely blood-drenched skulls, screaming their defiance! At the end of the row, dressed in kingly garb, were two huge skeletons who seemed almost eight feet tall, and one carried the horn of Merlin. This horn had been stolen by the black knight Mordred who had sold it to a witch in exchange for powers in the black arts. The other demon from the court of Hell carried a huge sword. Some legends say it was Excalibur, others say it was a magic two-handed sword that had fallen from Heaven.

There at their feet lay an open tomb, and inside it was the golden-haired girl. She was awake, her eyes filled with panic yet her body frozen stiff with fear. The warlock told Sir Guy that he had to choose between the sword of God or the horn of Merlin. His instincts as a knight told him to take the sword and kill these monsters, but something stopped him and he grabbed the horn. Placing it between his lips he blew for all that he was worth as the hundred bony knights approached with swords, axes and cudgels. That was his final memory, for in a second he was outside Dunstanburgh Castle again, pounding on the door with his sword.

Whether he chose wrongly, or whether his curse for taking on the armies of hell was to remain outside forever no one is quite sure. Sir Guy remains desperately seeking a way into the castle. The long white beard of the old fellow can often be seen late at night, particularly between September and February, still hoping to rescue the fair lady. There have often been reports that King Arthur's castle Camelot was based in Northumberland, and other claims include the Hartlepool area. They seem far-fetched, yet we do have many tales of Knights of the Round Table being active in the area. If Camelot was on the South Coast, how come so many Northern tales exist?

* Marjorie McAlpine from Shieldfield, Newcastle, saw something odd in 1990. 'I was standing sketching Dunstanburgh Castle when I saw something at the gate. I was about 400 yards away so I couldn't make it out. The entire body seemed to glint in the sun, as if the figure was covered in metal, like a robot!' Or maybe a knight?

DEATH AT DILSTON

The North has suffered many treacherous acts over the centuries but none so vile as what happened at Dilston in the early 1700s. James Radcliffe was the Earl of Derwentwater and he was a quiet peace-loving man. Despite the endless wars and revolts, he kept himself to himself. Yet during the Jacobite rising his wife began to taunt the Earl, saying: 'There are great fortunes to be made. Join the revolt, unseat this cruel king and just think how powerful we could be!'

For months Radcliffe ignored his wife's urgings, but they seemed to increase in number in direct proportion to the number of her friends that had returned from battle loaded with booty. 'You're a coward,' she would scream, 'not even willing to fight for your own Dilston soil!' or 'You cannot love me if you won't fight to protect me!' or 'My husband is a traitor', every possible insult bandied around, to villagers, to friends and to his face.

Finally, the peaceable earl took up arms, gathered a small troop of local men and off he went to war. His wife was thrilled, spending night after night wondering what treasures he would bring home to her. She told some of her close friends that her husband could even become king if he went about things the right way. She was a social climber of the worst kind. Things certainly did not go according to her plan. As the rebellion folded James Radcliffe was captured by the king's men, and even though he was a most unwilling rebel, he was sentenced to be beheaded on Tower Hill. It is said that on the day he placed his neck on the chopping block and the huge axe was swung down upon him, the gutters of Dilston Castle ran red with blood during a fierce thunderstorm. On that bitterly cold morning, thousands of adders swarmed along the River Derwent, where no snake had ever been seen before. Now centuries later you still see the occasional adder at Dilston, said to be the trapped soul of one of Radcliffe's men, sent to his death by a foolish greedy woman.

*There have been over three hundred sightings of a group of forty or so men riding over the Northumbrian countryside near Dilston. It is said to be the Earl riding off with his men. On dark nights you can often hear them laughing and joking, obviously in high spirits, not knowing the horrors that lay ahead.

*Dilston Castle has the ghost of the earl's wife, who on wet and thundery nights stands on the battlements wringing her hands in grief and anguish for the husband she sent to his doom. Many believe it was anguish for the lost power and riches, rather than concern for the earl.

*In August 1986 Frances Docherty was visiting her family in Hexham when she was driving near Dilston and saw in her rearview minor men on horseback, dressed in period costume, ride across the road behind her.

ELLINGHAM: THE FRIED FRIAR OF PRESTON TOWER

Preston Tower stands near Ellingham, Northumberland, and it was built to replace Preston Hall that was burned to the ground in 1782. The truth is quite straight forward, but I did come across one legend that bears repeating. It tells of the reason why the Hall was torched. It seems that local monks had been very critical of the family who lived in Preston Hall and had warned the family that if they refused to mend their ways, the wrath of God would descend upon them. The family continued treating the locals like peasants, and it is said that two brothers and the father had incestuous relations with the two youngest girl children aged eleven and seventeen. A monk entered the house late one evening and built a fire out of table and chairs at one end of the long hall. That part was entirely consumed by fire, and now only two towers out of the original four are still standing. There have been several ghostly sightings, usually of a monk, including one of a monk who was on fire (seen in the 1950s).

THE CURSE OF THE ELSDON GIBBET

There can be few experiences more eerie than driving through fog on a dusky night. Imagine how much more frightening it would be should you come across a tall gallows with a head hanging from it. Such is the case of Elsdon, near Otterburn, where a wooden head hangs as a reminder to wrongdoers of the fate that once awaited them. The ghost that is said to walk at Elsdon is that of a gipsy, William Winter, who had slit the throat of a woman by the name of Margaret Crozier. It had been a very bloody deed, for as she struggled for her life she had grasped at the knife, cutting her hands and fingers to the bone.

The crime was not too hard to solve, as witnesses had noticed Winter with a huge skinner's knife. He was arrested along with other gipsies who were conspiring to create an alibi for Winter. On searching their caravans they found goods belonging to the murdered woman and their fate was sealed. They were tried at Moot Hall in Newcastle where it was decreed that they all be hanged by the neck until they were dead. The two women, sisters by the name of Clark, were hanged at Westgate (now Westgate Road) and their bodies sent off for dissection, as surgeons attempted to glean what they could about the workings of the human body. Winter's body would be taken back to Elsdon, where the murder had taken place and left to rot. As Winter was being taken off towards the gallows he turned to the small gathering of onlookers and said 'You'll be seeing me again, I'll come back and haunt the bloody lot of you! A curse on your houses and damn you to hell, that's a gipsy curse that is, a gipsy's curse will see you to your grave.'

So the Elsdon stob, as it became known, was the place where visitors would recoil in horror on seeing this sturdy man being eaten away. Some locals claimed that as the broken body hung there in chains, crows would land on it, pecking out the eyes to feast on the jelly within. As they did so the corpse would shake until the birds flew off. Other people said that as the stench became too great they used to throw water on it, to make it easier to bear. It became a swarming place for flies, who laid eggs in the decaying flesh, food for their maggots. As you passed the tormented figure the socketless eyes seemed to watch woefully, and the skullish grin appeared almost to taunt the Elsdon folk. Once most of the flesh had gone, and the local children had snapped off many of the bones having used it as target practice, Winter's body was buried. Some say Winter's bones lie directly at the foot of the gibbet, others say that farmers fearing that his curse would transform their fields into wasteland ordered them to take the body up into the hills and to pack it beneath some scrubland. The curse may have carried some weight as eight of those who helped try the gipsies died within twelve months of the case.

Elsdon Gibbet, known by some as Winter's Stob, is still awaiting visitors who make a macabre pilgrimage often at dusk, to capture the gallows on camera, as night begins to fall. When the mist comes off the moors, wafting around the gibbet, there are fewer sights that can make your heart beat faster.

In 1832 a woman from Newcastle decided she would swing on the Elsdon Gibbet. As she showed off to her friends, her hands slipped on the dewy rope and she fell scraping her neck and cutting her hands down to the bone, the same places were injured on the murdered woman Margaret Crozier's body.

In 1907 a national magazine sent a reporter to interview locals about the 'alleged ghost of a knife murderer' after they had written a short feature called 'The Gypsy's Curse of Northumberland': The locals refused to mention whether they had seen anything,' and only one farmer would even speak to him and he told him to **** off!'

You don't make light of things that are part of people's lives. If you don't believe you should keep your opinions to yourself.

In 1987 a teacher from Northumberland called John Harbottle agreed to host a gathering of 'Night Owls' from Metro Radio at the Gibbet, from about 9.00 pm to 2.30 am the following day. He said at the time: 'It was incredible the response, people spent hours trying to find the place because it was so tucked away. They came in cars and vans from Scotland, Teesside and Cumbria, gathering in their kagouls and raincoats, and watched as the skies became darker and darker. At first, you think it's just a laugh, but as the night progressed more and more people were getting really jumpy. A girl screamed because she swears she saw the head hanging from the gallows turn and look at her! We did hear a lot of noises and rustling, and shadows always seemed to move, but I didn't see any ghost. It was still a terrific memory.'

THE EMBLETON PIPER

The tiny hamlet of Embleton has always been much as it is today, quiet, peaceful and happily out of the hustle and bustle. However back in 1393 the Scots began flooding into Northumberland laying waste to any village they came across. They were not just content with stealing cattle and carrying off the young women, they also laid waste to the fields, putting them all to the torch. The people of Embleton had not been bothered in any way, yet nor did they want to be, so landowners collected £40 and built a tower with a huge bell, to act as a warning of Scottish raids to all the villages. The pealing of the bells saved many lives and gave early warning to gather resistance to the marauding Highlanders. There were many battles in and around the village as hostilities continued, but the locals were so well organised that they managed to discourage the attacks more often than not.

It was during such an attack that a young Scot was captured and returned to Embleton in chains. The men had kicked and punched him until he was a mass of bruises, and he sat surrounded by villagers as they cursed him. He was quietly spoken and said that he was a piper and that he took no part in any fighting. Unlike any Scot, they had seen he did not have a claymore, not even a small dagger. They brought out some Northumbrian pipes, saying if he was a piper he could play those. After some effort, he managed to strike up a tune and by the end of the afternoon, he had the entire village of Embleton dancing and feasting. Although he was classed as an 'enemy' the locals took him to their hearts, and eventually removed his chains, allowing him to live freely within the village. The young Scot was happy to do so and decided to stay and help out local farmers. They paid him with food and a stable roof over his head.

Visitors to Embleton were surprised to see a kilt-wearing Scot living amongst Northumbrians as they were so very often at each other's throats. Many believe it is thanks to the people of Embleton that the Northumbrians and the Scots live so comfortably together side by side, sharing many of the same problems to this day as they did then.

In the early 1400s, there was an outbreak of fever in the village that took the life of the young Scot, and from that day it is said that if you stand in Embleton village late at night you can still hear the piper summoning up a tune. The music wafts across the fields towards the sea and those that hear it cannot help but tap their feet.

THE FARNE ISLANDS AND CUTHBERT'S GHOST

When Cuthbert the Bishop of Lindisfarne came to live on the Farne Islands in the year AD 6, his goodliness and Godliness forced all of the ghosts and spirits to flee. Although countless sightings of Cuthbert's ghost have been seen on Holy Island, the Farnes have had far more sinister spectres. All of those unhappy spirits that Cuthbert drove out took refuge on the outlying islands close to the Farnes. When it is late people have often heard terrible cries of pain and agony as these lost souls shriek out in torment. Local boatmen and fisherfolk claim to have seen ugly, deformed demons lurching across the rocks, sometimes riding on the backs of wolves and goats, two animals normally associated with Satan. Many think that these souls belong to sailors lost at sea, who were unable to find their way to heaven, and had not sinned quite enough to reach hell. Instead, they infest the craggy rocks like sand crabs, leering out at anyone who passes by.

*Women can suffer quite a harrowing experience when visiting the Farnes, for Cuthbert never liked women after the daughter of a Northumbrian farmer claimed that he had raped her. Some women have felt someone touching them, others have felt warm breath on the back of their necks. The wild birds are also more prone to swoop down on women visitors rather than men. Ornithologists suggest that this may be because they dress in brighter colours or are noisier. Others think that it is all part of Cuthbert's revenge.

*There is an ancient curse appertaining to any woman who sees his tomb. It is widely thought that any female who sees it will die a horrible death. This is after one woman died of a heart attack whilst out with a party of men.

HAUGHTON CASTLE'S MAN WHO ATE HIMSELF

Out in the wilds of sixteenth-century Northumberland stood Haughton Castle owned at that time by Sir Thomas Swinburne who was Lord of the Manor. Those that lived on his land would have been happy were it not for the gangs of robbers and Border reivers that plagued the entire area. Many of these Scots had been forced out of their own country by the various religious altercations that were becoming commonplace. The most troublesome clans were the Robsons, the Dodds, The Bilious, the Charltons and, arguably the worst, the Armstrongs.

On a dark November night, Sir Thomas Swinburne led an assault on a reiver encampment, killing dozens of men and capturing Archie Armstrong, their chief. After they had locked Armstrong up, in a dungeon, they passed the night in feasting and celebration, before Sir Thomas sped off to York early in the morning.

At this point, there are variations in the story. Some believe that Swinburne walled Armstrong up in the dungeon to be left to starve to death. Others declare that on nearing York he remembered that he had left no instructions for the prisoner to be fed, so either sent back one of his representatives or returned to Haughton Castle himself.

The timescale, too, varies; some say that the representative arrived back a week later, some say it was only days later, others say it was a month later. What they discovered was quite disgusting. The dungeon lay in silence, and on pushing the door open they found Archie's lifeless body in the corner. He had been so desperate to survive that he had attempted to eat his own arms and legs, and drunk his own urine and blood. He sat there covered with human bite marks; he had even chewed away half of his cheek. What Archie had started both rats and weevils had continued. His eyes hung down his cheeks, vermin having eaten away his eyelids; and as Swinburne stood at the dungeon door, they stared horribly at him.

It was said that Sir Thomas was so horrified by the way his prisoner had died that he refused ever to sentence anyone to those cells again. The door was sealed, and often his private staff would claim to hear strange moanings and screams.

The castle was exorcised but ghostly happenings occasionally still occur.

THE HALTONCHESTERS LIGHTNING CURSE

West of Haltonchesters near one of the Roman garrison's milecastles lies a heavy carved stone block with the markings FVLCVR DIVOM, a shortened derivation meaning 'Lightning of the Gods'.

It is believed that many years ago during a fair held nearby at Stagshaw bank, the rain began to pour from the heavens. As this monsoon became an electrical storm, with roaring thunder and countless bursts of forked lightning, the huge crowd ran for shelter. So swiftly had the squall hit, that the sky transformed from day to night, and the scurrying swarms of people began to panic. The people of this area were primitive in their beliefs, and this seemed to be an evil omen. They rushed to their homes, and if anyone fell they were trampled into the mire. One young Roman soldier watched as a child stumbled and was promptly trampled to death. No one took time to see to him, for they were all far too concerned with getting out of the rain. So this unknown trooper stood on a grassy knoll and ordered everyone to stop. To emphasise the point he drew his sword from its scabbard and held it above his head, trying to be heard against all the elements. At that very moment, there was an almighty crash and a blinding flash of lightning coursed its way down his sword and though his body.

One legend tells us that the young man exploded into millions of tiny balls of flame, others that he seemed held motionless for some seconds before collapsing to the ground, baked brown and dead.

It is said that a person wearing anything metallic who stands at the spot during a thunderstorm will be struck down too.

*During a live show in 1988, I tried this carrying an old-fashioned spear. Admittedly I was wearing rubber gloves and rubber boots, but even so, I wasn't struck to death. Having stood there for an hour through driving rain I did come back with something – flu! No wonder this country is up the creek, we spend about £50 million on medical research and closer to £1 billion on 'Get Well Soon' cards!

*Local farmers do claim that some cows were once found dead close to this spot, apparently struck by lightning, but no cases of human injury have been reported.

HALTWHISTLE: HERE COMES THE BRIDE

It is said that one of the most beautiful women in Northumberland was Abigail Featherstonehaugh of Haltwhistle who was madly and passionately in love with a young man from the village. This was not such a great problem until her father, a rich and powerful man, got to hear of it, and banned Abigail from ever seeing him again. Medieval England was known to be a man's world in which women were seen but rarely heard. Fathers ruled the roost, and women would merely do as they were told. A rich man's daughter would not be allowed to associate with a penniless waif, only the very best would do. This was a time when arranged marriages were common, and he was positive that she would marry for better, rather than worse.

The lover was a farm labourer with bright blue eyes and a waspish wit, and he was not going to allow anyone to stop him meeting his true love. They would meet in secret and the romance blossomed until one day Abigail's father overheard her telling a friend how much she was in love. This was the final straw, and in a rage the father slapped Abigail and locked her in her room. The house in Haltwhistle was soon regularly visited by young men of rank, wealth and position, invited expressly to meet young Abigail. She was still deeply in love, but her lover had disappeared without a trace. Some believed he had been bought off by her father, others say he was forced out of the parish by threats of death if ever he showed his face again. Rumours also abounded that the young labourer may have been Featherstonehaugh's illegitimate son, and so was Abigail's half-brother. The scandal would not have been good for the rich man's image as a God-fearing pillar of the community.

After pining for almost a year Abigail was betrothed to a fine gentleman from Alston, who was kind and generous, all the things her father was not. The banns were read and everyone in the Tyne Valley knew that they were finally to be married in a church at Alston. The arrangements were made for a fine procession, aboard a finely painted blue coach for the groom to collect his bride, then they would ride together to church. They would be accompanied by three outriders, his best man and two brothers. As their respective families gathered at the church, talking excitedly about the pair about to be wed, Abigail was slipping into a fine white gown bought in Newcastle for a king's ransom. If ever there was an angel in white it was her, and the staff gasped when they saw how beautiful she looked. Her life had been difficult, living out in the wilds, totally dominated by a cruel and heartless father, but finally, she was to leave it all behind. A cart was being piled with all of her personal belongings; this was to be carried to her new matrimonial home on the outskirts of Alston. Her fiancé arrived and, bedazzled by her loveliness, stumbled and stuttered a greeting, then kissed her hand and they walked arm in arm to the coach. Once aboard the staff and villagers threw rose petals at them, as the bridal procession set off.

The sun was shining and leaves of differing hues glistened. The couple were happy too, truly happy! He because he was marrying a woman of such intense beauty and sparkling personality. Life would be full of joy with a woman who loved to laugh, and who was able to spread that spark of excitement to everyone she met. She was equally content, for she was on the verge of marrying a good man, a man who would love her for what she was, and not for the dowry. They looked at the rolling hills, the birds soaring into the sky rejoicing at being alive, all of the smiling faces of those they passed and the horses plodding through the grass. A marriage made in Heaven!

What they didn't know was that a glimpse of hell was waiting around the corner. As they approached the crossroads that led them ever nearer to the church in Alston the procession reached a group of men waving and cheering. The couple waved at them until Abigail spotted the man at the front of the throng. It was her previous lover, he was drunk and his anger exploded within him as he led an attack on the wedding party. The riders were forced to flee, outnumbered by their assailants, leaving the bride and groom to the mercy of a rejected lover. That mercy was not forthcoming, and they were both hacked to death. The cart was set on fire and their bodies left in the mud.

Many travellers between Alston and Haltwhistle have seen a ghostly wedding procession, with two lovers ripped and bleeding heading towards a marriage that would never be. Some have mistaken this for a real parade, only to be shocked as it neared, to see blood pouring from open wounds, trickling down her shimmering bridal gown.

*Marje and Frank Coles belong to a caravan dub and whilst holidaying in Northumberland they heard strange music as if played on a lute. Marje continues 'We had stopped for our tea, early in November 1989, when we heard this strange music. We were parked just outside of Knarsdale, halfway between Haltwhistle and Alston, when we were aware of something coming our way. We had a small gas bottle cooker on the boil, and couldn't see anything else as it was pitch black. Then in the distance, we saw what we thought was an old horse and cart, yet when we shouted, we got no reply. Frank started walking towards the cart, and actually stepped aside to let it past. It never reached me, it just disappeared!' Frank added "There seemed to be two figures slumped over in the cart, I thought they were sleeping. I heard noises following behind and glanced over to see a man on a horse, and I looked back towards the caravan, exactly where the cart should have been, it was nowhere to be seen!'

HAZELRIGG: WE ALL FALL DOWN

'Ring a ring o' roses' is one of our oldest children's games, created by listing how folk had died of the plague, yet there was a major panic in 1972 when the climax of the game struck down children at Hazelrigg in Northumberland. It was a bright sunny day and the carnival had arrived in the tiny village. Colourful stalls were selling homemade jams and cakes, the travelling roundabouts had been installed and their music put everyone in good spirits. A field had been put aside for egg-and-spoon races, sack races and a dog show. Some of the villagers were organising games for the children and there were 152 children playing games when suddenly for no apparent reason every single one of them collapsed to the ground. They were dazed and couldn't understand why it had happened. To this day no one has given any reason how such a thing could happen. Yet the day it took place was 9th July 1972, when the power stations at Blyth and Newcastle both experienced power surges for no apparent reason. In Alnwick, three streetlamps burst open with a crash. Were they all connected?

A tiny inch-square newspaper reports the following day: 'A small Unidentified Flying Object was sighted by Graham Appleby from Newcastle. He said, "It was very high, bright orange, and although I was in my car, I could feel the heat coming from it. It vanished off in a northerly direction. It was at about 1.15 in the afternoon."' Within thirty minutes all of the other things had happened!

THE HEXHAM WALK OF DEATH

Many visitors to historic Hexham believe that they have witnessed strange apparitions. The earliest reports date back as far as 1350. Yet beneath the streets of Hexham, literally a yard beneath their pavements, there are the bodies of people buried hundreds of years before. The Yorkshire prophet Thomas Addison once wrote: 'In a year after 1990 the dead of Hexham's streets shall rise and revenge themselves on those that walk upon their bones.'

Hexham Castle is said to be occupied by a bent and twisted servant, who looked after the soldiers, providing them with wine and food whilst they patrolled the battlements.

Hexham Gaol was set up to hold Border Reivers along with the residents of the archbishop's land, who regularly couldn't afford their rent. So unfair were the rulers of Hexham that the peace-loving citizens rose against them, actually attacking the gaol in 1515, as there were over 150 people in cells built for no more than fifty. The squalor and filth were unimaginable. Over the years hundreds died in there of disease and malnutrition. Extra rations were not allowed, but often friends would hurl bread and sausages up at the bars, hoping their loved ones could catch them. When they did they often had to fight to keep them once inside. For the past two hundred years, people have heard the sighs and moans of the prisoners, as they suffered at the hands of the wealthy. People have also seen the ragged shapes of living skeletons, as they remain chained to the wall.

TRICKY DICKY OF STAWARD

An ex lead miner turned poacher, known as Dicky of Kingswood, is said to haunt Staward Pele, the ruins of a tower some ten miles from Hexham. It is wedged between two rivers and was the perfect place for catching fish and trapping game. This wasn't his only occupation: he also stole cattle and horses. He was a cunning man; once confronted by a farmer whose sheep he had stolen and who was threatening to kill him, he swore that if his life was spared he would reward the farmer with a gift worth more than the sheep. The farmer let him go. He visited another farmer, stole a string of goats and presented them to the first farmer. On another occasion, he had stolen two prize oxen from a homestead at Denton Burn village and sold them for gold to a Cumbrian farmer. During the transaction, he noticed that this farmer owned a beautiful black horse. So, late that night, he crept back and stole it. As he was fleeing from the Cumbrian he ran smack-bang into the man from Denton Burn whose cattle he'd half-inched. He didn't panic, however; he coolly sold the Newcastle man his newly acquired horse so that he could chase the man who stole his oxen. He then pointed him towards the Cumbrian so hot on his tail. The two victims cut each other down, and Dicky was there to take both of their horses, as they lay battered and bleeding.

Dicky is known to play practical jokes on anyone who goes to see ruins of Staward Pele. He takes things from people's bags, putting them into other people's pockets.

THE KRAKEN OF HOLY ISLAND

The causeway between the Northumberland coast and Holy Island is notorious for taking people's lives over the years. It has many myths and legends attached to it.

One legend, once fashionable but now out of vogue, was that a sea monster would come and eat those poor souls trapped on the causeway when the high tide swept in. Occasionally people would claim to have seen the huge brown beast swimming just offshore between the mainland and Holy Island itself. The stories began in the 1100s when bodies of drowned people were often washed up on the shore. On examining the body the eyes were always missing and often the bodies seemed ripped apart. Everyone began talking of this sea serpent that would tear you to pieces if you mistimed the tides and were trapped on the causeway. By the 1200s they began to attribute the ripping of the bodies to them being bashed on the razor-sharp rocks on the coast and those that run on a shelf between land and sea. The eyes were likely to have been taken by the many crabs that forage for food all along that coastline.

THE HOLY ISLAND SEA SIRENS

In 1934 two fishermen called Jackie Stokes and Bob Armstrong told friends that while out fishing in a Coble (a small boat) they had watched a parade of phantoms gliding over the water where the causeway would be. Bob explained, 'It was a foggy night when Jackie yelled to me that he could see someone walking on the water. We never have drink aboard so I knew he wasn't stottin' [drunk] so I left the cabin and went out to see what was gannin [going] on! As true as I'm standing here I could see at least a dozen shapes in the fog. Men, women and children walking along, all grey and they seemed to stand oot in the fog. It definitely wasn't just the fog itself. I was reminded of that part of the Bible where it says "One day the sea will give up its dead." I still divvn't [don't] know what it was, but we weren't frightened. It seemed peaceful, it wadn't [wouldn't] do nee one [no one] any harm!' Jackie Stokes added: 'When you spend your life working with nature as we have, you see a lot of things that ye can't explain. That's the thing, everybody expects that God has shown us all of his wonders, yet every day someone catches a glimpse of something new. I feel well pleased that he's seen fit to show me something no one else has ever seen. I divvn't care if you believe us or not. We know what we saw!'

THE BIG-NOSED GHOST OF HOLY ISLAND CASTLE

The castle on Holy Island was built to be the hammer of the Scots, to protect the Northern seaboard against an assault on land or sea. Huge iron cannons stood guard over the causeway and the nearby estuary. They had gun batteries pointed out to sea and landward. In the 1600s a great deal of money and time was spent to restore it to its former glory. Yet almost as soon as it was completed England and Scotland were joined by the Act of Union under King James I. Rather than consider all of that money wasted it became very much a fortress of the new regime. To preserve and protect the new wave of monarchy and to bring together the two feuding sides. One of the governors of Holy Island, in charge of two dozen men, was a rugged, ugly man called Captain Rugg. His nickname was 'Old Bottle Nose' as his bulbous beak resembled the shape of the beer bottles of the day. Rugg never died on Holy Island but may well be featured in two of the most well-known tales of the strange and bizarre.

* Gwen McIntosh of Amble visited Holy Island for lunch and a day out, back in August 1978. After eating at a small, rather crowded cafe she set out to explore the entire island. She sat down close to the tiny church and graveyard and looked out across the sand towards the sea. There on the sand, she saw a tall man with arched shoulders walking back towards the island itself. She describes what she saw: 'He was wearing high boots, at first I thought they were wellies. His trousers were tucked into them and he wore a bright blue jacket. As he got closer I saw he had very sad, wrinkly eyes and the biggest nose I have ever seen on any human being. It was so big it looked as if it was deformed. Not just long, but wide across his cheeks too!' Mrs McIntosh knew nothing about Captain Rugg!

* A fellow sceptic, Father Flanagan, an Irish priest, visited Holy Island in September 1987 (helping me prepare a radio Halloween special) and spoke to an elderly lady who did not wish to be named. She claimed to have shared her house with the spirit of a gentleman for over forty years. She said this when Father Flanagan interviewed her: 'I know that ghosts exist because I live with one. We talk every night, and he's rather like any other houseguest except he doesn't need food nor a bed for the night. In the 1950s he even saved me from a house fire. I was asleep in bed and woke after being shaken about by a pair of firm hands. It was the ghost! I dashed downstairs to find my living room full of smoke because some washing had fallen onto the open fire. Thanks to neighbours we put it out, and they helped me redecorate. Had that ghost not stirred me I'd be a ghost myself now!' she laughed. Father Flanagan then told her how he doesn't believe in ghosts at all, and gently suggested she may have invented a spirit to keep her company. It's a lonely existence living alone, especially on an island so regularly cut off from the mainland. Her reply surprised him. 'As God is my witness I am telling no lie! This ghost, I call him Billy, joins me every evening – you can meet him if you like.' After ringing me, I suggested he stayed the evening, and see what there was to be seen. He called at the lady's humble two-up, two-down terraced house at 7.30 pm that evening. This is his report: 'I sat down and was instantly presented with tea and sandwiches, followed by a scone with cream and jam. Then she looked past me saying: "Billy, there you are, come and meet the nice gentleman." I froze, as it did feel very draughty, the chill in the air was noticeable. Then the lady added: "No, don't worry about that, just come in, this chap says he doesn't believe you exist." She then began talking directly towards an empty chair. For a second I thought I saw the cushion move, just a fraction. Maybe my imagination was running riot. I spoke to this chair, to reassure her that I didn't think she was senile. So I asked her to look at "Billy" and tell me what she saw because I saw nothing. I must say I was dumbstruck when she told me what she saw: "He is a tall man wearing a blue blazer. He has tall black leather boots.

He is about mid-forties with baggy eyes and a very large nose. You don't mind me saying that do you Billy!" Once again, this frail old lady had no knowledge of Captain Rugg, yet she had described him to perfection. I had researched into Mrs McIntosh's story and they both matched up exactly. Yet neither had ever met. I still don't believe, yet I cannot offer a reasonable alternative explanation!' So ended Father Flanagan's report.

Many other sightings have been claimed on Holy Island, but the most recurring is of the tall man with the big nose'

HOLY ISLAND'S GHOST OF ST CUTHBERT

Lindisfarne is otherwise known as Holy Island because it is there where Christianity began in Britain when St Aiden arrived there in AD 635. Yet despite Aiden being buried there, it is one of the bishops who followed him who is regularly seen there. Cuthbert had once been a noble soldier and witnessing so much death and despair led him to join Melrose Abbey, which in turn took him to Ripon, preaching to and in some cases even healing plague victims. He returned in triumph to Melrose and was named as Prior. He decided that his calling was at the monastery on Holy Island, and moved there for a sabbatical. King Ecgfrith of Northumbria heard that Cuthbert was staying there and crossed the causeway to persuade him to become a bishop. He lived in a tiny hermitage, rather than share the monastery with his fellow monks, and lived a very private and secluded existence. Cuthbert worked tirelessly as bishop for two years until falling desperately ill, returning to Lindisfarne to die. On the day he died he was declared a saint. St Cuthbert's ghost seems to prefer seclusion at least as much as did the living Cuthbert, always appearing way out on his own, walking along the sand, in the Priory, on the peninsula at Heugh Hill or his favourite haunt sitting on the rocks by Hobthrush.

*St Cuthbert's ghost was once spotted by eight choirboys as they were rehearsing. They all scattered amongst the pews and three quit the choir because of it!

*It is said by islanders that St Cuthbert can be seen any night when the moon is full, and the tide is about to roll across the causeway. They say he is always somewhere on the island, wandering in Godly thought!

*Pat Robinson from Suttons Dwellings, Benwell, said in 1967: 'I went to Holy Island for a day last summer and I was having a paddle with the bairn when I walked past this monk. I even said "Hello" but he didn't answer. He seemed thoughtful, so I didn't pester him again. I turned around a few moments later to see where he was, and he'd just disappeared.'

*A ghost monk has been seen countless times, but whether it is Cuthbert, no one knows. They say that as the Bible speaks out against spirits, no saint could possibly go against the word of God.

*A string of ghost-monks was witnessed walking across the causeway in 1921, 1933, 1934, 1956, 1981, 1982, 1988 and 1989 (three times). These could be monks on their many pilgrimages, others suggest they are the souls of the monks butchered on the countless Viking raids that plundered Lindisfarne over the centuries. It may be nothing other than a lot of tourists with over-active imaginations.

THE TREASURE OF BROOMLEE LOUGH

Near Housesteads fort there is said to be a box of treasure at the bottom of the lake at Broomlee Lough. Everything about it is a mystery and I can merely recount the many variables so you can make your mind up as to whether you believe any of them. On researching this particular legend I was told that the treasure was:

*The Holy Grail deposited there by Sir Galahad for safekeeping when Arthur became close to death.

King John's treasure rescued from The Wash and carted to the North by Reivers.

*The collected treasure of the man known as Robin Hood. He had believed that his men were about to betray him, so he arranged for all of his most valuable gold and jewels to be placed on a boat and sunk in the middle of the lake, which was then believed to be bottomless.

*The Ark of the Covenant, secretly brought to Britain whilst the body of Christ was moved and buried beneath Rennes in France.

Whichever path you choose to take the treasure is certainly worth uncovering. On several occasions throughout history, they have tried to remove the treasure, and in the process horses, donkeys and dogs have been killed in efforts to drag the bottom of the lake.

*Mrs Ivy Hall from Saltburn visited the lake and paddled at the water's edge on a hot sunny day in 1953. She had suffered from verrucas and ingrowing toenails yet on removing her feet from the water, to her surprise these afflictions were gone.

*Locals say that it is a religious artefact, blessed by God, that lies in the lake and those who believe in God who bathe there will be cured of whatever ails them.

MEG OF MELDON

It is not unknown for people to marry for money, and such was the case when Sir William Fenwick of Wallington wed plain-faced Margaret Selby. Her father was one of the richest men in Newcastle and had tried to marry her off for some time with little success. It was the answer to his prayers when Sir William, suffering many financial problems, decided he was in love with this decidedly dodgy-looking woman. His high living came to an abrupt halt when Sir William died, and Margaret became a most powerful and rich woman. She inherited Meldon Hall, Hartington Hall, and over thirty other large properties in the locality. The longer Margaret was left alone the more paranoid she became, believing that everyone wanted to rob her. Unable to trust even her most loyal servants she proceeded to hide jewels, gold and riches whenever she could, filling her houses with secret passages and panels brimming with her inheritance. The servants began to call her 'Mad Meg' or 'Meggie of Meldon'.

Being so keen on protecting her family treasures it wasn't long before Meg returned in spirit form. She was found near her own grave sitting on the horse trough at Newminster Hall or wandering around the corridors making sure that no one had discovered where she had stashed the cash. Anyone who tried to find the countless hidey holes would ultimately be face to face with the pallid form of Meg, most displeased at their impertinence. There was gold in wells, churches, halls, houses, stables, schools and under gravestones. It took over 50 years for all of her secret caches to be found, and only once this had happened was the ghost of 'Meg of Meldon' allowed to return to the spirit world never more to walk the earth.

*If you visit the church in Meldon you can see a statue of Sir William Fenwick. They also say that if you glance at it late at night, the figure blinks!

THE HAUNTED LOVESEAT MORPETH

The road leading towards Telford Bridge that brings you onto Morpeth's main thoroughfare, Bridge Street, has several seats backing on to Carlisle Park. You should think twice before you sit on them, but you should particularly avoid those attached to the castle wall.

According to local legend, a man named Turnbull was resting after having walked from Hepscott with monies for his employees. This portly man was puffing and panting, trying to gather enough strength to complete his journey, when a local bandit crept out of the park, grasping the man by the head and slitting his throat with a skinning knife. In a state of shock Turnbull clenched his wound tight, and although he was badly cut, neither his windpipe or his main artery had been cut. With blood pouring from the flapping slit on his neck he gurgled with pain, falling several times.

He staggered down to the inn (now known as The Waterford) where he begged for help. The villain escaped without a penny, and Turnbull made a full recovery. Even so, that seat has caused a few problems:

*In 1919 Frances Wills of Bedlington claimed that someone had pulled her hair while she sat on the seat. They tugged so hard that a huge dump fell out. Her scalp was so badly damaged the hair never grew back. On looking around no one was there.

*In September 1965 Joan Marsh from Morpeth was having an ice lolly when her throat was grasped by someone from behind, who almost choked her. Once again, her attacker was never seen, but she was so badly attacked you could make out the fingermarks of her assailant. In 1986 she said, 'I never went to the police because they wouldn't have believed me!'

*In May 1991 on Metro FM's 'Night Owls' show an apprentice at a Cramlington engineering factory, Paul Smith, claimed that he felt as if someone was strangling him while he sat on the seat in Morpeth.

THE BATTLE OF OTTERBURN

In the 1300s one of the bloodiest battles of all time took place at Otterburn and ever since, huge armies of phantom soldiers have been witnessed by hundreds of different people. There have been cases where drivers have suddenly had their car engines cut out, when phantom soldiers, beaten and bloody, began marching across the road.

*Gwen Dougray of Stannington reported in 1964: 'I was on my way to see a friend in Otterburn, and halfway along the A68 approaching Raylees when the car began to splutter. So I pulled over to the side of the road and heard this tremendous racket. It sounded like a heavy industrial factory. There was clattering and banging and then I started to hear men's voices, and they sounded in tremendous pain. Then all around me, I saw men fighting each other with swords and spears. The terrifying thing was that I was in the middle of it. They were within yards of me and the car. The funny thing was I seemed to be more worried about the car than about my safety. I hadn't had it long, and it cost an arm and a leg. Arrows were flying about, people throwing spears. Then all of a sudden it was gone. I hadn't been drinking or anything, and I knew about the Battle of Otterburn but wasn't thinking about it as I drove. I was looking forward to a barbecue that was planned for me at my friend's. If what I saw were ghosts, they were as solid as you or me!'

Hundreds of similar reports exist, and so common are the reports (averaging twelve a year) that some locals take the sight of the battle for granted now.

THE GHASTLY CAVALIER OF ROCK HALL

Rock Hall would surely be everyone's idea of the ultimate country residence, as covered with plants and ivies it remains one of the North's little jewels. Yet this rural paradise once housed a murderer that many believe still walks the shadowy corridors to this day. Members of my family once worked 'below stairs' at Capheaton Hall and many stories circulated there about the goings-on at Rock Hall, as they always have amongst the domestic staff of the great houses.

The English Civil War divided many families and villages, some believing in good old King Charles I, others wanting the new order under Cromwell. The North has always been furthest away from government, so it really didn't seem to matter to the average man and woman in the street, but in the stately homes of old England, a change in the order of things could have dire repercussions.

One of King Charles' most loyal captains, Colonel John Salkeld, used to own Rock Hall. Colonel Salkeld led battalions of Royalist troops in many skirmishes with the New Model Army. This prominent man of means hated and despised the master of Capheaton Hall, John Swinburne; some say he was jealous of his fortune, others that they shared love for the same woman. Whatever the grudge between them it was Salkeld who acted first when he grasped Swinburne from behind and forced his knife upwards into his heart, murdering him. This act was witnessed by many people, all underlings and peasants who wouldn't dare speak out against someone as powerful as the colonel. Word did eventually reach the king that one of his trusted aides had committed murder, but so desperate was the Royalist cause at that time, the king had no option other than to let the crime go unpunished.

When the Royalist cause crumbled Salkeld became silent and kept away from any confrontation with the new Roundhead regime. This kept him alive until he reached the age of fifty-nine. When he was buried it was said that noises could be heard from his coffin as it was being interred. Since then things in Rock Hall have been known to move, whispering is sometimes heard late at night on the upper floors, and from time to time people have glanced at the figure of a cavalier prancing through the house, always brightly dressed with a cockade in his wide-brimmed hat, which fades as soon as it is seen.

*When I related this tale on air a caller from Berwick phoned to say that they believed that it was the ghost that started the fire in the 1750s. The ghastly cavalier realised that the Royalist way of life would never return, so he chose to make mischief and burn it to the ground.

THE SALTSKIN OF SEGHILL

In the early 1400s, Seghill Tower was one of the largest in the entire country, standing three storeys tall, with battlements, and a bell to give warning of unwanted guests.

The legend I have been told came from a Scottish gentleman called Roy McIntosh from Glasgow, whose relatives came from Seghill.

The country had been at war with France and King Henry V was just about to snatch their crown too. He had married Catherine, the daughter of the imbecile French monarch Charles VI. Henry would have become King of England and France on the death of Charles, but fate intervened. Henry became seriously ill and died aged only 35. One day England had a strong soldier and military genius as her king, the next the entire nation was fearful of a total collapse of their international authority.

Groups of armed soldiers decided to use Henry's death as an excuse to loot and pillage, and although the North Country seemed more peaceful than the south, the residents of Seghill were fearful that all their foodstuffs would be stolen by marauders. So they asked the keeper of Seghill Tower to protect their stores, by locking them, with him, in the tower. The building was believed to be unassailable, so high was it, with walls three feet thick. A single man, an ex-soldier, Allen, maintained the tower, living in the vault, and keeping vigil by day. He readily agreed to help his friends protect their stock. Within a week, Seghill Tower was full of corn, wheat, oilseed rape, flour, salt, vegetables and fruit of every kind.

Then one day from his vantage point he saw horsemen approaching at speed and rang his warning bell. The villagers were ready for that sort of emergency and ran out into the fields and countryside. Not one of the fifty or so locals remained in Seghill, except for Allen safe in his tower. In ransacking the village, the looters came away with only a handful of chickens and nothing of value at all. They pounded on the thick wooden door of the tower, but Allen wasn't even going to reply. Instead, he was on the top of the battlements heating some pitch to pour down on them should they try to batter the door down. The battlements had huge stockpiles of rocks and missiles to hurl at potential enemies, and Allen was the man to use them.

The marauders spent the night sleeping in the beds of the locals. At three o'clock in the morning, believing them all to be drunk, Allen crept out to do vengeance to them as they slept. He took a dagger and a sword and slit the throats of several of them. But he was overheard by one who roused the camp. As Allen ran back to the tower, they were only yards behind him. He slammed the door shut behind him, and fastened bolt after bolt in a cold sweat. Then he raced up to the battlements to hurl rocks down at the villains. He had taken a risk, but it had paid off, surely, he thought; they would never come back to Seghill.

Yet it was at that very moment that he felt a blow to the back of his head. He tried to turn but blackness swallowed him up. One of the marauders had crept in while he had been out paying them his murderous visit. He awoke to find himself tied to a post in the storage yard, and all around him cavorted the marauders, drunk and wild with rage at how he had despatched their comrades. They took turns to peel the skin from his body. Each time he passed out with the pain, they would wait until he regained consciousness before beginning again. Then when he stood there naked, completely peeled, they gouged out his eyes and hurled him into the huge mounds of salt he had agreed to store. The extremes of agony he went through are unimaginable; suffice to say that he died within minutes. Minutes that must certainly have appeared like years.

*It is said that Allen, 'the Saltskin of Seghill', still occupies that vault today, protecting everything inside. Strange noises and cries have been heard, but more commonly just a very white apparition gliding along from wall to wall.

The vault has been used as the storage cellar for the Blake Arms Hotel.

THROPTON: GOING BOO FOR THE BOOZE

In 1867 a strange incident took place in Thropton near Rothbury in Northumberland, that may have left its stain on subsequent generations. A man called Douglas Moffat fought in the main street with Frank Ford, a visitor to the town. The resulting exchange of blows left Ford unconscious on the ground. Moffat, a tough from a nearby village, simply walked away. Unbeknown to the thug, on hitting his head Ford had suffered serious brain damage, and although he was still able to walk, his speech and behaviour drastically changed. Ford was taken to hospital and had to leave his job. He would return regularly to Thropton where he would drink at an inn, now known as the Cross Keys. Ford had always been prone to feel the cold so would hog the fireplace, always sitting directly in front of it, staring into the flames. He had said to his mother that it was 'his favourite place in the whole world.'

Previously he had been a very decent gentleman, kindly and not the least bit aggressive. Some believe that this was the very reason that Moffat had picked on him, as he was viewed as 'a nob from the city'. Since his assault he was a pest, driving many drinkers to distraction by moving their drinks, slamming doors, hiding in the toilet to lurch out at people when they least expected it. Sometimes he would pick up plates and smash them against the wall. Eventually after several incidents over the months, regretfully the landlord ordered Ford from his inn and barred him for life. The problem was that Ford loved that pub with a great passion, and although it was linked with his health problems he felt that he couldn't live without it. He took to his bed in Hexham and chose to die. Within the month plates were once again smashing at the Cross Keys and doors slamming and banging. So it has been through the years.

*In 1961 Martin Flahsted visited the pub on a walking trip with fellow Scandinavians. He knew nothing of the legend, yet he said 'My plate lifted from the table with all of my food still on it, then crashed into the fireplace! I had to pay for the damage, but it was not me.'

*In November 1988 landlord Peter Hillier spoke out about the variety of phenomena he had witnessed, as reported by Newcastle's Evening Chronicle. He believes that things only really began to heat up after he removed a fireplace to extend the pool room, the very fireplace where Ford had always warmed himself. He told of strange footsteps walking across wooden and stone floors when no one else was in the building. Regularly doors would rattle and slam. The various electrical gadgets would switch themselves on and off for no reason, once boiling an electric kettle when it wasn't even plugged into the mains. The television would change channels.

*Regulars at the Cross Keys were having a quiet pint or three with the landlord when an ashtray exploded into a thousand pieces showering them all with glass. Fortunately, no one was hurt. Peter Hillier told Chronicle reporter Mike Barron: 'He's causing trouble, and I'd like to bar him, but how can you do that!'

QUEEN MAB OF WHITTINGHAM

Stories of fairy kings and queens are commonplace the world over, yet Queen Mab has been named by dozens over three hundred years. She is said to live underground at Fawdon Hill close to Whittingham. It is said her kingdom stretches for miles underneath most of Northumberland, hundreds of thousands of fairies rarely ever seeing the light of day as a protection against the killer people – mankind.

It all started in the 1400s when a farmer heard strange music and on following the strange sounds came upon a hill completely covered with what looked like a million tiny people. When Queen Mab, their leader, spotted the human she ordered that a huge cup be filled with wine and taken over to their guest. Eight tiny pixies carried over the huge tumbler and handed it to the farmer. Terrified the man slapped it away, and grabbed his scythe, and swishing it all around him, slicing thousands of fairy folk into pieces. They were running in every direction, shocked and disgusted that any creature should act in this way having been shown only kindness. It is believed that 200,000 of them died, the rest scuttling into fox holes to be eaten, climbing trees to be taken by rooks and crows. There were only about a dozen left, including the sad old Queen Mab, who ordered that the fairies should live far underground, where the killer people could never harm them again.

So if you visit Whittingham, far beneath your feet there lies the court of Queen Mab where the fairy folk, now back in their hundreds of thousands, dance and sing, and keep well out of our way!

WHO WALKS AT WARKWORTH

One of Northumberland's fiercest strongholds for centuries was Werceworde, named after a witchy woman with magical powers called Werce who first settled on the spot now called Warkworth.

The history of the castle is amazing. It was given by King Ceolwulf of Northumbria to monks to use as a safe refuge against the Picts, Scots and Norsemen. This is how it stayed for hundreds of years until the Percy family took it over in the early 1330s.

The 1st Earl of Northumberland and his son Harry Hotspur lived there. Hotspur made his name as the hero of the battle of Otterburn Hill, where he saved hundreds of lives, and claimed at least that many from the Scots.

So powerful were the Percys, particularly the gallant Harry Hotspur, that it was merely by putting the name behind Henry of Lancaster Hotspur was instrumental in the deposition of Richard II.

All went well for the Percy family until they began to disagree with the actions of the man they had helped place on the English throne, and conspired to overthrow him. Henry IV knew full well of the romantic hero-worship felt for Hotspur by everyone in the north, so brought armies to face him. Harry Hotspur was hacked to death during the bloody battle of Shrewsbury, as the King marched on towards the north to destroy the seat of Percy power - Warkworth.

Warkworth Castle would never ever be quite the same again; the glory days were over.

Although much of the castle is in ruins, tales have been told by visitors and staff alike of the ghost of a young and vigorous man, running along the walls, loping up the stairs two at a time, or keeping vigil at the Great Gate Tower. You rarely get a chance to ask a ghost his name, but wouldn't it be grand if this was Harry Hotspur, arguably one of the North's greatest ever heroes.

*In 1972 on a school trip outing to Warkworth Castle, schoolteacher Mrs Gibson met a man wearing tights and a chainmail shirt. She takes up the story: 'I told him how pleased I was that someone had taken the trouble to dress up for the children. The man just looked puzzled and walked up the stairs ahead of me. On reaching the tower I found no way out, but the man had disappeared. Believe me, he was no ghost; he looked like solid flesh and blood, but I can't explain where he went. I said nothing at the time, not with thirty-two youngsters in my charge!'

*In 1991 Jean Coles from Cullercoats phoned Metro FM's Night Owls programme to tell of how she was once knocked off her feet by 'something' at Warkworth. It was a bright sunny day, she had been walking across the grass inside Warkworth Castle when she felt 'a force hitting her tummy' that knocked her down. She had not been drinking, she wasn't within twenty feet of another person and is still puzzled as to what it was.

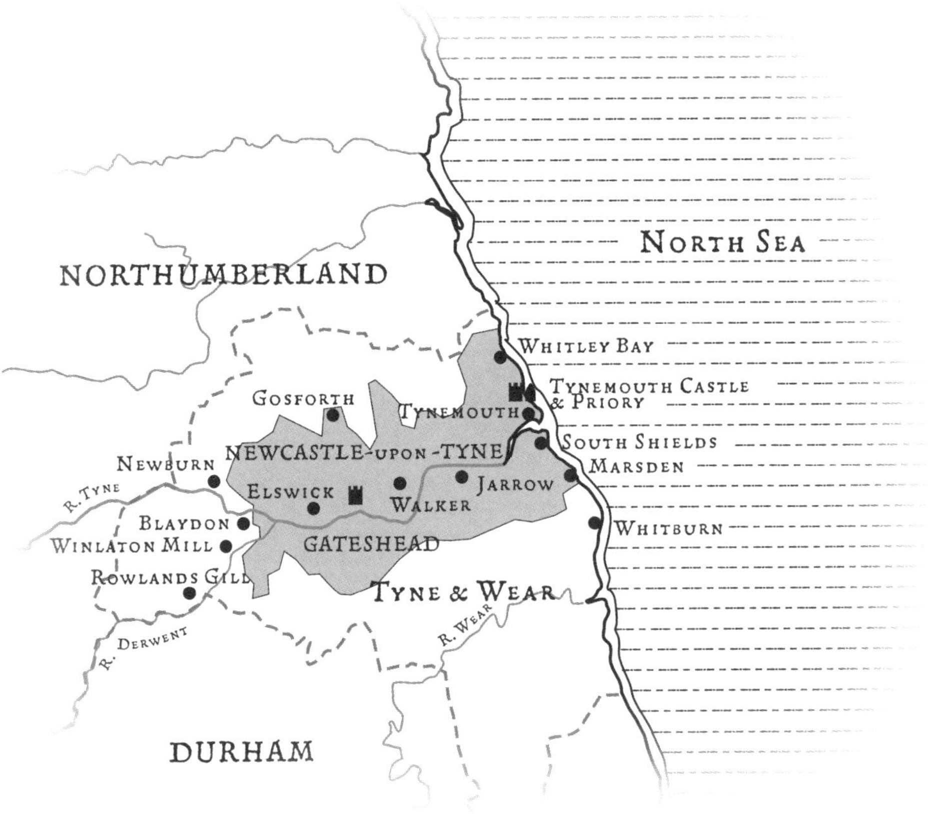
North Sea
NORTHUMBERLAND
Whitley Bay
Tynemouth Castle
& Priory
Tynemouth
Gosforth
South Shields
Marsden
NEWCASTLE-upon-TYNE
Newburn
R. Tyne
Elswick
Walker
Jarrow
Blaydon
Winlaton Mill
GATESHEAD
Whitburn
Rowlands Gill
Tyne & Wear
R. Wear
R. Derwent
DURHAM

TYNESIDE

THE BLACK MAGIC WOMAN AND THE GEORDIE

Newcastle lad Barry Hunt was on holiday in Jamaica in 1972 when all hell let loose in a small village on the outskirts of Montego Bay. He was sunbathing when newspaper men began following a portly black woman who was approaching the beach. She removed a wrap-around skirt and went in for a swim. The newsmen snapped away until a group of Jamaicans arrived to push them away.

The woman was called Mamma Yepo, a native Jamaican who had recently visited New York to find a young man who had made a Jamaican girl pregnant. She did manage to track him down using a map given her by reading chicken entrails. On finding him she ripped his face twice with a chicken's claw, and within two days the boy was dead.

No cause of death could be found other than fright. His hair had turned white and his face was contorted in panic.

Mamma Yepo returned to Jamaica where she was already renowned as a witch queen, a voodoo lady, schooled in the dark sciences.

Mamma Yepo had conducted surgery on people without using any medical instruments and had successfully cured people suffering from cancer, tuberculosis, growths and had even conquered a gangrenous limb. One of Mamma Yepo's proteges had once attended actor Peter Sellers, helping him with a back problem.

Barry visited the same beach during his stay in Jamaica, Doctors Cave Beach, and each day Mamma Yepo would appear with her entourage for a swim. One day she dropped a small black pouch and Barry spotted it and picked it up. He grabbed his towel and chased after her. He was stopped by two tall Jamaicans who would not allow him within ten feet of the large voodoo queen. When he explained that she had dropped her pouch she thanked him and offered to help him with his knee.

Barry was gobsmacked, no one knew he had a cartilage problem; he didn't limp or show any other visible signs. She gave him an address and told him to be there at nine that night.

He arrived in a very seedy part of Montego Bay by taxi and entered a blackened room covered in spiders' webs. In the light of flaming torches, her eyes shining like polished ivory, her skin like ebony, he saw Mamma Yepo. He was aware of dozens of pairs of eyes watching his every move, but couldn't go back now.

She told him to sit and hold up his knee. He was wearing shorts so there was no need to undress, to his relief. She began to chant and threw things on to a small fire that crackled and spat as it consumed them. Barry felt no pain at all but almost fainted when Mamma Yepo seemed to open up his knee near to the bone with her bare hands. He watched as skin and sinew peeled back in the same way you would remove a banana skin. He saw her scrape the bone with what looked to be a small potato knife; she then removed what looked to be gristle, and placed both of her hands over the open wound. When she moved her hands away the wound was closed. The knee was swollen and a little stiff, but not painful.

Mamma Yepo told him to rest that night, and in the following morning, all would be fully recovered. He did and it was.

On returning to Britain he visited his hospital who X-rayed it and told him he did not need the operation that only three weeks earlier they had said was essential if he wanted to remain walking normally.

That was Barry's last contact with Mamma Yepo. Not long after that incident the Jamaican government became frightened of her immense power and made arrangements to have her arrested. However, she had supporters in the police force who warned her of the plot and she fled to Cuba. Before she left she phoned the police chief and cursed him. The most successful young police officer ever to serve in Jamaica, at 38 he was their youngest ever police chief.

He committed suicide four days after receiving that telephone call.

THE DISCO-DANCING MONK OF NEWCASTLE

A Middle Eastern monk is said to walk the streets of Newcastle to this day, most upset that they closed his favourite disco!

The 'monk' is believed to have travelled to Britain after having been converted to Christianity in the Holy Land. His name was Yusef, a dark-skinned six foot five, and only capable of broken English. He journeyed to the monastery in Blackfriars in Newcastle City Centre having arrived aboard a trading ship at Hull. On reaching the monastery he was banned from entry, as the Christian monks believed he was still a heathen, despite his conversion to their faith. This giant had journeyed for almost eight months to reach 'a house of God' and had been shunned by it.

His faith was so strong that he decided not to be put off and took a job on the Newcastle Quayside to be able to afford a dirty upstairs room near the monastery. The room was situated in the building that later would become La Dolce Vita.

Yusef was never allowed to join the order of monks that he so desperately wanted, and his demise was said to be at the hands of one of the monks. He had become a thorn in the monks' side, many locals having realised that his faith was far stronger than any of the monks. They used to take money from the poor to feed themselves, while the Moor Yusef would give his last penny to any beggar that would ask for it. He was truly a Christian man, and as showing the monks up for the greedy egocentrics that they were.

Some tales tell us that Yusef choked on some food and died, but the most common explanation is of a rather more murderous end.

The monks visited Yusef saying that they were to allow him to join their order. They had brought food and wine to celebrate. Yusef was in joyous spirits, at last, his dream was about to come true. The monks shared a drink, but the food was eaten by the Moorish giant. He unsuspectingly ate two half-chickens and some fruit. Such was his stature and constitution that the poison in the food only made him groggy, and was far from being fatal. Realising their plot was about to fail, one of the monks wrapped a knotted rope around Yusef's neck and began to pull and twist for all he was worth. In his doped condition, Yusef could not fight back and the life was squeezed out of him.

The following morning one of the monks told people that Yusef had returned home, having been rebuffed by their order. No one would question the powerful monks, and nothing else was ever said about it. Yusef's body was taken away in the night and buried on the land that now houses Blyth's Keel Row shopping complex.

*Patricia Brown used to visit La Dolce Vita in Newcastle twice a week for almost ten years and claims to have seen 'a swarthy-skinned man' with a long robe, on several occasions. 'Everybody saw it,' says Patricia, he was common knowledge to all the regular customers, and some of the staff told me his name was Joseph.'

*Bill Hardy was a temporary barman at La Dolce Vita. 'Everyone said I was pissed at the time, but I did see Joseph, a ghost in a long monk's habit, dancing amongst the crowds at the disco. He didn't have the modern steps, he moved more like one of those African tribal dancers, but he was dancing! ... I know what I saw. I've not made money out of this, and everyone thinks I'm either stupid or a liar. I did see it, and I don't care what anyone says!'

*Viv, a regular caller to the Night Owls programme on Metro FM claims to have seen Joseph/Yusef in Blyth.

THE GHOST OF THE BLAYDON RACES

I actually took part in the Blaydon Races in the sixties commemorating their centenary. I took part in the egg-and-spoon race in an attempt to win a plastic Stingray you could float in your bath. I came second, winning merely a colouring book, and I would have won had I boiled my egg as the winner had done. Mine was raw and light, his was boiled and heavy and clung to his spoon. Life is but a whirlpool of injustice, is it not?

Yet a man mentioned in the song is supposed to haunt Blaydon Burn. His name was Jackie Brown and he used to be verger at the parish church of St Cuthbert. He was a real likely lad who would act as town crier, arrange charabanc trips to the music hall, and days out into the 'country for old and young alike. He was a close mate of Geordie Ridley who used him as a 'plugger', giving him tickets on commission to fill out his shows in Newcastle and the Blaydon area. So when Geordie Ridley penned the song 'The Blaydon Races', one of the North's great anthems, he couldn't miss out Jackie Brown.

Why he should haunt Blaydon Burn no one is sure, yet it was one of the places where he had arranged picnics and 'treats' for the bairns. He was seen walking there three years after he had died and has popped up from time to time ever since.

THE HOPPINGS' HEAD BOY

Europe's largest fair, 'The Hoppings', comes to Newcastle's Town Moor every year, but in the early 1900s, a smaller version came into the city. One of the most popular stalls belonged to a young traveller called Mo. It was called 'The Emporium of Freaks' and featured sheep with five legs, dogs with two heads, and other rarities. After having handed over your money, you discovered that all of these animals were either stuffed or pickled in jars. The stuffed creatures were more often than not composites made to order by a taxidermist. Putting two dead sheep together to create an apparent bizarre freak of nature.

More gruesome were the human heads Mo displayed in jars. The cards told the public that they were the heads of mass murderers stolen from their graves. The police had been called several times to the fair as it travelled the country, yet each time they left satisfied that the heads were just models. However, while the fair was at Newcastle, one visitor to the Emporium recognised the face of one of the heads – it was her father! He had died the previous year when the fair was in town. Mo must have spotted a fresh grave and taken the opportunity to add to his exhibits, severing the head roughly with a spade.

She screamed and caused a huge rumpus, demanding that the police investigate. Mo tried to quieten her down, claiming that the heads were only clay, but this didn't placate her.

The following morning the police arrived, but Mo and his emporium had gone. On locating him three days later at Alnwick, they searched the tent for the heads but they were nowhere to be seen; neither were the specimens – which included babies – in glass jars. Nothing could be proven.

*The descendants of Mo still have a regular plot at travelling fairs.

THE BLACK PLAGUE OF ELSWICK

In 1836 the plague entered Elswick, killing more than half of the entire plague victims of the Newcastle area. Out of a population that stood at barely 12,780 at the time, 1,960 people died, one person out of every six. They did indeed have men with kerchiefs over their mouths to avoid contamination pushing handcarts through the lanes, calling 'Bring out your dead' or tolling the bell. It was the poor that died like flies, the rich had prepared well. Knowing that it was a water-borne affliction, many of the well-to-do had private wells, others had water barrels brought down from rural Scotland. The people of Elswick were pumping their water directly from the River Tyne below Scotswood, the most heavily polluted stretch. In the 1800s another water contamination took over 1,500 lives.

It is said that if you walk through the West End of Newcastle late at night you could meet Coughing Jack or 'Coffin Jack', said to have been one of the few men to catch cholera and yet survive it. He would be out with the handcart, manhandling the dead bodies and taking them close to the West Road for burial, believed to be somewhere near Rutherford School. He didn't need to shout or ring a bell to let you know he was coming for any corpses, you could hear his bronchitic chesty cough. 'Coffin Jack' is supposed to still walk along Armstrong Road between Atkinson Road and Suttons Dwellings. If you don't get the chance to see him you will hear his slow shuffling footsteps as he drags his feet along the pavement, then that wheezing cough cracking into the silence of the midnight air.

Jack's grave is supposed to be in Elswick Cemetery. If you're going to try and find it, take some linctus along just in case. The residents of Elswick would thank you for that!

THE FLAMING GHOSTS OF GATESHEAD

On 6 October 1854, a fire started at a wool factory on Hillgate, Gateshead, and the touchpaper was lit to one of the great tragedies of Tyneside. Within three hours huge explosions were heard as far away as South Shields and Hexham. Mushrooming into a sky that was as black as pitch for miles went countless chemicals that had been stored in warehouses right in the heart of Tyneside. It had been a time bomb just waiting to go off. As the fragments of twisted metal and burning timber landed on a house or factory within seconds it was yet another problem for the fire service that at that time was hard-pressed to contain one serious factory fire, let alone such a major catastrophe. The fire brigades were called in from Newcastle and Durham, and troops were sent from the Albemarle barracks with whatever equipment they could gather. Many drums of chemicals hurtled through the air, landing on people and property alike, pouring out their explosive contents and creating a fireball that consumed them in seconds. People clutched at their belongings trying desperately to evacuate the scene, many leaving it too long, and ending up trapped behind falling beams, burning wildly. Their screams would begin loudly, then fritter away into nothingness. Everyone who could lend a hand did so, trying to rescue those trapped, giving homes to the families safely removed from the furnace that was once their town. This was turning into 'The Great Fire of Gateshead'.

The High-Level Bridge shook, and rivets popped along its structure as the heat began to reach staggering temperatures. Burning heaps of wood would fall in clumps that could weigh anything up to twenty tons. Those boats that were moored along the banks of the Tyne were almost destroyed, some were sunk and others hurled onto the opposite bank, starting a chain of fires there too.

It was like Dante's Inferno. Families were wiped out, people ran in all directions, some naked, hoping to get anywhere out of the fire. Many were running to their deaths, as often they were surrounded by the blaze. Doctors and nurses gathered trying to help those that suffered such horrendous burns, arms and legs ripped off by the thousands of explosions. It was a nightmare of Biblical proportions. The hospitals didn't come close to coping either, up to a hundred people an hour were pouring in, some with minor burns, others with red-hot metal buried in their scorched flesh.

The firefighters saw scenes that would haunt their every hour, awake or asleep: tiny babies trampled to death by panicking hordes, other babies charred and burned, human bodies torn in half, eyes out of sockets, mothers clinging to their children, cremated where they huddled. The fires in Newcastle were beginning to spread, as explosions fired flaming wreckage into Pilgrim Street, Blackett Street, Grey Street, Market Street and Dean Street. Most of Newcastle Quayside and all of the streets that lead from it were totally incinerated.

By the end of the day fire engines, ambulances and assistance had gathered from Scotland to Lancashire in an attempt to bring this fire under control. Over the following twenty-four hours it seemed to be more a mixture of the weather conditions, wind, rain and good fortune that the fires burned themselves out. Seasoned firemen said at the time 'It just shows how futile we are when faced by nature at its worst!' Practically every family lost a friend or a member of their family, entire family lines were snuffed out, as many of the houses destroyed were home to not only parents and children, but also grandparents.

Over the following century, there have been countless reports of ghosts and phantoms throughout Newcastle Quayside, and more particularly in Gateshead.

*In 1911 Joseph Armstrong was walking along the banks of the Tyne towards the bridge when he felt very warm indeed. It was a chilly January morning, and he put it down to the topcoat he was wearing and the pace he was setting. Yet he cast a glance over his shoulder and could see flames licking over the skyline and could see people in the windows of a wooden house, begging for help. He didn't hear a sound, only the murmuring of the River Tyne as waves lapped up against the quay. He blinked, looked again and it was gone!

*According to a church magazine published in 1952, Mr and Mrs D. Gill of Greenside were looking for business premises on Oakwellgate in Gateshead, when they heard people screaming in a warehouse they were about to inspect. They hurriedly opened the door to see if they could help, and although the screams were still echoing through the eaves of the building there was no one inside.

In 1986 Graeme Anderson of Newcastle rang Metro FM 'Night Owls' phone-in show to tell how he had been dancing on the Tuxedo Princess, a nightclub on a ship ship moored on Gateshead's Quayside, when he glanced out and saw something he couldn't believe. He saw a man on fire walking in agony along the bankside, high above the ship. He had this to say: 'At first I thought it was a reflection of all the lights of the ship, but he kept walking and then fell, landing on the quayside. He rolled over and over again with flames and sparks coming off him all the time. It scared me so much I told a bouncer what I'd seen, and he thought I was drunk. I went out and looked but there was nothing there!' I told him about the Great Fire of Gateshead, and he had not been aware that there had been one!

IT'S RAINING DOSH!

For centuries there has been a kind of friendly rivalry between Newcastle and Gateshead, both at opposite ends of the Tyne Bridge. To this day many shopkeepers believe that far too much money has been spent on the renovation of Newcastle City Centre while Gateshead's town centre has been allowed to run down. When money is brought to Gateshead it seems to start and end at the Metrocentre, Europe's largest and classiest shopping centre.

Yet the good people of Gateshead did have something that Newcastle has certainly never experienced: a shower of money! Granted, the North does tend to have its fair share of rain, but back on 17th February 1957 in between snow flurries it rained money! It wasn't pennies from heaven, but Gateshead was halfway there. Thousands of halfpennies fell all over Ellison Street hitting men, women and children hard on the head. No one knows where they came from, they just heard the clang and clatter as they hit the ground and began to roll and spin. The children started to cry, then realised that the blow that had struck them could buy a good few ice creams, began to collect the sky's peculiar outpouring.

In 1962 it also rained seashells all over the Sheriff Hill area of Gateshead. It was thought at the time that a severe storm way out at sea had sucked up thousands of tiny shells from the sea bed and they had been carried on strong winds inland, falling over the town. If that were the case why were there no fish or pebbles or seaweed, just small limpet and cockle shells? Moira Thomas from Sheriff Hill reminded us of the story in 1989 saying, 'I was washing my car at the time then all of a sudden I heard a noise from the bonnet as if someone had thrown small stones at it. I was angry and looked to see who it was. Then the rattling just went on and on. When I felt them hitting me, I ran under my porch, and saw hundreds of thousands of these tiny shells bouncing off the car and off the path, and almost covering my lawn like snow. The front of my car was scratched by them!'

GOSFORTH'S SINGALONGAGHOST

They say that children can sense things that adults can't, and maybe it's a sixth sense that we forget how to use later in life. This gets very creepy indeed when a five-year-old girl starts telling you about an old man who talks to her in her bedroom. At first, it is discounted as 'an imaginary friend' or 'a vivid imagination'. The youngster was always telling people how 'the old man' had told her this, how they had played games together, how he sat on her bed and told her a story. Like most mums, Sandra Cunningham believed she would grow out of it, as any other action may blow things up way out of proportion. So real was the child's description that they even considered that maybe a burglar was breaking into the family home. Dorrington Avenue in Gosforth had its fair share of break-ins. Gosforth has always been considered 'well-to-do', a place where people get their cauliflowers delivered by Interflora, where even the police are ex-directory. So better safe than sorry! They checked all windows and doors to no avail. Still, children are amazing when they set off on a flight of fancy, and a good imagination is to be encouraged. However, Sandra was pleased when December came along, at last something to take the bairns mind off this `old man'.

Christmas morning can be a trial to any parent of a five-year-old, especially when every twenty minutes from 4.00 am the children are shouting 'It is time to get up yet?' or 'Has Santa been yet?' Sandra had saved up to buy the tot what she had always wanted, her own cassette recorder. She was thrilled with it and spent almost all day walking around the house taping the television, the radio and records. So when bedtime finally came around, and mum wanted to tidy the house up, the youngster was put to bed with her beloved tape recorder. As Sandra collected together the remnants of Christmas paper, all of the sweet papers and dirty plates, she could hear the child singing her heart out into her tape. Every nursery rhyme and song she knew was sung over and over again. It had been a happy day, with no talk of 'the old man'. At last, the child was over this stupid obsession.

Boxing Day is a family day, a slow lazy day to help you recover from your over-indulgence. People call with compliments of the season, then after another belt-busting meal, everyone lies down in front of the television. At this stage it doesn't matter what is on, even if it's the sixtieth rerun of The Sound of Music everyone's too full to move!

Sandra thought to herself what a perfect Christmas it had been. The family were all pleased with their presents, good times were had by all and finally things were coming together. On to her full tum leapt her five-year-old, full of love and kisses, telling her mummy how well she had sung the night before. 'Well let me hear!' said Sandra, as the youngster ran into her bedroom returning with the cassette recorder. At first 'Baa Baa Blacksheep' was performed with maximum cuteness, through gaps in teeth. 'That was lovely,' said her mother, supportive all the way. The next song started and Sandra could clearly hear that her daughter was not alone. There singing on the tape was an old man. A nursery rhyme duet, followed by a childish laugh and an old man's cackle. The rest of the tape featured the old man encouraging the little girl to sing 'just one more' until she fell asleep. The very last words on the tape were the old man's 'Night night little one!' When Sandra began to make enquiries about the house, she discovered that the old man who used to live there had died in the back bedroom – the very same bedroom her daughter was using as her own.

NEWCASTLE'S PHANTOM OF THE THEATRE

Newcastle's Tyne Theatre is a beautiful building now restored to its former glory, having been a soft-porn cinema for many years.

The ghost that resides in that building is rather like the Phantom of the Opera, often seen, but never witnessed. It is the ghost of a theatre-goer who was less than fortunate in his inadvertent 'audience participation'.

Many years ago during a performance of a play, an old-fashioned gadget was used to create the sound of thunder. It was a metal track that swung around the top of the set over the heads of the upper gallery, 'the gods', and back behind the stage again. How it worked was very simple, you merely placed a heavy bowling ball on the top of the slide, and as it ran over the metallic channel it 'thundered'. One night, however, the track was very slightly buckled, and as the bowling ball built up speed it hit the buckle and flew off hitting an unfortunate man in the audience and killing him.

The apparatus was taken apart so no similar accident could occur, and an alabaster figure was placed in the seat of the dead man, as for years people refused to sit in that spot.

*The spirit that resides in the theatre has been seen by thousands, including the theatre's cleaners, one of whom told me in 1984:

'Once I was cleaning the stairs when he walked past me. I thought it was one of the staff, I turned to tell him to watch his feet on the slippy floor when he just disappeared!'

*It is said that the ghost is a bit of a pesky poltergeist too, stealing props, hiding items of clothing and making things move of their own accord.

One year impersonator Jessica Martin couldn't find her woollen jumper and suspected an unkind joke. No one had the guts to tell her it may not have been something earthly that had half-inched her pully.

*Young actress Sharon Percy, who starred in the title role of the very successful stageplay Annie, said, 'I was very young, and felt a lot of strange things. As if someone was pushing past you, yet when you look there is no one there. You'd put a brush down on the table, next time you look it's on the chair. Stuff like that is common at the Tyne.'

*The Tyne Theatre were kind enough to allow me to place two listeners to Night Owls, my late-night chat show, in the theatre overnight.

So two total sceptics, Sandra and Marjorie, both bundles of fun, were locked in and told to keep by the phone and awake.

The telephone in the theatre went berserk, lights flashed on and off and their radio began to suffer the most dreadful interference. This made them begin to get the wind up, but things were to get much worse. Sandra tried to take a photograph of Marjorie sitting next to the alabaster figure, but the camera wouldn't work, even though it had worked perfectly an hour before. They took the camera outside and it worked perfectly there.

NEWCASTLE'S WILLIE WATCHER

At the end of Nelson Street in Newcastle, there is a pub that used to be called the Cordwainers that had a most peculiar and playful phantom. It waited until you were in the gentleman's toilet then it would begin playing games. Sometimes it would turn the light out on you. Other times it would push you into the urinal stall, soaking your trousers and making you piddle down your legs.

The scariest of its tricks would be to wait until your yellow river had begun and then tap you on the shoulder, breathing a foul beery stench into your face as you turn around.

Other customers had had pennies thrown at them while seated in the cubicle, yet they knew they were the only ones in the toilet.

Customers regularly complained that whilst in the toilet they felt as if someone was watching them. Occasionally they even chose to use the toilets in nearby Eldon Square rather than spend a penny in the Cordwainers.

One Saturday morning they were hosing the toilet walls down, after a particularly messy Friday evening and something turned off the hose half-way through.

Once the bar manager found a red sludgy substance on the bannisters, which he couldn't remove. It took four people a week to get it all scraped off and destroyed. Having seen the film Ghost Busters, they thought it similar to ectoplasm.

The Cordwainers was known for having long lights hanging down about eight feet from the ceiling. One night an entire pubful of people were terrified when every single light began to swing from side to side, without anyone having touched them!

It has been renamed, since then there have been no episodes reported ... yet.

THE PHANTOM OF WINDOWS ARCADE, NEWCASTLE

A girl called Carol who had worked in a shop in Newcastle upon Tyne's Royal Arcade (often known as 'Windows Arcade' from the music store J. & G. Windows that takes up much of the space) for years and told me how she had often seen something rather eerie. Each evening after six, when she had completed her paperwork, she would walk through the building and let herself out of the huge metal gates that were secured each evening. She was usually the last to leave and witnessed on at least thirty occasions an odd and terrifying apparition. I asked her to jot down her story back in 1982. 'Each time I've seen him he has been bleeding from the head and mouth, and he's wandering about as if he was blind, walking with his arms held out. The people in the Arcade say that someone was murdered in here, but I don't know anything about that.'

Carol once dared to challenge whatever it was: 'It was in September 1977. I saw the man coming towards me so I shouted out, "What do you want? Can you not just leave me alone!" As soon as I raised my voice the figure just vanished. I didn't see him again for almost a year.'

I made a few enquiries as to whether there had been a murder or a death in the Arcade and apparently there had been. A clerk for the Trustees Savings Bank had been beaten to death. The man, Joe Millie from North Shields, was found in his office in the bank, his skull shattered to pieces and his face battered to a pulp, the carpets soaked with his blood. He had been murdered with a poker hat lay at the scene covered with his blood, hair and sinew.

Whether this is Millie's ghost or not remains uncertain, but it sounds pretty close.

THE JARROW REAPER

Jarrow had the honour of having the last gibbet ever built in England, yet they tore it down in 1856 when they were building Tyne Dock. It stood for many years at Jarrow Slake, and saw many a cut-throat and bandit walking in the air.

The legend of the Jarrow Reaper goes back to this scene some ten years earlier to 1846 when a criminal by the name of John Adams disrupted a meeting held at the gibbet by shipyard workers. He claimed to have killed dozens of Jarrow residents in their beds, by placing a pillow over their faces. The lads from the yards thought he was mad, so discounted his story, gave him a bit of a slapping and sent him on his way. In various pubs throughout Jarrow, he repeated the same story and eventually he was questioned by the police when of course he clammed up altogether. He was an arrogant, thick-set man, who had this need to regale all and sundry with his criminal exploits, as if he half-expected them to say that they thought well of him because he was a burglar, a thief, and, if his story was true, the murderer of elderly ladies.

He told everyone that he had helped Louis Napoleon to escape to England after escaping from a chateau in Amiens, France. He described how he had hidden him on a small fishing boat, landing in Whitby, then carrying him by coach to London where his supporters could successfully hide him. The locals of Jarrow thought this was merely boastfulness, Adams was such a braggart. Yet when the newspapers announced that Louis Napoleon had indeed escaped from France, and had been spotted in Piccadilly, people began to think that maybe the boastful man had committed the crimes he claimed.

This enflamed an old quarry worker known simply as Big Geordie who had lost his mother about eight months earlier. She had died aged only sixty-eight and had been perfectly fit the day before, yet died in her sleep that night. The quarryman believed that she had been murdered, he had cleared her house and many of her items of jewellery and her money had not been found. Adams had been very shrewd, never taking anything from these ladies' homes that would have been noticeably missed.

Big Geordie followed Adams that evening to his circuit of public houses, where he spoke of his exploits, trying to impress some of the drunken women, in the hope he could take one home. That night he had some degree of good luck, that would be far outweighed by the bad luck he would endure later. He left a public house with a prostitute known as Clara and after having a drunken knee-trembler with her down an alleyway off the town centre, he made his way home. All the while the quarryman had followed, watching his every drunken move. He was about halfway home when Big Geordie approached him saying 'Hello John, where are you going?' Adams was startled by such a huge man and failed to register his face, so asked if he should know him. Geordie said: 'Of course, do you not remember last week we had a drink together and spent the night talking?' 'Of course,' said Adams, still none the wiser, but he was so often drunk he could have talked to the prime minister Robert Peel without remembering it.

'Come on,' said the quarryman, 'I know where there's a party tonight, lots of ale, lots of women and lots of dancing, surely you can't be for your bed yet?'

Adams took little persuading as the large fellow led him towards the gibbet on Jarrow Slake. Big Geordie suggested they sit there awhile and rest as they still had a fair way to go. As they chatted he asked Adams to tell him again how he raised money from killing little old ladies, and the loudmouth never needed asking twice.

'I am the Jarrow Reaper,' boasted Adams. 'I do the killing for God. Any old woman who deserves putting out of her misery I will do her in. There is never any struggle, I climb into the house while they're asleep, kneel on their hands and force a pillow over their faces until they choke to death. Then if you're careful you can take most of the money, the best pieces of jewellery and nobody ever thinks there's been a crime committed!' On being asked how many women had died that way, he replied that he would kill 'about once a fortnight to keep bread on the table and beer in the glass'. At this, Big Geordie wondered if he'd killed a woman eight months ago who had a huge ruby ring on her hand. Adams said 'Oh yes, a fat woman she was. That ring I sold in Newcastle for thirty shillings,' quite a sum back then. That was the moment that Big Geordie placed a rope around his neck, and began punching his face, over and over again. Adams sobered up fast and begged Geordie to release him, but the furious quarryman was in a vengeful mood. Each time that Adams tried to remove the noose, Big Geordie would push him to the ground and stand on his hands until all of his fingers were shattered and broken. Then he slowly winched Adams up onto the gibbet until his legs began running in mid-air.

'Remember this,' said the quarryman, 'for it is the last thing you ever will remember. When you take a life, your life is forfeit and now as life is being choked out of you, you will know what pain and fear you made my mother suffer! To the Devil with you!' At this, he tied the other end of the rope to a lamppost and watched for five minutes or so until Adams's aerial contortions ceased. On checking that his heart had stopped Big Geordie walked down to a nearby shop, emptied a cloth sack of its rubbish and placed Adams's broken body in it. He took it down to the banks of the Tyne and began digging into the silt with a heavy wooden plank. Having removed a huge trenchworth, he filled the sack with rocks, and threw it in. Then he collected ton after ton of stone and hurled it on the top, then replaced a top layer of silt.

No body was ever been found there and Big Geordie was never charged, yet it is said that a few people saw what went on that night. Many heard Adams's confession too, and all chose to keep it to themselves. The police were never informed, and Big Geordie returned to the quarries where he reached retirement age. Such was his popularity a large heavy crane was named after him!

JARROW'S BLACK DEATH

The church of St Paul is built directly on the site of a monastery first built in AD 681 and dedicated to St Paul by a Saxon bishop. It is said that the very first Germans ever to take Christian teachings were taught by the monks at Jarrow. All went well until AD 733, the time when St Bede lived in the town. A traveller from the South arrived at a local inn, he was suffering from the fever and passed out in the town square some hours later. After being carried to his room it was discovered that he was suffering from the Black Death, his body was covered in septic boils, and he was coughing his germs into everyone's faces. Within a month half of Jarrow was dead or dying. Bede did his best to help the suffering, but all to no avail. It wasn't until all of the bodies and their belongings were burned that the town could begin to battle through it.

*In 1887 a drayman was returning home from work when he met a man who stood in his way. His face was covered with angry-looking boils and his face was distorted with pain. The clothes he wore were nought but rags and his skin looked 'slippery'. The drayman reached out to touch him only for his hand to go through the stranger's stomach. He felt nothing but turned and ran.

*In 1988 Shirley Gallagher contacted me about something she had experienced while waiting for her husband on a Wednesday evening outside The Clock public house. 'I was a bit angry with him for keeping me waiting. I had rushed to get ready and he swore blind he wouldn't be late. I was standing looking down the road in the direction that I thought he'd be coming when I felt him standing behind me. I felt two arms cuddling me in, and said: "Where the hell have you been?" At that I turned around and saw this horrible man holding me, he had almost no skin on his face at all, it was nothing but lumps. I screamed and ran into a bar, they must have thought I was mad, but I did see him. He felt real, but as soon as I yelled he just disappeared.'

THE SPIRIT OF THE SWAN

One of the best-known park areas in Newcastle City is Jesmond Dene, with its river curving through it, the pets' corner and the endless varieties of trees, shrubs and vegetation. One of the joys of the Dene were the swans, at one time half a dozen. One black swan used to be the centrepiece. Yet one of the sicknesses of modern society is the behaviour of people who fail to value things of great beauty. One by one these morons have killed the swans, some by polluting the Dene, others were shot with a crossbow. How it can possibly be clever to kill a bird that is so tame it swims within a foot of you is quite beyond me. The swans may well be replaced, but to many locals, it will never be the same again. The Dene was created by the last remnants of glaciers that melted during the final years of the ice age. The river has been used for wild birds since then, and even though mankind was neanderthal way back then, they weren't so pathetic as to kill off the birds. Even so, the Dene is glorious and is well maintained, and a place visited daily by thousands.

Whilst giving a talk at a school in Wideopen in 1987, I spoke to one of the children's mothers, Hilary Chapman, who had heard of my interest in all things strange and downright wacky, and told me that she often sees the 'ghost swans'. Humouring her, I sat beside her at the entrance to the school as she related the story. At twilight each summer evening she sees two huge flapping apparitions, that fly not just up above the tree line, but actually through it. At first, she thought it was merely the beams of headlights as cars took a corner near her home, but often she would see the shapes on nights when the roads were quiet. Hilary lives overlooking Jesmond Dene and says that she has seen this amazing event 'hundreds of times', believing it to be the freed spirits of those birds butchered by the scum that infest our streets.

*There is a legend from Northumberland that ties in regarding swans. In the area north of Alnwick they believed in the seventeenth and eighteenth centuries that when people die they take on the shape of birds, usually swans, to fly to heaven. So maybe the strange figures flying skyward are the souls of those freshly buried in the huge cemetery that leads down to Jesmond Dene.

THE NEWBURN SCREAMER

No one quite knows when Newburn Hall and the tower was built, but it certainly goes back to at least the middle 1400s. It was established there because the River Tyne could be forded at that spot. It has since been demolished when Spencer's Steelworks decided to expand, needing the extra area. Yet the workers often mentioned that they had heard a strange screaming cry, coming from the vicinity of the waterside.

This was supposed to be the ghost of a young man called Frankie Johnson who was seeking the attentions of a young housemaid, employed at Newburn Hall in 1497. Once he had been found in her bed-chamber and the master of the house had ordered him never to return, concerned that one of his young children could have walked in on them. So they used to meet down by the Tyne, and kiss and cuddle in the moonlight. He would light a candle on the south side of the river, when she arrived she would wave, and then he would wade across. Yet that September had been a very rainy one, and the Tyne was uncommonly deep, so Frankie took his time. What no one could have known was that it had poured for almost twelve hours in the mountains, and all of that extra water, aided by a returning tide, was gushing down the Tyne. It caught Frankie midstream, and hurled him off balance, down to the sea. His body was never found.

Many believe that they can still hear Frankie's cry late into the night, as his spirit journeys along the river frightening fishermen.

THE GHOST OF THE BIGG MARKET

Newcastle's Bigg Market is known by the cynical as the place where children go to drink, so they can pretend to be men. A visit these days can be a dicey business, with the young crowd in designer clothes all trying to out-pose each other. Fighting in the streets is all too common, yet throughout history, it always has been. Even in the 1700s that Newcastle street was full of inns and taverns filled with every kind of villain, hooligan and vagabond.

There is supposed to be the ghost of a Scottish soldier called Macdonald who had murdered a local cooper outside a tavern at the spot where the Bigg Market forks with the Groat Market. The Scot had been lampooned by locals for dressing in full kit, the kilted garb of the 43rd Royal Highlanders. He took only so much, but after countless remarks and several flagons of ale his temper had snapped. Macdonald was hanged and his phantom is said to have been seen by several shopkeepers and pub landlords.

The story varies depending on who you talk to, some say Macdonald was hung three times and failed to die, so was released. On the day he returned to the Bigg Market one of the murdered man's friends clubbed the Scot to death. Other tales tell of him not being killed by the hangman and having to be finished off with a hammer as he was placed on the table in the morgue.

Either way, several reports tell of the Scot walking the Bigg Market.

*In the mid-1800s an inn was exorcised because of troublesome spirits that had frightened customers by spilling drinks, pulling their clothes and breathing on them.

*In 1984 Jean Curry from Stockton-on-Tees wrote to a women's magazine telling of how she had seen a ghostly figure in a short dress beside the old toilets halfway down the Bigg Market. When she approached it she saw the figure had a beard. It is not likely that this was a ghostly transvestite, so maybe the dress she witnessed was, in fact, a kilt.

*In 1986 two people in a pub called The Pig and Whistle claimed that they had watched a Scotsman in a uniform walk into the pub and go straight into a wall. They blamed the drink at the time, neither one mentioning it to the other until the following day. Frank Gibson said, 'We were having our Sunday dinner at a pub on Archbold Terrace called The Royal Archer when I just mentioned to Si that I'd thought I'd seen this Scottish bloke the night before, expecting him to laugh. Si froze stiff and said, "Bloody hell, I saw him as well!"

THE GATESHEAD GRUNT

In the early 1700s when Gateshead was very much Newcastle's poor relation, times were hard and only those with money ever prevailed. One such man was Charles Henderson who used to buy and sell goods from both Scotland and the south, selling them at a huge profit to anyone he could. He created an early form of 'car boot sale', taking his goods on a horse and cart to homes and villages as far afield as Durham, Stanley, South Shields and Hexham. Within a year he was wealthy, within five years he was rich. Henderson's 'gallowa's' (horses) were renowned, people believing that they were getting bargains. Admittedly the things he sold were only available in the big cities, so to find fine fabrics, delicate ornaments, luxury food items, etc. in a back lane in a small village was bound to create interest. The richer Henderson became, the more he delegated the work to younger men, all quite poor and keen to earn any kind of living.

By 1755 Henderson was in his late thirties, rich, yet still unfulfilled, so he took himself a bride. Her name was never known; some say he bought the young girl from her father for a sum of five shillings.

Henderson's close friends were introduced to a staggeringly attractive brunette whom he called 'Sophie'. She never left his house on Windmill Hill, just out of the centre of Gateshead, overlooking the River Tyne. Her only visitor was the old tinker who had 'provided' her, who claimed to be keeping check on his daughter's progress.

Within a year she was pregnant and Charles Henderson was thrilled; he would have an heir and all of his hard work could become a 'family concern'. Everything was going for him, he had started providing coal carts and coach services, his 'gallowa's' were still pouring profit in his direction, and overtures were made to him to go into politics. When in November 1756 the Duke of Newcastle resigned as Prime Minister, the groundswell of northern opinion was that Charles Henderson would put himself forward. This he refused to do, claiming 'This war with France will ruin many men but not Charles Henderson'. William Pitt became Secretary of State and gathered other northern ministers to face the French threat.

Charles Henderson was very much his own man, and despite it being totally against tradition, he attended the birth of his son. The delivery had been difficult, and on seeing the child, Henderson reeled back in horror. The infant's face was horrifically deformed. Storming out of the house, he ran along the street crying out, 'God has cursed me with a devil for a son!' He was found by friends sitting in an inn on the corner of what is now Charles Street, where he was trying to drown his sorrow; he then sobbed uncontrollably into the arms of an old woman. Some say he refused to return home for almost a month, but when he did his demeanour was very different from that of the loving man he once was. He became an ill-tempered brute of a man, hurling abuse at servants, and behaved contemptuously towards his wife. His son was named George after the composer Handel, but Henderson refused to call him that, preferring to call him 'Grunt'.

Young George had one eye higher than the other, his nose was completely flat and a cleft palate had viciously twisted his mouth, causing him to talk in a low 'grunt'. Henderson consulted physicians but none had the expertise to do anything for the youngster. As the boy entered his teens his problems increased; it seemed the taller he grew, the more stooped he became. On his sixteenth birthday, the terrifying truth emerged. During a vicious argument, Sophie told Henderson that George was not his son. She had been carrying such a great burden, and it all spilled out like a leak in the Atlantic. First, Henderson learned that Sophie's mother was also her sister, who had been the victim of incest since she was twelve years old. And once Sophie reached that age, their father turned his attentions upon her. Even after her marriage, he had been visiting her and having sex as he had done throughout her childhood. Sophie had been too frightened and ashamed to tell her husband. The child was deformed because of inbreeding.

It was as if someone had wrenched out his heart. Henderson grabbed his silver-topped cane and went straight to the slums that existed on what is now Gateshead bus station. He entered the home of the tinker and beat him to death. He then set fire to the hovel and left.

The authorities interviewed Henderson who admitted to beating the old man but claimed to have left before the fire started. Such was his influence that charges were never brought against him.

From that day young George was never allowed out of the old mansion on the Windmill Hills and remained confined to his twelve-foot room. He died of influenza at the age of only 39 in 1795 having been hidden away for almost 24 years. Henderson never slept with Sophie ever again, and she ran off three months after her son died. It was believed that she set up home with a butcher in Saltmeadows Road.

Henderson's financial empire crashed around his ears; he had no appetite for it any more, and he allowed various parts to be taken from him by his own employees, who struck out on their own. In 1789 there was a mysterious fire that burned down the businessman's mansion, and despite a thorough raking through the ashes, no one ever found the body of Charles Henderson. Some say that his spirit will not rest until it is found.

Two ghosts are said to walk Windmill Hills – one, the grief-stricken old man with a silver-topped cane, who can be heard weeping or seen holding his head in his hands in doorways. The other desperate ghost is said to be that of George Henderson, who hammers on doors begging to be released, clawing with bloody fingernails at heavy wooden doors.

*One of the buildings built on the site of the Henderson home later became an unemployment benefit office, and an ex-employee who wishes only to be known as Tom said, 'I worked there for a good few years and often heard, late in the afternoon, doors slamming, and hammering coming from upstairs. If you followed the sound it came from one of the rooms on the very top floor. Despite our radiators, it was always bitter cold. Occasionally people claim to have seen glimpses of a man with a hunched back hobbling around. Once one of my colleagues, a woman in her fifties, actually fainted while sitting in the ladies loo because she heard a man behind her grunting in a sexual manner. We had to burst the lock on the door to get in, dress her, then take her to the Queen Elizabeth Hospital outpatients. She had such a shock she was off work for almost a month. She came back for a fortnight, then found a job with the local Electricity Board.'

*Whilst walking her dog past Windmill Hills one cold Sunday morning in 1982

Mrs Kathleen O'Connor experienced something very strange. She claims that she heard a woman screaming, and flagged down a police car. She pointed police towards the old house, telling them she had heard shouts of 'Father, no! Don't do this to me!' followed by screams of agony and torment. The police checked the scene yet found no evidence of wrongdoing. Had that been the horrified pleadings of young Sophie, raped yet again by her incestuous father?

AULD CLOTHIE OF THE COOPERAGE

Close to Newcastle's Quayside stands the Cooperage, a rough and ready wood-beamed building renowned for live music and a good atmosphere. This building has had dozens of phenomenon reports of all kinds for almost seven hundred years. It was one of Newcastle's earliest buildings, so, therefore, probably hosted millions of human inhabitants, and now a good number of phantom ones too. The staff claim to have become immune to the strange spectres that drift past them. A dozen or so 'silkies', women in long gowns who glide along the corridors, men in Edwardian garb with high-necked collars, a hooded figure that looked like a monk but had the face of a child. Strange noises are heard almost nightly, ghosts moaning, whining, laughing, giggling, crying and shouting. This is not a place to spend the night. The entire Newcastle Quayside is known to have thousands of strange apparitions, and countless reports are made every single year.

The most famous tale of that area concentrates not so much on the Cooperage itself, but the alley that runs along beside it. It seems only to be used these days by struggling road crews, who pack their gear into the pub's tiny rooms.

Yet in the 1500s a press-gang was running rampant across Newcastle, snatching any able-bodied men and forcing them to serve on board ship. A local cooper, Henry Hardwick, was grabbed, and as he and twenty or so other hapless Novocastrians were being pushed towards the quay, Hardwick decided to fight back. Breaking free of the sailor who held him, he rallied the other Geordies who punched and kicked at their kidnappers. A gallant act indeed, but all to no avail, the sailors were armed to the teeth and soon the uprising was under control. As a warning to others they nailed Hardwick to the back door of the Cooperage, gouged his eyes out, and whilst he was still alive, severed his testicles. A spectre has been seen walking along Newcastle Quayside, his eyes just bloody sockets. I'm not sure it was Hardwick, as surely he certainly wouldn't be walking too well, would he?

THE LAUGHING CAVALIER

During the Civil War when the Roundheads under Oliver Cromwell were in the process of defeating the cavalier forces of King Charles I, many battles were fought both in and around Newcastle. The cavalier newsletter of the day Mercurius Aulicus printed the story of a cavalier called Roger Weatherly who led thirty soldiers into battle with over a hundred Roundheads in the City Road area of Newcastle. He was victorious, and the newsletter declared 'Had we a hundred like Weatherly, the war would already be won!' Many years later swords, cannons, human remains, and musket balls were found buried at the site.

Between the Great Siege of Newcastle and Cromwell's rout of the king's forces at Naseby some ten months later, Weatherly became quite a hero, greatly loved by his men. The cavaliers were really up against it in Newcastle, totally outnumbered and with no chance of reinforcements. On 27th October he and eleven others were hidden in Sallyport Tower, and most of his comrades were either dead or prisoners of the New Model Army. He decided to make a run for it. Rallying his injured and tired men, they stole horses that were tethered close to what is now Claremont Road and began to ride in the direction of Carlisle, hoping to slip into Scotland. As black fortune would have it they rode straight into a Roundhead patrol. They faced them off at Kenton, Weatherly shouting 'There are thirty of you and only twelve of us, we know the battle is lost. Let us on our way or certainly, most of us will be dead within the hour!' The captain of the Ironsides thought awhile and said 'Good sir, were it my choice I would seek no more blood on our hands but is my duty sworn unto God, so let us have done with it!'

At that, the Roundheads charged, and Weatherly's men cut into them. On getting through their ranks five men made a break for it. As Cromwell's men turned to give chase, their route was blocked by Weatherly. His horse rearing in front of them, Weatherly was laughing. This unsettled many of the Roundheads, who died at his hands. He was unseated from his horse and took to bringing down horses as well as men. Finally, he stood over a mound of bodies, torn and gory limbs piled high, cavalier and Roundhead alike. Four honsides stood there facing him, and Weatherly roared with laughter: 'Well some of my lads have made their escape, so I am well satisfied!' The captain, carrying an arm wound, said: 'So now you must surrender and face trial.' Weatherly declined their invitation and shouted: 'Well, come to me my bonny boys, let's finish it. My men are many miles away and I have some catching up to do!' His sheer effrontery continued to nag at the soldiers' confidence.

The captain turned to his three troopers saying 'We have done our duty, it matters not to me if one more rebel escapes, the day was ours!' They turned to walk away, as Weatherly mounted a horse and rode on, laughing and smiling all the way. Fate was ultimately unkind, as he was robbed by vagabonds as he slept three days later. They stole his sword, two rings and the few pounds he had in his pocket. The ghost of the Laughing Cavalier is said to walk through various parts of Newcastle particularly around the Royal Victoria Infirmary up towards Kenton. Other sightings have been made on City Road, Sallyport Tower, the Quayside and even as far out as Woolsington.

THE MASSACRE OF THE MOOR

The reason why gipsies visit Newcastle's Town Moor year after year is now purely for Europe's largest funfair, The Hoppings, but throughout history, travellers have been drawn to this massive stretch of open parkland close to the city centre. The truth could be linked to the fact that Newcastle's Town Moor was used for almost fifty years as the place where 'The Judgement of the Witches' took place. In the mid-1600s over a hundred and fifty witches died there, mostly hanged. Everywhere you looked there were self-designated Witch-finders, seeking out those wise women who were widely respected in their towns and villages. Fifteen witches were hanged at the largest public witch execution in the North in August 1650. These women were not witches, but could not prove that they were not. The prosecution also couldn't prove that they were, but that made no difference as they still went to the gallows. Their bodies were buried in holy ground to 'purge their evil' in St Andrew's churchyard. Many other witches were hanged at Gallowgate, the site currently occupied by Newcastle United Football Club.

In 1653 a woman by the name of Beth Bell lived in the tiny suburban village of Delaval. She was a very God-fearing woman, yet she owned a black cat, and that was sufficient to cost her her life. Each Witchfinder was paid a bounty for each witch he located, so he found plenty! A witch was once burned at Delaval Hall, a building now known as The Mitre. The building does have a 'silkie'-style ghost, yet three women were supposedly burned to death by a Witchfinder in 1659. He had found three women bathing naked in a nearby pond late at night. Although it was fairly innocent 'skinny-dipping' he declared they were summoning the Devil.

The local people campaigned for their release, yet many felt to fight too hard would win them nothing but another place in the fire. So ultimately the fire was lit, and it went out, it was lit again yet did not take. After four attempts it finally took hold but burned very slowly, and the agonies of those poor women were long and drawn out. It took them almost three hours to die. There have never been any sightings of burning ghosts, yet strange noises and howls of pain have been heard by many visitors to the hall, pub and disco all in the same grounds. The only common 'phantom' is the Grey Lady, who doesn't do much other than float about, and occasionally appear at the upstairs window.

*As young lads on the bus to school each day we would ride past Delaval Towers and would always say: 'Look there she is – it's the Grey Lady!' Imagine doing this for close on six years. Then one day we went to investigate late on a Saturday night. We had claimed to see a face at the window thousands of times, so we set off to see if it were true. On arriving we sat eating our jam sandwiches and drinking a bottle of lemonade. By the time we had finished we had forgotten about ghosts and were talking about having a game of football under the lamppost in the back lane down in Benwell village. At that moment a curtain twitched, and a woman's face peered out of a downstairs window, not ten yards from where we sat. Our sandwiches were flung in the air, pop bottles flew in all directions and we were almost a mile away by the time the first one hit the ground. For years we swore that we had seen the Grey Lady. I have since discovered that the Hall was occupied at that time, and it was more likely just the owner wondering what all the noise was!

THE FLOATING FACES OF THE NEWCASTLE FLOOD

When God had wanted to start from scratch again he sent a Great Flood, having prepared Noah and his family for that terrible day. Well, he decided against warning the people of Newcastle one day in 1339 when a swollen river tore down bridges, sunk boats, and swept people off the riverside. For centuries the locals had said that could never happen again. The Quayside was much higher, all the homes more stoutly built. Yet happen it did in 1771.

It was the rainiest November in the history of Newcastle, the level of the Tyne rose on average between six and ten feet. As the tide proceeded to go out, swollen by the torrents of water pouring into the upper Tyne Valley from the hills, it was the early hours of the morning. The city slept, happily unaware that disaster was about to strike. Many people merely awoke to find that there was an inch of water on the floor, others were shaken out of bed as their homes were crushed, buffeted and ultimately consumed by the water that killed thousands as it gushed mercilessly towards the sea. You could no longer tell where the water ended and land began. Ships were washed up sidestreets, others were chewed into matchwood as the water rammed them into the sides of houses.

As homes crumbled into the water the cascading tidal wave became even more dangerous, destroying everything within thirty feet of the riverside. You could barely see the surface of the water for debris mixed with screaming people, horses, boats and farm carts all being swept along. Almost all of the old bridge that stood on the site of the Swing Bridge was carried off. It took almost forty years before Newcastle was remotely like it had been before, and since that day they have been very careful about constructing homes near the river.

A most amazing story was told me by Maureen Donaldson who lived in Dunston. She has claimed to have the gift of second sight and says it has been passed down her family for many years. Scots by birth she arrived in Gateshead in 1975 and knew nothing of the town's history. Yet one Sunday in November she was standing looking down from the High-Level Bridge towards the bustling Quayside Market that stretches for almost a mile. She looked down into the river and couldn't control the scream that tore from her throat. She could see no water at all, just thousands of people crying in pain, begging for help, all raising their hands and moving like liquid down towards the sea. She could hear a thousand screams, all drowning and in torment. She felt so weak she had to seek help at The Bridge Hotel just across the bridge in Newcastle. Bolstered by a brandy she made her way across, yet each time she crossed that bridge the same thing happened. Ultimately her fear got the better of her and she moved back to Falkirk rather than face those poor lost souls. She never knew of the flood yet painted an accurate picture of what had gone before.

THE BODYSNATCHING BUSINESS (TYNESIDE) LTD

All over the North-East in the 1800s the criminal element discovered an easy way to make money – stealing bodies. At first, each criminal gang would claim a graveyard as their 'turf' then as soon as a body, was interred, they'd have it out of the ground, into a box, and on its way into the hands of a surgeon. They needed bodies to use as human guinea pigs, as they researched how the body worked. A warehouse on City Road was once filled with over thirty corpses in boxes waiting to be moved to medical scientists as far away as Manchester. Lloyds Bank on Collingwood Street was a stopover point for coaches, many of them carrying the decaying corpses of the recently deceased. Those brigands that couldn't take control of their own graveyard would take matters into their own hands and would murder to order. Should a surgeon say 'I need a ten-year-old girl child!' they would kidnap and murder one, delivering it within an hour. Let's face it, nowadays it's hard to find a pizza company that can manage that sort of speed!

Countless disappearances, hundreds of bodies stolen from their graves, all for the sake of science. There were so many itinerants from Ireland, Scotland and abroad in the North it is impossible to number how many were murdered, but it is estimated to be thousands. Many graves from around that period in the city are empty, their occupants long since having helped some medical student learn how to cut flesh, how to sew a vein or set a bone!

THE CATHEDRAL PHANTOMS OF NEWCASTLE

Whenever anyone mentions a cathedral in the North, you can bet people are thinking of York Minster or Durham, yet Newcastle-upon-Tyne has the beautiful St Nicholas' Cathedral. There has been a church on that site since the Norman invasion, and there are still fragments of the original dating back to 1091. Between 1870 and 1950 there were countless reports of moaning and groaning, yet you can't simply blame a tiresome sermon, as often the noises can be heard when the cathedral is empty. These reports were discounted out of hand by the clergy, who refuse to give the building any emphasis other than as a place of worship.

A possible answer to the phenomenon came from Archie Knox of Glasgow who told of how the Scottish army, made up of mainly Lowlanders, attacked the walled city of Newcastle in harness with the parliamentarians, and had surrounded St Nicholas' Church (before it was given cathedral status), and fired arrows at it, many aflame, but the structure, being mainly stone, withheld.

So over thirty cannons were rolled into position and the Scots warned that they were about to turn the church into rubble unless it was surrendered. The mayor of that time was John Marlay who, in the hour's grace he was given by the enemy, gathered together over a hundred injured Scottish prisoners and filled the church with them. When the hour was up Marlay roared out his defiance, telling the opposing army that if they bombarded the church they would be massacring their clansmen. The Scots continued peppering the Newcastle city walls, but not a single cannonball hit St Nicholas'.

The siege did claim many lives, often through disease and starvation as it was impossible to get food through enemy lines. It is believed that many of the Scots taken to St Nicholas' Church to protect it from those cannons, died as a consequence of being moved and being ill-fed. It is thought that these poor wounded Scots remain in spiritual torment, because of the heartless treatment shown to them by their captors.

*A friend of Archie Knox gave one account: 'I have visited all of the cathedrals across Britain and have had only one unpleasant experience, and that came in Newcastle. It was a Sunday, and I had shared the service and had asked if I could wait until the cathedral cleared, to take some photographs. It was a very wet and stormy day in September 1966, and it seemed almost like night, hardly any light shone through the stained glass windows. I engaged the flash on my camera and started taking standard shots when I heard something odd. At first, I thought it was a small dog yelping, yet it persisted. Then another noise joined in, and it sounded much the same as noises I have heard many times in my job. I used to work in an accident and emergency department in a hospital – There were sounds of men in great pain, and I searched that Cathedral, and it was not a practical joke.'

*During a bus trip in 2018 with seventy radio show listeners visiting Newcastle's scariest buildings, we ended the tour just outside the Cathedral, where I told the final story. About how the starving Scottish prisoners hammered on the walls, screaming out for passers-by to give them water or bread. Jesting, one young lad began banging on its wall, shouting "You can have my sandwich". The laughter on his face changed when he felt something hammer back with a growl. Three others with him heard it!

THE BLACK FRIARS OF BLACKFRIARS

In the thirteenth century monks set up a friary right in the centre of Newcastle-upon-Tyne. They helped the local community and lived a very unadventurous existence until King Henry VIII decided upon the dissolution of the monasteries. Having had several run-ins with the Church, particularly the Pope, over his wish to divorce, Henry decided to smash their power once and for all. He sent his commissioners all over Britain interrogating nuns, monks and friars, declaring that they were 'profoundly bawdy and drunken knaves'. They were accused of whoring and using church funds for 'their own depraved devices'. Thomas Cromwell decreed that the Newcastle Monastery was such a place, and demanded that all its riches and assets be removed. The friars were thrown out and forced to leave the city.

One story that has been passed down since 1600 tells of how armed men came upon a group of monks near a small well (now known as Swalwell) and attacked them. As the monks ran off into the undergrowth one shouted 'We shall all meet again back at our home!' So the monks would separate and return in secret to the remnants of the monastery. Three monks were finally cornered by the thugs, loyal to King Henry. They taunted the monks about the alleged womanising, drinking and how friars had stolen from the people for centuries.

The monks remained silent, even when they were beaten across the face with a club. They were told that they were going to die, so sank to their knees and began to pray. Some of the ruffians wavered, saying that maybe these were true God-men', but their leader shouted 'If they are God-men, let God stop me from spilling their blood!' With a mighty swing of an axe, he smashed into the skull of one of the monks. As he fell, still with the axe embedded in his skull, he pushed against one of his friends, gushing blood all over him. At this the two remaining monks took to their heels, both covered in gore. The other attackers caught one and hacked into his back with their swords until he was silenced forever. The third monk fought his way through the tangled undergrowth managing to reach the area around Winlaton Mill, where he threw himself into a lake and began to swim out into the middle. At this three of the king's men began to fire arrows at him, so he ducked under the water. They watched carefully for him to reappear for air, but it never happened. They camped at the side of the lake for three days, and the body was never seen again.

Back at the monastery, now known as Blackfriars, it is said that the ghosts of those three monks returned to seek out their friends who waited for months in hope that they had escaped. They saw them waiting, but as they were new to the world of spirits, they couldn't make themselves be seen. When the surviving monks began their trek into Northumberland, to set up a new order, the spirits remained tied to the building.

Over the past four hundred years, countless people have seen the figure of a monk or monks wandering the corridors of Blackfriars. It is also fairly commonplace to see monks disappear through walls where doors once stood.

THE GHOSTLY ELOPER

Newcastle's Quayside has taken on a new look in recent years and is now a haven for the nightclub poseur, the trendy bistro customer and the occasional lager lout. The nature of the quay is now as bustling as it once was when the banks of both Newcastle and Gateshead were lined with tall ships. The Tyne was one of Britain's biggest trading ports, goods from all over the world were landed there, and millions of tons of coal were shipped out.

My great-grandparents were from a family of boatmen, who would see the tall ships coming into sight, then row out into the estuary, taking their cobles ashore and tying them up. This story comes directly from them and was a much-repeated tale all along Tyneside in the late 1800s.

It centres around a house that still stands at 41-44 Sandgate in Newcastle, the road that sweeps up to Dean Street then on to the city centre. It is the amalgamation of two sixteenth and seventeenth-century merchants' houses that were converted into one. This was the house of one of Newcastle's raging beauties, Bessie Surtees. Her father was a rich banker, businessman and entrepreneur and had transformed his daughter into a real lady, whose good manners and startling appearance turned many heads. Her father had tried to persuade her to marry countless men, all much older than her. One was so old he deserved a mention in the Book of Revelations, so strong-minded Bessie was having none of it. She wasn't going to share her life with a man so old he had cobwebs under his arms, she wanted the exciting life, with a man closer to her own tender years.

It wasn't easy for Bessie, as the nature of her father's business only ever brought older men to the house, and opportunities to meet her own age group were few and far between. Most fathers who lived near the quay were very protective of their daughters as they knew the reputation of the floods of sailors pouring along the streets every night. Many of them not having seen a woman for up to a year at a time. However as she shopped in Newcastle she did become the nodding acquaintance of John Scott, who lived in Love Lane, in the poorer quarter of the City. As the friendship developed, Bessie knew that her father would forbid her to liaise with anyone who was from an area so rough that if you had two socks you were called a snob!

All Hell was let loose when neighbours alerted the Surtees family of seeing young Bessie with John Scott holding hands and kissing. Such affection was only ever allowed after the banns had been read, and it soon became the scandal of the city. It was then that Bessie's father ordered Bessie never to see John again. Each evening her father would bolt the heavy wooden door, padlocking it so that Bessie couldn't sneak out in the night. Every single day she was accompanied by her mother or a series of aunts. They say 'Absence makes the heart grow fonder' and such was the case, for John Scott planned to rescue Bessie from that tyrant that was her father. Having sent a secret message through Bessie's cousin, John Scott had arranged to elope with her on a dark evening in 1772.

It was almost 11 pm on a Tuesday, traditionally the quiet time of the week, when the clatter of a horse's hooves rattled over the cobblestones, stopping outside Bessie Surtees' house. There at the first-floor window stood Bessie, her long hair flowing down over her shoulders. She had waited almost two hours for him, and there he was. First, she threw down a small cloth bag that John Scott tied firmly to his saddle, then began to panic as the height between the window and the horse seemed so very great.

The legends differ, as they tend to: some say Scott climbed on to her window ledge and lowered her down onto the horse's back; however the more common story tells us how Scott stood on the back of his horse, one foot on the saddle, the other on the wall, guiding her down beside him. At this point, her father heard a kerfuffle and alerted friends and neighbours to set their dogs on them. They mounted their horses, and with their hunting dogs began the chase.

They galloped along the Quayside, with Bessie clinging on to him for dear life, and as the throng neared them, slowed down by two people on one horse, Scott turned his mount towards the stairs leading up to Newcastle's Castle Keep. These are some of the steepest stairs in Britain, not easy for even the fittest man, but surely impossible for any horse. Yet driven, some say, by the power of love, the horse clattered its way towards the top, sweating and foaming as it reached the top. The other horses just couldn't make it, tumbling back on top of one another injuring many and throwing their riders. The dogs did manage to reach the top, but having done so and finding none of their masters to run them, they merely made their way back down again. Bessie and her man had done it! Those stairs are now known as the Dog Leap Stairs.

Having rested on the outskirts of what is now Ponteland, they began a long and tiresome journey to Scotland, John Scott walking much of the way, allowing the horse to carry only the weight of Bessie. They were married in Scotland, sending a series of letters home to both sets of parents to explain. It took the families almost two years to come to terms with what had happened, but they did eventually rally round, accepting the marriage. It was just as well they did as John Scott, driven on by his beautiful wife, eventually made his fortune, becoming Lord Eldon, the Chancellor of all England.

It is said that after her death Bessie Surtees returned to that old house on Sandgate, and each evening relives the same adventure. She waits at her window, longingly awaiting her lover to steal her away into the night. She has been seen by tens of thousands over the years. English Heritage has taken over the building in recent years, and that haunted window is marked with a pane of blue glass. If you gaze towards it at 11 pm on a dusky evening you can make out that beautiful face, waiting, always waiting, as she will do until the end of time.

Throughout history, theologians have said that a place can trap the most intense emotions of any incident that has happened. Could this be such a case?

* Mark Fothergill from Leeds was visiting Newcastle's Quayside market on a Sunday morning in 1954 when he chose to run up the Dog Leap Stairs. He began to tire halfway up and decided to stop and catch his breath. On doing so he heard an incredibly loud noise, the sound of horses on concrete approaching him. All he could see were stairs up and stairs down, yet the volume of the horses' hooves almost deafened him. He said in a church magazine: 'I am a Godly man but I am sure of what I heard. The noise of horses breathing heavily, then some cried out as if they were in pain. It was almost as if one rode past me too, for as soon as I turned I heard a clattering higher up the stairs too!' He was shouted down by a few people because there were some horses on the Quayside that morning, but they remained at the opposite end near the warehouses.

* Elaine Murray was dining with Philip Harvey in a restaurant called the Red House, that once occupied the same floor that Bessie Surtees eloped from. They were eating when Philip saw a woman in a long flowing dress and commented on the fact to Elaine. She turned and said she could see nothing. All the while Philip could see a beautiful girl, with long flowing hair, and even asked a couple at the next table if they could see it. Once again they saw nothing. Philip was getting quite frightened, as he was so close to this 'whatever it was' that he could see the colour of her eyes and a mole on her cheek.

'I have seen nothing like it since and I'm bloody pleased about that. Elaine thought I'd been drinking, but I hadn't. I had the car and was on orange juice. I saw a woman in a black dress with white shoulders, long hair, blue eyes and a mole. She was as solid as you or I, and I'm not saying it was a ghost, because I don't know what it was. I thought because it was an old house one of the staff had dressed up, that's all!'

THE GHOSTLY HEAD OF EARL GREY

Grey's Monument is just about the centre of Newcastle-upon-Tyne, everyone knows where it is and it has become the universal meeting place, along with the fire station next to Worswick Street Bus Station. It was built in 1838 to commemorate Earl Grey, a Geordie lad who became prime minister and from it some of the most breathtaking views can be seen, once you have climbed up the 164 steps inside the column to stand on the gallery just below the statue itself, almost 120 feet above the City. Earl Grey's hair looked permanently white thanks to the pigeons, and whenever you looked at the statue there was always a bird sitting on his head. Yet during a particularly severe electrical storm in 1941, a bolt of lightning severed the earl's head and it plummeted to the ground, narrowly missing crowds of shoppers scurrying to get out of the rain.

Whilst the head was being resculpted by a man by the name of Ralph Hedley, passers-by claimed that they had seen another head on the statue. They claimed that the head had looked both to the right and to the left, as if still alive. People travelled from Sunderland and Teesside, many claiming they had seen this strange phenomenon. It may have been an optical illusion, or mass hypnosis, or just a rumour that spreads with no substance. Yet since the replacement head was installed you never see a bird sitting on Earl Grey's head. Had the old earl got sick of these birds doing the dirty on him, and thrown down a bolt from the heavens to discourage them once and for all?

* It is said that if you see a bird sitting on Earl Grey's head nowadays, it gives an omen of either good or bad fortune. Any white birds, such as seagulls, doves, etc. mean that anyone who sees them will have good luck; any black-coloured birds such as crows, rooks, pigeons or blackbirds mean that ill-luck is about to prevail.

GHOSTS GALORE AT NEWCASTLE'S CASTLE

The original 'New' castle at Newcastle was at the bridge head. Despite the Romans having had a fort on the area taken up between Dean Street and Collingwood Street, it was a Norman fort constructed in the 1100s that gives the city its name. There is nothing left of the original castle apart from a very few basic foundation stones. Yet it is the building that is now called the Keep that seems to house countless restless spirits. The legend tells of how that building was used for many years around 1400 as the prison for Newcastle and the surrounding district. Due to a shortage of space, criminals of all kinds were held together, the other buildings being sectioned off into the High Castle and Moot Hall.

Stories abound of murderers being placed in the same cell as those charged with theft, and how the killers would strangle the thieves or beat them to a pulp. Occasionally women would be put in cells with fifteen to twenty men, where they would be raped. Disease was always a problem too, as should one unfortunate catch a virus or suffer from fever, everyone else did too, and many fatalities took place. So Newcastle's Keep was home to a great deal of suffering well into the early 1500s, almost a century.

It shows you how bad conditions must have been when a prison reformer John Howard wrote in his report in 1787 (almost three hundred years later): 'They are kept in dirty, damp dungeons, having no roof in the wet season, and they sit in up to six inches of water. The felons are chained to iron rings hammered into each wall.'

Over the years ghosts have been witnessed of every shape, size and kind. Norman soldiers, Scottish Highlanders, raggy-dressed women, witches, little children arrested for stealing apples, an endless list of sad spectres.

We should remember that in those times even if you were innocent, you'd often be dead long before any trial. There is one tale about a young flower-seller called Briony, an Irish girl who had fled from Ireland during troubles in the 1600s. Each day she would go out into the countryside (the area that is now Gosforth) and collect wildflowers, making them into posies, and then she would bring them into town to sell. This gave her just enough money to scrape through. One day a rich merchant bought a bunch of flowers for his daughter, and out of the bunch flew a bee that promptly stung him on the nose. The merchant recoiled in pain and saw that young Briony was laughing at his predicament. He was incensed to such a degree that he had her arrested for assault. She was carted off to Newcastle prison where they found that the women's cells were full, yet there was room in another cell occupied by around twelve men. The men were smugglers sentenced either to hang or to hard labour in the colonies; none had anything to lose. Briony was in that cell with them for eight days. Every single day she was raped by each of those men, often over and over again. When she was brought to court this child, barely fifteen, was so badly injured that she was unable to testify. She was taken to surgeons where she died in their arms. So much for justice. They say that her ghost along with hundreds of others still cries out in pain along the corridors of Newcastle's Keep.

Another of the castle's ghosts died because of the portcullis of the Black Gate. The gate was constructed in 1247, and convicts were often led through it towards a stinking underground prison. Yet in the early 1300s one of the Sheriff of Northumberland's men was walking under Black Gate when the rope holding the badly rusted portcullis snapped, crashing down on him and slicing him in two. Following that episode, the Sheriff ordered a complete renovation. It is said that no one dares to close their eyes whilst standing under the arch of the Black Gate. First, you will be swept back to those dark days, then you will hear the squeal of the rusty portcullis screeching down upon you, and your heart will not stand the strain, 'bursting its chambers in terror' as the legend goes.

THE WITCH HOUSE OF CLAREMONT ROAD

If you should take a trip up Claremont Road you will suddenly come upon Newcastle's only windmill. It was built in 1782 and directly overlooks the Town Moor. It was originally used as a tower mill, to work on the grain stocks collected from the nearby fields. Yet there is a strange tale about the building that involves a group called 'the Sisters of Satan'. This story is universally denied, yet has been told to me on two separate occasions. During the First World War, a group of seven women gathered together and created their own mystical order. The ladies lived in houses on Beaconsfield Street, Arthur's Hill and Corporation Street, and were all interested in magic, ghosts and spirits Their association had begun innocently enough by the using of ouija boards, then reading tarot cards and ultimately taking part in seances. As the war progressed they discovered they were able to communicate with men who had been killed in battle on the Somme, Ypres and elsewhere.

The relatives of the bereaved flocked to their meeting place, believed to be the back gardens to the old windmill. The 'Seven Sisters' would take each relative by themselves into the garden, fill their heads with mumbo jumbo, deliver their 'alleged' message from the grave, and be handsomely paid for the privilege. This went on for the last two years of the war, and only stopped after one message was passed over about a John Darling who had supposedly been lost in action back in 1917. The 'sisters' gave a long and complex message from John Darling, who three weeks later returned to his home in Fenham. Overnight their credibility was blown, and their source of income had dried up.

It was around December 1918 that they began creating curses, praying to the Devil and giving blood sacrifice. They started to treat the windmill in Claremont Road as if it were a black shrine. They would sacrifice cats, dogs, sheep, goats or cattle to Satan, always within sight of the windmill. Some say that the Devil came out of the pit in Newcastle appearing in front of the 'sisters' in an unholy vision. Others believe the 'supposed' messages from the grave were merely Satan's trickery, trying to win new converts to his cause.

Their undoing came in 1923, and this is where the tales I was told differ. One story tells of how the leader of the 'Seven Sisters' died of a heart attack, and the other sisters drank her blood, then bathed in it, stark naked, dancing around the windmill. Locals were terrified and called the police who arrested them, placing them all in an asylum. I checked this out, and there are no records to prove it.

The other version tells how they decided that animals were no longer suitable as a sacrifice to 'the Prince of Darkness', so they began stalking human prey.

They came across a small child at Newcastle Central Station, a small Scottish chap who had got off the train believing Newcastle to be Edinburgh. No one knew he was there, there were no witnesses, he was the perfect victim. The youngster had been crying, having been put on the train some fifteen hours earlier in London, and wanting to see his mother and father waiting for him at the railway station in Edinburgh. The 'sisters' tried to cheer him up, giving him sweeties, and lots of hugs. Yet as night descended the young boy was woken up and told that his parents were waiting for him.

The young chap was ecstatic, he hadn't seen his parents for almost a year, having been sent to school in London. He raced downstairs and together with the 'Seven Sisters' he walked to the shadowy back garden of the Claremont Road windmill. The women said his parents were to meet them there at midnight. Slowly but surely that time arrived, and the twelve-year-old was grasped firmly by the women, his shirt ripped open and his heart cut out. It was so swiftly done that it was still beating as one of the 'sisters' held it in her hand.

Whether they ate the boy or merely disposed of the body, no one knows. Yet it is said that some locals had witnessed what had happened, and had forced the 'Seven Sisters' out of Newcastle. A group of over thirty men and women confronted each one direct, telling them that if they didn't leave the city forever they would inform the police. Within an hour the seven sisters of Satan had moved out, and once again the windmill was free from the Devil's sign, and Newcastle folk could breathe a sigh of relief.

The sails of the windmill were taken down within months of this event, and it is thought that should they ever be replaced, the Seven Sisters would return from hell to begin their evil work once again.

THE POWER OF THE NORTHERN MIND

The Reverend Joe Poulter and I decided to try a totally different night of radio, by trying to channel the brainpower of the North in specific directions. I for one didn't believe it was possible and, deep down, neither did Joe, yet we agreed to give it a go. We targeted certain things that everyone in the North knew about and told the listeners to think about them very hard, to concentrate on that article and nothing else. It sounds weak even telling you about it now, yet it actually worked beyond our wildest dreams. What I am about to relate are the facts, the things that worked and the things that didn't, but I swear to you it's all true.

We targeted Blyth Power Station, telling people to concentrate on turning off the lights. Those lights by law have to remain on due to low-flying aircraft, yet after channelling energy we took them out of commission for nearly an hour.

We targeted Stockton High Street, brightly lit until midnight when a time switch turned all the lights off to save electricity. It is impossible to alter this time switch without visiting each shop individually. Our listeners positioned in the street in their cars told us at 11.15 pm after we had turned our attention to them: 'The lights in some of the shops are flashing on and off as if they are shorting!' By 11.35 pm they reported: 'Two-thirds of the street is in darkness, and even the traffic light twenty feet away from the car is permanently stuck on green!'

We targeted the brightly lit folly at the top of Penshaw Hill visible from almost twenty miles in all directions. We targeted our concentration on that, and the lights went out. I was later informed that a bloke who maintained the lights had switched them off. It seems that he wanted to take part in the fun aspect of the evening.

We targeted church bells and made them ring, despite the fact that no one pulled the ropes. We targeted countless things and amazingly we didn't fail to score once. Even when callers said 'Why not switch the lights off in my local church, the cinema in town or the restaurant at the end of the street?' In each case, we either did it, flickered the lights or created some inexplicable disturbance.

Our most remarkable happenings took place in Morpeth when we targeted the clock tower in the town centre. It is situated in such a place that you could see all four sides. There are two doors in it, and before we started it was checked as being completely empty. The evening had gone so successfully that by the time we turned our attention to Morpeth's clock tower about two hundred people had gathered around it. So the weight of the million or so minds were channelled into action. What I had wanted was to stop the clock. This we didn't do, but at midnight it showed one o'clock. Then instead of showing one the pointer moved to two, at one o'clock. Yet by the time 2 am. came around, the clock was working normally again. The crowds of people couldn't believe it, and quite frankly neither could I! It didn't stop there, for we knocked off the lights at several shops on Bridge Street. We began to receive complaints from people living nearby that their radio reception was poor and their televisions had actually gone off. Then cars began to break down, three vehicles ground to a halt, each one within a hundred yards of the clock tower. All this within twenty minutes of our energies being channelled there. Motorist, Terry Gee wrote in two days later: 'You really put the wind up me. I was driving through Morpeth on my way home to Pegswood when on approaching the clock tower my engine just petered out. I'd just had the car serviced, it was in perfect nick, and I was due to drive to Manchester the following day. So there was I stuck, and I couldn't phone the AA because you had crowds of listeners ringing you from the phone box. So I was getting quite enthralled by all this myself and began chatting to other people there. I discovered that a lad called John from Seaton Sluice had broken down, with exactly the same problem, not thirty feet from my car. As your show ended I decided to give my car one final try before walking down to the next phone box, and the engine turned over first time. So I drove down to John's car, and offered him a lift home, yet when he tried it his engine started too! I can't explain it, I don't know what you did, but it was quite incredible.'

The magnitude of what happened took almost a fortnight to add up. Apart from all of the things we've already noted the following occurrences were reported by either phone call or letter:

Twenty-seven people told me their watches or clocks had stopped.
Nine other cars broke down.
Thirty-four television sets packed in.
Seventeen people suffered serious radio interference.
A young girl in Jesmond made a spoon bend, just by looking at it.
A local cinema had a total power cut.
Eight people complained that electrical gadgets in their house switched themselves on.
Twenty-one people with hearing aids experienced high-pitched feedback.
A police car siren switched itself on and couldn't be switched off.
Sixty-seven homes said their lights either flashed or went off altogether.
I'm still not sure I believe what went on, but I've listed what information I received.

ROWLANDS GILL: THE GHOST THAT WOULD NOT BE RECORDED

During one of my earliest ghost hunts, I was pointed towards a picturesque part of the North, Rowlands Gill, to visit the nearby Gibside Chapel.

In the 1960s a study had been made by two scientists who tried to seek out the paranormal. They had recorded, or so they claimed, heavy breathing, panting and moaning from the building, and swore that it was haunted by not just one soul, but by many. This seemed to be the perfect place to investigate, as in the middle ages many monks had met an unpleasant end, hacked to death by the men of Henry VIII during the dissolution of the monasteries.

So a huge outside broadcast team was asked to investigate and set up a live radio show from the site. We set up a truck, two sound engineers installed, and everything was going according to plan. Over three hundred ghostly sightings in two hundred years at the Chapel, so we were sure it would be a most interesting evening.

We tried and tested all of the equipment time and time again; everything was in perfect order. Our feed cable was lined with four layers of rubber so even had a forty-ton truck driven over it, it could not have damaged the minute fibre cables inside.

At 5.00 pm we tested the link, at 7.00 pm and 9.00 pm we tested it again. Then at five minutes to the hour, I donned a set of headphones ready to host the programme. I was given a hand signal to pick up after the 10 o'clock newsman gave me my cue. 'My name is Alan Robson, welcome to . . .' when the power completely failed.

The electricity supply was still there, the gear was in perfect condition, yet why was this not happening? A quick dash back to the studio to replace a terrified stand-in D.J., who had just been playing segue after segue of music, to cover the grade-one fiasco.

The following day the twenty yards of power cable was stripped of the three-inch-thick covering of rubber, and it was breached in three places, six inches between each one. Over three hundred tiny cables were cut, all at the same place, times three – impossible to do beneath three inches of rubber, without leaving a mark. Every six inches, 6-6-6. A beastly number, or just an incredible coincidence?

THE VIKING OF ROWLANDS GILL

There is a romantic tale about a Viking family who had fallen out with their warlord Hagga and had escaped to the north of England, setting up home at Gibside. They erected a small lean-to, and with the tiny stream nearby they could survive, hunting in the woods and growing some basic food crops.

The locals were at first very worried about having a full-blown Norseman living beside them. A fearsome-looking mountain of a man, Bidor stood well over six foot tall, and had muscles in his spit! His beard was so bushy it was if he was looking over a hedge.

After almost a year had passed the people began to accept him and his family into the fold and often went with him on his hunting trips. Legend says that he could hurl an axe almost 200 feet, and struck down many a stag or wild boar.

One autumn day a Viking longboat sailed up the Tyne, docking at Swalwell (where the Marina is currently sited) and the wild men from Scandinavia poured off to steal, rape and ravage. By chance one of the Vikings spotted and recognised Bidor's son, and began chasing him, as the youngster tore off into bushes. The boy was barely fourteen and they trailed him to Gibside, bursting in on Bidor's wife as she prepared a meal. Treating the entire family as traitors they disembowelled the boy in front of his mother, slaughtering the other two children in their cots. They tied Breda, Bidor's wife, to a tree outside the hut, and lay in wait for the Viking refugee to return.

Bidor and his fellow hunters had been told of the Viking landing and were rushing back to their homes, none more keenly than the Norseman. What made him stop no one will ever know, but instead of returning home he made his way down to the Tyne where the longship lay at anchor, guarded by three burly Vikings. Bidor approached them cheerily, they reciprocated, but once he got aboard he swung his axe taking off the heads of two of the men with a single stroke. The third drew his sword but had no time to use it before he too was downed.

As, one by one, the Vikings drifted back towards the boat and stepped aboard, Bidor would kill them, rescuing dozens of young girls taken as slaves or bedwarmers.

Finally, one of the Viking leaders rolled up to the ship, drunk and swearing, laughing at the times he had had ashore. Bidor grasped him by the throat and told him never to return to the Tyne again. The Viking spat in his face, so Bidor brought his body down on his knee, breaking his back. The Norseman wasn't dead, but his spine had snapped, and he couldn't move anything but his eyes, which darted to and fro in a panic.

Bidor had killed most of the crew, and there certainly wouldn't be enough men left to guide the ship home, so he returned to Gibside.

Nearing his hut, he heard talking in one of the bushes, and he crept stealthily through the greenery, to see a carefully laid trap. Four men on one side, two across the other side of the clearing, directly behind a tree where Breda was tied.

He saw a huge red stain on the ground, and there in the middle of it was his eldest son, his eyes looking up to the skies but seeing nothing. He knew that they would have killed his babies too, and a volcano of emotion welled up inside him. Although he was barely ten yards from the four Vikings Bidor stood up and roared his pain and torment to the world. With an axe in one hand and a sword in the other, he was with one bound amongst them, swinging and swinging until the four Vikings lay in pieces before him.

The other two ran towards Breda shouting, 'Kill her, kill her!' As the first neared the petrified woman, he raised his sword to hack her to death when Bidor's arm swept down in a flash sending his axe spinning through the air, deep into the Viking's chest. The other Viking turned to run, yet tumbled into three of Bidor's friends who lived in the Gill, and they were swift to club him to death.

It is said that Eider's heroism saved the people of the valley from further Viking attacks, and they all saw out the rest of their lives in peace.

I sent a friend, Father Flanagan, to visit the site, and he claimed to hear strange voices, not speaking any language he could identify. He doesn't believe for a second in ghosts, but that language could have been Scandinavian. "It is believed that my family line began in that part of the world: many people think that I still have a face like a Norse!

THE JACKHAMMER MAN OF SOUTH SHIELDS

If you lived in or around South Shields in the 1840s you would know Jack the Hammer, a traveller who picked up manual labour as he found it. He would carry out any jobs such as carpentry or repairing pots and pans. Although everyone felt comfortable to have him around he never managed to gather any friends around him. He lived in a part of South Shields that is now known as 'The Nook' and remained almost a hermit in his own home.

He never answered a knock at his front door, merely stared down from his tatty net curtains, a tall blond man with sagging shoulders and a huge beak-like nose, grimacing at anyone that dared bother him. People were so often rebuffed that they simply stopped calling on him. Neighbours never heard a sound from him, even when he was at home for long periods. When, in his fifties, he suffered a bout of flu he remained in bed and tried to sleep it out of him. All that happened was that he became weaker and weaker, eventually dying from lack of nourishment.

His neighbours were not aware that he had died, and the body began to decay in the rocking chair that he died in. Eventually, though, a pungent stream of mixed bodily fluids began to seep down on the couple that lived below him. They were eating lunch when a dripping began, dropping into their soup. At first, they thought it to be condensation, but it built up to be a fair old stream, stinking out the lower flat.

On investigating they discovered the man almost mummified. He was covered in cobwebs and sat there palely as they shrieked in horror.

He was carried out of the house in the chair, covered with a sheet, and taken away for burial on the back of a cart. In due course, the house was sold and nothing untoward was reported. However, many of the South Shields people claim regularly to see the shape of a stooping man at around six in the evening, walking along 'The Nook'. Some said that he appeared on the riverside during times of thunderstorms and gales as a sign that someone is about to be lost at sea.

Other tales tell of how he hammers out a warning of impending doom on the wall of any house occupied by a man who goes out to sea.

*In 1941 Mrs Margaret Brown heard tremendous hammering sounds on the side of her home in South Shields. Two days later she received a letter saying that her son had lost his life aboard the HMS Hood sunk by the Bismarck when only a handful of the 1,421 crew managed to survive.

*In 1982 Mr Roger Douglas of Tynemouth was staying with his friend Paul Somerville in South Shields. He was woken by a loud hammering on the wall of the house, and immediately looked out of the window as the hammering continued.

There was no one there.

The following Saturday Paul received a letter from an aged persons' home to say that his mother had died.

THE PHANTOM FORTUNE OF SOUTH SHIELDS

There is nothing more terrifying than discovering that there is something' lurking in your very own home. One young lady in Thrift Street, South Shields, discovered this on a warm August evening. She heard a strange noise beneath the floor, so set off to investigate. On reaching the top of the stairs she saw a figure in the blackness, a very old woman, who seemed to be shivering with fear. The young girl was trembling too, but soon direct contact was established, when the old woman begged her not to bring a candle down the following night and told her that if she didn't it would be well worth her while. Quite how that young lass managed to sleep that evening is well beyond me, but sleep she did. So once night had fallen she left her candles and set off down those mould-laden cellar steps. Imagine how scared she must have been stepping into the unknown with a strange spectre. Yet it was a most courteous phantom, very grateful to the girl for showing sufficient respect for the old lady to have kept her word.

Although the girl could hardly make out any shape or form, she felt the old lady pull her head down, as if to whisper, and was given precise instructions as to what she had to do. Then the lady vanished, leaving the girl, arms outstretched, searching for the steps so she could escape the deathly hush of that echoing chamber.

On climbing out of the pit, she ran into a back bedroom, long neglected by the household and currently being used as a storeroom for old chests, trunks and old clothing. The elderly lady had told her to reach into a huge crack in the fireplace wall. On doing so she felt a cockroach scurry over her hand as it sank into a mass of cobwebs. Yet there in the flue of the fireplace someone had hidden scrolls of paper and a tightly fastened leather pouch. On close investigation, the papers were the deeds to the house that she was renting. So now she was the new owner. In the leather purse were over fifty golden coins worth a small fortune – certainly sufficient for someone who owned their own house to live comfortably for the rest of their life. The girl quit her job and became one of the 'grand ladies' of South Shields. Yet she never ever returned to that cellar, in case the lady could remove the fortune as swiftly as she had provided it. She nailed down the cellar door, and despite the bumping and banging she heard from time to time, she never dared investigate again!

SOUTH SHIELDS OLD HALL AND THE SIGNS OF MURDER

In the 1770s a wealthy merchant was hacked to death by one of his ships' captains whom he had just sacked. As the old man worked through the books, he failed to hear the footsteps as the spurned skipper stood looking down on him. The merchant saw a flash of wire, then the garotte dug into his throat, and he desperately clawed at the wire managing to get two fingers inside to protect his neck. As he did, the seafarer put his foot on the back of the merchant's chair and heaved with all his might, pulling the chair towards him, severing the fingers and wrapping the wire around his spine. Blood spurted from his neck like a geyser and two bloody fingers and a thumb landed on the mantelpiece.

The sailor returned to his vessel, his crew and other members of the company not knowing he had been sacked. He resumed his career and was never found out, being long at sea by the time the body was found. It is said that if you look closely at that selfsame mantelshelf you can still see the bloody marks made by the old man's fingers. No matter how often you paint it, varnish it or smear it with cleaning fluids, the prints return.

The Old Hall in the West Holborn area of South Shields has a catalogue of ghosts ranging from a blue nun (I presume that is one with filthy habits), an old World War I soldier, a lady in white, a Roman soldier and a howling dog.

TYNEMOUTH'S VIKING PHANTOM

Nowadays you need a string of references even to get an interview for a job, yet in days gone by this sort of check was rarely done. How else could a Viking murderer and rapist possibly take charge of Tynemouth Priory? Yet this is exactly what happened. A young Viking had been injured during a murderous raid on the area around Melton Constable and as the Danes escaped back to their longship, he wasn't able to make it. Rather than be killed for the part he played, the teenager was nursed back to health by the canny Northumbrians and began to live amongst them. His name was Olaf, and he was so taken by their kindliness he embraced their faith, Christianity, and became a monk.

Viking raids up and down the North East coast were commonplace, and each time Olaf saw that curved sail on the dragon-headed boats; he shuddered, for there lay his villainous past, and little did he know his deathly future.

'Beware the men of the North wind!' was the cry when a sail came in sight, and deep down Olaf knew that one day he would meet his countrymen again. Whenever the winds blew Easterly he knew that the longships would be on their way, filled with bloodthirsty cutthroats ready to rape, murder and steal.

Tynemouth Priory seems to be well protected against any adversary, yet little did they know the determination of the Norsemen. Olaf, his monks and many of the villagers huddled in the priory, gazing down as two Viking longships began spewing out their deadly cargo. Men armed to the teeth, their swords and axes glinting in the mid-morning sun, half sang, half shouted their way as they wended up the cliff face, their hair long and ragged, their coats cut from animal skins. These raggy-faced men, many with beards down below their waists, these savages were finely tuned killing machines. Their leader was reputed to be Eric the Red, who had discovered America long before Columbus.

When the Vikings pounded on the priory gate, they ordered that its occupants open up at once, lest they be totally destroyed and no mercy given. Olaf knew that the Vikings weren't merciful anyway, so chanced his arm by ignoring their instructions. Within seconds spears, arrows, rocks and axes were flung over the walls, raining down on the unfortunate Tynemouth citizens. They had set the huge wooden gate on fire, and the searing heat forced the monks back from it. At that moment they knew they were finished unless with the grace of God they could keep the Vikings out.

Despite being God-loving men they had prepared a surprise for the Viking raiders, in the form of barrels of boiling pitch and huge stones dug out of the wall loosened in readiness to drop on their assailants. The boiling pitch had softened the Danes' resolve, but the final straw was when their infamous leader Eric was thrown to the ground when one of the priory's stone blocks had crushed him with a fatal blow. The Vikings backed away in horror when their leader, who had been given the power of Odin, found himself unable to defeat a handful of monks. The monks managed to capture the crushed Viking leader and began to tend his severe internal injuries. This would all be to no avail: his spine was severed, his ribs shattered and he gasped for air, his lungs cut to ribbons by bone fragments. At this point, the legend takes two paths. One tells of how the Prior Olaf held the body of Eric the Red high above his head on the battlements, shouting out in Danish how he would take the life of any other Viking ever to dare attack Tynemouth again. The Danes then slunk back to their longboats, returning home to name a new leader.

The other route taken by storytellers is a little more flowery. They say that once Eric the Red was safely inside Tynemouth Priory Olaf began to wipe away the blood, in the hope of saving his life. As he did so he recognised the Dane as the brother he hadn't seen for over twenty years, and Olaf had taken his life. He was consumed with guilt and remorse, for surely had Eric known he was attacking his brother, all hostilities would have stopped. Olaf prayed for the life of his long-lost brother, but the prayer wasn't answered. Eric's injuries were too great, and he died in his brother's arms.

The monks buried Eric the Red in the grounds of the priory, a grave lovingly tended by his brother until his death. Olaf was buried next to his brother so they could reach heaven or Valhalla together. Despite Olaf being a Christian prior, he still hedged his bets, asking for a sword on his deathbed. No Viking can enter Valhalla without one.

Olaf has been sighted in the priory thousands of times over the centuries; some say he's keeping guard over his brother's corpse. At the time of his death, many locals thought it inappropriate that a Viking murderer was buried in sacred ground, and had wanted his body removed.

* In 1974 Gill Trueman from Stockton-on-Tees was in Tynemouth and said: 'I saw a figure in a white robe standing by the sea wall. He had a long beard and little hair on top!' Despite Gill not knowing anything about the story of Olaf, she had described him perfectly.

* A group of schoolchildren from Rutherford School in Newcastle spotted a strange figure near the gate to Tynemouth Priory in 1979. They even pointed it out to a teacher who refused to believe what she saw. Thirty-two youngsters saw the shape vanish into the door, even though the door was locked shut!

* In 2017 we put several radio listeners into Tynemouth Priory in the evening. We had done something like this fifteen years earlier with great success, yet second time around things seemed far quieter. Until with ten minutes to go a scream went up, as fourteen people all saw a man dressed in hides walk through a wall into what is now the Priory shop.

WALKER'S WEEPING MADONNA

In Catholic countries, a statue that cries a vision of the Virgin Mary or the sight of a monument that bleeds is instantly declared as a miracle. A shrine is established and millions of travellers from around the globe flock there on their pilgrimage. Yet something more than odd took place on Tyneside, that came close to following such famous examples.

A canny Tyneside housewife, Mrs Theresa Taylor, lived in an ordinary terraced house in Walker, Newcastle, and used to pray to a plaster statue, believed to have been bought at one of the city centre's Bible shops. She was on her knees praying on 10 October 1955 when the Madonna opened one of her eyes and began to weep. A tear began to fall down the cheek of the sculpture and on to the floor. Mrs Taylor refused to believe what she had seen so she called in her neighbours and friends who all testified that the statue was not just shedding an odd tear but dripping with water from the eye. Over eight months thousands of people visited her home and dozens of them claimed that it was real and that they had witnessed the Mother of Christ weeping. Local professors claimed it was condensation caused by the plaster reacting to the high temperature in the house, and bringing any liquid still trapped in the statue to the surface.

Whatever the truth Catholics travelled from as far as Spain, Mexico and America to witness this amazing statue that cried. Throughout Walker, many hundreds are willing to swear that a miracle did take place in Mrs Taylor's living room on that warm October evening.

THE FIRE WOMAN OF WHITLEY BAY

When a scream shattered a peaceful evening in a quiet street in Whitley Bay in March 1902, no one could have guessed the controversy about to unfold. The cry seemed to come from the home of the Dewar sisters, and soon Margaret had rushed down the path of her neighbours' home and hammered on the door. Margaret Dewar was in a total frenzy and blurted out how her sister had been burned. Taking this calmly the neighbours walked around to check on Wilhelmina Dewar, as they had suffered from burns themselves and knew how to tend them. At this stage, they were getting nothing comprehensible out of Margaret at all. They sat her down, and gave her a gin, as she muttered and mumbled about 'the terrible fire.'

It was hard for the neighbours to believe that there had been such an inferno, as the building was still standing and there was no smoke whatsoever. They presumed that Margaret had had such a shock on seeing her sister give herself a bad burn, that she had become unhinged. Yet the sight they saw when they opened Wilhelmina's bedroom door made them sick to their stomachs. They were not prepared for the woman's body being charred beyond recognition. There were the remnants of a foot and you could decipher the shape of something that was once human, but it was impossible to identify. The most amazing thing about the case was that the actual bed, including stiff cotton sheets, was not burned or damaged at all. The rest of the bedroom was completely intact and unharmed except for some smoke damage to the ceiling. When the police and coroner attended the scene they refused to believe that this woman had just burst into flames and had caused so little damage to her surroundings. If anyone had lit a fire on a bed the entire room would be ablaze within minutes. It was no surprise when both police investigators and two separate coroners declared that they refused to believe Margaret Dewar's story.

The newspapers hounded her, the neighbours whispered stories of foul play, the police kept pushing one interrogation after another. Although Margaret knew what had happened she had to admit to lying, although she had not, just to get the case over and done with. She changed her story, saying that she had found her sister in the living room on fire and had covered her with a blanket to extinguish the flames, then had carried her up to the bed, where she had died due to the extent of her injuries. The coroner said, 'See, I told you I was right!' and a verdict of accidental death was posted.

The truth of what really happened was in Margaret's original statement. All of the evidence points to it. Margaret later sold her story to an American storyteller called Ripley and swears that it was the truth. She had been putting clothes away when she looked in on her sister Wilhelmina who was lying on top of her bed reading, just as she looked in, a fire began at stomach level. Wilhelmina looked up at Margaret and yet she didn't seem in pain, rather more startled! The fire had engulfed her within ten seconds, and she didn't panic or move one inch from the bed. Margaret explained: 'It was as if she was almost happy about it. I tried to grab hold of her, but the heat was too fierce. So I ran down to the tap to wet a towel, but on returning to her room less than a minute later, there was nothing left of her!'

Many think that spontaneous human combustion is far more common than the authorities would have us believe. Fire is a major killer, and how can we be certain that when a building bursts into flames and people are killed, the catalyst of that building's destruction was not a human incendiary?

The coroner's case regarding Wilhelmina Dewar is easy to destroy:
- a) If she was that badly burned in her living room how come there was no sign of damage whatsoever?
- b) How could Margaret carry her sister upstairs as she was barely 5'3" and seven stone, but her sister was 5'5" and closer to ten stone?
- c) If she could carry someone that badly burned, how come there was no trail of ash and skin up the stairs?
- d) To create the amount of heat to make bone crumble into ash, you would need an incinerator at least, to come close to the victim's condition.

There are more questions than answers, but it seems certain that Wilhelmina Dewar was prey to a condition that no one truly understands. Was it internal gases that exploded into flame, was she struck by a fireball, was it human electricity in the body going haywire, or was it an act of God?

No one is sure, but the fact is that without ever visiting a crematorium Wilhelmina Dewar of Whitley Bay was turned to ashes whilst lying on her bed, without as much as singeing the crisply starched sheet!

THE WITCHES OF WINLATON MILL

There is still a coven based in Winlaton Mill, many people are connected to it and it has been claimed that they have tremendous powers including the ability to kill those who try to attack their creed. The heritage appertaining to witches began in the Winlaton area back in the eleventh century, when it is said that witches flew around on broomsticks and each owned a black cat.

It is said that Scotland's most famous witch, Isobel Gowdie, visited Winlaton to impart the Devil's power to the coven, a mystical power that would last forever.

The witch queen of Winlaton was Suva, who would be seen wearing a long black cape to protect her anonymity. She had been known to those that lived around that area, owning a house in Rowlands Gill, yet when she became Suva only those who were witches could look upon her face without dying. They would gather together, cursing those whom they hated and giving the Devil's blessing to those that had done well. They would disembowel sheep and goats in the nearby woods and occasionally would tear at someone's face with a cockerel's claw. To do this was to execute unbelievers. It is claimed that dozens died over the years.

Suva would make a stew from the rotting remains of newly buried corpses, rats, spiders, slugs and woodlice, and feed it to her flock of witches to make them impervious to the will of man. Suva was the demon goddess; it was she and she alone who controlled these people. It is believed that this coven carried out murders, including the smothering of babies at birth. Once the babies were buried, a witch would dig up the remains and store them in huge pickle jars. Suva, whose real name was Sally, died in her nineties and the coven became less apparent, but hundreds of years on it still exists.

* In 1986 a witch claiming to belong to the Winlaton Coven cursed me, and I received a paper with blood smeared across it. They said that I would die within the year. It's been a long year!

* In 1988 an anonymous caller claimed that his life was being threatened by the witches of Winlaton Mill. His dog had already been stolen and returned to him in pieces. He was in such a state that he claimed he was going to take his life, the police were called and traced his number. While I was still talking to him on the air you heard the police burst in and take him away for medical help. He was sectioned and placed in a mental hospital for six months and has since moved to Suffolk. Whether modern-day witches have any power at all I don't know, but as long as a single person believes they have power, then harm can be done.

WHEREVER YOU GO YOU'RE SURE TO FIND A GEORDIE

Three days before Harry Fallon died, he sent me an old wrinkled document about his great-great-great-grandfather.

Robert Fallon had travelled to America and had earned a basic living as a carpenter in and around San Francisco in the 1850s. To supplement his earnings he would go into saloons and play poker. The West was still wild and woolly in those days, and selecting your opposition was impossible. So you took a chance, some nights you could win a fortune from cattlemen or merchants, on other evenings you would be fleeced by cardsharps and gunmen. Over an average week, he was well ahead.

But while he was playing a game at the Bella Union saloon one of the other men in the game, known as 'Wildeyes', pulled back the table to see an extra card on Fallon's lap. He stood up, drew his Colt, and slowly pulling back the hammer, he fired four shots into Fallon's head and chest. Cheating at cards was almost as heinous a sin as stealing a man's horse or hitting a woman. Shootings were fairly common in San Francisco, so the body was covered up and put in a backroom until the undertaker and the Sheriff could arrive.

Rather than let it spoil the night, the blood was wiped off his chair, and they shouted along the bar to see if anyone else wanted to play cards.

Most people were reluctant to take a dead man's place, but one young man stepped forward, sat down and began to deal.

By the end of the evening, he was quite a rich man, having cleaned out his opposition. The amazing coincidence was that he was Joe Fallon, the son of the man who had been shot hours before. He had not seen his father for years and was not aware he was even in San Francisco.

Joe Fallon returned to England after spending ten more years in America as a professional gambler. Fate certainly played a hand on that bloody night, when a son filled his father's shoes.

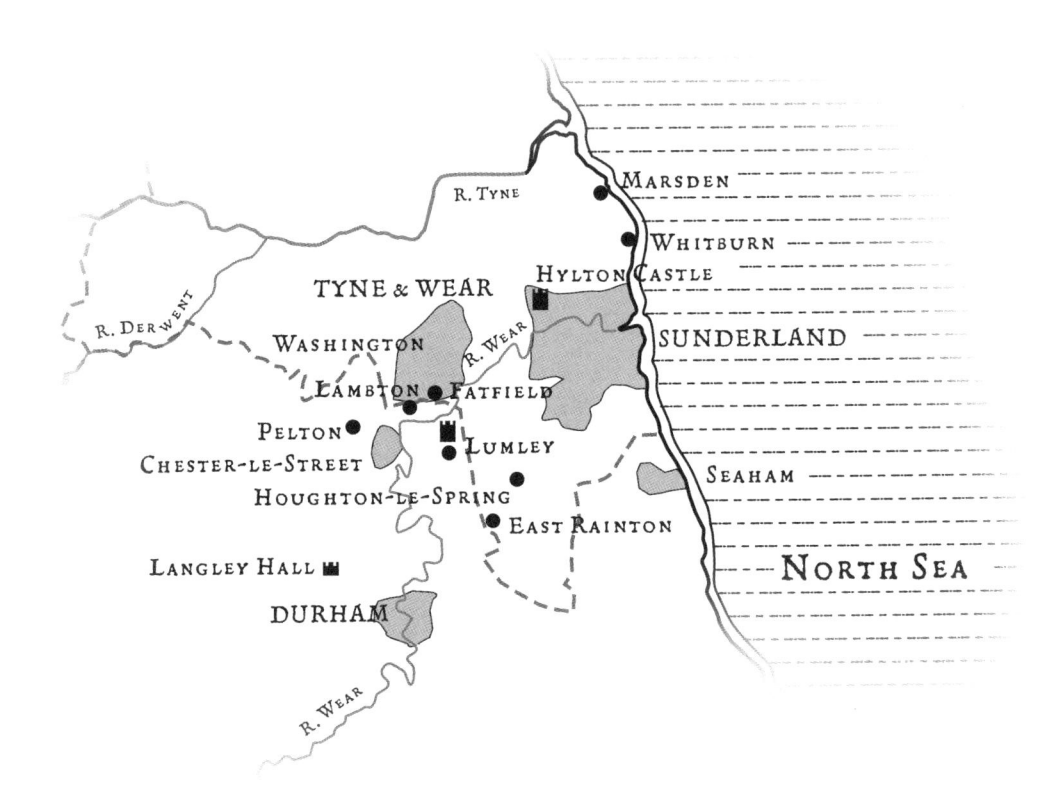

Marsden
R. Tyne
Whitburn
Hylton Castle
TYNE & WEAR
Sunderland
Washington
R. Wear
Lambton Fatfield
Pelton
Chester-le-Street Lumley
Houghton-le-Spring
East Rainton
Seaham
North Sea
Langley Hall
Durham
R. Wear
R. Derwent

WEARSIDE

THE PESKY POLTERGEIST OF CHESTER-LE-STREET

Around 1978 an architect and his family moved into a house a few doors away from the Lambton Worm public house, intending to completely refurbish it. Within days the place was full of workmen ripping down partition walls, building alcoves, installing coving and new light fittings, in readiness for it to become the new family home. The house had been empty for many years and had that musty smell that lets everyone know of its neglect. It had been owned by an old seaman who had been what his neighbours had called 'a right old sod!'. He had given them a good few years of 'Don't play football in the street', 'Turn down that music' and 'Don't think you can leave those bin bags out there!' He was a real crusty old bloke who did his best to plague the residents. He would send nasty notes through their doors, curse at them across the street, always in a petulant mood. His demise was not particularly sad, in fact, Roger Harper, who ran a mobile shop in the area, said: 'I couldn't stand the old bugger. Whenever I arrived in the street you'd find him trying to jump the queue, and if you tried to put him in his place he'd tell you how much he'd done in the war for people like me! I caught him slipping some food in his pocket, even then he turned it around saying it was my fault. Hell's teeth, this is a mobile shop, not Tesco's. Two days before he died he told me that I should take down the pictures of fruit and vegetables in the van because the apples I was selling were a different colour than those on the van.'

Buyers were reluctant to take on the salty old sea dog's house. The walls were painted bright white and he had no pictures on the wall, preferring the neatness he had come to expect on board ship. Mrs McIntyre, one of the few elderly ladies that could put up with the old chap, once brought in a few landscapes to brighten up the place, yet within a day of the gift they were stored in his attic, never to see the light of day again.

So the revitalisation of the house was now complete, having taken over eight months at a cost of around £10,000, a fortune in 1978. The very last touch was to dress the living room, place ornaments on the furniture and choose the exact position for their pictures. The last picture was that of white horses running through sea foam. The nail was hammered in and the last piece of the jigsaw completed the layout of their home. Yet later that day when they returned to the house they found the painting lying in the centre of the floor. So it was re-hung using a stronger bracket, yet as soon as they left the room they would hear a crash and the painting would fly across the living room to crunch down on the carpet. They tried hooks, nails, clips, all to no avail.

Later in 1978 Mum and Dad decided to take a holiday leaving two teenage daughters and a teenage boy to fend for themselves. All went well until one Wednesday afternoon when the girls found that the living room had been trashed. The pictures were down from the walls and every ornament that had been so delicately placed was lying in pieces on the floor. The girls knew that their folks would presume that they had had a party and invited the wrong crowd. That evening as they lay in their beds they could hear things moving across tabletops, things breaking and that awful sound made by a boot walking over broken glass. The doors and windows were all locked and the burglar alarm on, yet there was someone or something in the house.

On their return Mum and Dad soon realised that these strange incidents seemed to be increasing, so they moved from their custom-built dream house into the Chester Moor Pub. They were confident that they had left whatever irksome spirit had plagued their life, yet on Christmas Eve the young lad was sitting watching the action movie on television and was being distracted by the random flashing of the Christmas Tree lights. 'I wish they'd stop flashing', he said to his parents, and at that very moment they went out altogether. Other strange happenings occurred for a while, and only when the two daughters left home did they stop altogether. Medium Joyce Clavell said: "It is well known that spirits are often attracted by the strong life force of young girls and young women. Only when they mature are they able to shake off the contact, allowing it to seek out another younger girl!'

EAST RAINTON: THE GHOST OF MARY ANN COTTON

During a live radio conversation with Doris Stokes in the early 1980s, she mentioned to me that I was related to Mary Ann Cotton. At that time being a Newcastle lad, I had never heard of her story, and I remember saying to her: 'Well, I'll ask my parents, but I don't think so!' When I eventually learned about who she was, it made me feel less than comfortable.

Mary Ann Cotton was the daughter of Michael Robson, a miner at the Hazard Pit in East Rainton and most of my family was connected to mining or the coal industry. She was married at the age of nineteen and poisoned four of her five children. The doctor put the deaths down to gastric fever. Soon after, Mary was collecting decent insurance for her husband William Mowbray who had complained of stomach pains for months. Within a month of her husband's funeral, his body not even cold in the ground, she married a lad from the local shipyard who had four children. Once again they seemed a picture of domestic bliss. Then again, before their first wedding anniversary, all of the children were dead. This 'gastric fever' was a deadly condition. Her husband kicked her out after he saw an insurance policy taken out on his life. Still, the penny had not dropped. The locals were sympathetic and tried to help where they could. Having moved from Rainton to Sunderland centre, she moved on again. She took up with a man from West Auckland, Fred Cotton, who soon after died of `gastric fever'. Lodgers soon passed away, the signs were there for all to see, but no one believed that this stern-faced woman could be such a cold-hearted murderess.

Mary Ann Cotton even seemed to flaunt her crimes without shame or fear, and once scolded her son in front of half the street, warning him that she'd kill him if he didn't behave. By the end of the month, her seven-year-old was dead. This time there was a lot of talk and a post mortem ordered by a local magistrate. On finding arsenic in his stomach, further post mortems were carried out, and it was later discovered that she had killed sixteen people. While she was in prison, she even tried to poison her baby, in a hope that it would delay her execution. It didn't and she died a particularly unsavoury death. They say it took her almost five minutes to die. She fought death every step of the way until the rope finally choked the last evil gasp of life out of her. After her burial stories began to circulate that while she worked at Sunderland Infirmary a lot of people died of 'gastric flu'. The number of those who had dealings with Mary Ann Cotton we will never know. Her ghost is said to walk in two places, one being St Mary's School (the building was that infirmary all those years ago) and the other East Rainton where she spent much of her childhood.

* **It is said that if you are in East Rainton at midnight near the church if you recite the children's rhyme,**

'Mary Ann Cotton, she's dead and forgotten, She lies in a grave with her bones all rotten. Sing, sing, what shall we sing,

Mary Ann Cotton's tied up with string!'

she is supposed to show herself and many people have dared to speak the first three lines, but not many have ever finished it.

* **Another rhyme exists about her, a song is sung by little girls skipping or playing two-baller:**

'Mary Ann Cotton, Mary Ann Cotton, killed her children, will never be forgotten. Her blood was cold, her soul was rotten Mary Ann, Mary Ann, Mary Ann Cotton.'

FATFIELD: THE HORROR OF THE HAVELOCK ARMS

During the 1970s there was a string of tales involving The Havelock Arms in Fatfield. Customers and staff witnessed a strange floating shape that appeared to glow. All of the standard ghostly signs were apparent, a frosty chill would descend on rooms with the heaters on full. In 1974 a customer said that a ghost physically walked straight through him as he stood at the bar. He saw a dark figure walking towards him, and moved back against the bar to allow him past. Instead of moving around him the figure, looking completely solid, walked through him, through the bar and into the wall.

The press once again picked up on a story in 1976 when a man by the name of Brian Proudlock was lying in bed and he became aware of a man standing over him. He awoke with a start and cowered beneath his quilt. The figure seemed to be glowing but was clad in nineteenth-century garb, including a fancy 'maverick-style' waistcoat. It was later discovered that a previous landlord of The Havelock Arms, who had died in that very bed, was called Long John and his gimmick for the public was to wear a variety of very fancy waistcoats. Once the ghost had been identified, things would move from the bar, taps were left running, the hosepipe would switch itself on long after it had been switched off and electrical gadgets would suddenly glow.

The Havelock Arms has a continuing history of events including ghostly figures appearing in mirrors both in the bar and in the toilets. There have been sightings in 1978, 1980, 1983, 1985, 1986 and 1989.

THE FAIRY MINSTREL OF HOUGHTON-LE-SPRING

Close to Houghton le Spring, between the tiny villages of Eppleton and Hetton, there is a fairy mound for centuries believed to be the home of Quicksilver, the king of the fairies. The stone escarpment has a centrepiece known as 'the fairies' cradle'. It was believed that whenever a new fairy was born it was brought to this mound; a mound, if you are human size, certainly a mountain if you're only a tiny fairy. Once the baby fairy was placed in the cradle, Quicksilver would appear flying into the air playing on his pipes of Pan. The music was intoxicating and any human hearing it would fall into a deep sleep for twenty-four hours. This magic guaranteed that no 'giant' could ever disturb their rituals.

In the eighteenth century, despite great unrest with the locals, two scientists sent a pair of Jack Russell dogs into the holes dug deep into the hillside. No fairies were found but the dogs had eaten something whilst down there. Had they feasted on fairy flesh or had the wee folic given them food to protect their colony? Since that day no one has ever come forward with any sightings.

THE SPOOKS OF HOUGHTON-LE-SPRING

The ghost of an old man who caught the plague is said to walk through Houghton-le-Spring on the evening of Halloween. This poor old soul is literally rotting away before your very eyes. Over forty people have claimed to see him over the years and many more have smelled rancid rotting flesh and felt a 'presence'. He wears a long brown coat and his fingers are rotting to pieces, his face is eaten away down to the skull, and his eyes are sinking into their sockets.

There is also a pub called The Robbie Burns where some serious poltergeist activity was apparent in 1984. Mrs Janet Porteous reported in the press how there was 'something' lurking in her bar cellar. She had been bending down to count the stock when that 'something' cracked her on the back of the head. She screamed thinking that she had stumbled in on a burglar and struggled back to the stairs, yet when she looked around there was no one there.

On relating this story locals told of Thomas Caldwell who had worked in The Robbie Burns. During delivery of barrels, he was waiting in the cellar to ease them down and store them, when one barrel slipped off the tracks crushing him to death. His friends found him with his head staved in, jammed beneath a heavy wooden cask. Even though half of his head had caved in, he still begged for help. Yet once the cask was removed, the air flooded into his smashed open skull and he died instantly. It was rumoured that it was his restless spirit that inhabited the cellar.

The husband, a likely lad called Stuart, didn't believe his wife but did humour her, as he was well aware that she had had a shock, but wasn't convinced it was some ghostly mugging. It was during the nights that followed that he began to be convinced that something was wrong. One night he was awoken by what he described as 'a noise like a crash of thunder' from downstairs. Doors would slam shut for no reason, trays would rattle, within the walls there came a tapping sound. It was like living above a carpenter's shop. Clocks crashed from walls shattering on the solid floor, other clocks stopped, the television experienced problems, the one-armed bandit went berserk and would play all by itself.

Within a month more than three separate ghosts had been seen by various people. Things quietened down until 1982 when a bar cellar-man had his hand stood on whilst in the cellar. He saw no one but did feel a foot on his hand badly bruising it. If this is the spirit of Tommy Caldwell he still has not come to terms with his untimely death.

* The ghost of a mine worker called Dobson is said to haunt the main street in Colliery Row just outside Houghton. He was returning up from the black coal face at Murton, in the very early days of the pit opening, when a friend tripped and his head hit the wall of the shaft, almost ripping the top of his skull off. In the darkness, the others were splattered with blood and couldn't assist him until they got to the surface. On seeing the extent of his injuries they called a vicar from the local church who arrived too late. His body was returned to Colliery Row on a horse and cart, and his widow blamed the pit owners and cursed them. Since that day the ghost of Dobson the miner has been seen over the past century. Often the only thing they see is a tiny light from his pit helmet glowing in the dusky streets.

THE SEXY SPIRIT OF HOUGHTON-LE-SPRING

In May 1989 a pretty twenty-nine-year-old, Lynne Arkley, decided to send for the exorcist as things in her house were going far beyond a joke. It all started when Lynne moved into her council house and began making it into a home. At first, she believed that it was merely a dream, common enough in red-blooded folk, but fairly soon she started having more and more extreme experiences. She would wake to feel frozen fingers touching her naked body in all its most intimate places, and it was obvious to her it was something wanting sex. Lynne said at the time: 'It felt like a boyfriend making love to me, yet when I looked there wasn't anybody else in the room!'

On the occasions Lynne invited a boyfriend to the house, this jealous spirit was swift to vent its anger. Once while she was in bed with her partner the doors started slamming, and he didn't stay long. The only way that Lynne could stop the ghost sexually assaulting her was to leave the light on, for then it never touched her. This was the only way that she could get any sleep at all. At that time Lynne's daughter was only four, and she believed that the spirit had to go before it caused her youngster any problems. She had suffered various gropings and spooky sexual advances for two whole years, never thinking that anyone would believe what she had experienced. Eventually, a Pentecostal pastor called Norman Humphrey exorcised the house. Some weeks later Lynne said that she believed that the ghost was still there, but now it had merely a platonic friendship with her!

THE TERRIFYING TRIO OF HOUGHTON-LE-SPRING

Many pubs believe that a ghost is good for business, a talking point for punters, and a bit of living (or dying) history. The Robbie Burns pub in Houghton-le-Spring has not one, but three ghosts on the premises.

The hauntings – as recounted in my first Grisly Trails – began back in 1984 when the manageress was down in the cellar collecting a crate of soft drinks when she felt a tremendous crack to the back of her head. She spun around, but there was no one else to be seen in the cellar. She had a lump on the back of her head as big as a goose's egg to show for it. Every evening from then, strange music could be heard, a banging and crashing too, yet whenever you investigated there wasn't anything out of place.

*In 1984 the figure of an old woman wearing black was seen; she melted into a wall.

*In 1985 one of the one-armed bandits in the bar went beserk. No one had put any money into it yet it started playing itself, the handle going down, the wheels spinning, and often pumping out a fortune in ten-pence pieces.

*In 1985 two customers and one of the staff saw the silhouette of man, yet within the shadow, there was nothing at all. They watched it as it walked through the pub.

*The third phantom was that of a young child with fair hair, wearing baggy, Victorian-style shorts.

'Since then countless other things have happened: various electrical appliances have caused trouble, notably the bar pumps, the television and the radio. Things have moved of their own accord, including a clock which threw itself from a wall and smashed in the middle of the floor.

MANEATER OF SEAHAM

One of the toughest 'grisly trails' to follow was the story of a merchant seaman from Seaham Harbour on the North East coast. A man known locally as 'Slavvery Jack' had started visiting a girl called Beatrice Robinson, much to the disapproval of her puritanical father, who ran a grocer's shop. Jack's nickname 'Slavvery' had come about because he always flirted with the local women, calling them 'my dear lady', 'you sweet poppet', 'princess' and his favourite phrase, 'precious buttercup'. This did nothing to endear him to Mr Robinson. Fortunately, Jack was at sea for most of the year and would appear for no more than six weeks a year. During Jack's time aboard ship, Mr Robinson tried to matchmake his daughter with any suitable young man in the vicinity, all to no avail.

In January 1909 Beatrice was thrilled and Mr Robinson horrified when Jack announced he was giving up the sea and settling in Seaham for good. He even dared to enquire if Mr Robinson would employ him in his grocer's shop; the reply he received was far from polite. Finally, Mr Robinson told Jack that he could never marry his daughter, and swore that he would see to it that she never saw him again.

Within days Jack was off to sea again, his last trip before seeking work on the land. Beatrice knew that his ship was leaving the Wear to travel to Africa, and decided that she would smuggle herself aboard ship. This she did, and made herself known to the ship's captain only when they were three days out at sea, and couldn't turn back.

Her father knew what she had done, and each evening around six he would walk along Seaham Harbour wall waiting for his daughter to return.

Jack and Beatrice were married at sea on 21st April 1909, little knowing that they would be married for less than 48 hours. Beatrice fell ill with food poisoning, and the ship had to land on the Gold Coast, where during a fever fit she choked on her own vomit and died. She was buried close to the beach, and Jack was allowed to stay there until the ship returned to collect him on the way back. Jack was inconsolable; his only ambition had been to settle down with the woman he loved, and now she was planted in a strange land hundreds of miles away from the home that she loved.

At that time Africa was firmly under the thumb of the white money men who ruled with the lash and the gun. So Jack was treated well, and a local tribe gave him shelter and food. What Jack didn't realise was that he was being fed with human flesh. Lost in his grief he would sit out in the sun at temperatures of up to 115° Fahrenheit, his hardened skin flaking from his body. He seemed impervious to pain; he once stood on some sharp coral which sliced off his smallest toe, yet all he did was bind the wound then continued his walk.

Almost three months passed, and the ship returned to find a stranger waiting for them. Jack had grown a long white beard, his face was blistered and burned, and his eyes were mad and staring. At first, the Captain refused to believe this was the man he had sailed with for almost fifteen years and had it not been for a distinctive anchor tattoo on Jack's shoulder he might have left him there.

When the ship got back to the Wear, Jack ran off into the town centre, without his pay or belongings and was never seen again. Or was he?

This is where the stories differ, the first version of the tale tells of how Jack returned to Seaham and told Mr Robinson of his daughter's fate, whereupon the old man suffered a heart attack and died. It is said that on foggy nights you can see the shape of a rotund old man waving a lantern towards the sea, in a desperate attempt to beckon his child home.

In 2019 Richard Horseborough of Durham was walking along Seaham beach when something horrific happened to him. It was dusk on a muggy night, a little sea fret just starting to roll in, so Richard decided to make his way back along the beach, up to where his beloved Land Rover was parked. He saw an old bedraggled man sitting at a brazier, and he was eating something. "As I approached I shouted 'Hello' but got no reply. I had no choice but to walk past him to the car. As I got close it looked like he was biting flesh of a cooked human arm. There was a second one cooking on the fire. It all looked totally real so I began to half run past him, fumbling to get my phone out to call the police. As I turned and looked back there was no one there. The golden glow of the fire was gone. I cannot explain what the Hell it was I saw!" He had never heard the story of 'Slavery Jack'.

THE LAMBTON WORM

The story of the worm has changed over the years and is embellished annually, and only the song ever remains the same. The worm was, in fact, a wurm, or dragon. It is believed that one day young Sir John Lambton was out fishing in the River Wear, deciding that he was going to skip church for one Sunday. However, his luck with the rod seemed cursed right from the start and he was not able to catch one single fish. The only bite he had all day was from a weird green wriggling worm-like creature, with a huge toothy head. Far too embarrassed to take this strange creature home, he threw it down the nearest well. Some years later 'the bold and brave' Sir John Lambton went off to the Holy Land to fight in foreign wars, unknowingly sentencing his homeland to untold grief and misery, for late one night the creature he had cast into the well had grown large enough to climb out. For months he slithered around the countryside eating men, women, children and sheep and terrifying everyone. It was said that when it was thirsty it would milk a dozen cows.

Such was the terror felt at home that word was got to Sir John, who promptly returned to the North to face this horrible creature. By this time it was said to be so large that it could coil itself ten times around Penshaw Hill. There is some disagreement over this, as the people of Fatfield, near Washington, say the actual hill was called Worm Hill, where the grooves made by the Lambton Worm's body can still plainly be seen.

Many people had tried to kill the worm, yet every time it was cut in two, it simply joined itself back together again and gobbled down its attackers. Sir John met up with an old wise woman known to some as the Lumley witch, to others as a Sybil, or, as Panto would later described her, Elspeth of the Glen, who told him the only way the dragon could be killed. This wise woman did demand some conditions from the valiant fighter. She said that he must destroy the creature on its own rock in the middle of the fast-running River Wear. He also had to promise that should he be successful in his quest he would have to kill the very first living creature he saw afterwards. So after discussing it with his father this was sealed with Sir John's word. Failure to keep to his word would assure the early death of the next nine Lambton generations. Sir John was confident of keeping his word; his problem was being able to survive the monster. Sir John managed to corner the dragon by the banks of the Wear. His armour was covered with spines, so that when he attacked, the worm wrapped itself around him, impaling itself on the spikes. The battle was fierce and bloody as Sir John stepped into the rain-swollen river, hacking the beast into pieces, the spikes wouldn't allow the worm to join together. Sir John hurled the pieces into the Wear and the monstrous Lambton Worm was no more. John sounded a deer horn so that his father could send a hound, sacrificing its life rather than a human's. However, thrilled and joyous that his son was safe, Sir John's father ran into his arms, long before any dog was on the scene. Sir John couldn't kill his own father, so he killed a hound instead, shattering the promise he had made to the witch, bringing down a full curse on the Lambton name.

*The curse did indeed carry out its threat – Sir John's beloved son died in a drowning accident when only young.

*Other Lambtons would die in only their twenties on various battlefields around the world.

*Henry Lambton was just arriving at Lambton Castle when he suffered a stroke and died in his carriage.

*There is said to be a curse connected with anything to do with the Lambton name. In May 1973 Lord Anthony Lambton resigned after admitting that he had associated with prostitutes. Despite many MPs having done likewise the story became a scandal after the husband of one of the prostitutes sold photos to the newspapers. The joke of the day told how the pub The Lambton Arms would be renamed The Cock of the North.

*During 1988 myself and several top local actors were involved in a pantomime called The Lambton Worm, and although it became Britain's longest-running panto of that year (a full six months) it was 'cursed' by misfortune. Baddie Jimmy Swan fell from the stage very badly bruising his arm and side. Dame Denny Ferguson and I also had tumbles during its preview fortnight at Gateshead Leisure Centre, before it moved to the prestigious Newcastle Playhouse. At the Playhouse, the leading man 'the bold and brave Sir John' played by Joe Caffrey (star of Byker Grove on television) suffered a nasty fracture during a stage tumble.

*Due to popular demand, a follow-up panto was written called Revenge of the Lambton Worm and once again countless problems arose. Despite the audience having a whale of a time, once again Joe Caffrey was forced to miss a show because of a severe tummy bug. Denny Ferguson was attacked, I was beset by troubles and yet again the Lambton name seemed to act as a catalyst for trouble.

* Metro FM held a live late-night vigil on Penshaw Hill, next to the gigantic folly erected on top of the mound. The structure resembles the general shape of a Roman building, with huge pillars and a rectangular shape. I had heard that on this particular night there was to be a meteor storm, and I decided to link it to a UFO skywatch. The entire population of the North seemed gripped by the idea and they could take part wherever they happened to be. What I wasn't told was that on a Sunday night the top of Penshaw Hill was frequented by drunks, punks, and various strange characters. On reaching the brow of the hill I found myself surrounded by a crowd that would have been at home in The Rocky Horror Picture Show. We set up camp, and before long over a thousand people were thronging Penshaw. Due to the high cloud, the meteors were lost to us all, and the drunken thugs began to cause problems. So taking an executive decision I was forced to abandon the UFO Skywatch, not for my sake, but for the sake of hundreds of parents and children who could have been at risk had I allowed things to get out of hand. On returning to my car with my Night Owl telephonist, Jayne Steel, we proceeded to drive to another Skywatch site close to the Hancock Museum in Newcastle. Whilst I kept the show going, my outside broadcast vehicle, manned by producer Jim Brown, had its thirty-foot antennae snapped off. The tent we had used to keep the microphones wind-free had been kicked down the hillside and the rowdies were going crazy. One of the first calls on air following that came from Diane from Winlaton, who claimed to belong to a witches' coven and said: 'The Curse of the Lambtons covers Penshaw Hill, no good will ever come of it!'

THE GHOSTLY AVENGER OF LUMLEY VILLAGE

One of the main reasons that I am so sceptical about ghosts is the reason they choose to return! They seem to transcend the great beyond to tell us the colour of their socks on the day they died, they remind us of trivial details about a holiday or give us information that we already know. If we already know these things what is the point of coming all that way back to tell us? Yet to return for vengeance I could fully understand.

The North's best-known example of this goes back to the early 1600s. A mill owner called James Graham was just finishing off a hard day's work when he turned and there right in front of him was a girl. Startled, he jumped back and began to absorb the horrific sight that had confronted him. There stood a girl with serious head injuries, blood gushing down her pale grey gown and her face contorted in silent agony. His first thought was to give her medical aid, but when his eyes fully examined the scene, he realised that he could almost see through the figure, and she had no feet, floating eight inches or so off the ground.

He turned seeking a place to run, but this ghastly apparition remained to hover directly between him and the front door of the mill. It moved even closer to him, and he could see the full extent of her injuries. Her skull was completely caved in at one side, one eyeball was missing and alongside the blood, a grey stream of brain matter oozed like treacle across her shoulder.

The tale she told certainly equalled the dreadful sight before him. In a quiet well-spoken voice, the apparition told him that her name was Anne Walker and that she had been murdered by her cousin William Walker. Graham found all of this mindboggling, but the spirit continued to urge him to take the information to the authorities. She gave him every single detail including the name of the man hired to do the killing, a coal miner (believed to work at Dawdon Colliery) called Mark Sharp, though his mates called him Wacky'. Anne Walker's phantom explained how she had been William Walker's secret lover for many years, despite his having a lovely new wife. On hearing the news that Anne was pregnant, Walker was furious, claiming she had fallen on purpose just to spite him. To have your family name disgraced in the 1600s was tantamount to ruin and this social-climbing landowner would have none of that. So as the beautiful young girl walked through the Old Mill Wood near Finchale Priory, Macky Sharp leapt out on her and battered her to death with a pickaxe. The irony of this was that Sharp had seen young Anne Walker around the village and thought she had the most beautiful long blonde hair. Yet for a paltry sum he had mashed her head to pulp, carried her lifeless body to a redundant mine shaft and thrown it down. The miner knew where all the old diggings were, and also knew that no one ever examined them, so the likelihood was that the body would never be found.

The ghost did say that it was less than a perfect crime, as so vicious was the assault that Macky Sharp was covered with her blood, and after a fruitless attempt to wash off the offending stains in the River Wear, he had merely stripped down to his underclothes and wrapped his bloody shirt and trousers around her body before hurling her into the abyss. Anne Walker had returned to avenge herself against the man who had done her so violently wrong. When alive it is very hard to endure hatred without resentment and a wish to reciprocate, and it seems that is the case when you're dead, too! They say that revenge is sweet, but if that is so, why does it leave such a bitter taste?

Poor old James Graham was so confused he went straight to bed firmly believing he was losing his mind. How could a man of his standing go to the local magistrates with a story as far fetched as this one? He would be the laughing stock of the county. Surely no one would ever speak to him again. So he pretended that the whole episode had been merely the creation of overwork and a tired mind, a flight of horrific fancy that certainly wouldn't happen again. He made a conscious decision not to take on quite so much work again. Almost two months later, after the first snows of a particularly mild winter, he was cuddling up to his wife on a lazy Sunday morning when his slumber ended in dramatic style. The bedclothes were ripped off the bed, the warm bedroom flooded with freezing air, and there, standing above him, was the spirit of Anne Walker, her one eye burning with a fury that cut him to the bone. The ghost began sobbing and begging him to alert the police to the horrendous crime that had been committed. Up until that stage, the family of Anne Walker believed that she had run off with her secret lover. They had long been aware of a liaison, but she had steadfastly refused to name the object of those secret trysts. The figure disappeared as soon as it had come, and not once had Mrs Graham awoken. Still, he had no proof, and this led him to ignore the dead girl's pleas once again. The last straw came when he was walking through woodland close to Chester-le-Street. He whistled a tune as he ambled through a light covering of snow, casually collecting snow from hedgerows, firming it into snowballs and throwing them at trees.

Stories differ over this next episode. Some believe the ghost of Anne Walker reappeared, pinning him to a tree with such force he was almost knocked unconscious; others that she shouted and abused him, swearing to haunt him forever unless he told her story. The third version tells of how Graham saw the body of Anne Walker standing in the snow, and the blood pouring from the smashed skull dripped onto the white snow, turning it into a sea of red that surrounded him. He began to feel as if he were sinking into it. On begging for his life the spirit made him vow to see that justice was done.

Whatever happened in that wood, it certainly did the trick. James Graham scuttled to the local magistrates and blurted out the entire story. No one believed him, but as he was such a pillar of the local community they felt that to humour him, was the best step forward. So believing it to be a complete wild goose chase, they sent out a team of local men to the disused pit shaft. They attached a rope to a twelve-year-old boy, in the first year of his apprenticeship, and began to lower him down. He had not been down more than twenty feet when he cried out and they swiftly pulled him back to the surface. The tar-covered torch had come unwrapped and the hot covered cloth had burnt his hand, forcing him to drop it. They supplied the youngster with another tallow-dipped flame, and down he went again straining his eyes through the darkness. Almost 150 feet down the boy's scream surfaced yet again, and cursing his clumsiness they began to pull him back to the lip of the shaft. This time the boy's face was ashen white and his hand covered in blood. At first, they thought he had hurt himself, but on examining him, he was without even a scratch. So next three men went down and returned with the broken and twisted body of Anne Walker, her head staved in and her hair matted with blood.

Despite a total lack of any substantiated evidence the miner Macky Sharp and Anne's cousin William Walker were charged with her murder at Durham assizes. The locals still tell how when the sentence was passed in that court how many of them saw Anne Walker standing beside the judge. Members of the jury also claimed to have witnessed this awful apparition. Sharp and Walker were hanged by the neck until they were dead in November 1632.

* In 1967 Harry and Cissie Reid from Birtley were in a wood outside Chester-le-Street when they saw a woman covered in blood lying on the ground. Cissie had this to say: 'We thought she had had an accident, and I got a bit frightened, so Harry ran across towards her. He was standing directly above her when she just disappeared. I wiped my eyes, and he turned to me in shock. We still don't know what it was, but we know we saw something. It was a bright summer's day, we had the dog out for his walk, and when you see something that vivid you don't forget it!'

THE PHANTOMS OF LUMLEY CASTLE

Out of all the northern castles, Lumley is one of the best-loved, and with fine banqueting facilities and a golf course, it is a favourite resting place for many well-heeled travellers. The staff have helped me out on many occasions, providing children's parties for the underprivileged and so on. They allowed me to bring a huge party of wheelchair-bound people to meet top rock band AC/DC and several ghost hunts there have raised a fortune for charities.

The history of their hauntings changes with every person who tells it, so I intend to tell you the most likely candidates. The most common tale involves Sir Ralph of Lumley who was the governor of Berwick on Tweed, and his beautiful and bright wife, Lady Lily. Being the wife of an influential man she believed it was her duty to educate herself so she would fit in with her husband's guests. This she took seriously, some would argue too seriously as it ultimately cost her her life. Having worked her way through much of the Lumley Castle library she came across a copy of Wycliffe's translation of the Bible and spent much time reading it. The book was only for the eyes of men; as it had many meanderings away from the established beliefs of the day, it was not considered suitable reading for any mere woman. The monks from Durham Cathedral and Finchale Priory were so grossly offended that a woman was allowed to read such top-secret literature that they demanded that she recant. As an educated woman she believed that she was intelligent enough to make her mind up and decide what she believed. This did not come close to placating the irate men of God who, failing to turn the other cheek and 'forgive her her trespasses' promptly hacked her to death.

To this day we're told of similar scenarios, books held by the Vatican that no member of the public is allowed to read, many of the Dead Sea Scrolls have been played down and are seemingly censored, so to understand this degree of fear and superstition isn't hard.

So once the lovely Lady Lily of Lumley was chopped to pieces they threw her body down a well. You can still see this well as you enter the reception to Lumley Castle. To cover up their wicked deeds and to provide a body to be interred in the family plot they murdered another woman from the village and used her corpse to cover up the dastardly deed. Sir Ralph was away on business when all this happened and was told on his return that Lady Lily had taken ill and died in her sleep, and had since been buried. Yet the woman in the family tomb is not known, it certainly isn't Lady Lily.

The second version also involves Sir Ralph and the lovely Lily who were married even though she did not belong to the same faith as her husband. Sir Ralph was a devoutly religious man, taking a great deal of advice from the local order of monks at Durham and Finchale Priory. So when it was revealed that Lily disagreed with their religious teaching she was ostracised, and Sir Ralph tried to make peace. He travelled to London to discuss the situation with all of the leading bishops, only to find on his return that Lily had been murdered by three monks. This was around 1560. They had imprisoned her in her own home, Lumley Castle, then after a summary trial they had executed her, throwing her lifeless cadaver into the dungeons. The dungeon was later excavated to make a well and can be seen in the entrance to the castle. Some legends say the monks had raped her, others that she was a Devil worshipper: all they agree on is that she was indeed murdered. The tale continues that Sir Ralph ordered his castle guard to seek out the monks and execute them. They were brought under the castle walls and begged Sir Ralph to spare them, making the excuse that they had saved him from hell's fiery furnace and that they had only done God's will. This was to no avail as they had their heads cut off, and they were thrown into the nearby burn, to the left of the castle. Having visited the castle on a sunny day, it smells as if they're still in there! The ghosts are manyfold, Lady Lily certainly walks the castle walls, and there have been over three hundred sightings over the years. She is said to wear a long silkie' gown that glows an eerie greeny-white. Other regular ghostly sightings include a group of monks, sometimes three, at other times up to twelve, walking from the path at the right of the castle straight into the wall. The castle in the 1500s and 1600s had a door at that precise spot.

* Whilst there on a ghost hunt a hotel porter told me that one day he was asked to take a couple's bags up to their room, while they had an evening meal. He went up to the room, used a house key to open it up, and on entering the room saw someone fast asleep in the bed. Believing the room to be occupied he apologised, and rushed downstairs to get another key for another room. The receptionist insisted that the room was empty, so accompanied him upstairs. Once again he opened the door after knocking, and the bed was empty. He said: 'There is no doubt to anyone in this place that it is seriously haunted, but we've just got to live with it.'

* The scariest experience I had in the dungeon of the castle was during a ghost hunt in 1985. I was broadcasting live and having linked up listeners situated at many other haunted places, it had become quite an interesting situation. I had insisted on an old medieval candlestick as my only light. Two out of the three huge candles had gone out, and the flickering light made shadows dance and shapes appear in every corner or cubby-hole. This was the first time that anyone had linked eight of the North's most haunted houses and castles, and some religious figures believed we were opening the gates of Hell and letting the wicked run rampant on Earth. To us it was an experiment in the subconscious, to see if being in a situation like that would or could make things happen. Is it your imagination that makes you see these things?

Well, I had discussed ghosts for nearly four hours when suddenly I noticed a light at the top of the stairs that led down to my dungeon cell had gone out. At first, I thought nothing of it, then through the bars, and through the grey murk of the stairs, I saw a shape. It looked remotely human, and it was coming through the greyness towards me. My description was a mixture of fear, half swearing with fright and blind panic. My outside broadcast producer Jim Brown heard me describe it and ran into the corner of the cell seeking to escape by crashing into the wall. He's built like a Russian war memorial but so involved in the evening were we that our imaginations were running riot. All the time this thing kept coming, you could hear no footsteps, all that I knew was that this black something was floating down the stairs, getting closer and closer to the barred door. I reached towards the door, about to surrender to my fear and force it shut. At that moment the door swung open hitting my thumb, and with a mixture of pain and surprise, I squealed. For weeks afterwards listeners phoned and wrote of how they screamed too, not knowing what was happening. As the door swung ever wider this black shape became a man, a man in the uniform of a hotel porter who said: 'Hello Alan, just checking you're all right!' My heart was dancing to the beat of a Motorhead record, my stomach resembled a tumble drier and I refused to breathe in deeply in case my trousers held more than they were designed for!

* Another experience I had at Lumley Castle involved fancy dress. As I have been involved in countless escapades bungee-jumping from bridges, hang-gliding, abseiling down bridges and buildings, I have a nickname given me many years ago of 'The Flashing Blade'. There are other reasons too, but I'll leave that to your imagination. So a newspaper decided to get me dressed in cavalier garb, put me on a horse and situate me at Lumley Castle for a photo session. It was 6.30 am on a

misty Sunday, the photos had to be taken then because the castle was being used as a conference centre for Levi Strauss. The first photos were to be of me as a cavalier marching down the drive away from the castle. The photographer using a long lens was a hundred yards away, close to the trees. As I marched down, one of the sales reps from Levi's began walking up, having popped into the village for a newspaper. He was reading the sports page and hadn't noticed me until I was level with him. He looked up, did a double-take then gasped: 'Are you real?' I replied 'Why not touch me and find out!' He ran back to the castle, presumably looking for a clean pair of Levi's.

*In 2020 during the Covid-19 virus lockdown, Mary Hall from Birtley took her dogs there to walk them. As she threw a ball for them to chase someone grabbed her from behind. She screamed and screamed, yet a hand started to cover her mouth and she began to panic. Her cries were overheard by staff at the castle who came out to find her rolling on the grass as if she was trying to get someone off her. They saw nothing and helped her pull herself together. Mary said "A monk came out of nowhere with wide staring eyes, grabbed me and tried to tear off my clothes. When I fought back, suddenly he was gone! It was one of the scariest things ever to happen to me!"

THE CURSE OF THE MARSDEN GROTTO

It was nearing Hallowe'en when I was told of a classic ghost story set in one of the North East coast's favourite pub/restaurants, The Grotto, between South Shields and Seaburn. The pub wasn't always there, the maze of caves was once the residence of an ex-miner from Allenheads called Jack the Blaster who couldn't afford a home for his wife and family, so moved into the caves. It was said that in around 1788 he carved out the first stairs from the beach up to the clifftop. The stairs carry his name to this day. It would not be long before this sheltered cove became popular with visitors, and now that there was access to the beach, thanks to Jack, it became a place for day-trippers and sightseers. Two hundred years ago this sleepy cove was one of many places used by smugglers to bring illicit goods ashore. The innkeeper knew very well what they were doing, but it was good for business, and often he would buy kegs of ale and rum, at very much reduced rates. Just off the shore stands Marsden Rock, covered with nesting sea birds, and surrounded by water whenever the tide is in. This was used as the cubby-hole by smugglers to hide barrels of booty smuggled ashore until it was safe to move it.

One day a smuggler walked into the inn straight from the beach and ordered a tankard of ale, and was drinking it when in walked a soldier. The smuggler presumed he was the tallyman to arrest him, so he pushed him to the ground and sped along the beach. The soldier got to his feet, aimed his musket and fired. The lead ball struck the smuggler in the back of the neck and he fell dead to the ground.

The landlord emptied the pewter tankard and nailed it to the wall of the bar, built directly into the rock. He said: 'This tankard is cursed. Let no other man drink from it otherwise evil will befall him too!' The ghost of that smuggler returned to the inn every night, and so regular were his visits they would leave him a mug of ale. Every morning that mug was drained of every drop, and the ghost would cause them no trouble.

I decided to investigate this particular story and spent Halloween in the cellar bar. Whilst live broadcasting I took down this pewter tankard, washed out all the spiders and dust of two hundred years, filled it with ale and drank it down. I challenged whatever spirit was there to do its worst. As I expected, nothing happened. I had placed listeners, alone, in other haunted places throughout Britain and an interesting evening of ghostly tales transpired. Throughout the evening the landlord and his wife became more and more nervous about what I had done. He was a portly chap, with a stomach that has sunken many a pint, but he was not prone to flights of fancy. A realistic man who said that the ghost story was good for business, but he didn't really believe it. Even so, his wife seemed to be rather perturbed by any summoning up of people from beyond the grave. Nothing drastic happened that evening, apart from the fact that we'd alarmed a few people with our tales of things that went bump in the night.

So business went on as usual for everyone until three days later the landlord phoned to say that he was in trouble. The wine cellar of The Grotto is a locked room at beach level, it is built into rock with no windows and only one door. The only key is worn around the landlord's neck, and he was sleeping when something woke him. He checked that the burglar alarm was switched on and it was, so he patrolled the premises. He found nothing wrong so returned to bed. On getting up in the morning he opened the door to his cellar to set up the bar for the day ahead. He was shocked to see that all of the metal casks were opened, the corks had popped from hundreds of bottles, cans had exploded and gallons of alcohol flooded out into the bar. The walls looked as if they had been sprayed with green slime, he wasn't sure what this was. The insurance man was called, and could not believe that this was all done by accident, and a battle ensued for him to be recompensed. I thought this strange, but none of my business, I commiserated and said my goodbyes. Then I was told that the landlady had been hit on the back of the head by a flying ashtray. She was alone in the bar when a glass ashtray rose up and crashed into the back of her head causing a lump the size of a goose egg to prove it.

A week to the day of our live outside broadcast, I received another phone call to tell me that the family in The Grotto had watched a black magic rite being carried out on the beach. A group of hooded men and women had sacrificed a chicken, painted symbols with blood on the pub and left the disembowelled thicken hanging from the door. By this time the landlord's wife was having palpitations at every creak of a floorboard, or every time the wind whistled through the timbers.

On the third week after the show there was more ghostly activity, customers felt as if something was pushing them away from the bar. One customer Jack Harris from Whitburn said: 'I was having a bottle of Pils when the glass in front of me slid along the bar and tipped over. No one touched it, and I wasn't drunk, but I know what I saw!'

One month to the day that I visited the pub another phone call informed me of the last straw that had broken the camel's back. The landlord and his lady were getting a good night's sleep, and at seven in the morning were still in the land of nod, when they got their rudest awakening ever. A disturbed young man who had just been dumped by his girlfriend had decided to commit suicide, so he stood on the Marsden cliffs, took one final deep breath and dived headlong towards the rocks below. He never reached them, instead, he plunged through the ceiling of their bedroom, and hung above their bed, bleeding down on them. Within two days they had acquired a pub in the North Riding of Yorkshire, never to return to The Grotto again. Since then things have been very quiet. The publican and his family still leave a pint of ale on the bar each night, and every morning it's gone. It's a small price to pay for peace of mind!

PELTON'S METAMORPHIC SPRITE

If you live in Picktree, near Felton, you may well know of the Picktree Brag. Some say he was a pixie, others a poltergeist, yet all agree he was a complete pain in the backside. He could change shape into any living creature other than a human. Sometimes he would become a horse, and when someone mounted him he would hurl them to the ground, transform back into a sprite and run off laughing. He turned into donkeys, goats, sheep, owls, hawks and once even a dairy cow. He allowed himself to be milked when suddenly he began to urinate into the milk bucket, ruining its contents. Then he turned into a sprite, scaring the dairymaid, who ran off to get her master. As the Picktree Brag was male, I wouldn't like to think how she was milking him!

THE MIRACLE OF THE SUNDERLAND SAND EELS

It was one of those days that makes you just want to roll over and go back to sleep. From around five in the morning, you could hear a monsoon-like rain pound down your windows, flooding gutters and pouring in torrents along the roadway towards the sewers already full to overflowing. Every pothole and dip was filled with water as thousands of people from Hendon forced themselves out into the rain to plod their way to work. It was uncommon to have this amount of rain in August, yet 1918 had been a year of many surprises. The papers were telling of how some women were striking for war wages in London. The Wearsiders thought this was disgusting, as not long before British, American, Canadian, Indian, French and Australian troops had started their final push in Amiens, the Germans had begun surrendering in their tens of thousands, and at last, the war seemed close to an end.

The bus stops were filled with people, the streets heaving with those scurrying forms, trying to get from place to place with the minimum soaking. Yet at that moment a woman screamed, then another, umbrellas were ripped and people bruised by something that felt very sharp, that fell from the sky by the hundred. Close to a thousand sand eels, long dead and as stiff as a board, fell on almost half an acre of ground in that Sunderland suburb. At first, it was believed that they had been pulled out of the sea by a 'twister', and deposited on Sunderland. Had that been the case they would have probably still been alive, but these were long dead. Had they been pulled out of the sea surely fish, shells, weed and so on would have been taken up too? No one has come up with a reason for this since.

THE CAULD LAD OF HYLTON CASTLE

In Sunderland's Wear Valley stands all that's left of the once imposing Hylton Castle, a place responsible for many a ghastly experience over the years. The story began in 1588 when a group of local barons gathered for a feast in the Great Hall. They supped ale by the bucketful, gorged themselves on what seemed an endless supply of partridge, pheasant, quail, venison and beef. The room was throbbing with activity as a quartet of musicians played and the drunken elite sang along tunelessly. Servants scurried to and fro, the girls were goosed and groped by the lecherous crowd, the men taunted and punched in this orgy of the worst kind. The barons believed that they were the superior ones and everyone else must bend to their will or face the consequences. It is frightening to believe that purely by an accident of birth, scum like these controlled much of the North. They had been known to set their hounds on small boys as 'sport' if they couldn't find a fox. If the child was killed it was a 'terrible accident' and 'greatly regretted' and the family would be bought off by the rich men with more money than sense. This may sound vile, yet it still exists in a watered-down form. Each year hundreds domestic dogs and cats are killed by local hunts, often in their own gardens, and it is 'greatly regretted' and 'a terrible accident'. Then a financial settlement is offered.

Those dark days of the sixteenth century also allowed some of the more villainous barons to take a bride's virginity before she was allowed to marry. It was a loathsome practice hated by everyone, yet such was the power of the landowners any sign of dissent could cost humbler folk their homes and futures. If you know the background of this tale, you realise how these spoiled and moronic men gained much gratification from humiliating and shaming hardworking, honest people. It must have been 3.00 am when it was decided to end the Bacchanalian revelry, as these drunks made their way to bed. Up the hard stone staircase, they staggered, vomiting as they went, one baron firmly grasping the hand of a serving wench. He would honour her with his body that night. Despite her screams, she would be raped and none of the staff dared to intercede. It was rare to have so many of the county's rich and famous under one roof at the same time, so a day of sport had been arranged.

It was barely six hours before the boar hunt was due to begin around Penshaw a particularly good spot for such activities. Between 3.00 am and 9.00 am, the castle's staff had to clean the place up, removing the vomit from the floors and then washing them with rose water to remove the smell. Scented candles were lit to take the gut-rotting stench from their nostrils as fifteen men and women laboured to put right the Great Hall. It looked as if a hurricane had ripped the place asunder. The dishes were taken away, food scraps removed from everywhere. Pools of stale urine had to be mopped away from the hall's decorative corners. Halfway through cleaning, the young scullery maid appeared at the top of the stairs, her dress torn and her eye blackened. The baron had bitten into her neck as she had fought him, leaving huge curved teeth marks in her flesh. The old cook cradled her into her buxom chest, as the bairn cried uncontrollably. This was life in the raw. If you had money you made the rules and everyone obeyed you. You didn't have to be fair and just, only rich!

It was nearer 10.00 am when the first of the hungover barons began to appear for breakfast. The staff had not slept for forty-eight hours, they had prepared quails' eggs, pork chops or porridge and still were cursed for being slow. The older staff were conditioned to the long hours, snatching sleep where they could, but the youngsters could barely keep their eyes open.

So when Hylton's lord and master commanded that his horse is saddled in readiness for the hunt, the staff told him that the stableboy had already done that. Little did they know that the child, all of fourteen years old, was fast asleep on a straw bale. The lord became more and more impatient and decided to go to the stable for his horse, as there was still no sign of it coming to him. On getting to the stable he saw the youngster snoring like a buzz saw, and kicked him hard in the stomach. 'I don't pay you to laze around!' growled the lord, still half-sozzled from the night before. 'I'll teach you a lesson you'll never forget!' he screeched and shouted at the child, lashing out with fist and riding crop. He was just about to land a blow squarely to the boy's nose when the lad ducked, allowing the master's fist to smash into a metal bucket with a clang. The lord looked at his scarred knuckles, as tiny trickles of blood ran down into his clenched fist. His fury was welling inside him like a volcano set to explode, and this was the final straw. The boy was trapped in a stall backed against the wall, tears streaming from his eyes as he gazed in terror as the lord's anger detonated. As the boy begged forgiveness he watched as the surly brute of a man picked up a hayfork and hurled it at him. The fork pinned the boy to the wall as he gazed at the man who glared at him. The boy's vision began to fade. Colours melted into one, then suddenly that flicker of light was snuffed. When the lord realised the gravity of his actions he sobered up, unpinned the boy's body from the wall and buried it under a huge mound of hay, placing heavy corn sacks on top so it wouldn't be disturbed. He saddled his own horse and rode into the courtyard exclaiming how he had thrown the stableboy out into the cold, never to return to Hylton Castle. Within the hour the hunt had begun and the episode of the stableboy was put firmly behind him.

Later that night, when all the barons had returned to their homes, Hylton Castle returned to normality. The staff were able to bed down early, and the lord had been almost pleasant to them. Little did they know that late in the night their master would sneak downstairs, across the yard to the barn, to recover the child's lifeless corpse. He was well prepared, he wrapped it in a huge horse blanket so as not to stain his silken shirt with blood, threw it over his shoulder as a butcher would an animal's carcass, and walked towards an old abandoned well. One second his burden was making his shoulder ache, the next the package was falling, down and down until over 150 feet below there was an echoey splash.

There were no strange apparitions until well over twenty years later when Hylton Castle's other well began to give problems and they decided to reopen the original water provider. The baron of Hylton Castle, mindful of what was down there, put off any excavations until it could not be avoided. The workmen were sent down to dig out a new water supply, adding to the depth of the well, and on reaching the bottom, buried in mud and sludge they found the cadaver of the murdered boy. At first, they screamed and yelled, but eventually, they calmed down enough to lash the boy's body, still wrapped in the horse blanket, to the bucket cable and he was winched to the top. An inquest was carried out by the coroner in July 1609 and after hearing the baron's story they decided it was accidental death. Had that boy been killed by any other member of staff they would have been executed the same day, but once again money and power won the day. In September of that year, the baron was pardoned by the courts.

Maybe it was that final injustice that made the stableboy of Hylton, who had forever complained of the cold, return to remind everyone of the wrong done to him. Despite the horrific way that he met his end, he isn't a vengeful spirit and has always been mischievous rather than bad. Sometimes he would just create noises, strange banging and crashing late into the night. Snoring was heard from the barn almost every night.

Everyone believed it was 'the Cauld Lad', yet it was more likely the horses! It surprised everyone when centuries later they got rid of the horses, and the snoring stopped too. Rather than admit that it had been the horses all along, they said that 'the Cauld Lad' had stopped sleeping there once he couldn't use the horses for warmth. The lad's party trick was to wreck tidy rooms. Kitchens, halls and bedrooms were turned upside down by this Wearside Will o'the Wisp. Those that saw him described him as about fourteen, wearing a green cloak and raggy shoes. Many versions of this very old legend tell of how he used to row people over the River Wear, as a spectral ferryman. Occasionally he would disappear as soon as they stepped on board, other times he would remove his head and frighten people so much they leapt into the river rather than look at this horrible sight. Over the years hundreds of people claimed to have been ferried across the river by 'the Cauld Lad of Hylton'. The truth is rather more mundane, the local ferryman, aware of the story, dressed his sons up in a green cloak, and had them playing the part of the Cauld Lad'. Only once was someone brave enough to grab the boy, and on finding he was solid demanded his money back!

* A historian visited Hylton Castle in 1966 with Rosalind Douglas, a medium who knew nothing about the legend of the stableboy, and who began communing with spirits. She told the historian that she could see the bodies of hundreds of murdered peasants hanging from the wall. She saw a ghost too, that of a woman dressed in grey, walking the battlements. She mentioned a knight from the middle ages, unhappy at how he had died in battle, shot by an arrow fired by his own men. Not one shred of truth, not one fact that could be proven.

*Although Hylton Castle is now in ruins I have placed ordinary members of the public there on two occasions. In 1987 a young girl spent the evening there linked to me by walkie-talkie. She was a total sceptic, not believing for one minute that there was such a mischievous ghostly sprite or 'brownie'.

She wrote in her report: '11 o'clock: the castle is very cold, I'm glad I brought my parka, the first hour has passed without incident, although I'm sure that a mouse ran over my foot. I did scream at the time, but I would have done that had it happened in my kitchen in daylight. Midnight: although most of the building is solid stone it does make an awful lot of noise. If it was windy I could understand it. Yet one moment it's so quiet you can hear your heartbeat, the very next second there are creakings and groanings so loud you would not be able to hear yourself speak. Still nothing supernatural though! 1.00 am: my soup flask is empty and I'm still hungry, I wish I'd brought more food. The noises have come and gone, but I feel OK. Bats are flying around overhead, you never hear them but do see strange shapes whizzing across the sky, too small to be birds. The longer I am here the eerier the place appears. I have seen or experienced nothing but I do feel very strongly that a terrible wrong was carried out here. I know the story and realise that this is true. Yet I feel this sadness, I am not unhappy yet I feel this strongly. It's probably just my imagination.'

On getting home in the early hours of that morning Sandra Marshall, a 27-year-old secretary from Newcastle completed the last and most intriguing entry about her four-hour 'expedition'.

'2.00 am: I was standing at the gate to be let out of the castle by the caretaker, a bit disappointed not to have seen anything at all. I had enjoyed myself strangely. It was then I heard footsteps walking down the road and the jingling of keys, I would be back in my car very soon. Yet at that very second, I felt someone tickle me from behind, the way you do when you creep up to someone, one hand squeezing each side of their waist. I must have flown six feet into the air, I screamed and the elderly chap who let me out started running to get the door open. He tried to calm me down, saying: "There, there, don't frighten yourself, there's nothing behind you!" I looked around and there wasn't but at first, I believed that maybe "the Cauld Lad" had been toying with me, allowing me to think there was no one there, then proving his existence at the last possible opportunity. The more hours that pass, the more confused I am, maybe it was my imagination, but I can tell you I have never been more terrified in my life. Yet it was obvious that if this "Cauld Lad" exists, he is a playful sort. Maybe I am going mad, it was the very last thing I expected from the night. Now I certainly will keep an open mind.'

* This pattern proved itself the following year in 1988 when instead of one lady, I allowed two young girls to spend the night of Hallowe'en in Hylton Castle. Once again we were linked by mobile phone (they were very much in their trial stage which caused us a great many problems). The crackling, growling and interference on them made general chit-chat impossible. We were lucky to get anything from them at all. The two girls' names have been lost in my filing system, as it borders between mayhem and total disorder, yet I remember that one of the girls worked with her mother in a fruit shop in a Newcastle suburb, probably Coxlodge. I met the girls at 2.15 am after they had returned to the radio station by taxi, I calmed them down and gave them a coffee. I was joined by the Reverend Joe Poulter who is usually my partner on such forays into the unknown. Joe is a canny bloke, witty, wise and always able to keep his head in times of crisis. We sat next to the girls as they told us quite a bizarre tale that runs an interesting parallel with our experience of the previous year.

'We were messing around, cracking jokes, trying to frighten each other, and drinking coffee from our flask, and nothing had happened. It is creepy being in a castle like that, but we didn't see any spooks or anything. Yet it was about twenty to two when we both decided to split up and have one last look around before being collected at the gate. We were about a hundred yards apart when we both screamed simultaneously and ran back to where our packs were. We were both in an absolute panic. I said to my friend that I had felt as if someone was standing right behind me, I could feel breath on my neck. I could smell that breath too, it stank of rotten cabbage. I heard a noise like you would make if you were trying to frighten them, "uh-huhhhhhh!". I spun around, saw no one there, screamed and legged it. We crashed into each other and fell on the floor. She told me that at precisely the moment I had felt that, she had exactly the same happen to her. At 1.40 am. prompt.'

The following evening I received a phone call from the girls' mother who had listened to the radio show, as the entire thing was broadcast live, and she realised that we were not able to talk to her daughter due to the dodgy mobile phone. So she was enjoying the other strange stories that were being discussed, yet at 1.40 am she sat up in bed and screamed. Her husband was still downstairs listening to the radio, and he ran up to find her shivering and quaking. She said: 'My bairn, something has happened to my bairn!' When I pulled up at her door the entire house was up waiting to make sure she was all right! The coincidences continued the following day, for as mother and daughter worked in the greengrocers', the electric clock stopped at precisely 1.40 pm!

THE SUNDERLAND BODYSNATCHER

One of the strangest ghosts said to walk the yards of Sunderland shipbuilders belongs to arguably Britain's most renowned body-snatcher. William Burke and his partner William Hare provided over five hundred corpses to Edinburgh physicians between 1815 and 1828, yet when the amount of funerals couldn't fill the demand, Burke and Hare took matters into their own hands. They murdered between eighteen and forty-nine people to supplement their graveyard thefts and made a good living out of dying. Iris said William Burke learned his craft in the cemetery of Holy Trinity Church in Sunderland, providing bodies for local doctors to carry out medical research. Many believe that he only left Sunderland when the authorities began preparing a case against him after a young man had died.

William Burke was a Sunderland man who had worked on the banks of the Wear preparing stone to be used in the construction of the pier. It is there that legend begins to merge with fact. It is said that an eighteen year old had slipped whilst working with Burke and had broken his neck. As he had no relatives in the area his body had been placed in a stone storage room until burial could be arranged. After its second night, it mysteriously disappeared and no one could say where it went. A local stonemason had witnessed Burke loading a handcart, and instead of carrying stone towards the horse-drawn carts, he had walked with it in the opposite direction, towards Sunderland town centre.

Burke explained this to his gaffer by saying: 'I needed the cart to move some furniture, having done that I returned to my work.' In the light of his later activities, many believe that he had used the cart to transport his very first victim across Sunderland to a doctor in Hendon.

The site of that workplace on the banks of the River Wear is now a shipbuilder and steel stockholders, and many witnesses say it is haunted. The ghost is said to be that of a stocky, ugly man whose arms appear rather too long for his body. He has been seen on cranes, walking along a variety of steel structures and the most terrifying case was told on 'Night Owls' on Metro FM by a foreman for the firm. Later I caught up with Raymond Phillips, a Seaburn man, who said: 'I was working the backshift, which meant that I had to take my lunch break at about eleven o'clock at night. I was sitting alone in the small wooden cabins provided, chewing away at a cold bacon sandwich when I heard the toilet door slam shut. So I walked outside the cabin to the small toilet and hammered on the door telling whoever was inside to take it easy. There was no answer, so I called out the names of the three lads working for me, and still no answer. I looked across the yard and could plainly see all three lads working away, so pulled the door open thinking I'd trapped an intruder, and there stood an ape of a man. He was crouched over and he ran at me so I lashed out with my fist and with the momentum I tumbled into the toilet and almost cracked my head on the pan. There was no way he could get past me unless he went through me. I'm certain he did!'

GHOST SHIP ON THE WEAR

Plato's crew had been devoured by sharks, and the rest had managed to row their lifeboat from island to island in search of food and water. Each evening they would light a beacon in the hope that they could attract the attention of a passing ship. On one island they were welcomed by a tribe of natives, who provided them with bread, fruit, coconuts and pawpaws, gave them all fresh water and seemed to be very happy with their guests. This was no great surprise, as they were cannibals, fattening up their guests for their own table. On realising their predicament the sailors tried desperately to reach their ship. After a mad dash to the boats they were stopped by the swifter native canoes and herded like cattle back to the shore, where they were cut down by the crazed villagers.

Those who managed to keep ahead of the natives were killed by a hail of arrows. Able Seaman John Collins was the only survivor, despite arrows sticking out of his chest, arms and legs. He watched as the bodies of all his friends including that of his captain were dragged out of the sea and carried ashore. That night as young native girls swabbed his wounds, huge bonfires were erected, and the bodies of Sunderland men were roasted over fires and eaten by over five hundred wild-eyed, dancing natives. The feasting lasted almost a week, and Collins was given meat to eat, but refused, choosing fruit instead.

Some weeks later a Royal Navy vessel was in the area, and on hearing that an Englishman was held prisoner by natives they decided to plan his rescue. They wanted to get a few men onshore to sneak him out of there, but that proved impossible due to a lack of a suitable landing site, so they merely bombarded the native encampment with cannon, until they cleared out and John Collins was brought limping aboard. They listened in amazement to his stories of how 41 of his friends had been devoured by this cruel camp of cannibals and demanded that they take action. This they did that very night, having sailed out of sight, they returned around the cove and let go with an entire broadside of shells peppering the native camp. Round and round they went until the entire camp was flattened. More than content with their night's work the Royal Navy schooner returned to base, putting Collins on the first boat home.

In reports they told of how the entire village of cannibals had been destroyed, this was true but many of the cannibals escaped into the interior. Within eight years seventeen other ships from various ports had gone missing in that vicinity including another ship from Wearside, a tea clipper called the Maitland.

For anyone to claim to see a ghost ship is quite rare, yet to see one and be able to identify it is even rarer. This seaman who witnessed such a thing knew nothing of the fate of the crew of the Plato yet did place it in the mouth of the river that gave it birth. Is that beyond coincidence?

Philip Franks decided to investigate the story and set off into the South China Seas from Hong Kong with a crew made up of Chinese low life, murderers, thieves and vicious assassins. He was determined to see if these cannibals still existed, hoping to sell the story to the press. His vessel was never seen again, fuelling more rumours of how the cannibals were feasting on more Englishmen. The truth was more likely that his own crew killed the man who hired them, then scuttled the ship and returned to shore by longboat.

Franks's mother in Sunderland received a final letter from her son that read: 'Don't worry, this is just another one of my adventures. A journey that will make me a very rich man. As soon as I return to Hong Kong I shall be selling the story and my remaining business interests and coming home to Sunderland!' He was either murdered and fed to the sharks or eaten by cannibals. Whoever got him, I hope they suffered terminal indigestion!

THE FREEMASONRY PLOT

In 1717 the Freemasons established themselves in London, claiming that the organisation had existed since the dawn of time, directly associated with the sons of Adam and King Solomon's master mason Hiram. In fact, it is part of their creed that Hiram was executed by Solomon because he refused to tell him the secrets of his society. The Grand Lodge set itself up in a pub called The Goose and Gridiron in Covent Garden. They sent off many of their 1,400 Freemasons into the provinces to set up lodges there. At first, they were established only among the wealthy. Many rich Christians refused to join, believing many of their rituals to be pagan and appertaining to the Devil and not to Christ.

In 1718 some Freemasons decided to set up a lodge in the outskirts of Sunderland. They had gathered a dozen or so of the wealthiest men and swore that they would help each of them become even richer than their wildest dreams could imagine. On explaining the highly secretive and elaborate ritual, each of them agreed to join. Yet when a noose was placed around the neck of the first man, Terence Somerville, a retailer from Pallion, walked out. He had witnessed the ceremony and had to be dealt with. That evening following the induction, all of the masons gathered outside his home and called him out. He appeared carrying a sword, and told them to go home saying: 'You may have time for these devilish children's games but not me!' At this, he noticed that his home was on fire and he ran inside to rescue his wife and child. As he did so the masons started fires around the front of the house too, and they were all burned to death. The ceremony and the 'Masonic Word', the secret handclasp, remained a secret.

WASHINGTON'S LADY IN RED

In the 1700s there used to be a huge house in a place that is now known as Cooks Wood in Washington. It was said to belong to a soldier who had fought alongside General John Burgoyne who had fought for British interests in America. Following Burgoyne's surrender at Saratoga in October 1777, over six thousand soldiers were captured, including John Taylor, from Cooks Wood. Despite the most civil and courteous treatment by his jailers Taylor suffered a severe fever and died.

On receiving the news, some months later, several family members tried to claim the house as theirs. Taylor had not been married but was engaged to Elizabeth Gill, the daughter of a local farmer. The wedding had been planned for his return. Although she was living in his house, it seemed that Taylor's envious sisters were putting pressure on her to move out. Dorothea and Marjorie Taylor had agreed to share the large house between them.

Elizabeth Gill was inconsolable; not only had her future husband died, but now she was stripped of her home and her future too. It was on the day that she was moving out that disaster struck. Elizabeth was leaving the room that was to be their honeymoon suite when Dorothea began to taunt her. She shouted across the upstairs hall how common she thought Elizabeth was, how her brother must have been mad to fall in love with a 'common peasant' like her. Normally 'a placid soul, Elizabeth snapped and ran at Dorothea and caught her a blow square on the chin, knocking her to the floor, her pantalooned legs waving in the air under her crinolines. At this Marjorie appeared and thrust Elizabeth up against a door jamb and screeched obscenities at her. The farmer's daughter was made of sturdy stuff, and kneed her in the stomach, winding her, then crashed a double-handed blow to the back of her neck. As the shocked sisters looked up at this Rambo in female form, Elizabeth said 'You want me to leave the place that should be my home, yet I will be here a thousand years after you're gone!' At this, she smiled and turned to the huge staircase and dived into space. The sisters gasped in disbelief to hear Elizabeth laughing as she hurtled to her own certain destruction. The laughter ended in a crash as the young girl impaled herself on the banisters' decorative edge, almost fifty feet below.

Shocked and horrified, the Taylor sisters brought in the authorities, who on seeing their injuries, Dorothea's black eye and Marjorie's split lip, presumed that a dirty deed had been committed. Rumours abounded for weeks, but nothing could be proven. So life at the hall returned to normal, until the first anniversary of Elizabeth's death. Dorothea was working on a tapestry when she heard laughter from the upstairs hall. On reaching the bottom of the stairs she looked up to see Elizabeth Gill walking towards what was once her bedroom, wearing a long red silken gown. She rubbed her eyes, and looked again, just in time to see the farmer's daughter make her way into the bedroom. Dorothea rushed into the garden to collect Marjorie and together they climbed the stairs and opened the bedroom door. There standing before them, looking as solid as she ever had been, was Elizabeth Gill. The phantom walked directly towards them, and as she neared the sisters could see almost straight through her skin, the outline of her skull was plain to see. 'I told you this is my house, get ye gone!' At this, the ghost held up its fists and strode menacingly towards them. The two sisters crashed into the door opening, fighting with each other to get through first. They ran towards the stairs when Marjorie stepped on the hem of her own dress and tumbled, Dorothea crashing into her, and they both fell onto the balcony rail. The sheer weight of the sisters cracked the wood and they burst through into space. Marjorie shouted 'Bugger me!' as she plummeted to meet the same fate as Elizabeth Gill. Dorothea had been marginally more fortunate, managing to cling to the rail, as she dangled precariously over the stairwell. Despite her bulky gown she was managing to pull herself up when out of the bedroom stepped the lady in red. 'What are you waiting for?' asked the spirit. 'I'm waiting for you in hell!' Dorothea's face whitened and her hands just seemed to lose the will to hold on as she slipped away. The silence of her fall was truly amazing. It was almost as if in slow motion as her billowing underskirts failed to stop her landing on her sister's broken body. They lay there together, entangled around the very bannister where Elizabeth had died. After this event, no one offered to buy the Hall. It went into decay and was demolished in the early 1800s. Cooks Wood is still said to have the ghost of the lady in red.

*Mrs Rose Duggan from Albany in Washington told me: 'I have visited Cooks Wood ever since I was a little girl, and knew all about the ghost. I have seen her on at least thirty occasions since I was about seven. She isn't scary or anything, she just walks past you, smiling and almost laughing, but you never hear anything! I know you'll think I'm crackers but I have seen her.'

*In July 1991 an anonymous caller from Washington told a radio audience that he had once witnessed a strange red light floating through the trees of Cooks Wood. It had no particular shape but was bright red.

WASHINGTON: THE GHOSTLY PILOT OF NISSAN

Nissan's gigantic factory was constructed on the old site of Washington airport, used by pilots during World War II and long afterwards. The ghost is believed to be that of a Canadian pilot George Hamilton, who died in one of two ways. He either crashed his aircraft during take-off, exploding into the hangar, or he was actually standing on the roof of the hangar and fell off. Having spoken to three different contacts, the most likely was the crash on take-off. The ghost currently haunts the old Lamella hangar and has been witnessed by staff in the old Flying Club a good few times. Despite never having visited the cellar in his lifetime, Hamilton often makes his presence felt down there, while barrels are being changed. We tried to find where George Hamilton was buried, as the majority of those killed on or near the airfield are buried in Castletown Cemetery yet there is no trace of him there. Andrew Parkin of the Aircraft Museum nearby said, 'We think he must have been flown back to Canada for burial.'

*A fireman was once locking up the hangar for the night and caught a glimpse of a man, dressed like a pilot, hovering about a foot from the ground.

*It is said that the Nissan guard dogs will not go near this particular hangar!

*One man who works at Nissan, who prefers not to give his name, said: 'I have seen the pilot three times, and have taken some stick for saying so, I can tell you! I think a lot of the blokes now believe in him but haven't the guts to speak out. He's about 6 foot 1 inch tall with brown hair, blue eyes, and a bit of a moustache. I walked into him just about, we were eye to eye. I presumed it was someone else who worked here. Then when we nodded at each other, I turned and saw he was wearing air masks hanging around his waist, and a flying suit. As I watched he just faded away and I nearly s**t myself!'

THE SILKIE OF WASHINGTON HALL

One of the buildings visited by most Americans in the north of England is Washington Old Hall, filled with memorabilia of the early days in America's history. It was given prestige when the then President Carter visited it, and said: 'It's a great place, a piece of home abroad!' Yet it has a 'grey lady' that glides along its long corridors upstairs, and in 1977 she literally passed through a cleaner. The cleaner was spraying polish onto the wood panelling when she saw a woman in a long dress sweeping towards her. She didn't have time to move or get out of her way, and the figure passed straight through her.

*There is a painting of an unknown woman in Washington Old Hall; she is believed to be the spectre.

THE WHITBURN POLTERGEIST

It seems that poltergeists have chosen to live on the North-East coast rather than other parts of the country. The Bloxham family suffered at the hands of such a phenomenon in 1983. Three different newspapers covered the events, plus a story featured on Metro Radio.

It all started one day when William Bloxham was walking outside his pub The Jolly Sailor in Whitburn and a huge electric lantern crashed from the wall on to his head, which later needed several stitches. A door slammed into his face, and his wife was in the bathroom when a cabinet crashed on to the floor absolutely terrifying her. There were countless strange oozings, odd smells, plumbing problems, fires, electrical difficulties and then a variety of inexplicable noises. The Bloxhams were convinced that they were haunted, though some regulars thought it beyond belief.

TYNE & WEAR

• Ebchester
• Beamish

R. Derwent

• Whaskley Moor
Langley Hall
DURHAM
• Brancepeth
• Shotton Colliery

R. Wear

DURHAM

Hartlepool

• High Force
Witton Castle
Bishop Auckland
• Ferryhill
R. Skerne
• Sedgefield

NORTH SEA

• Bishopton
Stockton on Tees
MIDDLESBROUGH
Redcar
Handale •
Guisborough

R. Tees

DARLINGTON
Teesside Airport

• Stainmoor Forest

• Sockburn

NORTH YORKSHIRE

DURHAM AND TEESSDIDE

THE SHEPHERD AND SHEPHERDESS AT BEAMISH

Beamish Open Air Museum is renowned throughout the world as one of the finest ways to take a trip back in time, seeing the old North as it really was. They have bought old homes, reconstructing them on the site brick by brick. With the old shops, a drift mine, funfair, farm and working steam railway, it is no surprise that it has won many plaudits. Yet just along the road stands a public house called The Shepherd and Shepherdess with matching statues. Having viewed the museum, so accurate in every detail, you may spot that these statues are standing on the wrong plinths. The Shepherd is on the Shepherdess's stand, and vice versa.

It is said that every night these two statues came to life and ran across the road into the woods to dance with the fairies. They did this every night for years until one evening they had enjoyed themselves too much, and the sun began to rise. So the Shepherd and Shepherdess rushed back to the pub and jumped back onto the pedestals. However, in their haste, they mounted the wrong ones and they remain frozen there to this day.

THE BISHOP AUCKLAND BOAR

Talk to any fisherman and he'll be swift to tell of a monster pike as large as a house that lurks in a particular stretch of water. Every hunter has a similar story of a giant stag, a monstrous moose or a giant elephant on the Kenyan veldt. Such was the case around Bishop Auckland amongst the boar-hunting fraternity, in this case, an eight-foot-long killer boar with tusks up to eight inches long that had taken many lives. He was known as the Pollard Worum', said to be an Old Norse phrase for monster or dragon.

Many hunters had started to hunt the local wild pigs, only to become the hunted themselves. Many stories told of hunters being tipped off their horses by this devilish hog. On one occasion a most gallant knight was thrown from his horse when it confronted a mighty wild pig. As the knight lay on the ground, unable to get up for the weight of his armour, the pig rammed him over and over and over again, knocking the life out of him. The king was made aware of this monstrous beast stealing the lives of his knights and offered a huge reward to anyone able to bring its stuffed head to the palace. The Bishop of Durham had lost over twenty of his congregation to the creature, and so added a further sum to the king's booty.

It was a young man called Pollard, a hunter from Bishop Middleham, who came forward to take up the challenge. Other bounty hunters had tried, only to be gored to death by this huge animal so adept at turning the tables on any human pursuing it. Pollard tracked the creature to a hollow on the outskirts of Byers Green where it was feasting on the body of a young farmer. Standing above the creature on an outcrop of rock he hurled a net over it, entangling the beast and leaving it lying there helpless. Having climbed down he drew his broadsword and held it above his head ready to strike when a smaller boar ran hard into his legs, knocking him face down upon the beast. It whipped and turned its head trying to kill Pollard with its tusks, but he was too agile and grasping at his sword he stuck the hard blade into the beast's neck.

Again and again, he hammered the sword blade home, hacking the ensnared hog into pieces. Lost in the bloodlust that often comes with life-and-death struggles he was unable to return to the king with the creature's head. It lay in hundreds of pieces. Only the long tongue remained, over a yard long, and Pollard set off to London to claim his prize. The king refused to believe his story and would not pay up.

The Bishop of Durham lived up to his part of the deal, giving Pollard a patch of land and presenting him with a new broadsword, blessed and ready to protect the people of Durham should they ever need his services again.

THE CURSED LAND OF BEAMISH

In the year 1293, the Vikings were seeking ways to hit back at Britain after a couple of notable defeats; they were known as the 'Wild Men of the North', even getting their title 'Norsemen' from an old Northumbrian cry 'Beware it's the North Men'. Well, that year they gathered their longships all with bright sails and headed for Lindisfarne, the Holy Island. The monks had been alerted by local fishermen and began running along the causeway. Fortunately, the tide was out. The Vikings landed, sacked the monastery and slaughtered as many monks as they could, this was the first of many more invasions to come. The Vikings had a favoured method of intimidation. They would invade a church and capture a Christian priest. Then in front of his church, they would strip him naked, hold him down and skin him alive, taking great care to keep him conscious as the razor-sharp blade scooped under the skin until it was all off except the head. Some Norwegians say that if the priest had been brave and had not squealed too much, they would finish him with a stab to the throat. If, however, he had cried or shown signs of weakness, they would continue skinning his face and scalp, gouging out his eyes as they did. The blanket of human flesh was then folded up and nailed to the door of his church as a warning for what they could expect when the Vikings returned. Some years later, a group of Vikings, who had pretty much stripped coastal towns and villages bare, decided to strike inland to see what they could steal. Usually, it was gold artefacts, women and livestock, in that order, Three longboats had landed in what is now Dunston on the River Tyne, and started a forced march to the town that is now Chester-le-Street. At the time, it was a busy market settlement that attracted traders from all over northern England. Yet as the Vikings had no map and guessed their whereabouts, they instead entered a small village, barely half a dozen wooden huts by a small stream on land that is now next to Beamish Hall. Locals from nearby farmsteads had run away into the forests, or they had armed themselves to defend their land and women from the invader. The Vikings numbered around 120, and even though almost three times that number had gathered to fight them, the battle was no contest. The Vikings, all trained killers armed with double-headed axes, longbows and swords were the comfortable victors against farmers with scythes, clubs and crudely carved wooden spears. There was a trail of blood and bodies stretching over a mile and a half, as the Vikings not only fought through them but on reaching that stream they washed, raped women and then turned back to their boat with what little booty they had managed to snatch.

As they wearily plodded through the heavy countryside, they were attacked again by a dozen heavily armed men, but the Vikings soon overwhelmed them. The leader, a brown-haired, heavily freckled man called Malcolm was captured wearing a round Viking helmet and carrying one of their swords. In his pack around his waist, there were eight human noses and a hand, presumably, they were evidence of his Viking kills, in exchange for a bounty. It was soon evident that profit rather than defence of their realm inspired this group. The Scandinavians decided that this man would suffer their most terrible vengeance. Firstly, they staked him to the ground, hammering crude wooded pins into his hands, holding him to the ground. They ripped open his shirt and cut him open from his breast bone to his navel, as his intestines rolled out of his stomach into a slithering, slippery mess on the grassy floor. Then they tore his rib cage apart, so he resembled a spread eagle, this is where the phrase derives. The rib cage was folded back and broken as their victim lay awake but in agony. None of us could possibly imagine. Then the raw flesh was sprinkled with salt to increase the pain, then the Vikings spat on his insides and left him to die. Although this was easily bad enough, what probably happened would be even worse, as the hungry dogs that scavenged to survive from the local villages almost certainly would have found him and eaten him alive. Their muzzles scooped out the salted meat from his stomach cavity whilst the helpless man could do nothing but watch.

Three remaining crews marched home pretty much empty-handed, tired, bloodied and not in the best of moods. This was unfortunate for the hundreds of friends and family who thought the Vikings had gone, so they crept out of the hills and forests to tend the wounded and, recover what livestock they could. Some were putting their homes back together when the Men of the North were suddenly among them. Unarmed and defenceless, they had no choice but to surrender. Over fifty local women were taken back to Norway, many with children. Any men aged 14 and over were put to the sword. The Vikings believed it was more honourable for them to die, and they would not be waiting for them on their next trip to farm the people of northern England.

From the Norman Conquest up until 1268, Lord de la Leigh was Lord of Beamish. All this during the reign of King Richard. Many northern knights fought with him against the French. It was there Richard's gallantry won him the title 'Coeur de Lion' the Lionheart. None of these knights ever returned home and their wives and lovers waited and waited, yet never see their loved ones again. This became the thread woven into the history of Beamish Hall, for it is littered with tales of unrequited love and an unbelievable longing that seems to have soaked into the very stone walls of the place.

In 1268, Lord de la Leigh allowed his daughter to marry Sir Guiseard de Charron, Knight of Northumberland, and the Hall was given as a dowry or 'marriage portion', on payment of a single penny at the nativity before the wedding service. It was common at that time for many noblemen to be of French ancestry as England had been occupied by the Normans (French) for over a hundred years.

Sir Guiseard de Charron's son took over his fathers estates. Eventually, they gave the Hall to his daughter Joan on her marriage to Sir Bertram Monboucher, another Knight of Northumberland in 1309. Many of Monbouchers men would fight alongside King Edward the Second, or Longshanks, 'the hammer of the Scots', and it was he who had given John Sage his first commission as Lieutenant, long before he became torturer at Chillingham Castle following his disablement.

Yet Monbouchers life, it seems, was not a happy one, certainly not domestically. It is believed that this arranged marriage was not of Joan's choosing and that she had been, what Monboucher described as 'an icy mare'. Some say the sudden cold spells found in Beamish Hall are caused by her spirit trying to run from the husband she loathed.

Yet, they had children and five generations of them lived in the majestic Beamish Hall. They say that none of them particularly loved their men, and the building acted like a sponge soaking up all of that dissatisfaction and a longing to find true love. The building has a mood all of its own. It is blissfully romantic, yet if met with a love that is not true, it seems to react against it.

On the death of the very last Monboucher in 1400, the building passed on to a sister Isabella, the wife of Robert Harbotel who was Grand Sheriff of Northumberland. He was responsible for agreeing on a law to hand over heretics to the secular authorities in 1401. Over the next twenty years, he permitted the witchfinders to pin and burn over forty witches. At Beamish, a pyre was built in 1405 and six young women, all denying any involvement with witchcraft, were tied to a tree and burnt alive. Rumours of the time claimed that Harbotel and one of his closest friends had had relationships with these girls and they had conspired to blackmail them. The problem was easily solved as the torch-lit the kindling at their feet. There are regular sightings of strange lights, white-faced women hiding behind trees and dreadful shrieking late at night, right here at Beamish.

On her deathbed in 1450, the estates became the property of Bertram Harbotel of Sutton on Trent. Eleanor Harbotel married Sir Thomas Percy, youngest son of Henry, the fifth Earl of Northumberland who was executed at Tyburn in 1537 for his part in a rebellion. This was part of 'The Pilgrimage of Grace' where many noblemen fought against King Henry the Eighth. The King decreed that many Catholic clergies were 'profound, bawdry, drunken knaves', more obsessed with money and wealth than serving God. This was, in essence, reasonably true and gave Henry the chance to create his church, the Church of England. Any nobles who rebelled against the new order were hung by the neck until they were dead.

Eleanor sought mercy for her husband, at last, a Beamish woman who truly loved her man. She would never see him again and stayed in misery at the Hall, dying of a broken heart. Her sobbing is commonplace on the upper floors where she often shows herself to those who share her melancholy mood.

Beamish Hall then became the property of her son Thomas, Earl of Northumberland, who was beheaded on the pavement at York in 1572 for leading the Northern Rising in 1569. Thomas had a girl he had sworn to marry waiting for him, all that returned was his head in a bloody grey sack, as the Crown confiscated the bulk of his land and kicked her out on her ear.

In 1572, Queen Elizabeth the 1st, the Virgin Queen gave Beamish Hall and the estates to Sir Henry Gate who had suppressed the rising and stayed loyal to her. His son would later sell the Hall to Henry Jackman of London. Already, the Hall was known for ghostly activity, and many reported sightings of strange entities, odd noises and unearthly screams. Perhaps this had been the reason it was sold to someone who had no idea of its bloody history. Eventually, the Jackmans sold the estate to Sir William Wray who died in 1628. His son Thomas was a colonel in the service of King Charles the First. On losing the Battle of Worcester to Oliver Cromwell's Roundheads, the estates were again forfeit and claimed by the state. Many Royalists were taken from Beamish Hall, jailed, tortured and later 'disappeared'. As the Hall was taken over, all of their wives were dragged out and made homeless.

Twenty years later, George Wray, the brother of Thomas, repurchased the Hall only to see his son sell it on to Major William Christian of Unerigg, Cumberland in 1671. Many claimed he was a cruel man who beat his wife and regularly abusing chamber staff. It was believed that some of his money funded slavers belonging to the Royal African Company who captured people in Sallee, Morocco for sale in the Caribbean to plantation owners. You could buy a man for £15, a woman for as little as £5 and a child for a shilling.

In 1682, Major Christian sold the place to Timothy Davison. He became Lord Mayor of Newcastle and knew Christian as he was Governor of the Merchants Company of Newcastle who had dealings with the more established businesses of the wealthy Major.

His son William Davison lived at Beamish Hall with his first wife Elizabeth, an aggressive pairing that would lead to five children and an acrimonious ending. His second wife Dulcibella was the daughter of John Morton, Rector of Sedgefield with whom he had five more children. She was said to be a rather dull but obedient woman, quite the opposite of his spirited first wife. Their daughter Mary lived at the Hall with her husband Sir Robert Eden in 1739. The Edens lived there up until 1904 when on the death of Mr Slingsby Eden, who choked in his sleep the estate passed to Captain Slingsby Duncombe Shafto.

He was succeeded by the famous Mr Robert D Shafto. The song 'Bobby Shafto' was the story of his life and begat a story of heartbreak that still lingers at the Hall. 'Bobby Shafto went to sea, silver buckles on his knee, he'll come home & marry me, bonny Bobby Shafto' Well he did fall in love with a beautiful if rather poor local girl, she was head over heels too with this fine, handsome man. He was rich too, what a bonus for a girl from a family of potato growers. Yet he had to prove himself as a man and decided he would go to sea and would return to marry her. Off he went and after almost three years returned to his home Beamish Hall. His beloved had stayed true and waited for him, but on his travels, he met another woman from a wealthy family and vowed to marry her. His poor girlfriend was bereft, destroyed, humiliated and desperate. She went to the gates of the Hall to try and see the man who had loved her, begging to be heard. Well, Bobby Shafto's new bride to be, heard that his ex-girlfriend wanted to see him and ordered staff to keep her out. One day she managed to slip into the estate and into the house too. A search was called to find her and throw her out. Terrified and yet determined to get her man back, she raced down into a cellar room, that had once been a dungeon. She heard footsteps behind her so climbed into an old trunk until they had gone. Unfortunately, the old box had a latch that had clicked shut. She was trapped in a part of the Hall where no one regularly went. No one knows how long it took her to die, almost thirty years later, the partly mummified body was found lying among old wedding dresses stored in the old trunk. The soul of this trapped girl is the most commonly experienced phenomenon that Beamish Hall has to offer. Regular sightings have been reported for over a hundred years. During a radio show, 'Grisly Trails' dozens, photographed entities and felt a presence as the ghost seems to enjoy the notoriety of her great unrequited love.

Now Beamish Hall is used for weddings and it seems the irony of this is not lost on the spirits that reside there. They love love, and it is said that those who celebrate their wedding night in the Bridal Suite enjoy the greatest sex ever. As the energies trapped in the Hall, all desperate to love and be loved, generate an amazing charge.

In recent times there have been reports of water running without reason, noises of parties when the entire building is empty, glasses flying off counters and smashing, visions sitting at chairs and people being touched by unseen hands. Most recently a photograph was taken of a bride and bridesmaid floating in mid-air.

THE FAERY FOLK OF BISHOPTON

The nearest most of us get to meeting a fairy face to face is when we're young and have a tooth out at the dentist. Then we place it under the pillow and find the tooth fairy has rewarded us with ten pence, fifty pence or a pound, depending on whether the tooth fairy is working or not!

My father wears false teeth and told me that one night he fell asleep with his head under the pillow and the fairy took all of his teeth out. Whether we choose to believe or not is not the point, for it is catalogued in books around the world that one of the largest faery colonies in the world was at Bishopton in Teesdale, on Castle Hill. People travelled from as far as Asia and America to see thousands of tiny burrows cut into the hillside, supposedly the tiny pathways used by the faery folk.

The local people have heard strange music from the hillsides late in the evening, seen the tiny lights of minute campfires, and watched in wonder as thousands of tiny bodies whirled and danced to the weird music. The first Northumbrian pipes were said to have been invented 'to create the sounds made by the Bishopton Faeries'.

BRANCEPETH: BOBBY SHAFTO AND THE LOVE HE LEFT BEHIND

A fragile young woman called Mary Bellises was a most insecure girl, always believing that she wasn't quite as good as everyone else. She lived in the family home at Brancepeth, Durham, with her father and mother, where she kept herself very much to herself. The truth of the matter was that she was an heiress with a bone china complexion, who had she had the personality, would have been the toast of the North East. She fell in love with a rather more worldly man by the name of Robert Shafto, who was loud and adventurous, always dreaming about foreign travel and the times he would have.

They became very close, and he would revel in telling her tales of the great travellers, and how he would have loved to emulate them. Soon an understanding was reached that was unspoken. They would indeed marry, but only once Shafto had sampled the life of the adventurer. So he arranged to board ship and sail to strange exotic ports, sampling the wild life aboard the tall ships. He sailed from the Wear and young Mary wept as she saw him waving back at her from the ship's stern. Bobby Shafto went to sea, with silver buckles on his knee. She believed that he would return to marry her. He had sworn to her that he would return, and some years hence he did. Within weeks of his ship docking, he married someone else. Shafto did well for himself too, eventually becoming MP for Durham between 1760 and 1768. Young Mary Bellises died of a broken heart, her love unrequited. It is said that the silken dresses often heard rustling along the streets of Brancepeth belong to this sad young girl.

DARLINGTON'S CURSE OF ST BARNABAS

June 11 is St Barnabas' Day, and normally these pious saints protect people and allow them to do very much what they want. Yet on the outskirts of Darlington, close to the River Tees, there are four deep, murky pools known to the locals as 'Hell's Kettles', the last known resting place for a farmer and his entire family.

A poor Darlingtonian had gathered together his crops for the great market, but could not manage to finish collecting all of the vegetables until St Barnabas' Day. He knew that he had to get them to the market or his competitors would make all the money, and he would not have enough to feed his family for the rest of the year. So he ordered his entire family to load his four hay wagons with all of the produce, barrels of corn, corn cobs, carrots, peas, potatoes, apples, pears, lettuces etc. It had been a great year, and each wagon was full to capacity.

A local monk warned them that it was St Barnabas' Day, and all pious people must not work. So desperate were they to survive that the entire family, men, women and children, ignored his warning and headed into Darlington where the market would begin in the morning. As they neared the Darlington suburbs, almost in sight of where the market would be held the ground opened up beneath them, sending all four wagons and all the people upon them down into Hell. The holes eventually filled up leaving what is known as 'Hell's Kettles'.

TOUCH OF THE DEAD

One of the most common legends attached to Beamish Hall is that of the witches coven based in woods behind the hall. This was one of the countries leading covens for almost 200 years from 1650 until around 1780 over two hundred years of Satanic worship and the wood is now permanently stained. Whilst most witches and Pagans were peace-loving, this coven was one of the very few that had a history of human and animal sacrifices. Those who often travelled between stately homes begging for alms gave Beamish a wide berth, not because the hall owners were inhospitable, purely because they had heard the stories of what happened to those who walked the woods nearby.

In several local church manuscripts of the time, there are details of those the church refused to bury in sanctified ground. Instead, they were buried beneath the trees in the woods. In the early 1700s they found a horse hacked open and staked out surrounded by Satanic symbols, goats horns (the symbol that they had raised the Devil) nailed to a tree. That tree is said to be still there, high in its branches the goat's horns overseeing the land and keeping it a place sacred to 'dark walkers'. So severe were the stories of the dark arts that in the late 1700s the ground was blessed by the Bishop of Durham. From that day the spirits of the dead began to show themselves between the trees and scaring locals by touching them. Many felt pushed or stroked by unseen hands. During an experiment in 1984, thirty people stood in various areas of the wood and closed their eyes, holding their arms outstretched. After one hour, twenty-three had felt something, it made the local press and brought many to a search of spirit in this area, ground the Christians now consider sacred, as do witches... it is doubly blessed.

THE DURHAM FORCEFIELD

Readers of Newcastle's premier morning paper, the Journal, may remember the weird case of Dilys Cant and her strange episode at a car park in Durham City. It took place on 7th December 1975, when Dilys was visiting the city to purchase some Christmas presents and some clothes and drove into the parking area close to the centre. Finding a car parking space in Durham can be tricky at the best of times but towards Christmas it can be almost impossible. Once I saw a man lying face down in a car parking space. When I asked if he were alright, he replied: 'Yes, I'm fine, but it's taken me two hours to find a car parking space, so the wife's gone home for the car!'

So Dilys was indeed fortunate to find a vacant spot and drove past it to reverse in. On doing so she felt a bump to her back wheels, as if she had hit a kerb, or run over a cone. So she got out of the car and took a closer look, but there were no obstacles at all. Her daughter stepped out and walked towards the parking space and bumped into something she would later describe as a 'forcefield'. As it was impossible to get into that space, Dilys drove out and watched as other motorists latched onto the space. But they couldn't drive into it. One bent his rear bumper trying to do so. Two days following the incident, representatives of Durham Council went to investigate. By this time the parking space was back to normal and had a car sitting in it!

DURHAM: THE STORY OF MARY O'BRIAN

During the darkest days of the Great War, there were many horrific stories, tales of terror and death, yet none come close to this.

Mary Delaney had come to live in England with her two brothers when her parents had died in County Cork in 1911. Life was far from easy. She had tried her hand at a variety of jobs, serving in shops, grafting in factories and working as a barmaid. In 1913 she met and married a soldier, John O'Brian. Her life suddenly began to blossom, and they settled in a small village on the outskirts of Durham City. Mary believed that she was the luckiest woman in the world. She was madly in love with a good man, had a home of her own, her brothers lived nearby and she could finally put the struggle and squalor behind her.

The August Bank Holiday of 1914 was one the family would never forget. John O'Brian had taken his wife and two brothers to Whitby to sample the cockles and mussels, play football on the beach and spend a happy evening in the pub. Too drunk to go home, they stayed at a boarding house and John and Mary celebrated their first-ever night away from home. Money was still tight and they were determined to squeeze as much pleasure as they could from this amazing Bank Holiday weekend. On returning home they sat around the O'Brian kitchen table full of excited chatter about their summer adventure. It was then that the bombshell broke, the Prime Minister Herbert Asquith declared war on Germany, and within days John O'Brian would be sent to France as part of the British Expeditionary Force led by Field Marshal Sir John French. Surprisingly there was euphoria on the streets, huge crowds gathered and sang, every one certain it would be all over by Christmas. Drawn by the wave of patriotism two young Irish boys, Mary's brothers Pat and Philip Delaney, joined up as soon as they were able. Amidst the optimism, Lord Kitchener had warned that the war could turn out to be a long, drawn-out struggle, and very soon he would be proven right.

Mary O'Brian was filled with terror, for every single person who meant anything to her was off in a foreign land fighting for their lives. The neighbours tried to help her cope with the worry and anxiety, but it ate away at her, and as the war completed its first year the reality of what could happen hit her.

The daily routine for everyone in the village was to rush to the local church where the names of those lost in action or wounded were affixed by an official from the council. In silence, the crowds of men, women and children waited until the man in the suit, stiff-collared shirt and pencil line moustache tacked the three hand written sheets to the noticeboard. Day in, day out the fear worsened. Entire families were on the verge of nervous breakdowns, and the churches filled with the masses begging the Lord to spare their husbands, brothers, fathers and sons.

Despite Mary O'Brian knowing that her brothers and her beloved John had survived almost four years of the bloodiest war in history, she still had this anticipation of doom. The fiery flame hair had turned to white with worry, the soft-voiced colleen had become a shrieking banshee, and most of her friends would avoid her when they could.

It was on a chilly Sunday morning, 12th May, that Mary waited at the church hall for the lists to be posted. There on the list was her older brother Philip, he had been killed on the Western Front at Amiens having choked to death by mustard gas. Mary cried for weeks and was slowly coming to terms with the fact that her big brother wasn't coming home when a neighbour hammered on her door. Pulling herself together as best she could, she opened the stiff wooden door. She found herself being dragged towards the church, where another list had appeared. Dizzy and confused, almost drunk with grief Mary read down the list, and there was the name Pat Delaney. He was lost in action, drowned in the thick mud during the Allied counter-attack on the Western Front on 18th June 1918. The scream surely could be heard back in Cork. A doctor gave her a sleeping draught, and she remained in a local cottage hospital for nearly a month. The tender loving care didn't seem to be able to rescue Mary from the dreamlike state her torture had driven her into.

The war was finally coming to an end, the nurses took every opportunity to reassure her that her darling man would be home within weeks. At last, this began to hit home, Mary started to regain the thread of hope and every news report seemed more and more positive. The Allies had broken through German lines, Bulgaria had surrendered, Lawrence of Arabia had galloped into Damascus, it was inevitable that Germany would surrender soon.

On Bonfire Night Mary spent her first night at home in months, cleaning, polishing, washing, making sure the house was ready for the return of her conquering hero. On 11th November her heart soared, the shackles of fear were smashed wide open, Germany had surrendered! Mary worked through the night on a new dress, made from the scraps of material she'd collected over the months. The world stopped on 15th November, factories, shops and offices closed their doors, the war was over. The centre of every town and city was jammed with people singing, dancing and waving flags. Durham was no different – in the market square thousands gathered to celebrate, in the centre of it Mary waving a Union Jack and singing the National Anthem. Sharing a drink with strangers, treating everyone as if they were old friends, the gush of relief fuelled the most amazing party Durham had ever seen.

The following morning Mary was awoken by a knock on the front door. Glancing through the curtains of her upstairs bedroom window she saw an army uniform. Grabbing her dressing gown she ran down the stairs to greet her husband returned from the war. She threw the door open so hard it crashed against the wall, and was about to dive into his arms when she saw it wasn't her husband. It was the son of a neighbour, asking her to go with him to the church. She presumed it was a celebration service, so quickly dressed and accompanied the young man. On getting to the church she was drawn to the list roughly pinned to the board. Four men had died of influenza on a troopship on its way home. One of those men was John O'Brian.

The news failed to register, and when Mary was told again she ran back home, dashed inside and closed the door.

Mary didn't cry, she simply gathered all of her husband's letters, photographs and mementoes, the photograph of her brothers horsing around in the sea at Whitby, the orange faded picture of her parents and her wedding dress. All her memories of the joyous times surrounded her. It was then that she walked into the back yard to the shed, where she picked up a long-handled axe and walked back inside. She wedged the axe between two heavy armchairs with twine, and after saying a short prayer she threw herself onto the axe. Her head was almost severed, hanging onto her body by a grisly thread. The blood and there was much of it, poured down onto the photographs and letters, oozing into the paper as the family became one again, united in death.

Concerned neighbours found her body the following day, and within the week she was buried. Mary knew that a John O'Brian had died, but it was not *her* John O'Brian. Husband John had landed with other troops in Southampton and was on his way home. John had become used to death, but it was over now, no more pain, no more blood, no more horror. He turned his key in the door, and neighbours gasped as they saw the burly soldier return from the grave. On finding the crimson stain on the carpet he asked what had happened, and his world crashed. The victory he had suffered to win was worthless, the light in his heart had gone out.

Even in that small Durham village, they were aware that war had changed many men, often pushing them over the edge into madness. John O'Brian was enveloped by his sorrow and refused to leave the house for months. Then suddenly neighbours heard laughing, John's voice in conversation and music being played on the piano. It was as if the house had burst into life again. John O'Brian was seen walking up the road to the local shops laughing and joking, the only thing wrong being that he was by himself. He'd say hello to everyone he passed and became engrossed in conversation with his non-existent companion. The local policeman was informed and was urged into action by concerned neighbours.

At 3.30 pm on Wednesday 11th December the policeman visited John at his home and took him into custody. It was thought he should be placed in a sanatorium for his own good. While the officer waited for a doctor to attend, John O'Brian said from his cell: 'Mary won't let you keep me here! She'll get me out!' The policeman nodded, feeling so very sorry for the shellshocked soldier. That evening at 8 o'clock the door to the tiny police station burst open, papers flew in all directions and the surprised policeman ran to secure the doors. Thinking it to be a freak gust of wind he collected the various reports scattered across the floor. He looked up to see John O'Brian looking down at him, his cell door was open and he walked calmly to the door. 'I told you Mary would come for me!' said the grinning soldier. The policeman tried to grab him, but something pushed his hand away, he tried again and again only to find himself thrown back against a wall.

He couldn't move until John O'Brian was out of the building. Darting to the window he watched as his prisoner walked down the dimly lit street, seemingly with his arm around someone. The police-man's heart was already beating so loudly he could hear it, so when the doctor arrived the following morning he decided to hand the entire case to him. The doctor noted John O'Brian's address and said he would call on him that very weekend.

Almost a week later that police officer received the doctor's report, which read: 'I visited John O'Brian today at his home, both he and his wife made me very welcome. We chatted at great length and I can assure you he does not need a sanatorium. The O'Brians merely need a little time to put their lives in order again.' A shiver involuntarily rocked the constable, and he chose not to investigate further. From that day on neighbours would often catch a glimpse of Mary O'Brian at the window, and would hear her singing or laughing. They became so used to her they would always send her a Christmas card and gift, and she always reciprocated. I was told this tale by Catherine O'Brian, their daughter!

SANCTUARY DENIED IN DURHAM

The huge lion-headed door knocker on Durham Cathedral is renowned for offering sanctuary to anyone who needs it. All a man had to do was grasp the metal ring and cry 'Sanctuary' and the staunchly religious folk of the late 1700s and early 1800s would respect God's will, and allow the person to seek refuge inside.

Things didn't quite work out that way for Mad Jack who lived in a tiny lean-to he had built near the Mill House on the Wear in Durham city. Everyone knew Mad Jack and had a lot of affection for him, as he was a harmless soul. He learning difficulties, acting like an eight-year-old rather than his forty or so years. This all supposedly stemmed from his birth: his mother was also his sister, who had been involved in an incestuous relationship with her own father, giving birth to Jack while barely thirteen years of age.

Even though everyone knew that Jack wouldn't hurt a fly, there had been talk that he had accidentally pushed a young girl into the river. She hadn't hurt herself much, but her mother was shocked and tried to get Jack run out of town. Within a fortnight or so the fuss had died down, and Mad Jack was back at his manic best, collecting farthings on the bridge, dancing and singing out of key. The little money he raised paid for bread and milk, and with the gifts of soap and cakes from the citizens of Durham, he lived a fairly comfortable life. He had no education but did know that if anything happened he could race up the hill to the cathedral and ask for sanctuary. All he had to do was grasp on to the door handle and then no one could hurt him. His mother had drummed this into him ever since he was tiny. She was right to do so for he would eventually need it.

The mother of the child who so hated Jack bumped into him one day as he sat in a hedgerow (close to where Dryburn Hospital is now built) and she proceeded to shout at him. Screaming curses into his face, passers-by could see him getting very upset. He may have had the body of a man in his forties but his mind was that of an infant, and he began to cry. Mad Jack ran off into the fields sobbing, as the screeches of the mother flew after him like arrows. This woman was obsessed with getting rid of 'the retard', as she called him. She began to rally others behind her. Despite everyone knowing that Jack was harmless, a petition demanded his banishment from Durham.

Durham was the only place he had known, it was his security, it was his life. He didn't understand what was happening when all his 'friends' began to turn against him. The little old ladies who would bring him soup each week slowly stopped coming, the few coppers he would earn on the bridge stopped too. He was starving and didn't know how to save himself. He ate berries, apples from the woods, mushrooms, literally anything to keep him alive. There may have been no great intelligence in the man, but his will for self-preservation was strong.

The mother was furious that all of her actions hadn't managed to move Mad Jack from the community, so one day she spent an entire morning ripping her clothing, and she inserted a pair of scissors into her nose until it bled. Then she ran headlong into a wall knocking herself unconscious. She was still dazed when she staggered out into the street shouting 'Rape!' Her face was rainbow-coloured with bruising, the clotted blood from her nose trailed not only down her face but all over the bib of her gown. The local men gathered with staves and clubs to track down whoever it was; there was no way anyone could have doubted her, so convincing were her injuries. They demanded that she tell them who was responsible for this heinous crime. The answer was a foregone conclusion: 'Mad Jack,' she cried.

Poor Jack was on the bridge where he always was at that time of day, dancing and singing in the hope of persuading the people of Durham to part with their pennies. He saw the throng of men striding down the hill towards him. They were still five hundred yards away when he heard one yell: 'There he is, get him!' and they proceeded to run. In a panic, Mad Jack turned and ran, back across the bridge, through the city centre and up the hill towards the cathedral. He remembered the only lesson ever taught him by his mother. He was heading for sanctuary.

The rabble were close behind, as he scrambled through bracken and hedge to reach the mighty door to the cathedral. He reached out and grasped the lion's head door knocker, screaming 'Sanctuary, sanctuary!' Over the years thousands had demanded and received help in this way, and despite being surrounded by dozens of club-wielding men, he felt relieved, so relieved that he let go of the knocker before the door to the cathedral could be opened. As he did so he felt his leg being pulled. Frantically he reached back to the knocker but was now inches away. His fingers stretched as far as they could towards the door, but they were pulling him further and further away until he tumbled down a slope, as the locals circled him. 'First you try to kill our children and now you rape our women. After all, we have done for you, you ungrateful wretch!' Then the blows began to rain down on him. He never understood for one moment what they were hitting him for. He didn't even know what the word rape meant. How many eight-year-olds do?

Despite reaching his sanctuary it was plucked out from under him, and there he was being pounded into pulp. He screamed for his mother to no avail. She had disappeared from Durham ten years before. Mad Jack was to die for crimes he had not committed. The screams and yells of all those blood-crazed men were the last thing he'd hear. He looked up at the scrum of faces over him, shouting and spitting hatred down upon him. Almost in slow motion, he watched as over and over again the fists and feet tore into him. Blood poured into his eyes from a major head wound and consciousness evaporated like spilt wine. Death mercifully claimed him, as he was kicked around like a rag doll.

Some say that Mad Jack occasionally pops up along the riverside at Durham and he hasn't learned his lesson. He's still mischievous and 'mad'.

* Mrs Jean Aitchison was walking along by the river at Durham in 1968, it was a hot August day. The Wear was full of boats as she sat on the wooden steps that lead down to the river. At that moment she saw her nine-year-old daughter fall in up to her waist. The girl believed that her mother had pushed her in, having felt a shove in the back!

* In 1979 Richard Freeman from Newcastle was at college at Durham and he said that on 28th September 1979 at 2.00 am he was walking back to the halls of residence when he saw a man dancing on the bridge. He walked straight past, thinking he was merely a drunk. Yet on looking back he saw the man just fade away.

THE EBCHESTER INCINERATION

They say 'Where there's a will, there's a relative' and such was the story of Robert Johnson, a rich landowner who lived on the outskirts of Ebchester in the 1760s. A hardworking and frugal man who didn't believe in wasting money, he spent the last twenty years of his life trying to instil this into his son, to no avail. The son, a spoiled brat, paid no heed to his father, buying drinks for anyone and everyone, spending a fortune on prostitutes, and gambling at every opportunity.

During a blazing row over huge sums paid to a local farm girl whom his sort had made pregnant, Robert Johnson changed his will to disinherit his son. This, he thought, would oblige the young man to work for a living, and perhaps give him some real character.

Legend has it that one Sunday, Johnson declared to the entire church congregation: 'May my right arm burn away before I give my son sixpence.'

Five years later his son had become a changed man, holding down a steady job, with a wife and young children. Robert Johnson decided to change his will again, reinstating his son.

Eventually, Johnson died, leaving his fortune to his son. Friends and relatives came to pay their last respects to the body lying in the library of his Ebchester home. As one of his cousins leaned over to give him a last kiss, she smelt burning. The undertaker rushed in to pull back the sheet, and saw that Johnson's right arm had burned away to nothing!

THE FAIRIES OF FERRYHILL

If you said that the people of Ferryhill were fairies in the town on a Saturday night you would see for yourself the skill and expertise of the staff in intensive care. Yet it is thought that the town got its name from a hill on the outskirts of the village where the fairies would gather for feasts. Fairy Hill it was called, and as the village spread it took on the name.

The most widely told tale was of a lady called Mrs Howe who found a fairy with a broken wing, so she took the strange elfin creature to her house in Ferryhill where she mended it with threads made from a cobweb, and butterfly wings and the fairy flew off into the woods again. Every morning until the day she died the fairy left food and a jug of water on her step.

THE FOOTLESS MAN OF WASKERLY MOOR

The courtesy of those around Consett is legendary in itself, as there's always a smile, a cup of tea or food if you're hungry. Such has it always been, and yet from time to time an incident occurs that can colour your view to the contrary.

It was a freezing December night when a traveller called Garston was caught on 'the Tops', the high moorland where the wind can cut you in two. He met another man also frozen with the cold, and they dug their way into an old badger's sett and kept each other warm. The following morning the second man, Dennis Phillips from Waskerly, spotted Garston's boots. They were very fine, far better than his. He knew that he would surely suffer from frostbite, should he face the knee-deep snow in his thin, leaky shoes. So as the man slept he began unlacing his boots. The problem was that his feet had swollen and the boots were impossible to remove. As Phillips tugged at his legs, Garston awoke but was unable to turn around in the subterranean burrow. At this Phillips panicked and drew his long fishing knife, plunging it into Garston's back. He ran out into the crisp fresh snow, and in an instant felt the water soak into his feet. At this, he reached down into the old sett and pulled out the murdered man's feet. He could not remove the boots by force, so proceeded to cut Garston's feet off, boots and all. He shoved the remnants of the corpse back into the ground and blocked it with rocks. Having cut the feet from the boots he began returning to his Waskerly home. The body was never found and is still believed to be located thereabouts. However a year later the Phillipses were celebrating a quiet family Christmas when a huge snowstorm was whipped up and the howling wind rattled through the eaves of the house. Phillips' wife Jean said that she could hear someone shouting, and gazing through the window spotted the lonely figure of a man, plodding through the snow towards the house from the moors. The farmhouse had a tiny hatch in the door, and Phillips yelled: 'Over here, over here!' As the shadowy figure neared the snow-covered dwelling Phillips shouted: 'Get yourself in here and warm your feet by our fire!' A voice returned: 'How can I warm them when you cut them off!' Looking down at the figure Phillips saw bloody footprints in the snow. The man was walking on the gory stumps. Phillips screamed, began to have a fit, and died in his wife's arms. 'When she opened the door there was no one to be seen. It is believed that Phillips was buried wearing the selfsame boots.

GOD'S ASSASSIN IN GUISBOROUGH

In the 1100s monks regularly used to use a secret passage from the crypt in Guisborough Priory to sneak out and dally with the local maidens. The tunnel used to come out at a field in Tocketts, a parish a fair distance to the north. Some of the good-time girls would be waiting to 'serve' their pious preachers and would make a lot of money doing precisely that. Some of the ladies were married to farmers, millers and merchants but knew that the monks wouldn't tell, so their reputations would never be tarnished. They were always paid in gold and would explain the extra money by saying that the monks were giving money to the community. This had a roundabout way of making the monks more popular with the community, as they could see people actually benefiting from their presence. Everyone within the Priory including the Abbot was known to frequent the silken loins of these ladies, and on several occasions had to buy their silence when they fell pregnant.

No one knows why their midnight manoeuvres ceased, for this is where fact ends and legend begins. It is said that after forty years of lewd and lascivious lusting, they kept a chest filled with gold in the passageway, to pay for whatever services they required. It was guarded by a black raven who would claw at the eyes of anyone trying to steal from it. Yet one day one of the ladies told her husband what had been going on and he decided to enter the tunnel at Tocketts and walk to the Priory to confront the monks. On getting halfway he saw the trunk laden with shining gold. He was just about to scoop enough to fill his pockets when the raven swooped down and landed on his chest. No bird would stop him having his money, so he swiped at it and the raven was transformed into the Devil. 'For the love of God, no!' cried the husband. 'I love no God', answered the Devil, 'for I will be his murderer!' At that moment he raised his hands and slowly the walls, the floor and the ceiling of the tunnel began to come together. The man ran for all he was worth to reach the entrance. Sprinting into the blackness, tumbling over tree roots and wheezing with fear, he could see the daylight through the bushes that masked the entrance. He was now doubled up to avoid the ceiling, he was within yards of escape, and that is where he remains to this day. So near and yet so far. It was said that his hand remained sticking out from the soil, grasping at the fresh air that he could no longer breathe!

THE SERPENT OF HANDALE

Some believe this to be the Lambton Worm under another name, yet there are even more versions of this story than that of the bold and brave Sir John Lambton's old adversary. Stories abound from as far back as AD656 so I've chosen my personal favourite to share with you.

The area around Handale is renowned for its beauty and solitude. As such it became a place that was frequented by the most beautiful women in all of England and Scotland. They were drawn by the beautiful clear springs and rivers, believed to have the power of giving everlasting life. It was often said that if a woman was aged over forty and looked barely twenty that 'she was touched by Han-dale'. Because of this, the town had around five women for every man, and all efforts were made to bring men in from nearby villages to seek a wife. It was never known if the spring water had a similar immortalising effect on the male sex, but it is believed not to be the case.

It was then that a black witch visited the town and was so disgusted by the sheer beauty that she decided to curse the place. 'Let the flower of womanhood shrivel in this garden of wonder. I send forth a poisonous avenger to sweep you all away!' The locals drove her from the town hitting her with rocks and stoning her to death. Had they done this before the curse a great deal of suffering would have been avoided. As it was, late into the night a loud hissing noise was heard, and as a couple stared out of their window they saw a monstrous green dragon with a winding serpent's tail sliding through the village, leaving behind it a trail of poisonous slime that killed any plant that it touched. Its track was always clear, stinking like a cesspit. As they screwed their eyes to see into the dark, their stomachs turned on seeing that there between its fanged jaws was a young woman, impaled on its teeth. Over the next few years, this creature preyed on women, killing and eating them one by one. Some tales tell of how it would tear the thatched roof from a cottage and steal a man's wife from her own bed, biting her head off and spitting it back to her husband. It didn't make any difference if they hid in cellars, or if they ran, the lashing snake dragon would find and kill them.

The murders continued until an ungainly knight arrived – some legends say he was one of King Arthur's knights. This would be quite hard to prove as the stories of this serpent existed a good two hundred years before he was born. Even so, this knight seemed clumsy, could not sit squarely upon the back of a horse, and looked far from attractive. Yet he was appalled at the degree of fear in the hearts of the locals so decided that he would seek out the serpent and kill it. The serpent had never killed any man but could disappear at will, so couldn't be trapped. He asked for a local girl to help bait a trap for the beast. At first, the girl was frightened, but he swore that he would protect her. Foolishly she believed him.

On arriving at a nearby river, she waited, wetting her arms and neck with water from the stream. Within an hour she could smell that gut-rotting stench that warned of the serpent's presence. She looked around for the knight and he was nowhere to be seen. She turned to run, falling over her long white gown, and tumbling to the ground. The serpent stood above her looking down at his latest feast. She was an attractive girl, shapely with short blonde hair in braids. He was just about to open his jaws and clench her in his fangs when the serpent felt a sharp pain. The knight had hurled himself off a cliff and thrust a lance through the serpent's tail, pinning him to the ground.

The monster swung around launching the girl into the air and she landed in the stream. The serpent couldn't escape this time. The knight drew his sword and tried as he could to stab the beast's chest, but couldn't get close enough as the beast lashed out with mighty razor-sharp claws. The knight swiftly took up his longbow and began to fire arrows at the creature's bead until he had pierced both of its eyes. It lashed out blindly now, allowing the knight to sidestep the dragon's flailing claws and he plunged the sword into its chest, bursting its pounding heart. The monster exploded with blood, throwing the knight into the stream too. He sat there and watched as the serpent shook and trembled in the final throes of death. He turned to see the young girl sitting in the stream beside him, and she kissed him tenderly. He pulled her out of the water, presumably before his armour rusted, and rode back to Handale in victory. Handale has learned its lesson though, for it has never been a vain village ever again, although the women are beginning to outnumber the men again.

TOAD IN THE HOLE, HARTLEPOOL

If there is a worse job than clearing sewage I have yet to hear of it. Thanks to modern plumbing systems you rarely have to delve beyond the manhole cover, as it is always possible to call an expert to clear the blockage. Such luxuries didn't exist in the 1800s, so it was finally decided that the old china clay channels would be cleared and replaced with more modern piping. This had followed scores of complaints from Hartlepudlians who had watched raw sewage running along the gutters. The excavations were very deep, some 25 to 30 feet below ground, and it was there they came across a layer of magnesium limestone. As the workers hammered into this huge stone block they were shocked to see a live toad hop out of it. The hollow where it had been was almost a plaster cast of the toad itself. Some zoologists claimed the toad had been trapped in the rock for between 5,000 and 6,000 years, having slowed its heartbeat in the same way toads do for hibernation. Miraculously there it was, not just alive, but very active too.

On getting it out of the hole into the daylight everyone could see that its eyes were glowing, and it was barking like a small dog with bronchitis. Its pale colour changed as it came fully out of its solid sleep, and returned to the land of the living. The toad was placed in Hartlepool Museum along with the piece of rock that had long been its home.

THE SAINTLY POLTERGEIST OF HARTLEPOOL

If you should ever visit The Cosmopolitan pub in Hartlepool, stay on the ground floor. Only someone foolhardy would ever choose to spend the night in the cellar, for it is there that countless individuals have confronted a list of ghostly apparitions. At first, it was believed to be that of a nun who was creeping out of a secret passage that had led to the old inn from a nearby convent. It was from this tunnel that the nuns could secure the purchase of food, drink and have the occasional sex sessions with the locals. The innkeeper turned a blind eye and was well paid for this service by locals and convent alike. Others say that the ghost is of the old Abbess, wearing purple robes and appearing in the twilight each evening for a few seconds. This figure has made many a bar cellarman run out, drop kegs and smash bottles.

* Another legend connected to The Cosmopolitan's cellar features Saint Hilda. The story goes that many years ago when Hilda was driving all of the snakes out of Eskdale, she had heard that all of the remaining serpents had secreted themselves in the tunnel between the convent and the inn, so she set off to seek them out and drive them away. She entered the convent and walked the length of the tunnel, as thousands of writhing, wriggling snakes slid out of the floors, walls and ceilings. She demanded that the tunnel be filled in afterwards, trapping one of the young nuns inside, and there she starved and suffocated to death. The ghost is still there, and she continues to plague those who enter the cellar, in revenge against the saint who condemned her to die.

THE HAWK OF HIGH FORCE

In the twelfth century, a violent murder took place on the cliffs overlooking England's highest waterfall, near Middleton-in-Teesdale. It involved a brute of a man called Bob Milburn who had long had a blood feud with the Robson family from Barnard Castle. Big Bob was a cutthroat of a rogue, who thieved, bullied and intimidated his way through life. He had no one to tame him or bring him to heel, so ended up totally out of control. Big Bob fought Tommy Robson on the rocks above the falls and eventually battered his head to a pulp with a rock. To cover up the murder he dragged the body across to the torrents of clay-brown water that feeds the falls, and pushed the body into the stream, and watched as it rocketed over the edge. It seemed to be the perfect killing. Bob Milburn looked around to see if there were any witnesses and there were none, save one hawk that seemed to hover directly over him.

The Milburns used to drink at the local inn nearby, and now, every time Bob looked up he saw the bird, bright eyes homing in on him.

But soon he was planning another murder. He invited Frank Robson, the leader of the Robson clan, to High Force for 'a chat'. However, for some unexplained reason, Frank's young daughter Elsie came instead. Milburn was disappointed as he'd planned a major coup against his most despised foe, now all he had was this child. She asked what he wanted, but he said he would only talk at the top of the falls. So slowly and delicately the young lady ascended the crudely built steps to the very top of High Force. Milburn's mind was working overtime, if he negotiated with a child his reputation would be destroyed. But, he thought, he could rape her, then send her back to the Robsons as the ultimate insult. On getting to the top of the falls, Elsie Robson removed her shawl to show a wimple. She was a nun.

This shook Milburn, but soon he had decided that to rape a nun would be an even greater show of disrespect to the adversary. Instead of talking, he walked menacingly towards her, pushing her back off the rocks on to the grassy knoll. She screamed and ran towards the edge of the falls shouting, 'If you come near to me I'll jump!'

'Then jump, you stupid cow,' barked Milburn. 'Why did you come instead of your father?'

'You would have killed him like you did his brother.'

'Aye,' said Big Bob, 'and like I'd have killed you!'

He began walking towards the girl and was just about to grab her when suddenly a hawk swooped down and clawed at his eyes. It flew back into the skies carrying the eyeball and some gory sinew. Milburn screamed in anguish and ran at the Robson girl, pushing her over the edge. The hawk swooped down again and seized the girl's dress in its talons, fluttering frantically to ease her safely on to the rocks nearby. Then the bird spotted its prey, the one-eyed monster on the cliff, and without a pause, flew at him.

Milburn tried to run, yet every which way he ran the hawk was there before him. Eventually, he was shepherded back to the edge and found himself falling, not over the falls, but on to a small shelf some twelve feet from the top. His relief lasted only until he discovered that there was no way off, except to jump about a hundred feet on to the rocks below. There was no way he could climb back up the cliffs.

'Save me, please save me!' he shouted to the Robson girl. She turned away, saying 'You are now in the hands of God.'

Milburn eventually starved to death, as no one who saw his plight thought he was worth saving. He was such a villain, everyone was glad to see him out of circulation. His body lay on the rock for almost ten years before a strong wind tore what was left of the corpse from the cliff face and sent it careering into the foam.

*Legend claims that the hawk watches over High Force to make sure that justice is done. Many hawks are seen there every day.

LANGLEY HALL: ANY BODY FOR ME?

The North is spoilt for choice when it comes to great halls surrounded by lush and lavish countryside. Such is the case with Langley Hall in Durham, a house steeped in history, but the phenomenon witnessed there is a mystery. There are at least eight different stories as to how the haunting began, and my favourite is this:

Long ago a man owned Langley Hall and he was having problems maintaining it as the revenue from his tenants did not match up with the needs of his opulent lifestyle. The solution to all of his problems lay with the daughter of a rich merchant who lived in nearby Durham city. He never really fancied her, but certainly did feel a close attraction to the dowry he would receive when he took her hand. She was a portly woman, around 5'2" tall and close to twenty-one stone in weight. Her face had two huge hairy moles on her double chin. The dowry duly came, his debts were instantly paid off and the wedding night arrived. She had prepared herself and was lying in bed in a long white gown awaiting her conjugal rights, while he prepared himself drinking gallons of ale to lull his sensitivities so he could face the mountain of flesh currently warming his bed. On reaching the bedroom he removed his clothes, put on a nightshirt and squeezed in. Honeymoon nights are normally lustful, but this was a disaster. There was no way he could function, so he leapt out of bed to sleep in the room next door. After breakfast, his bulging wife said she was going back home to her father, and as the marriage had not been consummated he had to return the dowry. She slammed the door to Langley Hall and began walking towards the stable to arrange for a carriage to take her home. He couldn't allow that to happen, as most of the dowry was spent and he faced total ruin should she say a word, so when the carriage pulled up at the hall he allowed her to board it, and the team rode away down the tree-lined lane. He mounted his horse and galloped after them halting the coachman half a mile down the road. He ordered him to drive over open fields towards Esh. There in a copse of trees he ordered the coach to stop. As his new bride began cursing at him he drew his sword and hacked off the head of the coachman. It flew down past the window of the coach, blood gushing out of his body. She screamed in horror as he opened the door and ordered her to come out. She refused, believing that he was about to kill her too. He demanded that she step outside so they could talk through what was going to happen. He swore on his honour that he would not harm her provided that she remained married to him. As her life was on the line she agreed to do this. So as she stepped out of the coach they walked together for a few minutes, then he held out his hand offering a handshake. She reached out her hand and he promptly sliced it off.

She shook as she watched blood ooze from the cleanly hacked stump, and she slumped to her knees. Surprisingly she could feel no pain, adrenaline had jammed all of her nerve impulses and all she could do was gape at the end of her arm. He approached even closer shouting 'Bitch' and as she looked up the sword swung again and her head was taken from her shoulders by the fine sharp blade. This copse 'of trees was surrounded by a marsh and already the heavy carriage wheels were half sunk in mossy slime, so he urged the horses to walk even further into the quicksand. It was then that they began to rear up and panic as their feet began to slide out from under them. They were making a terrible noise, and his every attempt to silence them came to nought. So once again he drew his bloody sword and hacked away at the horses' necks until they were severed too. The bodies and the heads were pushed further into the marsh until they were out of sight.

He returned to Langley Hall and reported that his wife had gone out for a coach journey and not returned. Witnesses saw the coach leave, so the master's story was substantiated. Her disappearance was never solved. Yet now at midnight at least once a month a ghost hearse pulls up outside Langley Hall driven by a headless coachman and pulled by two headless horses. It is believed the murderer was forced to take his own life by the apparitions which it is said will continue until the end of time.

* In the 1820s a marsh was drained near Esh by a farmer and the remnants of a carriage were found, plus the skeletons of two horses.

THE PICKLED PARSON OF SEDGEFIELD

In the 1700s every single man and woman had to pay tithes, a charge of roughly ten per cent of their earnings, directly to the church. The local rector and his wife were exempt, as he was a paid official of the church. However in 1747, the rector died literally days before the 'tithes' were to be collected, and as she now had to pay this sizeable bill, bigger than any poll tax, his widow decided to fiddle her way out of it. No one knew the rector was dead, so if she could keep quiet about it for a week or so, the church would waive any bills. The problem was that every evening the rector could be seen in the upstairs window of the rectory reading the Bible and waving at passers-by. How could his frantic wife keep the lie alive? Then it hit her. Why not preserve her husband's body in salt, then place him in his chair propped up with rope under his cassock? So every single afternoon she would sit beneath his chair, making him move ever so slightly, and occasionally picking up his hand to wave casually to the people that trundled down the lane.

Three days after the church had paid the rector's 'tithes' she said that her husband had died in his sleep. There was great unrest in that house in Sedgefield from that moment on, furniture being hurled across the room, pictures smashing onto the varnished wooden floors and a vile smell that would not go away. The wife lived most unhappily there until the church threw her out in favour of the new rector, who continued to suffer all that had gone before. Finally, in 1792 the rectory was burned to the ground. Some say it was struck by a bolt of lightning, as God took his vengeance on the widow's deceit. Others say that the rector believed the rectory to be occupied by wicked demons, so destroyed it. To this day the site where the rectory once stood, near the current churchyard, is said to have regular visits from the 'pickled parson' who is still angry at his wife for conning the church out of its money.

THE SPINNING SAUCER OF SHOTTON COLLIERY

Joanne from Jarrow contacted me in July 1991 with a true story concerning her mother back in Shotton Colliery back in 1978. Mum was caught short, as can happen to anyone, and she rushed to the nearest netty, ripping down her knickers. Not having had time to close the door she was shocked to see a strange shining object moving across the sky very slowly over Shotton Colliery. Having taken care of the business in hand, she dragged her drawers back on and stood up as this strange whirring craft swept across the sky. She looked down the road in the hope to see anyone else confirm the sighting but to no avail. The craft hung in the sky for almost seven minutes before vanishing over the horizon.

SIR JOHN CONYERS, DRAGONSLAYER OF SOCKBURN

In the year 1063 many local northern knights had gathered to form an alliance that some historians believe could have been the basis for the legend of the Knights of the Round Table. Knights from the Scottish Borders to Durham agreed on a code of loyalty and brotherhood. They would defend the weak, protecting women and fighting for God and country. It would be two more years before the knights of Europe agreed a similar code of morality and horsemanship, the French word for horsemanship being chivalric. Chivalry, as we know it today, began in the North all those years ago. So all of these knights newly sworn set forth to do good and seek out causes worth risking their lives for.

Sir John Conyers visited South Durham after hearing that a monstrous dragon was terrifying the populace, eating sheep, cattle, men, women and children. The Worm of Sockburn was a creature the size of a house, covered in green scales and breathing fire. He left behind him an acrid slimy venom that killed any grass or trees that it touched.

Sir John, wearing his finest armour and carrying a lance, faced up to the beast and despite huge puffs of fire he rode his horse straight into it, the lance piercing the monster's eye, through its brain and out of the back of its head. As the creature writhed and wriggled in torment, thrashing out at the knight, he dismounted and pulled out his sword. He said a prayer to God and plunged the point into the monster's chest, a coup de grace blessed by God. Apart from minor burns to man and animal Sir John Conyers was victorious and became known far and wide as 'The Dragonslayer'. If you visit Sockburn you can see a depiction of that very sword inlaid into a stained glass window.

STAINMOOR AND THE BLOODY HAND OF GLORY

Of the thousands of strange and bizarre superstitions that are commonplace in the North, surely the most disgusting was the 'Hand of Glory'. Every thief believed that this was as vital to their nefarious deeds as a jemmy, a skeleton key or a swag bag. For over three hundred years this loathsome practice was operated by thieves and rogues, eventually petering out in the middle 1800s. The villain would find the body of a hanged man, ideally still swinging on the gibbet, and he would cut off his hand. On getting the hand home the criminal would squeeze all of the blood out of it, then spend many hours carefully embalming it with a mixture of salt, pepper and saltpetre before allowing it to dry out in the sun. Many a stolen hand was to be taken and eaten by dogs. There is another storytelling of how a huge black crow once removed a hand as it lay on a wooden pallet near Selby in Yorkshire.

As the hand dried the skin tightened into the shape of the bones, and often turned a sick-looking pinky brown. Once this gruesome hand was complete they would begin making candles, some say they were simple wax candles, others have said they were made from whales caught in the North Atlantic, others describe ingredients such as Lapland sesame and something called blub wicker. Yet once again others tried to gather the human fat from the bodies of these hanged men, using them rather like a dangling DIY store. Once the candles were made they were wedged between the stiff fingers of the 'Hand of Glory' and lit as soon as the villain broke into someone's house. It was believed that the hand could open locks itself. The pungent scent acted like chloroform on the household and if discovered, the hand could render the thief invisible using its light to guide his escape The truth was that many households were woken by the light, or they would sniff the curious smell and go and investigate.

*In the early 1700s a 'Hand of Glory' was given to a monk in Durham, and it was said to have been stored in a vault in Durham Castle. Three days later the box had been opened and the hand stolen, presumably by a burglar who believed in its peculiar powers.

*Danby Parish Church in Yorkshire also had a 'Hand of Glory' found in a leather pouch by one of the parishioners.

*Over seventeen hanged men dangled from gibbets throughout Cumbria in the middle 1700s yet when inspected the day after their executions, all their hands had been severed, the criminal fraternity not missing the chance to gain this magical protection.

*A pub called The Old Spittal Inn, at Stainmoor near Bowes (now a farmhouse), once had a story about an old hunchbacked woman with a thin angular face who warmed herself in front of the fire. The landlord had treated her kindly but did become suspicious when he noticed she seemed to have stubble on her chin, and her right hand was bright green. Summoning up the courage he grasped the woman's hand, and to his horror it came off. The woman was in fact a man, and the green hand was his 'Hand of Glory'. He had sat there hoping to become invisible, all to no avail. The publican hurled the withered hand into the fire and he screamed as it proceeded to climb off the burning logs back onto the fireplace. The rogue spewed curses at the landlord and ran out of the tavern, as the hand proceeded to slowly walk on its fingers towards him. Fortunately one of his old serving ladies knew how such an evil spell could be broken. She snatched a jug of milk from the kitchen and picked up a very sharp carving knife. Using the knife she sliced open the palm of her hand and thrust it into the milk, watching as the wholesome white turned a fleshy pink. She hurled the contents onto the 'Hand of Glory' and it began to sizzle like bacon under a grill. The skin soon disappeared leaving the bones. The landlord crashed his foot down onto them, crushing the brittle joints into a thousand pieces. This sounds far fetched, yet the strange mixture of fat and chemicals pushed into the 'hand' could be sufficient to make it appear as if it were moving, and perhaps be enough to make it explode out of a fireplace. So maybe the serving woman cut her hand for nothing.

THE TEESSIDE AIRPORT SPOOK

Barney Concannon was one of British Midland's most-senior Captains, yet his rank didn't stop him being frightened out of the St George Hotel, Teesside Airport. He was trying to sleep one night in the hotel when suddenly he felt a coldness across his head and shoulders. At first, he pulled the bedclothes higher, thinking it was nothing other than a freak draught. Then he felt something or someone sitting across his legs. So he looked into the blackness and swore at whatever it was. As soon as he did so the pressure on his legs disappeared and the room temperature began to return to normal.

Many other crews from other airlines have experienced strange happenings in the room too. Yet despite the management saying that there are no ghosts in the hotel, other staff members over the years have reported doors cashing in the middle of the night despite being locked, curtains opening by themselves, things moving from one surface to another and even one case of a bed flying through the air. Having dined at the hotel I can testify it is a fine one, and whether it is haunted is not for me to say.

In 1951 an RAF pilot died when his plane crashed close to the site of the St George Hotel.

WITTON CASTLE GHOSTS: THE SURGEONS ROOM

There is a room in the Castle known commonly as the Fire Room that is linked to some sort of medical room. Yet the only record of the Castle being used for medical purposes was during the English Civil War when there are reports of men being taken there to see 'the surgeon'. He was said to treat both sides of the conflict, yet had only simple tools to do his job. Imagine sawing off men's legs without anaesthetic, how horrific that first stroke would have been and then the second and third until the bone fell away tearing any flesh still attached. Typical wounds at that time would be from a sword, musket balls, slashing, hacking and stabbing. The only full report was from a soldier called Turner who wrote "I brought my dear friend Holly to the surgeon who had a small room full of the wounded, the table was awash with blood and after each man was seen, a bucket of water washed the blood from the table onto the floor and it seemed to vanish into the castle itself. The room was crimson red as we put Holly on the table. His right arm hung by one thread of skin and we knew he had lost it. The surgeon who had thirty others to see after him just took a small blade and sliced it off. Holly must have passed out in the shock, twas a mercy to him. The surgeon used a hot iron to seal the wound and then pulled down the skin and stitched it together like a joint of beef. Holly was then lifted off the table and laid against a wall on a wooden seat. When he awoke the screams of agony were a horror to all that heard them. His pain was great. Three days later his wound festered and we brought him back to that surgeon who cleaned and cut away the bad flesh and stitched him up again. I just got him to Trimdon and he died after his first night in his own bed". They say that the blood that sunk into the castle transformed it into a living entity. Today, anyone who spends time in the room can feel illness, nausea, sickness and diarrhoea. There is a very particular smell too of tinny blood in this area. Screams have been regularly heard and on one occasion a visitor saw a man's face appear in front of them covered in blood.

WITTON CASTLE GHOSTS: THE STAGE ROOM

When TV mediums visited Witton Castle there was talk about horses in this room too, claiming that they 'felt' that there had been a woman hanged in this room, or stabbed because she was pregnant. They asserted that this happened because the girl was pregnant and therefore no longer of use to the household. This has nothing to support it historically as many grand houses were quite happy for their younger staff to have children as they would acquire loyal servants of the future for greatly reduced wages. Those who were unhappy about it simply sacked the girl and brought in another. Yet the link to pregnancy is an interesting one as in several ancient documents there are passages where locals claim to be taking their daughter to Witton to get the baby 'seen to'. An olde worlde phrase for abortion. Many castles had quite a large staff and on many occasions as the male staff had a patriarch figure to run them under control of the master of the house. The female staff had a matriarch figure, usually the senior housekeeper, who would look after and tend the needs of all of the women. In the early 1700s, for around thirty years, there was a woman in that position called 'Auld Jeannie' and as well as organising all of the jobs, she looked after the health of her girls too. She would tend them if they had a fever, pull teeth if necessary and was the woman who would 'see to' any unwanted children. The girls knew if they were married to another staff member and fell pregnant their position was probably safe, but if they fell out of wedlock they would be put out and be unable to get another position. So these crude knitting needle abortions were commonplace and often ended in septicaemia or other life-threatening situations. It is all conjecture at this time, but the Stage Room seems the likely place for a senior housekeeper to carry out such things under candlelight in conditions that were far from sterile. This room has had a major impact on visitors who are pregnant or young mothers. It seems many have felt very ill and some have heard babies crying or whimpering here. There is a distinct feeling of something bad having happened there.

A FINAL WORD
THE FIRST LIVE BROADCAST FROM A BLACK MAGIC RITUAL

I wanted to experience what happened at a black magic ritual, but how do you go about it? Jim Brown; a producer for Metro FM, found the leading witch in the country, who lived in the outskirts of Manchester. Off we set to obtain permission to broadcast something that never had been before. Television coverage had been refused point-blank as that would burst the bubble of secrecy, faces would be seen and the association smashed. But live radio had a chance.

As we drove through the rural suburbs of Manchester, the sun was shining and it was a great day to be alive. Yet there in the middle of a street bathed in sunshine stood one house on its own, and a black cloud hung over it! Other clouds seemed to amble across the sky, whilst this one remained welded to the house.

'That's the place,' I shouted. 'Turn in there!'

Despite the house being a standard four-bedroomed detached home, it gave you the same feeling you would get if you were visiting the Addams Family or the Munsters. It was your archetypal house of horrors.

One sound engineer decided to wait in the car whilst Jim and I ventured inside. We were greeted by a large portly woman in black with eyes that could see past your skin and almost stripped you with a glance. Most eyes you would list depending on colour, yet whatever colour her eyes were it was the black centres that seemed to force you to stare. Hypnotism could well be a tool that this lady was capable of using, so I was careful not to use eye contact unless absolutely necessary.

We discussed how we saw the programme and asked her what the chances were of covering a sabbat, a black magic gathering. At first she was shy of discussing anything, but once she realised we would treat the subject with respect, she began to make plans with us. Those of a strong religious belief will see this as placating Devil worship. Yet we are told to respect the beliefs of others, and thus we proceeded, with extreme caution.

In the front room of the house was an altar with black candles and a pentagram on the floor. Into this room they filed: a wine waiter from a bistro, a kitchen porter from a hotel, two Canadian students, an American lawyer and three tall shipyard workers. They sat around the pentagram chanting when in walked the Witch Queen with her daughter, a staggeringly beautiful girl, looking very gipsy-like in a black lace outfit. They chanted, talked in a strange tongue, then placed a snake in the centre of the star and fed it a live rat!

Within the hour they had agreed to arrange for me, and me alone, to take part in a black magic ritual.

To say we were glad to get out of that house was an understatement. The people were fine and had not given us cause to worry, other than the fact that most of them seemed to carry daggers. As a man, I showed tremendous interest in the daughter who had the shape of a young Bo Derek and the intelligence of a graduate. It was easy to see how people could be drawn into any group with her present. Those who say that these groups are ignorant people being led like sheep are far from the truth. Whether there is any firm basis for their strand of faith, I don't know, but their creed has existed since before Christianity, so maybe we should give it more credence than we do.

Several telephone calls were made to firm up details of what would happen, as the Queen Witch told me how she did not worship the Devil. She worshipped nature, the power that made things grow, the power that made the rainfall, the tides rise and the power that gives babies life.

The appointed time arrived. I was taken in a car, a Ford Sierra, driven by a stoney-faced man who pulled into a lay-by after driving through the Tyne Tunnel towards South Shields. There I was met by a tall man, built like a weightlifter and wearing a black ski mask. He asked if I had been followed. I swore that I hadn't and he instructed me to get into the back of a dark blue Ford Transit.

Inside was a young girl aged about seventeen who told me she was going to blindfold me, then remove all my clothes. Under normal circumstances, the thought of a gorgeous girl removing my clothes would have been more than acceptable, yet in this case, the blindfold caused me a great deal of concern. I felt embarrassed, humiliated and more than a little frightened. This young lass was very gentle, and she told me that she was putting my clothes, keys and money into a kitbag and that I would be given them back on the return journey. When she had finished I was completely naked, even to the degree that the chain was taken from my neck and my watch was confiscated, and all I had was a box of outside broadcast equipment. At that point, she instructed me to put my hands behind my back. They were tied very tightly, and then I heard her leave the van, to go and sit in the front with the driver. The journey took no more than thirty five minutes, and after driving over what my backside told me must be rough countryside the van came to a halt.

Once again the girl helped me out of the van. I was standing beside her and I could feel the dress she wore, yet I was naked. It crossed my mind for a second that this would be one hell of a stunt on Candid Camera. I was completely vulnerable, and it didn't feel good.

My hands were untied and the blindfold removed, and there before me, was a blazing bonfire in the centre of a copse of trees. The night was jet black, and around the bonfire sat about thirty men and women, all naked. I was greeted by a man who called himself Edge, who introduced me to people, never giving their names, though he did list their occupations. I had expected daft students keen for a cheap thrill, but nothing could have been further from the truth. I met businessmen, accountants, police officers, bank managers, heads of companies and secretaries, professional people aged between 17 and 60.

The girl who had stripped me was now also stripped, and yet all of the tingles that red-blooded men are supposed to feel refused to kick in. My brain kept yelling 'Now what?'

The ritual was over in seconds. A chicken was slaughtered by a woman wearing a tall hat and mask and its blood was smeared on her body before the carcass was passed around to the others to do the same. They began a chanting that started quietly but got louder and louder until it filled your head. They grasped each other's hands and did a sort of 'Ring a Ring o' Roses' until they hugged and caressed each other. Then they ate from a stew that had boiled on the stove. They drank from wooden goblets, then disappeared into the undergrowth, returning fully clothed.

All the time I was jibbering into a microphone while each word was recorded at the radio station. I was invited to sample the food, and did so, hoping it wasn't freshly chopped human or anything that was still alive. It tasted not unlike raw pork, and you had to chew for what seemed an eternity. It was fatty and raw, the two things I detest most about any food I eat. Still, I forced it down, and then a flagon was handed me. I looked inside expecting blood, but it was a pale yellow liquid, looking not dissimilar to urine. It was very cold and despite smelling disgusting tasted of lemon. I asked what it was, only to be told 'The ale of the earth.'

It felt as if I had been there only ten or fifteen minutes, yet on obtaining my watch I found it had been almost an hour and a half. I said my goodbyes and was blindfolded by the girl after being allowed to dress for my return trip. I had planned to take the number of the van, but the plates had been covered with rags, and on my journey home the girl gave no clues to where I had been nor where I would be dropped off. She was willing to talk about TV or pop music, and it was as if what had gone on that night was second nature to her, rather like going to church is for Christians. She'd been, and now she wanted to talk about other things.

This all opened my eyes and made me even warier of dismissing the so-called magical and mystical. These had been highly intelligent people, no mugs, who had devoted their lives to a creed far from the norm, yet who were totally sincere in their beliefs. They seemed to wish no harm to anyone, yet stood apart from society, despite living amongst us.

I saw that same girl three years later, working as a nurse at Newcastle General Hospital. She chose to pretend that she didn't know me, and avoided my glance.

So these people are in every strand of society, and could well be living next door to you!

INTERESTED IN LOCAL HISTORY!

If you are interested in history and heritage of north-east England and the borders of Scotland, Northern Heritage will have something for you. Choose from the most extensive range of books covering archaeology, Roman history, folklore, social history, sport and comedy. Whatever your interest, Northern Heritage has it all.

NORTHERN HERITAGE
www.northern-heritage.co.uk

Follow us on: northernheritageltd N_Heritage Tel: 01670 789 940